Santa's

Book Of Knowledge

Santa Al Horton

authorHOUSE®

AuthorHouse™
1663 Liberty Drive
Bloomington, IN 47403
www.authorhouse.com
Phone: 1-800-839-8640

First published by AuthorHouse 6/30/2011

ISBN: 978-1-4634-2404-6 (e)
ISBN: 978-1-4634-2406-0 (sc)

Library of Congress Control Number: 2011911242

Printed in the United States of America

Have you ever thought what the world would be like if I didn't carry that sack and make that sleigh ride each year? I know one thing; there wouldn't be a need for a Naughty and Nice list anymore. Can you imagine all those children and their sad little faces? I could never give up this cause because the children are so angelic with those bright and cheery smiles when they look at you or the presents you leave on Christmas morning.

-- Santa Claus

Table of Contents

The Business of Santa

Forward

Every once in a great while there is a Santa Claus who stands above the many others.

It's been said you can put a man in the "Red Suit" but only certain men own the "Red Suit."

Such a Santa is Al Horton and over the years here in the United States or in Europe, He had perfected the art of creating the character of Santa Claus. Santa Al is in character every day of year and any child who sees the wink of his eye or his impish smile knows immediately they are in the presence of the real man in red.

I first met Santa Al at the Santa Claus Academy in Atlanta, Georgia when he developed a curriculum of courses for the newest to the veteran Santa. What first struck me about Al was dedication to provide a high level of instruction delivered in a professional manner. His goal then and now is to raise the bar and make us all better at portraying Santa Claus.

I was also fortunate to teach with him and benefit from his accumulated knowledge. Al has that rare ability to condense material into understandable and useful information which you will find throughout the following material. His courses of instruction were always well attended and students were always eager to learn from him.

Within these pages Santa Al has put together a wealth of information to help Santas just starting their career and for those of us with a few seasons upon our beards. I'm sure you will find the information helpful and you will keep this book as a reference guide now and in the seasons to come.

Sit back, relax and let the magic of Santa Claus fill your mind and heart. Ho ho ho!

Louis.G.Knezevich
Santa Lou
Atlanta's Premier Santa

Merry Christmas.
Santa Lou

Introduction

Since you're reading this book, you are probably interested in either becoming a great Santa or improving on what you are already doing. Either way, this is a great place to start.

You have the calling to bring joy and happiness to the children. That is terrific and welcome to the brotherhood. This book is a collection of past experiences and helpful hints that are hopefully explained in terms that are understandable to everyone and enjoyed by all. This is a composite of some of the things that have been learned over the years from trials and errors and more errors, and embarrassing errors. Also you will find information that has been gifted to me by those consider to be the best Santas in the world.

Notice that the Reference in the back of this book gives credit to all the locations researched and to those who passed on information if not noted in each chapter where the explanation is needed.

Now, let's talk about representing yourself as Santa. It doesn't matter if you only want to do this for your children or for the office party. Maybe you have visions of being in the movies, television, or print, earning a bundle of money. It doesn't make a difference where you want to take it, what really matter is being the best you can be and always leaving the children happy, smiling and wanting more. After reading this book, you will want to keep it as a guide and future references.

What you will learn from this book will be important to you from the beginning of your Santa portrayal through the management of all the money you could be making if you choose to do so. You will first discover important facts of Santa, his reindeer, and many Christmas traditions that you can use to impress the children of all ages. You will find out how to look like a Direct Descendent of Santa and be given some information on where to look for improving your wardrobe. You will find some important facts about staying healthy and fit for longevity and the difference between putting the beard on as part of your costume and wearing a real beard year round. There is information on how to take care of your hair and beard, real or not? As you continue in this book you will find a list of the do's and don'ts of storytelling, whether reading or through improvisation. You will learn a little about your voice and how to use it properly. Just yelling HO! HO! HO! at the top of your lungs does not work and usually ruins the evening for the young children and their parents. Don't do anything to make the babies cry.

Have you thought about how to make an entrance? What about what you do once you have entered and have been announced? How to get to your special Santa spot and how to hand out the gifts is also important for you to know. Yes, there is a technique for all of that. This book will answer the question of giving out candy or not. Do you take a good picture? Inside this book you will find tips on how to take pictures that Grandma would be proud to show off. Have you thought how you might handle a problem child, a pushy parent or a scared or crying child? Great tips can be found within these pages.

Included within these chapters are tips and suggestions of getting yourself known. You will also discover about how and why you should be tracking your visits so you don't miss any and how to figure out what you need to charge. Also you will need to advertise. There are numerous methods to do that.

I initially created this book to help with the classes I teach and watched it develop into much more. Hope you enjoy reading it as much as I enjoyed writing it. I know the children I visit enjoy the things I do.

Did you know that to be successful, there are numerous things you should do throughout the year, not just put on the red suit in December. Earlier, we mentioned about being photogenic, well there is a section in this book that deals with the subjects of working with a mall or professional photographer and the child's parents photographic ability or just with someone who happens to own a camera and are trying to sell photos from their personal camera.

Do you entertain or do you just sit there. I have included a section of different things you can learn that will make your visit memorable and most enjoyable for the children. In some areas you will be shown how to perform specific activities, while others you will need to find someone to teach you or some other method to learn. There is a lot you can do. That is why this book has been developed. Let it be your reference and guide. When you are ready, review it and use the ideas to give you more ideas. The one thing that is constant with Santa is that things are ever evolving. The more you stay on top of the trends and try to anticipate them, the more you are the one everyone is seeking.

As stated earlier, there are things you should be doing year round. If you desire to portray Santa on a year round basis, there is a section that explains where else you may want to look for work. If you are going to work, then you will need to know how to build your Santa Resume. It's not as easy as you may think. Now looking for more work, spreading out in the Santa business may not be what you desire right now, but you will find some tips on how to set up your business. Now if you want to work as Santa but not set up a business, you can always look for an agent. There are cautions and helpful hints about finding and using an agent.

That is this book in a nutshell. I hope that you will enjoy and be entertained as you learn some new things. I can guarantee that the children you visit using these suggestions will thoroughly enjoy you and their time with you. You will be remembered forever.

Also included are some great stories and variations (or parodies) on Santa's *Night before Christmas*. There is a wealth of knowledge here and you will get out of this book almost anything you desire. It can be a reference or just a refresher to assist you with everything. The information is designed as suggestions to promote your thinking and ability to envision new and useful things and ideas. Go for the gusto and don't expect this book to make you the best. As with everything else, it takes work and practice.

Here is a sample of the type of stories and parodies you will find throughout this book. Now I don't believe this one bit, but a few engineering friends of mine tell me this is the truth. Well, I still don't believe it. I researched this and could not find an author. I am sure this has been passed around engineering schools for years before the internet came into existence.

An Engineering Perspective On Christmas

Author Unknown

There are approximately two billion children (persons under 18) in the world.

However, since Santa does not visit children of Muslim, Hindu, Jewish or Buddhist (except maybe in Japan) religions, this reduces the workload for Christmas night to 15% of the total, or 378 million (according to the population reference bureau).

At an average (census) rate of 3.5 children per household that comes to 108 million homes presuming there is at least one good child in each. Santa has about 31 hours of Christmas to work with, thanks to the different time zones and the rotation of the earth, assuming east to west (which seems logical). This works out to 967.7 visits per second.

This is to say that for each Christian household with a good child, Santa has around 1/1000th of a second to park the sleigh, hop out, jump down the chimney, fill the stocking, distribute the remaining presents under the tree, eat whatever snacks have been left for him, get back up the chimney, jump into the sleigh and get onto the next house.

Assuming that each of these 108 million stops is evenly distributed around the earth (which, of course, we know to be false, but will accept for the purposes of our calculations), we are now talking about 0.78 miles per household; a total trip of 75.5 million miles, not counting bathroom stops or breaks.

This means Santa's sleigh is moving at 650 miles per second -- 3,000 times the speed of sound. For purposes of comparison, the fastest man-made vehicle, the Ulysses space probe, moves at a poky 27.4 miles per second, and a conventional reindeer can run (at best) 15 miles per hour.

The payload of the sleigh adds another interesting element. Assuming that each child gets nothing more than a medium sized LEGO set (two pounds), the sleigh is carrying over 500 thousand tons, not counting Santa himself.

On land, a conventional reindeer can pull no more than 300 pounds.

Even granting that the "flying" reindeer can pull 10 times the normal amount, the job can't be done with eight or even nine of them -- Santa would need 360,000 of them. This increases the payload, not counting the weight of the sleigh, another 54,000 tons, or roughly seven times the weight of the Queen Elizabeth (the ship, not the monarch).

600,000 tons traveling at 650 miles per second creates enormous air resistance - this would heat up the reindeer in the same fashion as a spacecraft reentering the earth's atmosphere. The lead pair of reindeer would adsorb 14.3 quintillion joules of energy per second each. In short, they would burst into flames almost instantaneously, exposing the reindeer behind them and creating deafening sonic booms in their wake.

The entire reindeer team would be vaporized within 4.26 thousandths of a second, or right about the time Santa reached the fifth house on his trip.

Not that it matters, however, since Santa, as a result of accelerating from a dead stop to 650 mps in .001 seconds, would be subjected to acceleration forces of 17,000 g's. A 250 pound Santa (which seems ludicrously slim) would be pinned to the back of the sleigh by 4,315,015 pounds of force, instantly crushing his bones and organs and reducing him to a quivering blob of pink goo.

Therefore, if Santa did exist, he's dead now. Merry Christmas!

Now that I have left you this cheery thought, read on my friend. Read on and learn the magic of being Santa.

Basically Santa

This section is for the novice and a refresher to the Santas who have been performing for a long time. It is a terrific refresher to get your mind back into what is important for Santa.

For the beginner, don't take everything as gospel. Question everything you read and find more information for yourself. You can look up references from the Reference section or you can find your own. Either way, this is a marvelous place to start your quest.

I hope this book is a terrific beginning for those who will most likely let this become a passion and have a totally fun time with Santa. Even if you just review a few pages in October to get you ready for Christmas or read some of the poems, stories and jokes in November to put you in the mood. If this book is of any help to you, I will have considered myself successful.

Now sit back and enjoy some informative and entertaining reading. Let your imagination wander. Believe you are Santa and so will those around you. Act like you are Santa and the world will be banging on your door to get your attention. Now go out there and have fun being Santa.

One thing to remember, when with a group of Santas, never claim you are the real Santa. Now you may wonder why, well the simple fact is that every child of any age has their own vision of what Santa should look like. If you are not that vision, then the child will never believe in you nor will they trust you. But if you always say, "The Real Santa Is here and it up to you to find him," that leaves you still in the running. The child will have lots of fun trying to pick out the person they think fits their image of the real Santa. If it is not you, look to see what image the person they selected portrays and gear yourself more to look like that.

Now if you are in a crowd of Santas and someone ask if the real Santa please stand up, then by all means, join the crowd and stand. This is especially fun when there are loads of outsiders or non elf like persons hanging around.

One more hint, during the season, that is November through December, try to stay away from stores and places that have a Santa if you look like Santa. This will prevent any confusion with the folks and if you are a better looking Santa this will also prevent hard feelings. Be sure to say "Hi Santa!" if you see another while you are out. This greeting will get those around you who are not paying attention to look your way and that is what you want anyway. The more that look at you, the better off you are and the more the Christmas spirit is abound.

Always smile and keep that twinkle in your eye. It works magic for almost everything.

Chapter 1

The History

The following information is based on documented evidence and some folklore passed down from generation to generation. It is obvious as I researched this subject that the Pagan deities and folklore go back beyond A.D.; and the custom of gift-giving was practiced by the folks of that era for a long time. Thus this list is accurate but I still consider it incomplete. If you are particularly orthodox, you may not want to read this for it goes against many Christian beliefs. If you are curious, than read on and enjoy. Learn the truth as I learned it about how our current traditions began.

After reading this chapter, you may just come to believe like I do that Santa has no religion. It is the holiday and the season that has the religion. Read on my friend and discover how Santa and the season came about.

Like comparable figures of American legend (Daniel Boone, George Washington, Robin Hood)[1] Santa Claus's origins are shrouded in mystery. At the same time, it is clear that he is closely linked to a

1 Note that I did not include any sports heroes, movie stars or any other such modern day figures. They are mostly trash folks who are easily forgotten because they have the "me, me, me" attitude. Very few folks are around these days who think of others before themselves. That is way they are not mentioned here.

very good and prominent family. This was such a good family as to be an Olympian in stature. Of course, he has long since dropped all his foreign titles and decorations, his high office in the Church as a bishop, and all foreign associations generally associated with him. He has become a true democrat. Yes, I am talking about Santa Claus. He can be traced back to Odin, Poseidon, Zeus, Saint Nicholas and many more. Read on my friend and enjoy some interesting assumptions on my part. Yes, I did take some literary license in a few places, but that was just to further expound on my beliefs and explain some very important information I have found.

Are you curious about how some traditions began? Here are some interesting thoughts about that subject and more. Most of our current Christmas traditions began in ancient times during the winter holidays and festivals. The middle of winter has long been a time of celebration around the world. Centuries before the arrival of the man called Jesus, early Europeans celebrated light and birth in the darkest days of winter. The winter solstice was celebrated because the worst of the winter was behind them and the folks could look forward to longer days and extended hours of sunlight. Now bear with me on this. It will all come together soon.[2]

In the Scandinavian countries, the Norse celebrated Yule, the winter solstice, from December 21 through January. This was in recognition of the return of the sun. Fathers and sons would search for the largest log they could find and bring it home to light. Then everyone would feast until the log burned out, which could take as many as 12 days. The Norse believed that each spark from the fire represented a new pig or calf that would be born during the coming year. This is how the tradition of the Yule Log began.

We don't celebrate this tradition in America, but several countries around the world celebrate with a Yule Log. Look at the traditional candies we get at Christmas. Usually cheese and other foods are rolled

---

2 If you research the Winter Solstice, you will find it quite interesting. The pagans are given credit for most of this celebration, but there were others too. For example, the Romans were aligned with this event along with the ancient Greeks, Italians, and many more.

into a log shape. There are candies made to look like a log. Though most Americans don't have a fireplace to put a Yule Log into, they do celebrate it with the food they eat.

The end of December was a perfect time for celebration throughout most areas of Europe. This was the time of year, when cattle, sheep, goats, and other livestock were slaughtered so they would not have to be fed during the remainder of winter and the meat could be stored in the cold to help it keep longer. For many, it was the only time of year when they had an ample supply of fresh meat. In addition, most wine and beer[3] made during the year was finally fermented and ready for drinking. I knew there was a reason I loved the winter so much.

In Germany, people honored the Pagan god Odin or Woden during the mid-winter holidays. The German people were terrified of Odin or Woden because they believed he made nocturnal flights through the sky to observe his people, and then decided who would prosper or perish. Because of his presence, many people chose to stay inside. If you look at the modern interpretations of what Odin or Woden looked like, you can easily see our Santa there. Long hair and beard, brings gifts, flies through the skies, looks for who is naughty and nice, etc.

Who is Santa really? Well, he doesn't like it known, but Santa Claus (Sinterklaas, St. Nicholas, Father Christmas, Kris Kringle, etc.) actually started out life as sort of a Christian version of Poseidon[4], the Greek god of the sea and of all waters, also known as Neptune by the Romans. I'll bet you thought I was going to say Odin or Woden. Well Odin or Woden came a little later for the Pagans.

Now you ask, what does a god of the sea and all the waters have to do with Christmas and Santa Claus. Read on my friends and find out some interesting theories I and many others have developed. We embrace these theories because they make a lot of sense and have been

---

3 It wasn't actually called beer. In most places it was called mead. Read up on the subject and try making your own.

4 Poseidon was born, of course, into the first family of the world, son of Kronos and Rhea, and he had two brothers, Zeus and Hades. And as we know, Hades took the underworld, Zeus took the earth, and Poseidon took the kingdom of the sea, establishing himself in grand style in a golden palace under the waters of the Aegean Sea.

around for many years. They weren't created to push a religion or to make any one group or person a prominent person in society. They were made to follow along who society was currently acting and reacting to the world around them.

The early Greek Sailors were afraid of Poseidon because he could send them terrible storms at sea. But they also noticed if he was in a good mood, he would grant them calm seas and safe journeys in their little boats. They came to love him not only for his kindness but for the gift of the sea itself, will all its delicious goodies, and for the health-giving properties they found in salt water and air.

Ok, there is the first hint. He was kind and gave them the gifts of the sea and the health from the salt water and air. Keep reading, there is more information that helps with this theory.

Poseidon had charge over fresh water, too, and could strike a rock with his trident and make a spring of sweet water jet forth. He became known as a giver of all good things and of life itself.

So even back in the third century B.C., when people started erecting temples to him, he was already a kind of Santa Claus and his festival was celebrated by the Greeks and Romans on December 6 (which, after the fourth century A.D. became the feast of Saint Nicholas).

Now that is the pre-Christian version. It is well documented that as Christianity began to grow and spread, the priest needed to do lots of things to bring the Druids, old Romans and other Pagans to their cause and ideologies. This is why they started taking the Pagan festivals and feasts and attributing them to Christian ideologies.[5]

There is also a belief that Santa Claus is related to Thor. Mythologist Helene Adeline Guerber presents a very convincing case tracing Santa to the Norse god Thor in *Myths of Northern Lands.*

Thor was the god of the peasants and the common people. He was represented as an elderly man, jovial and friendly, of heavy build, with a long white beard. His element was the fire, his color red. The rumble

5 If you don't believe this, try looking up some of the theological history of early Christianity and see what actually occurred. Yes, they teach it in the different seminaries about how things actually evolved. Most accept the most current ideologies of the church and tend to forget the orgins.

and roar of thunder were said to be caused by the rolling of his chariot, for he alone among the gods never rode on horseback but drove in a chariot drawn by two white goats (called Cracker and Gnasher). He was fighting the giants of ice and snow, and thus became the Yule-god. He was said to live in the "Northland" where he had his palace among icebergs. By our pagan forefathers he was considered as the cheerful and friendly god, never harming the humans but rather helping and protecting them. The fireplace in every home was especially sacred to him, and he was said to come down through the chimney into his element, the fire.

The *unusual* and *common* characteristics of Santa and Thor are too close to ignore.

- An elderly man, jovial and friendly and of heavy build.[6]
- With a long white beard.
- His element was the fire and his color red.
- Drove a chariot drawn by two white goats, named called Cracker and Gnasher.[7]
- He was the Yule-god. (Yule is Christmas time).
- He lived in the Northland (North Pole).
- He was considered the cheerful and friendly god.
- He was benevolent to humans.
- The fireplace was especially sacred to him.
- He came down through the chimney into his element, the fire.

Even today in Sweden, Thor represents Santa Claus. The book, *The Story of the Christmas Symbols*, records: Swedish children wait eagerly for *Jultomten*, a gnome whose sleigh is drawn by the *Julbocker*, the goats of the thunder god Thor. With his red suit and cap, and a bulging sack on his back, he looks much like the American Santa Claus. Now doesn't that give a good accounting of Santa Claus?

6 Thor was built like what our imagination thinks a blacksmith would look.
7 Now stretch this thought of a chariot to a sleigh and the goats as reindeer and there you have him.

Thor was probably history's most celebrated and worshipped pagan god. His widespread influence is particularly obvious in the fifth day of the week, which is named after him – Thursday (a.k.a. Thor's Day).

It is ironic that Thor's symbol was a hammer. A hammer is also the symbolic tool of the carpenter – Santa Claus. It is also worth mentioning that Thor's helpers were elves and like Santa's elves, Thor's elves were skilled craftsman. It was the elves who created Thor's magic hammer. Now if that doesn't convince you, than nothing else in this book will do so. Have an open mind when reading and see if you can find other similarities.

There is also a popular belief growing that Santa Claus was created by using one of the devil figures associated with Saint Nicholas, Odin or Woden, Thor, Sinterklaas and many others.[8] There are some terrific articles about that theory, but I choose not to listen or accept them. In the meantime, let's move on to how the Christians changed Santa Claus.

The Christian Version

Fundamentally, I find that the Christmas celebration is based on the intertwining of two ethnic patterns, Roman transition rites and Germano-Celtic Yule (jiuleis) rites-feasting practice. First look at what the early Christians and Druids were sharing. The first known use of the word Christes-Maess was in England, 1038. The English titled Feast Days with Mass Days. No Saint's day listed for December 25th. Another interesting fact is that the abbreviation Xmas; X is Greek Chi, the first letters of Christmas--not X blank out, came into use.[9]

Most of our popular festivals and ceremonies are not originally

8 I prefer to not accept this philosophy, but if you read a lot about these characters and their sidekicks/helpers, you may find some similarities that you don't like either. I am sure my Christian friends will argue against these thoughts all day long and then some. Just research for yourself and come to your own conclusions.

9 To all you hard core Christians who believe that "X" as in Xmas is bad, need to research and find out the true facts about this subject.

of Christian origin. They may not be definitely part of any of the religion which Christianity replaced but were celebrations practiced by the people of the times. It appears that they are a mixing of existing festivals that everyone celebrated anyway in their own personal style. It could be that the apples and nuts in our Christmas stockings are the descendants of apples and nuts that grew on very old trees, trees older than history, perhaps there was a late harvest festival, or a kind of Pagan Thanksgiving, presided over by a beneficent elf[10], and accompanied by candling and feasting. We do not know for sure. I would love to have a time machine and go back in time to find out.

But we do know that as Christianity developed, the Church encouraged all the popular Pagan customs, or many of them, and took them over associating them with Christian holidays and events. This may have been a deliberate attempt of the priests to win the favor of the people and make the new religion really popular, or the people may have made the transfer themselves by the vague and untraceable but very real process of folklore and storytelling. Either way, the people kept their customs, traditions and they soon moved from the Pagan to the Christian beliefs.

Though generally assumed to be a date for the solstice, the original significance of the date December 25th (25 Kisleu Jewish calendar) is unknown. We know the day had important ceremonial and social significance, apparently unrelated to solstice activities. In pre-Christian Rome Mithras was seasonally reborn not on the day of the solstice, but on December 25th. The Romans had another deity for the solstice, the goddess Angerona. Her festival day is December 21st. I am sure if we continue to look, we could find dozen more examples.

After his introduction to Rome the composite Mithras, and perhaps his December 25 date of celebration, were again synchronized with *Solis indigeni* (a Roman sun god derived from the Pelasgean titan of light - Helios). This resulted in a composite being *Solis invicta*, the invincible sun. Mithras was the god of the regenerating sun and was annually

10 This is true because in ancient times, everyone believed in elves, fairies, gnomes, hobgoblins, the wee people and many other mystical and magical things and people.

reborn on December 25th. Aurelian eventually proclaimed Mithraism the official religion of the Roman Empire in A.D. 274 and *Natalis Solis Invicti* (Birthday of the Invincible Sun) became an official holiday. (This information was found in several locations on the internet. No specific source could be found for this discovery.)

To this day January 6 is the Eastern Church date to celebrate the unified date celebrating both Christ's nativity and baptism. Originally it was a nativity date established by Egyptian Christians in the 1st century and was apparently calculated from the belief Jesus died April 6, A.D. 29 (year inferred from Luke 3.23, date from Passover of that year) and "existed" on earth exactly 30 years from his incarnation. December 25th was later accepted date of Christ's nativity by eastern Christian churches (Orthodox, Ukrainian, etc.). Chrysostom states in AD 387 that the vacated January 6th had become the date of the Epiphany for the western church. This shift in dates was not due to Gregorian calendar correction. It was established by the church. (Again, this information was found in several locations with no specific reference given to one source.)

Representation of Epiphany in Western churches was based on the manifestation of Christ by Magi (whom many believe probably were Parthian astrologers and not kings). In the Eastern churches it was based on (1) Christ's baptism by John, and (2) his first miracle at Cana.

The twelve holy Roman days (actually nights, there are 13 days) established in 47 B.C. between the end of the Saturnalia (December 19th) and the Kalends (January 1st) eventually became the twelve holy days of the Christian Christmas celebration. They were officially adapted to the Christmas-Epiphany interval at the Council of Tours[11], A.D. 567. The Romans transferred the Saturnalia to the beginning of the year in the 4th century.

If we should wake on the sixth of December and find our stockings full of candy and toys we should think that the elfish old fellow who comes down the chimney has lost his marbles and arrived about three

11 This documentation is true. It is found even on the internet and describes what was discussed at the meeting. It made for some boring reading for me, but there were some interesting translations of the writings and records.

weeks too soon. But his arrival would be exactly on time to children in other parts of the world. For the feast of Saint Nicholas is the sixth of December, and how he became the patron saint of the "Day of the Saints", the Christ – Child, is another story.

Jumping back to earlier times, we should investigate the primary gift givers in our history. Let's begin with the most popular, Saint Nicholas. Others will follow as you learn about the traditions of other countries. I won't go into them as deep since very few folks know about these folks.

The Christian church created a fictional life history for St. Nicholas. He was given the name *Hagios Nikolaos* (a.k.a. St. Nicholas of Myra). Yes, I stated it was fictional. There are only stories, legends and hearsay information handed down. There are no official records in places where he supposedly went that indicated he was ever there. That is why the Pope removed him from the roles of Sainthood. In the early years of Christianity, Easter was the main holiday; the birth of Jesus was not celebrated. In the fourth century, church officials decided to institute the birth of Jesus as a holiday.

Unfortunately, the Bible does not mention a date for Jesus' birth (a fact Puritans later pointed out in order to deny the legitimacy of the celebration). Although some evidence suggests that his birth may have occurred in the spring (why would shepherds be herding in the middle of winter?), Pope Julius I chose December 25. It is commonly believed that the church chose this date in an effort to adopt and absorb the traditions of the Pagan Saturnalia festival. First called the Feast of the Nativity, this custom spread to Egypt by 432 and then to England by the end of the sixth century. By the end of the eighth century, the celebration of Christmas had spread all the way to Scandinavia. Today, in the Greek and Russian orthodox churches, Christmas is celebrated 13 days after the 25th, which is also referred to as the Epiphany or Three Kings Day. This is the day it is believed that the three wise men finally found Jesus in the manger.

By holding Christmas at the same time as traditional winter solstice festivals, church leaders increased the chances that Christmas would be popularly embraced, but gave up the ability to dictate how it was celebrated. By the Middle Ages, Christianity had, for the most part, replaced Pagan religion. On Christmas, believers attended church, and then celebrated raucously in a drunken, carnival-like atmosphere similar to today's Mardi Gras. Each year, a beggar or student would be crowned the "lord of misrule" and eager celebrants played the part of his subjects. The poor would go to the houses of the rich and demand their best food and drink. If owners failed to comply, these visitors would most likely terrorize them with mischief. Christmas became the time of year when the upper classes could repay their real or imagined "debt" to society by entertaining less fortunate citizens.

Saint Nicholas

Not much is documented about St. Nicholas, but his lore lives on. He is thought to have been the Bishop of Myra, imprisoned during the reign of Diocletian and released upon the ascension of Constantine as Roman emperor. Nicholas is said to have been famous for his generosity – one story has it that he provided the dowries for three Italian sisters by throwing bags of money through their windows. The tradition arose that he was a secret giver of gifts to children on his feast day, December 6th. Nicholas was one of the most popular saints in Europe throughout the middle ages, but following the Protestant Reformation, interest in him died out everywhere except Holland.

Nicholas was an actual person. Though he was the most popular saint in the calendar, not excepting St. Christopher and St. Francis, we know little about the man to whom so many lovely deeds, human and miraculous actions, have been ascribed. He was bishop of Myra, in Lycia, Asia Minor[12], in the first part of the fourth century of the Christian era. Asia Minor is the cradle of all Christian ideas.

Nicholas was persecuted and imprisoned with many other Christians during the reign of the Roman emperor Diocletian, and was released and honored when Constantine the Great recognized the Christian

12 This part of the world is now Afghanistan, Iraq, Turkey and other Middle Eastern countries. So if Santa Claus looks like him, how come he is not Arab looking? Try to answer that one for me please.

Church as the official religion and encouraged it. Now Bishops in those days were men of prominence and wealthy backgrounds. Nicholas was no different.

About two hundred years after his death Nicholas was a great figure in Christian legend Justinian, the last powerful Roman emperor in the East, built a church in honor of St. Nicholas at Constantinople.

This story of St Nicholas takes what seems as an almost humorous turn. Think about the three purses of gold. We now recognize them, in conventional form, in the three gold balls over the pawnbroker's shop[13]. Thus the holy man of the early Christian Church presides symbolically over a business which throughout Europe during the Middle Ages was conducted largely, though not exclusively, by members of the older Jewish sect. At first glance it does not seem quite appropriate that the charitable benevolent saint should become associated with a business, long notorious for exaction and usury, which the Mosaic Law forbade and which the derivative Christian morality condemned. One of the earliest acts of Christ was the expulsion of money-lenders from the temple: he 'overthrew the tables of the money changers' and scourged forth others who bought and sold.

But it may well be that the bankers and brokers wished to give sanctity and dignity to their business and so adopted the generous Nicholas as their heavenly protector. Every profession, guild, and trade made assimilations of legend to fact. This just simply happened and so far nobody knows just how. Nicholas was adopted not only by the more or less respectable brokers but by thieves and pirates. The sinner as well as the honest man had his heavenly benefactor. And it is no more strange in the history of mythology that Nicholas should have been invoked by thieves than that the Greek Roman God Mercury should have been the deity and god of robbers and tricksters.[14]

The most important role of Nicholas to us at the present time is his

---

13 Pawn broking included all forms of banking and money-lending with personal movable property as security.

14 I loved looking into mythology during my search. There are so many different stories out there that they would make wonderful modern tails if they were updated to days standards.

patronage of schoolboys, for this brings him close to us as Santa Claus, the bearer of gifts and the special saint of childhood. He was himself the Boy Bishop.[15]

So it is with Nicholas. He is honored and accepted with a kind of childish ignorance. Professor George H. McKnight of Ohio State University, who has given us the best account in English of the good St. Nicholas, begins his book by saying that strangely little is known of him in America. But he belongs to us by a very special inheritance. Our Dutch ancestors in New York – ancestry is a matter of tradition, not of blood[16] – brought St. Nicholas over to New Amsterdam.

The English colonists borrowed him from their Dutch neighbors. The Dutch form is San Nicolaas. If we say that rather fast with a stress on the broad double – A of the last syllable, a D or a T slips in after the N and we get 'Sandyclaus' or 'Santa Claus'. And our American children are probably the only ones in the world who say it just that way; indeed the learned, and very British, Encyclopedia Britannica calls our familiar form 'an American corruption' of the Dutch. I suspect, however, that we should hear something very like it from the lips of children in Holland and Germany; in parts of southern Germany the word in sound, and I think spelling might be something like, 'santiklos'.

Some religious historians and experts in folklore believe that there is no valid evidence to indicate that *St. Nicholas* ever existed as a human. In fact, there are quite a few indicators that his life story was simply recycled from those of Pagan gods. Many other ancient Pagan gods and goddesses were similarly Christianized in the early centuries of the Church. His legend seems to have been mainly created out of myths attributed to the Greek God *Poseidon*, the Roman God *Neptune*, and the Teutonic God *Hold Nackara*. "In the popular imagination [of many Russians] he became the heir of Mikoula[17], the god of harvest."

15 If you can call him a boy at the ripe age of 27 when he was appointed a Bishop.

16 What was meant by this statement is that the traditions and beliefs of the Dutch is how Saint Nicholas arrived on American soil and not by any actions he may have accomplished here.

17 Mikoula is legend to replace God, when God becomes too old.

The Roman Catholic Church (mainly the Pope) dropped Saint Nicholas from the honor rolls of Saints stating that there was no evidence that this man ever existed. Along with Saint Nicholas, went Saint Christopher who is highly revered in Ireland as the man who banished all the snakes from the island. So now we have the story of Saint Nicholas that even the church denies. I am sorry for my Christian brothers who so strongly believe in Saint Nicholas. They need to read the transcripts from the church when the Pope removed these two saints.[18]

The Birth of Santa Claus in America

Thomas Nast is a perfect example of the importance of knowing our heritage and just how many legacies one person can leave behind. Thomas Nast, through his wood engravings, sketches, and etchings helped to shape customs not only in America but also throughout the world.

Now we get to leave all the theories behind and the what-ifs of all the writings from earlier scholars and get down to the truthful business of discovering how Santa Claus actually was born here in America. I loved researching this part as much as I loved researching about mythology. Now let's get back to Thomas Nast and how this whole Santa Claus thing started and evolved. Yep, it evolved through the centuries to what we know of Santa today.

Nast was a pudgy little guy that had trouble speaking English and was assigned to draw Santa Claus one year. Not having an idea of what he looked like, Thomas drew him as the fur-clad, small, troll-like figure he had known in Bavaria when he was a child. This figure was quite unlike the tall Dutch Sinterklaas, who was traditionally depicted as a Catholic bishop. Nast may have actually drawn his first Santa depicting Saint Nicholas' dark helper, Swarthy, or Black Pete (a slang name for the devil in medieval Dutch).

The inspiration for how Nast's Santa should look came from the

18 If I can remember correctly, because I didn't write down this reference, that the Pope did this around 1955 to 1965. I wish I could remember better.

poem ‘Twas a Night Before Christmas, or known back then as a visit from Saint Nicholas. Since Thomas was lacking in reading skills, he had his wife read to him while he prepared his drawings and engravings each evening. On one occasion, Mrs. Nast read the poem to Thomas. That was all it took for inspiration. The rest is documented history.

For 24 years, Nast produced 76 Christmas engravings that were signed and published. He used the famous poem to put it all together in visual form; a sleigh, reindeer, jolly old elf, filling the stockings hung by the chimney, and so forth.

In addition, Nast used his own imagination to expand upon the Christmas theme. He was the first to establish that Santa’s home was in the North Pole. In this way, Santa didn’t belong to any one country -- he became a citizen of the world. The concept of Santa having a workshop and elves to help him was also Nast’s idea though they may have come from his Bavarian background.[19]

Prior to his engravings, all children received gifts from Santa. Nast conceived the idea that bad children didn’t get gifts from Santa. Again this could be because of his Bavarian background. The custom of sending Santa a letter is also due to Thomas Nast. Although the custom of kissing under mistletoe was known in Europe prior to Nast’s engravings, it was through his engravings in America that the custom caught on there.

Thomas Nast brought Christmas to a large audience through his engravings and subsequent publishing’s. The result of the impact that these drawings had on American’s is seen today in the well established practice of Santa Claus. In Europe, Christmas was observed for centuries on December 6. By the late 1800’s when Nast’s Santa Claus gained popularity, Christmas Day was legally established as December 25 in all states and territories in the United States. In addition, an extended school vacation during this period became a custom. It is said this custom began as a means for the children to write Nast and thank him for the season and vacation break from school.

19 Remember that believing in elves, fairies, gnomes and other such mythical creatures was part of his heritage and past life.

From this seed, Christmas began the move to commercial and economic interests. Stores began including drawings of Santa (though not necessarily done by Nast) in their ads and tying it in with Christmas sales and promotions. Soon to follow was the custom of sending Christmas cards. Without Nast and his Christmas drawings he brought to the masses, it is hard to tell what Christmas customs we would be celebrating today. We could all be looking for flying pigs for all I know and can think of.

Dates Associated with Christmas and Santa Claus

Now let's look at some real hard facts and chronology of Santa Claus and Christmas. Have you ever wondered where all our American traditions come from? Well read on and wonder no more. These next few pages give you dates of when things came about along with some background. If you want more information on any subject listed, look in the back of the book and see the references used. They will be very useful in your search for more information.

To keep the critics happy, I won't begin this chronological diatribe with Pagan thoughts. I will begin with the Christian philosophy and thoughts on Santa.

270-280 Birth of St. Nicholas. He was ordained Bishop as a very young man, and spent his life helping the poor and underprivileged. He loved children and often went out at night disguised in a hooded cloak, to leave necessary gifts of money, clothing or food at the windows of unfortunate families. Now this account of St. Nicholas brings us closer to what we know and understand about Santa Claus.

328-343 St. Nicholas died on the 6th of December. This is not a known fact, just legend from the Christian writings. I tend to believe it was more along the lines of being developed to sway the Pagans over to Christianity.

Bells. The kinds of bells that relate to Christmas are, (1) cup form Church bells, which appear ca. AD 400 in Italy, and (2) bells on traveling animals, a practice that goes back to antiquity. Bells are transferred from St. Nicholas's horse to Santa Claus's reindeer. There is no reference to Christmas in "Jingle Bells," recorded by J. S. Pierpont, Boston, 1857. The first Salvation Army donation kettle was present at Oakland ferry in 1891. The associated hand bells are not mentioned at this time.

4th century: There are two main, incompatible belief systems about St. Nicholas:
Among Roman Catholics and conservative Protestants, there is a near universal belief that *St. Nicholas of Bari* once lived in Asia Minor, and died in either 345 or 352. The *Catholic Information Network* speculates that he was probably born in Patara in the province of Myra in Asia Minor; this is apparently based on the belief that he later became bishop of Myra in Lycia (now Turkey). He is alleged to have attended the first council of Nicea; however, his name does not appear on lists of attending bishops. He is honored as a Patron Saint in Austria, Belgium, Germany, Greece, Italy, Netherlands, Russia, Sicily, and Switzerland. He is also considered the patron saint of children and sailors.

540 There was an elaborate Basilica built over his tomb, and dedicated to the saint.

600 The Saxons which invaded and settled Britain had the custom of giving human characteristics to the weather elements, welcoming the characters of King Frost, Lord Snow etc. to their homes in the hopes that the elements would look kindly on them. They would dress an actor in a pointed cap and cloak or cape, and drape him with Ivy, bringing him into their midst, and bidding him join their feast. He was to represent the Season, and would be treated with all respect, and drink toasts to him.

800 The Vikings brought with them their beliefs in the Northern deities and Elementals, and their main god Odin or Woden, who in the guise of his December character came to earth dressed in a hooded cloak, to sit and listen to his people and see if they are contented or not. It was said that he carried a satchel full of bounty which he distributed to the needy or worthy. He was portrayed as a Sage with long white beard and hair. There is no written proof of the fact, but it is probable that, like the Saxons, they dressed a man to represent Odin or Woden in his circuit of good works.

842 First written life of St. Nicholas listing all his miracles, by Methodius, Bishop of Constantinople.

850 The Clergy of Cologne Cathedral were commemorating the death of the saint by giving fruit and cookies to the boys of the cathedral school, on the 6th December.

987 Nicholas became Patron Saint of Russia. By this time, his fame had spread far and wide, and he was adopted by many guilds and groups as their patron, including: Sailors; Children; Spinsters; Pawnbrokers. All bearing a direct reasoning to the stories told about Nicholas. As patron saint of sailors, his effigy was the figurehead of many ships, and thus his cult spread across the seas to Britain, (and later to the New World).

1087 Italian Merchants steal the bones of St. Nicholas from his tomb in Demre, and take them to Bari, Italy. This was unofficially approved by the Church, which was anxious because the shrine of the saint was desecrated in the many wars and attacks in the region. Also, by that time, the break between the Universal Church creating Roman Catholic and Eastern Orthodox was a contributing factor. The Roman Church felt that the bones of this most popular of saints should be in their safe keeping!

10th century: The Christian author Metaphrastes collected and wrote many traditional legends about St. Nicholas.

1119 Life of St. Nicholas written by a Norman monk named Jean.

1120 Nuns in Belgium and France were giving gifts to the children of the poor, and those in their care, on the Saints Feast Day, 6th December.

1150 Guace, a Norman French scribe to the royal household, wrote the life of Nicholas as Metric Poems for use as sermons.

Yule log (usually of oak or ash), is a burning rite, probably of some antiquity, recorded in Germany in 1184 and later in the Italian Alps, Balkans, Scandinavia, France and Iberia. The ceremony is flourishing in Devon, England, by the 1630's and becomes associated with Father Christmas. Goose as Christmas food is probably a part of this tail too.

1200 Hilarius, who studied under Peter Abelard, wrote the first 'musical' play about Nicholas.
In the 1200s, December sixth began to be celebrated as Bishop Nicholas Day in France.

1300 Until this time Nicholas was portrayed with a short dark beard, like an Eastern Bishop. Belief in Odin or Woden, flying through the skies on his eight legged white horse, Sleipnir, with his long white beard flowing, was superimposed over the saint's characteristics, and he developed a white beard. In Germanic countries he was further overlaid with the character of 'Winterman' who supposedly came down from the mountains with the snows, dressed in furs and skins, heralding winter. This character was also known in Scandinavia, where the Laps believed that he herded the reindeer down to lower pastures, and this was a sign that the winter snows were coming.

Laps homes had one opening, which was both door and smoke hole. They were dome shaped houses, usually covered with skins, and usually with top openings. For this reason the subsequent romantic story that Santa comes down the chimney could have been developed.

Gift giving was common during the Roman Saturnalia. Nuns in

France started giving gifts to the poor on the eve of St. Nicholas' Saint's Day, 13th century. Gift giving was repressed by the medieval church.

1400 Over 500 songs and hymns had been written in honor of Nicholas by this date.
The first Europeans to arrive in the New World brought St. Nicholas; Vikings dedicated their cathedral to him in Greenland. On his first voyage, Columbus named a Haitian port for St. Nicholas on December 6, 1492. In Florida, Spaniards named an early settlement St. Nicholas Ferry, now known as Jacksonville.

1500 More than 700 churches in Britain alone were dedicated to St. Nicholas by this date.
There is some small evidence to support the fact that in Europe, street parades were held led by a man dressed in Bishops robes and Mitered hat, riding a horse, on the feast of St. Nicholas, in the late Middle Ages.

In Britain, each parish would employ a man from outside the parish to dress in long hooded guise, and go to each home leaving a small gift and taking back any important news of the needy to the priests.

1500's: People in England stopped worshipping St Nicholas and favored another gift giving figure Father Christmas. Over the centuries, St. Nicholas' popularity grew, and many people in Europe made up new stories that showed his concern for children.

The name Santa Claus was derived from the Dutch Sinter Klass pronunciation of St. Nicholas. Early Dutch settlers in New York (once called New Amsterdam) brought their traditions of St Nicholas. As children from other countries tried to pronounce Sinter Klass, this soon became Santa Klass, which was settled as Santa Claus. The old bishop's cloak with miter, jeweled gloves and crosier were soon replaced with his red suit and clothing seen in other modern images.

St. Nicholas had a difficult time during the 16th century Protestant Reformation which took a dim view of saints. Even though both reformers and counter-reformers tried to stamp out St. Nicholas-related customs, they had very little long-term success: only in England were the religious folk traditions of Christmas permanently altered. (It is ironic that fervent Puritan Christians began what turned into a trend to a more secular Christmas observance.) Because the common people so loved St. Nicholas, he survived on the European continent as people continued to place nuts, apples, and sweets in shoes left beside beds, on windowsills, or before the hearth.

1600's: The Puritans made it illegal to mention St. Nicolas' name. People were not allowed to exchange gifts, light a candle, or sing Christmas carols.

In the 1600's, the Dutch presented Sinterklaas (meaning St. Nicholas) to the colonies. In their excitement, many English-speaking children uttered the name so quickly that Sinterklaas sounded like Santy Claus. After years of mispronunciation, the name evolved into Santa Claus.

Winter festival food (original Christmas food at Jamestown, 1608) is oysters, fish, "meat," wild fowl and bread. Eggnog, originally egg grog (post-1750) is a later colonial Virginia concoction. It was made by adding rum to the French drink *lait de poule.* Traditional winter festival food is boar, roast, mince (meat) pie, plum pudding (raisin "hearts," no plums), sugarplums (originally greengage plums boiled in syrup and cornstarch, crystallized by cooling, but now considered to be chocolate coated cordials. The term survives from Moore's A Visit from St. Nicholas poem "with visions of sugarplums dancing" and The Nutcracker Suite "Sugarplum fairy"). Goose also included in the meal. Wassailing (salutation drinking from a bowl), is an Anglo-Saxon (at least the term) - Wass Hael, "Be in health." The bowl was to be kept full from Christmas Eve until the Twelfth Night.

1607 According to reports by Captain John Smith of Jamestown, Virginia, the first eggnog[20] made in the United States was consumed in his 1607 Jamestown settlement.

20 Nog comes from the word grog, which refers to any drink made with rum.

1616 Ben Jonson presented his play, 'Christmas, his Masque' at the Court of King James. In this the Season of Christmas is represented by an actor, and his entourage consists of the special characteristics of Christmas impersonate. Minced Pie, Plum Pudding etc. were treats of the day.

Harvest bounty food (supposed original food at Plymouth Rock, 1621) is turkey, pumpkin, corn, lima beans and cranberries. The only food items that have any documentation at the original meal, however, are venison and wild fowl (turkey?). Turkey was domesticated in Mesoamerica and was in England by 1524 and then to New England by early colonists and crossbred. Some original Pilgrims may have eventually known of domesticated turkey. To show the split in food pattern, Puritans banned mince pie in colonial and commonwealth Massachusetts. They believed the devil was baked in. It is now tolerated for Thanksgiving.

1626 A fleet of ships led by the 'GOEDE VROWE' (Goodwife), which had a figurehead of St. Nicholas, left Holland for the New World. They purchased some land from the Iroquois, for $24, named the village 'NEW AMSTERDAM' (Now New York), and erected a statue in the square to St. Nicholas.

1645 A Broadsheet appeared on the streets of London, taunting the Government by a humorous political 'scandal' about the conviction and imprisonment of Christmas, and the Hue and Cry after his escape.

1647 Christmas was banned in England, and the traditional mummers plays were visited by Father Christmas, who issued a taunting challenge to the government. "In comes I, Old Father Christmas, Be I welcome or be I not, I hope that Christmas will ne'er be forgot"

1651 The State of Massachusetts, settled by English Puritans, banned all observation of Christmas.

1664AD New Amsterdam was fought over and won by the British, who renamed the settlement, New York. They first banned St. Nicholas, and his statue fell. But later came to accept the pleasures of the festival of the saint, not associating it with Christmas, it being held on December 6th.

Candy Cane. Candy canes are replicas of shepherd's crooks. It was children's candy originated by a Cologne cathedral choirmaster in the 1670's. It is ideal in form to hang on the branch of a Christmas tree. In 1859 Amalia Eriksson, Granna, Sweden, devised the manufacture of alternating red (peppermint) and white striped rock candy. According to Nancy Baggett (*All-American Dessert Book*, Houghton Mifflin 2005) candy canes became popular in the United States in the 1920s when Bob McCormack of Albany, Georgia produced them in large numbers. His ingredients were corn syrup, sugar, peppermint flavoring and starch. In the 1950s his brother-in-law devised a machine that enabled him to undertake mass production

1678 A book was published in London entitled 'The Examination and Trial of old Father Christmas' and his clearing by Jury. It was from this book that the movie "Miracle on 34th Street" came.

From the 17th - 19th century it was the country mummer's plays which kept Father Christmas alive in Britain. With the 'cleansing' of religious popery, it is interesting to note that the saintly bishop, represented by the Parish gift-bringing visitor was replaced once more by the half Pagan Impersonation of the Element or Season of Christmas.

17th century: Dutch immigrants brought with them the legend of Sinter Klaas.

The American version of the Santa Claus figure received its inspiration and its name from the Dutch legend of Sinter Klaas, brought by settlers to New York in the 17th century.

1773 St. Nicholas first made the news in the New York Gazette which referred to him as otherwise known as St. A. Claus.

As early as 1773 the name appeared in the American press as "St.

A. Claus," but it was the popular author Washington Irving who gave Americans their first detailed information about the Dutch version of Saint Nicholas. In his History of New York, published in 1809 under the pseudonym Diedrich Knickerbocker, Irving described the arrival of the saint on horseback (unaccompanied by Black Peter) each Eve of Saint Nicholas. Black Peter (Zwarte Piet) is from the Netherlands. He is said to be the devil that Saint Nicholas defeated and now shackles him before the feast of Nicholas to do his bidding.

Colonial Germans in Pennsylvania held the feast of St. Nicholas, and several accounts do have St. Nicholas visiting New York Dutch on New Years' Eve. Patriots formed the Sons of St. Nicholas in 1773, not to honor Bishop Nicholas, but rather as a non-British symbol to counter the English St. George societies. This St. Nicholas society was similar to the Sons of St. Tammany in Philadelphia. Not exactly St. Nicholas, the children's gift-giver. The Saint Nicholas Society of the City of New York was founded by Washington Irving and others, as an organization to commemorate the history and heritage of New York, and to promote good fellowship among the members.

1804: The New York Historical Society was founded with St. Nicolas as its patron saint. Its members engaged in the Dutch practice of gift-giving at Christmas.

1805-1806: Here is where Major Livingston supposedly wrote his poem "A Visit From Saint Nicholas". Not that Santa Claus has been around for a while at this point. It wasn't until a few years later that Americans began to describe Santa and how he travels.

1808 American writer, Washington Irving, described St. Nicholas in his 'History of New York', in a description of the figurehead on the ship Goede Vrowe, as being ..."equipped with a low brimmed hat, huge pair of Flemish hose and a pipe that reached to the end of the bowsprit....."

Irving created a new version of old St. Nick. This one rode over the treetops in a horse drawn wagon "dropping gifts down the chimneys of his favorites." In his satire, *Diedrich Knickerbocker's History of New York from the Beginning of the World to the End of the Dutch Dynasty*, Irving described Santa as a jolly Dutchman who smoked a long stemmed clay pipe and wore baggy breeches and a broad brimmed hat. Also, the familiar phrase, "...laying his finger beside his nose...," first appeared in Irving's story.

After the American Revolution, New Yorkers remembered with pride the colony's nearly-forgotten Dutch roots, John Pintard, influential patriot and antiquarian, who founded the New York Historical Society in 1804, promoted St. Nicholas as patron saint of both society and city. In January 1809, Washington Irving joined the society and on St. Nicholas Day that year he published the satirical fiction, *Knickerbocker's History of New York*, with numerous references to a jolly St. Nicholas character. This was not a saintly bishop, rather an elfin Dutch burgher[21] with a clay pipe. These delightful flights of imagination are the origin of the New Amsterdam St. Nicholas legends; that the first Dutch emigrant ship had a figurehead of St. Nicholas; that St. Nicholas Day was observed in the colony; that the first church was dedicated to him; and that St. Nicholas comes down chimneys to bring gifts. Irving's work was regarded as the "first notable work of imagination in the New World".

Washington Irving's St. Nicholas may have strongly influenced the poem's, (*A Visit From Saint Nicholas*) portrayal of a round, pipe-smoking, elf-like St. Nicholas. The poem generally has been attributed to Clement Clark Moore, a professor of biblical languages at New York's Episcopal General Theological Seminary. However, a case has been made by Don Foster in Author Unknown, that Henry Livingston actually penned it in 1807 or 1808. Livingston was a farmer/patriot who wrote humorous verse for children. In any case, "*A Visit from St. Nicholas*" became a defining American holiday classic. No matter who wrote it, the poem has had enormous influence on the Americanization of St. Nicholas.

This is an Anglo-American adaptation from Dutch children having their wooden shoes filled with gifts. The "Hang up a stocking on the

21 A Burgher is a distinguished gentleman. In Germany, the Burgher Meiser was the town's Mayor or leader.

chimney," mentioned by Irving, 1809 is how this tradition evolved. The Pintard commissioned engraving by Alexander Anderson, 1810, shows a fireplace flanked by two oversized stockings. A poem, in whose meter Moore later copied his work, was published in a New York newspaper, 1815. It asks Santa Claus to bring gifts for children's stockings. This appeal may have been the crucial factor that suddenly allowed the shift of custom. There is a variation to the legend (see above) of St. Nicholas dropping gold coins through the chimney into stockings hung under the chimney to dry by maidens without a dowry.

1810 The New York Historical Society held its first St. Nicholas anniversary dinner on December 6, 1810, John Pintard commissioned artist Alexander Anderson to create the first American image of Nicholas for the occasion. Nicholas was shown in gift-giving role with children's treats in stockings hanging at a fireplace. The accompanying poem ends, "Saint Nicholas, my dear good friend! To serve you ever was my end, if you will, now, me something give, and I'll serve you ever while I live."

1812: Irving revised his book to include Nicolas riding over the trees in a wagon.

Perhaps nothing has fixed the image of Santa Claus so firmly in the American mind as a poem entitled *A Visit from St. Nicholas* written by Major Henry Livingston (1805). The Major drew upon Pintard's belief of the early New Amsterdam traditions and added some elements from German and Norse legends. These stories held that a happy little elf-like man presided over midwinter pagan festivals. In the poem, Livingston[22] depicts the Saint as a tiny man with a sleigh drawn by eight miniature reindeer. They fly him from house to house and at each residence he comes down the chimney to fill stockings hung by the fireplace with gifts.

Gift giving in colonial America was based on class differences, the

22 I am using Livingston here and not Samuel Clements Moore because Moore had not taken credit for this work yet. Livingston dies a few years before Moore took the credit for writing it. See later on in the book where I describe how I decided who actually wrote the book.

poor accosting the rich and demanding food, drink and money. In the 1820's, borrowing from the New York Dutch, gift giving was transferred to gifts for the children from parents. Livingston's poem may have been a factor in this. This started Christmas commercialization. Christmas shopping was encouraged to overcome the 1839-40 depression.

1821: William Gilley printed a poem about "Santeclaus" who was dressed in fur and drove a sleigh drawn by a single reindeer.

1822: Clement Clarke Moore is believed by many to have written a poem "*An Account of a Visit from Saint Nicolas*," which became better known as "*The Night before Christmas*." Santa is portrayed as an elf with a miniature sleigh equipped with eight reindeer which are named in the poem as Blitzen, Comet, Cupid, Dancer, Dasher, Donder, Prancer, and Vixen. Others attribute the poem to a contemporary, Major Henry Livingston, Jr.

This Dutch-American Saint Nick achieved his fully Americanized form in 1823 in the poem *A Visit From Saint Nicholas* more commonly known as *The Night Before Christmas*. The poem included such details as the names of the reindeer; Santa Claus's laughs, winks, and nods; and the method by which Saint Nicholas, referred to as an elf, returns up the chimney. (The poem's phrase "lays his finger aside of his nose" was drawn directly from Irving's 1809 description.)

Livingston had written the poem for the enjoyment of his own family, but in 1823 it was published anonymously in the *Troy Sentinel*. It became very popular and has been reprinted countless times under the more familiar title, *The Night Before Christmas*.

Santa Claus later appeared in various colored costumes as he gradually became amalgamated with the figure of Father Christmas, but red soon became popular after he appeared wearing such on an 1885 Christmas card. Still, one of the first artists to capture Santa Claus' image as we know him today was Thomas Nast, an American cartoonist of the 19th century. In 1863, a picture of Santa illustrated by Nast appeared in *Harper's Weekly*.

Nast continued to draw Santa Claus for several years. He created

75 prints of him in all. Said to be inspired by the poem, "A Visit From Saint Nicholas" Nast went on to create the foundation of Santa Claus: The North Pole, his workshop and elves as his helpers plus a lot more. The act of writing letter to Santa is also attributed to Nast.

Poinsettia, introduced to U.S. from Mexico by Joel Roberts Poinsett, Charleston, S.C., in 1828, while he was Minister to Mexico. It was considered to be the "flower of the blessed night," representing the star of Bethlehem to Mexicans in the 18th century. It is a common decoration in Mexican Nativity processions. The poinsettia as a potted plant was promoted by Albert Ecke, Hollywood, California, in the early 1900's.

Mistletoe, Connected to Germano-Celtic tree worship. Mistletoe is a common parasite on oak and ash trees. It remains green throughout the winter, thus symbolizing renewal. Kissing under mistletoe bough or sprigs was a custom of the English servant class in the 18th century until 1850 when it began to spread to the upper classes. Dickens describes the activity in the *Pickwick Papers*, 1837.

Holly[23], is used on festive occasions in Rome. Ivy was a common alternative, especially in England. Wreaths with berries originate with the Roman Christians. According to legend Christ's "crown of thorns" was of holly, the berries turning from white to red after crucifixion. Advent candles (four, one each Sunday before Christmas) in a wreath occur in Hamburg 1839, made by Lutherans. This custom may date back to 600 and may be the basis of the Advent Calendar?

1841: J.W. Parkinson, a Philadelphia merchant, hired a man to dress up in a "Criscringle" outfit and climb the chimney of his store.

In the 1840s, the Tomte or Nisei in Nordic folklore started to deliver

---

23 Commercial holly available today was hybridized by Kathleen Meserve on Long Island, New York in the 1950's. It is heartier than wild forms with brighter berries and glossier leaves. Also, unlike English holly, it can survive temperatures as low -20°F. It is called Meserve Holly.

the Christmas presents in Denmark, but was then called the "Julenisse", dressed in gray clothes and a red hat. By the end of the 19th century this tradition had also spread to Norway and Sweden (where the "nisse" is called *Tomte*), replacing the Yule Goat. The same thing happened in Finland, but there the more human figure retained the Yule Goat name. The Yule Goat relates back to Thor who road in a chariot drawn by two goats. The goats are killed and cooked for all his guests. Currently the goat is made of straw and lots of drinking before it is thrown on a bonfire and burned.

Christmas cards (approximately 1,000) were first printed in London, England. They were designed by John Calcott Horsley of the Royal Academy for Sir Henry Cole in 1843 and were sold at Felix Summerly's Home Treasury Office. The greeting was "A Very Merry Christmas and a Happy New Year to You." A portrayal of a child sipping wine in a toast on the central panel caused a stir with temperance groups. Cards were first mailed (to friends) by W. C. Dobson (Queen Victoria's favorite painter) in 1845. First mailings in U. S. were in 1846. Louis Prang, a Boston lithographer, marketed multicolored Christmas Cards in Europe in 1865 and in the U. S. in 1875. He made Christmas Cards popular. Mailing was expanded with the "penny post card," 1893. Half-tone engravings appear in 1900. The home photograph card begins in 1902 by Eastman Kodak.

The Ghost of Christmas Present, a colorized version of the original illustration by John Leech made for Charles Dickens's novel *A Christmas Carol* (1843).

Hubbard (winter) squash (from the Andes) is later food item and now thrives in the cool climate of New England. The "Irish" potato was domesticated in the Andes highlands and was introduced to America from Ireland after the Irish famine of 1845-46. The sweet potato was domesticated in northern tropical South America. It probably was introduced to the southern U.S. by Caribbean slaves in the early 18th century. The yam we are familiar with is not a true yam, but a variety of sweet potato.

1860's The English custom of a visit from Father Christmas was revived and established as the character visiting on Christmas Eve and leaving gifts for children in their stockings. Images, dolls and artwork from Germany helped to strengthen this custom.

The Germanic images showed him as a saint, in bishop's robes, as a winter man in furs, as a saintly old man, often seen in the company of the Holy Child, and as a gift-bringer in robes of every color from brown, white, green, blue to gold, pinks and red. Even in this latter guise, his countenance was serious more often than jolly, though laughing Santas did appear. These were usually those which were influenced by the American imagery, and intended for export to the USA.

1863 President Abraham Lincoln asked Nast to create a drawing of Santa with some Union soldiers. This image of Santa supporting the enemy had a demoralizing influence on the Confederate army -- an early example of psychological warfare. Thomas Nast created a political cartoon of Santa entitled '*Santa in Camp*', for *Harper's Weekly Journal.* Dressed in Stars and Stripes Santa had joined the civil war on the side of General Grant in the North.

Perhaps he could have also appeared (being Santa, and strictly neutral) dressed in rebel gray for the South, but if so it was a private drawing as the South did not have the publishing resources of the North.

In the South, by 1863, the Union had blockaded their ports and very little was able to get through. Southern families explained to their children that even "Santa" could not get through the blockade.

Thomas Nast, the well-known political cartoonist for the *Harper's Illustrated Weekly*, drew illustrations of Santa Claus from 1863 to 1886. In the Christmas season of 1866 he compiled a montage of drawings of Santa Claus. George P. Walker made five of these drawings into color lithographs illustrating a poem in a widely distributed children's book *Santa Claus and His Works*, ca., 1870 under the pseudonym George P. Webster. The poem steals in form, meter and style from the poem *A Visit from St. Nicholas*, but with different content.

1864-1886 Thomas Nast continued to draw Santa Claus every year, and became known as "THE" Santa Claus artist of the mid-1900.

Meanwhile Britain was importing illustrations and cards depicting Santa Claus from Germany. He was called Father Christmas by the English. He was usually represented as a tall, almost ascetic character, saintly and stern rather than the 'Jolly Elf' character being portrayed by the Americans.

1870's Santa Claus began to put in appearances in department stores in the USA and Canada.

1873 Louis Prang of Boston published the first American Christmas Card. His images showed Santa Claus much in the same tradition as the earlier American images, but with a softer, gentler look, more the saintly old gent than the jolly old elf.

1882 The world's first electrically lighted Christmas tree was decorated in the New York City home of Edward Johnson, a colleague of Thomas Edison at the then newly formed Edison Electric Company.

1885 Louis Prang, established the presently clad Santa Claus with black boots and belt, a bright red non-flannel white fur-lined suit and a white tufted tassel hat, in Christmas card illustrations. By the 1920's the red suit becomes standardized.

1885 a law was enacted giving federal employees Christmas day off. Christmas declared a legal holiday in U.S. late (1894 or early 20th century).

1889 The poet Katherine Lee Bates created a wife for Santa, Mrs. Claus, in the poem "*Goody Santa Claus on a Sleigh Ride*." The 1956 popular song by George Melachrino (of the Melachrino Orchestra), Mrs. Santa Claus, helped standardize and establish the character and role in the popular imagination.

In a Nast cartoon Santa Claus is sitting on a wooden trunk addressed

"Christmas Box 1882, St. Nicholas, North Pole." This continues the arctic cast of Santa Claus. There was enthusiastic acceptance of Santa Claus by Finns during Russo-Finnish War, 1939. They maintain Santa's winter quarters are at Rovaniemi, Finland, not the North Pole.

1890's General Electric, which had bought Edison's rights and his light bulb factory, began to promote Christmas-tree lights. These were individual bulbs shaped like the standard light bulbs of the time, which were smaller than those of today and had pointed tips. The services of a "wireman" (the electrician of the era) were needed to add the electrical wiring.

1890's Father Christmas began to appear in English Stores.

About 1890 Santa Claus' modern Christmas role becomes established. The first store Santa Claus was James Edgar, Brockton, Mass., 1890. Mrs. Claus created by Katherine Lee Bates, Sunshine and other Verses for Children, 1890, violating sainthood celibacy restrictions.

1892 A man dressed up as Santa Claus fundraising for Volunteers of America on the sidewalk of street in Chicago, Illinois. He is wearing a mask with a beard attached.

In some images of the early 20th century, Santa was depicted as personally making his toys by hand in a small workshop like a craftsman. Eventually, the idea emerged that he had numerous elves responsible for making the toys, but the toys were still handmade by each individual elf working in the traditional manner.

By the 19th century these two basic food traditions were blending in Europe and America. Though Dickens, *Christmas Carol* (1843), conveys a Winter Festival food tradition, Tiny Tim's family served fowl, and turkey is mentioned at end of the story. An ideal New Yorker (city) Christmas meal in 1875 was turkey stuffed with oysters.

1897: Francis P Church, Editor of the New York Sun, wrote an editorial in response to a letter from an eight year-old girl, Virginia O'Hanlon. She had written the paper asking whether there really was a Santa Claus.

It has become known as the "Yes, Virginia, there is a Santa Claus" letter.

1903. In the U.S., Miss Emily Bissell distributes Christmas seals, Wilmington, Delaware, Post Office, 1907. The proceeds were to fight tuberculosis.

1903 The ever-Ready Company of New York began manufacturing and marketing strings of lights, calling them "festoons."

1910 General Electric changed its miniature Christmas lights from standard light-bulb shape to a ball shape and added color by dipping them into transparent lacquer.

1920's: The image of Santa had been standardized to portray a bearded, over-weight, jolly man dressed in a red suit with white trim.

1922 Norman Rockwell created a perfect blend of saintly and jolly when he created Santa for the Saturday Evening Post.

In 1925, since grazing reindeer would not be possible at the North Pole, newspapers revealed that Santa Claus in fact lived in Finnish Lapland. "Uncle Markus", Markus Rautio, who narrated the popular "Children's hour" on Finnish public radio, revealed the great secret for the first time in 1927: Santa Claus lives on Lapland's Korvatunturi - "Ear Fell"

A communal Christmas tree was displayed on Mt. Wilson near Pasadena, California in 1909. General Grant redwood in Kings Canyon National Park was dedicated as the official Nation's Christmas tree, 1926.

1930's Christmas lights that flashed on and off became available.

1931: Haddon Sundblom, illustrator for The Coca-Cola Company drew a series of Santa images in their Christmas advertisements until 1964. The company holds the trademark for the Coca-Cola Santa design.

Images of Santa Claus were further cemented through Haddon Sundblom's depiction of him for The Coca-Cola Company's Christmas advertising. The popularity of the image spawned urban legends that Santa Claus was in fact invented by Coca-Cola or that Santa wears red and white because those are the Coca-Cola colors. In fact, Coca-Cola was not even the first soft drink company to utilize the modern image Santa Claus in its advertising – White Rock Beverages used Santa in advertisements for its ginger ale in 1923 after first using him to sell mineral water in 1915.

The American image of Santa Claus was further elaborated by illustrator Thomas Nast, who depicted a rotund Santa for Christmas issues of *Harper's Magazine* from the 1860s to the 1880s. Nast added such details as Santa's workshop at the North Pole and Santa's list of the good and bad children of the world. A human-sized version of Santa Claus, rather than the elf of the famous *Night Before Christmas* poem, was depicted in a series of illustrations for Coca-Cola advertisements introduced in 1931.

1931. In modern versions of the Santa Claus legend, only his toy-shop workers are elves. Rudolph, the ninth reindeer, with a red and shiny nose, was invented in 1939 by an advertising writer for the Montgomery Ward Company

Finally, from 1931 to 1964, Haddon Sundblom created a new Santa each Christmas for Coca-Cola advertisements that appeared world-wide on the back covers of Post and National Geographic magazines. This is the Santa we know and love today with a red suit trimmed with white fur, leather boots and belt, long white beard and a pack of toys slung onto his back.

1939 Copywriter Robert L. May of the *Montgomery Ward Company* created a poem about Rudolph, the ninth reindeer. May had been "*often taunted as a child for being shy, small and slight.*" He created an ostracized reindeer with a shiny red nose who became a hero one foggy Christmas eve. Santa was part-way through deliveries when the visibility started to degenerate. Santa added Rudolph to his team of reindeer to help illuminate the path. A copy of the poem was given free to Montgomery Ward customers.

1945-1950 "BubbleLites" were launched with much fanfare and for a few years in the mid 50's, sales were spectacular. Invented by Carl Otis, an accountant for Montgomery Ward, the bulbs contained methylene chloride, a liquid that will boil at the low temperature of a tree light.

1948 Department Stores in Britain increased the thrill of their Santa Grotto with train rides, sleigh rides, trip to the moon and elaborate animated scenes.

The concept of Santa Claus continues to inspire writers and artists, such as in author Seabury Quinn's 1948 novel "*Roads*", which draws from historical legends to tell the story of Santa and the origins of Christmas. Other modern additions to the "mythology" of Santa include *Rudolph the Red-Nosed Reindeer*, the ninth and lead reindeer immortalized in a Gene Autry song, written by a Montgomery Ward copywriter.

Commercially cut trees were in Philadelphia markets by 1848 and tree cutting in the Catskills by Mark Carr, 1851 created a market in New York City. The artificial Christmas trees, made of wire and covered with feathers, appear in Germany in the 1800s. The first artificial brush trees were manufactured by the Addis Brush Co in 1930s. A Christmas tree at the White House, Washington, D.C., was decorated by Franklin Pierce (friend of Nathaniel Hawthorne) in 1856. The annual lighting of the Christmas tree at the White House began in 1923. The tree was cut and sent to President Calvin Coolidge from Middlebury College in his native state of Vermont. National Living Christmas Tree was planted at Sherman Square near White House, 1924.

1949: Johnny Marks wrote the song "*Rudolph the Red-Nosed Reindeer.*" Rudolph was relocated to the North Pole where he was initially rejected by the other reindeer who wouldn't let him play in their reindeer games because of his strange looking nose. The song was recorded by Gene Autry and became his all-time best seller. Next to "*White Christmas*" it is the most popular song of all time. Rollo and Reginald were names also considered by May.

1950's English Father Christmas slowly gives way to American Santa Claus.

Since the 1950s, Santa has happily sojourned at Napapiiri, near Rovaniemi, at times other than Christmas, to meet children and the young at heart. By 1985 his visits to Napapiiri had become so regular that he established his own Santa Claus Office there. He comes there every day of the year to hear what children want for Christmas and to talk with children who have arrived from around the world. Santa Claus Village is also the location of Santa's main Post Office, which receives children's letters from the four corners of the world.

1970's Flashing midget lights, marketed as "Twinkle lights", became the biggest sellers in the history or tree lights.

1980's European traditions of Gift-bringers begin to give way to Santa Claus. Spain's Three Kings, Italy's Befana, and Sweden's Tomte in particular have all given way to Santa as the anticipated gift-bringer, sometimes even as an additional gift-bringer.

1993: An urban folk tale began to circulate about a Japanese department store displaying a life-sized Santa Claus being crucified on a cross. It never happened but became an internet sensation.

1997: Artist Robert Cenedella drew a painting of a crucified Santa Claus. It was displayed in the window of the New York's Art Students League and received intense criticism from some religious groups. His drawing was a protest. He attempted to show how Santa Claus had replaced Jesus Christ as the most important personality at Christmas time.

19th century: St. Nicholas was superseded in much of Europe by Christkindlein, the Christ child, who delivered gifts in secret to the children. He traveled with a dwarf-like helper called Pelsnickle (a.k.a. Belsnickle) or with St. Nicholas-like figures. Eventually, all three were combined into the image that we now know as Santa Claus. "Christkindlein" became Kris Kringle.

Before the communist revolution, large numbers of Russian Orthodox pilgrims came to Bari to visit St Nicholas' tomb. "*He and St Andrew the apostle are the patrons of Russia.*"

The Interesting Conclusion

In looking for the historical roots of Santa Claus, one must go very deep in the past. One discovers that Santa Claus as we know him is a combination of many different legends and mythical creatures. Make up your own mind as to what you want to believe. I prefer to think back to the Pagan times and how they celebrated before Christianity.

The basis for the Christian-era Santa Claus is Bishop Nicholas of Myrna (Izmir), in what is now Turkey. Nicholas lived in the 4th century A.D. He was very rich, generous, and loving toward children. Often he gave joy to poor children by throwing gifts in through their windows.

The Orthodox Church later raised St. Nicholas, miracle worker, to a position of great esteem. It was in his honor that Russia's oldest church, for example, was built. For its part, the Roman Catholic Church honored Nicholas as one who helped children and the poor. St. Nicholas became the patron saint of children and seafarers. His name day is December 6th.

In the Protestant areas of central and northern Germany, St. Nicholas later became known as der Weinachtsmann. In England he came to be called Father Christmas. St. Nicholas made his way to the United States with Dutch immigrants, and began to be referred to as Santa Claus.

In North American poetry and illustrations, Santa Claus, in his white beard, red jacket and pompom-topped cap, would sally forth on the night before Christmas in his sleigh, pulled by eight reindeer (which later became nine reindeer), and climb down chimneys to leave his gifts in stockings children set out on the fireplace's mantelpiece.

Children naturally wanted to know where Santa Claus actually came from. Where did he live when he wasn't delivering presents? Those questions gave rise to the legend that Santa Claus lived at the North Pole, where his Christmas-gift workshop was also located.

In 1925, since grazing reindeer would not be possible at the North Pole, newspapers revealed that Santa Claus in fact lived in Finnish Lapland. "Uncle Markus", Markus Rautio, who compared the popular "Children's hour" on Finnish public radio, revealed the great secret for the first time in 1927: Santa Claus lives on Lapland's Korvatunturi - "Ear Fell"

The fell, which is situated directly on Finland's eastern frontier, somewhat resembles a hare's ears - which are in fact Santa Claus' ears, with which he listens to hear if the world's children are being nice. Santa has the assistance of a busy group of elves, who have quite their own history in Scandinavian legend.

Over the centuries, customs from different parts of the Northern Hemisphere thus came together and created the whole world's Santa Claus - the ageless, timeless, deathless white-bearded man who gives out gifts on Christmas and always returns to Korvatunturi in Finnish Lapland.

Since the 1950s, Santa has happily sojourned at Napapiiri, near Rovaniemi, at times other than Christmas, to meet children and the young at heart. By 1985 his visits to Napapiiri had become so regular that he established his own Santa Claus Office there. He comes there every day of the year to hear what children want for Christmas and to talk with children who have arrived from around the world. Santa Claus Village is also the location of Santa's main Post Office, which receives children's letters from the four corners of the world.

Present day: Santa around the World.

Today's Santa looks like a happy grand-dad. He lives at the North Pole and has lots of elf helpers who work in his toy factory. He keeps a check on whether children have been naughty or nice so that he knows what to do when they write to ask him for presents. On Christmas Eve Santa fills his sleigh with presents and, pulled by flying reindeer, he delivers gifts around the world. On Christmas morning he enjoys a well-earned rest while Mrs. Claus takes care of him.

Throughout many countries in Europe, St. Nicholas/Santa distributes gifts to the children on December 5th, the eve of his feast day. In some countries, the gifts come at another times during Advent or on Christmas Eve.

In **Australia**, the holiday comes in the middle of summer and it's not unusual for some parts of Australia to hit 100 degrees Fahrenheit on Christmas day.

During the warm and sunny Australian Christmas season, beach time and outdoor barbecues are common. Traditional Christmas day celebrations include family gatherings, exchanging gifts and either a hot meal with ham, turkey, pork or seafood or barbeques.

Most **Canadian** Christmas traditions are very similar to those practiced in the United States. In the far north of the country, the Eskimos celebrate a winter festival called *sinck tuck*, which features parties with dancing and the exchanging of gifts.

Central America A manger scene is the primary decoration in most southern European, Central American, and South American nations. St. Francis of Assisi created the first living nativity in 1224 to help explain the birth of Jesus to his followers.

In **England**, Father Christmas delivers the presents. He is shown with holly, ivy or mistletoe. An Englishman named John Calcott Horsley helped to popularize the tradition of sending Christmas greeting cards when he began producing small cards featuring festive scenes and a pre-written holiday greeting in the late 1830s. Newly efficient post offices in England and the United States made the cards nearly overnight sensations. At about the same time, similar cards were being made by R.H. Pease, the first American card maker, in Albany, New York, and Louis Prang, a German who immigrated to America in 1850.

Celtic and Teutonic peoples had long considered mistletoe to have magic powers. It was said to have the ability to heal wounds and increase fertility. Celts hung mistletoe in their homes in order to bring themselves good luck and ward off evil spirits. During holidays in the Victorian era, the English would hang sprigs of mistletoe from ceilings and in doorways. If someone was found standing under the mistletoe, they would be kissed by someone else in the room, behavior not usually demonstrated in Victorian society.

Plum pudding is an English dish dating back to the Middle Ages. Suet, flour, sugar, raisins, nuts, and spices are tied loosely in cloth and boiled until the ingredients are "plum," meaning they have enlarged enough to fill the cloth. It is then unwrapped, sliced like cake, and topped with cream.

Caroling also began in England. Wandering musicians would travel from town to town visiting castles and homes of the rich. In return for their performance, the musicians hoped to receive a hot meal or money.

Finland *'Hyvää Joulua!'* Many Finns visit the sauna on Christmas Eve. Families gather and listen to the national "Peace of Christmas" radio broadcast. It is customary to visit the gravesites of departed family members.

In **France**, Père Noël distributes the gifts. In France, Christmas is called Noel. This comes from the French phrase les bonnes nouvelles, which means "the good news" and refers to the gospel.

In southern France, some people burn a log in their homes from Christmas Eve until New Year's Day. This stems from an ancient tradition in which farmers would use part of the log to ensure good luck for the next year's harvest.

In **Germany**, Weinachtsmann, *'Froehliche Weihnachten!* (Christmas man) is a helper of the Christkind (Christ Child). Christkind (Kris Kringle) means "Christ Child" in German and originally is applied to the Holy Infant who was thought to bring gifts on Christmas Eve.

Gradually, it evolved into an angelic helper who brought the presents. This figure carries a tiny Christmas tree. The household know he has been there by the ringing of a bell when the presents are all in place under the tree. He is expected each year by the people in Germany, Switzerland, Austria and with the Pennsylvania Dutch in America.

Decorating evergreen trees had always been a part of the German winter solstice tradition. The first "Christmas trees" explicitly decorated and named after the Christian holiday, appeared in Strasbourg, in Alsace in the beginning of the 17th century. After 1750, Christmas trees began showing up in other parts of Germany, and even more so after 1771, when Johann Wolfgang von Goethe visited Strasbourg and promptly included a Christmas tree is his novel, *The Suffering of Young Werther.* In the 1820s, the first German immigrants decorated Christmas trees in Pennsylvania. After Germany's Prince Albert married Queen Victoria, he introduced the Christmas tree tradition to England. In 1848, the first American newspaper carried a picture of a Christmas tree and the custom spread to nearly every home in just a few years.

Greece *'Kala Christouyenna!'* In Greece, many people believe in *kallikantzeri*, goblins that appear to cause mischief during the 12 days of Christmas. Gifts are usually exchanged on January 1, St. Basil's Day.

Italians call Chrismas Il Natale, meaning "the birthday." Befana, another character was added to the Saint Nicholas family tree. It was a very old woman by the name of Befana. She was a genial hag who searched the world leaving candy and sweets for good children, and stones and coal for the bad. A legend tells us of her history and how she met the Three Wise Men as they were searching for the Bethlehem Christ child. They invited her to accompany them in their quest, but she was too busy with her household duties. After they left, she changed her mind and searched desperately for them, but it was too late, they were well gone. Befana continues her search, hoping to fine the baby Jesus, leaving presents wherever there are children.

Mexico *'Feliz Navidad!'* In 1828, the American minister to Mexico, Joel R. Poinsett, brought a red-and-green plant from Mexico to America. As its coloring seemed perfect for the new holiday, the plants, which were called poinsettias after Poinsett, began appearing in greenhouses as early as 1830. In 1870, New York stores began to sell them at Christmas. By 1900, they were a universal symbol of the holiday.

In Mexico, *papier-mâché* sculptures called *piñatas* are filled with candy and coins and hung from the ceiling. Children then take turns hitting the piñata until it breaks, sending a shower of treats to the floor. Children race to gather as much of the loot as they can.

Norway *'Gledelig Jul!'* Norway is the birthplace of the Yule log. The ancient Norse used the Yule log in their celebration of the return of the sun at winter solstice. "Yule" came from the Norse word hweol, meaning wheel. The Norse believed that the sun was a great wheel of fire that rolled towards and then away from the earth. Ever wonder why the family fireplace is such a central part of the typical Christmas scene? This tradition dates back to the Norse Yule log. It is probably also responsible for the popularity of log-shaped cheese, cakes, and desserts during the holidays

In these countries, the holiday is considered the beginning of the Christmas season and, as such, is sometimes referred to as "little Yule." Traditionally, on the 13th of December, the oldest daughter in each family rises early and wakes each of her family members, dressed in a long, white gown with a red sash, and wearing a crown made of twigs with nine lighted candles. For the day, she is called "Lussi" or "Lussibruden (Lucy bride)." The family then eats breakfast in a room lighted with candles.

Any shooting or fishing done on St. Lucia Day was done by torchlight, and people brightly illuminated their homes. At night, men, women, and children would carry torches in a parade. The night would end when everyone threw their torches onto a large pile of straw, creating a huge bonfire. In Finland today, one girl is chosen to serve as the national Lucia and she is honored in a parade in which she is surrounded by torchbearers.

Light is a main theme of St. Lucia Day, as her name, which is derived from the Latin word lux, means light. Her feast day is celebrated near the shortest day of the year, when the sun's light again begins to strengthen. Lucia lived in Syracuse during the fourth century when persecution of Christians was common. Unfortunately, most of her story has been lost over the years. According to one common legend, Lucia lost her eyes while being tortured by a Diocletian for her Christian beliefs. Others say she may have plucked her own eyes out to protest the poor treatment of Christians. Lucia is the patron saint of the blind.

In **Russia**, under the influence of communism, St. Nicolas evolved into the secular Father Frost. He distributes toys to children on New Year's Eve.

Sweden *'God Jul!'* Most people in Scandinavian countries honor St. Lucia (also known as St. Lucy) each year on December 13. The celebration of St. Lucia Day began in Sweden, but had spread to Denmark and Finland by the mid-19th century.

In **Scandinavian countries**, the ancient Pagan Yule goat has transmuted into Joulupukki - similar to the American Santa.

From the heart of **Siberia** comes the legend of Dedt Moroz or Father Ice. Lore has it, a kind and gentle young girl was banished from her house to the frozen forest by her mean stepmother. As she began to freeze, a huge blizzard parted and Dedt Moroz appeared. Charmed by her Godliness, he showered her with diamonds.

The wicked stepmother immediately ushered her own daughter out to reap the same benefits. This ill-tempered, spoiled child disgusted Dedt Moroz with her behavior. He waved his arm and froze her for eternity.

Combining the elements of religion, history and folklore, the **Ukrainian** people give us this special version of St. Nicholas. With the acceptance of Christianity in Kievan Rus in 988 AD under the rule of Vladimir The Great, along came the customs and pageantry for all the religious holidays, including Christmas. Through the Centuries, Christianity spread North and Eastwards into the surrounding lands that would eventually become Russia. By the 1800's, the Russian St. Nicholas was a figure carrying the punishment of birch switches as well as gifts, symbolized by a Christmas tree. Now we can see both reward and punishment are retained in one elegant figure. *'Srozhdestvom Kristovym!'* Ukrainians prepare a traditional twelve-course meal. A family's youngest child watches through the window for the evening star to appear, a signal that the feast can begin.

In **North America**, Santa Claus rules, thanks to a certain brand of soda. Three cheers for Coca Cola and their Santa Efforts. If you ever have the chance and are in the Atlanta, Georgia area, visit the Coca Cola museum. It is wonderful and the Santa memorabilia are terrific.

In the **United States** and **England**, children hang stockings on their bedpost or near a fireplace on Christmas Eve, hoping that it will be filled with treats while they sleep. In Scandinavia, similar-minded children leave their shoes on the hearth. This tradition can be traced to legends about Saint Nicholas. One legend tells of three poor sisters who could not marry because they had no money for a dowry. To save them from being sold by their father, St. Nick left each of the three sister's gifts of gold coins. One went down the chimney and landed in a pair of shoes that had been left on the hearth. Another went into a window and into a pair of stockings left hanging by the fire to dry.

Twelfth Century Europe was a time of castles and Kings, Wizards, Jesters and Gypsies. During the Christmas season, castle gates were left open. Holiday travelers on foot and horseback were made welcome … especially Santa. The medieval Santa traveled through the countryside delivering his gifts from hamlet to town and spreading good cheer. Sometimes when his load was very heavy, folklore said he would be seen accompanied by the merry band of gnomes.

During the **Victorian era**, Santa Claus took extreme care and pride in his presentation to the public as a fine gentleman. With clay pipe, elegant costuming, and stylish manner, this Santa brought the finest gifts. The Victorian World each year awaited this man to spread lots his affluence and bring abundant joy. Lucky were the children that he visited.

More Recent Developments

It's possible that there will never be an ending to the evolution of Santa Claus. We keep seeing minor changes. In the 1930s the Coca Cola Company published ads of Santa drinking their product. These ads were very well received, and our perception of Santa changed once again.

The *Miracle on 34th Street* took away much of Santa's elfin quality. He became more human and it placed him in the department stores. This movie changed the way Americans look at Santa.

Since the world has seen Tim Allen's movie, *The Santa Clause*, there is no question in anyone's mind as to what Santa's workshop at the North Pole looks like. What can be next? Maybe I shouldn't ask for I am afraid of what may come. Not really, I am looking forward to the next generations of changes.

It's true that Santa brings joy to the faces of the children as we chat with them; however, the affection of the children and its reciprocal effect on Santa is, in itself, its own reward.

The list of movies goes on and on for what seems like an eternity. These Christmas movies are shaping what we believe in and what we expect when we see Santa. My only recommendation is to see as many of the Christmas movies as you can and always view the new ones that are coming out. This is not only the theater movies, but the made for TV movies also.

The Chronology of Santa Claus

John Pintard is the forgotten hero of the American Holidays. He was instrumental in establishing Washington's Birthday, the Fourth of July, and Columbus Day as national holidays, and helped to do the same for Christmas. In 1804 he established the New York Historical Society, with Nicholas the gift-giver as its patron saint. Read the interesting history of John Pintard and see how he worked and the many things he did in his lifetime.

Pintard was motivated in part by his nostalgia for Old Dutch custom and the "ancient usages" of New York. Saint Nicholas had been an important element of the Dutch celebration of Christmas in New Amsterdam, as New York had once been known. The name Santa Claus is believed to be an Anglicization of the Dutch nickname for St. Nicholas, Sinterklaas.

In Knickerbocker's "History of New York" by Washington Irving, Nicholas was first mentioned as the gift giver who rode his wagon pulled by two horses over the tree tops. He was first mentioned as coming to a Dutch explorer in a dream. After he gave the children their gifts, he sat down and lit his pipe. The smoke from the pipe covered a vast area and that is what gave this explorer the idea of building a city. New Amsterdam (now known as New York) was first envisioned in this tail. This is how the Dutch brought Saint Nicholas to America. They celebrated his vision every year.

Everything started coming together in "*A Visit from St. Nicholas*" (1823). Published in the *Troy Chronicles* under no one's name in particular, took the traditional person of St. Nicholas and mixed it with some if the ideas in the poem to provide a visual image of Santa Claus. Pintard's reintroduction of St. Nicholas was only for the upper classes, but this poem captured the imagination of rich and poor alike.

Eventually, this poem's image combined with other traditions around the country to create the figure we have today. The well-known newspaper cartoonist Thomas Nast drew illustrations of Santa Claus that were widely circulated in the late 1800's. Santa's image was solidified in 1931 when Haddon H. Sundblom began to draw his popular pictures of Santa Claus for the Coca Cola Company. By that time however, the image of Santa Claus in his traditional red and white had already become a standard figure

However, that may be, America owes the cheery saint of Christmas to Holland and Germany. In Belgium and Holland the festival of the saint is still observed on his birthday, December sixth, and the jollities and excitements are much the same as those we enjoy at Christmas, with some charming local variations. Saint Nicholas is not the merry fellow with a chubby face and twinkling eye, but retains the gravity appropriate to a venerable bishop. He rides a horse or an ass instead of driving a team or reindeer. He leaves his gifts in stockings, shoes or baskets. And for children who have been very naughty, and whose parents cannot give him a good account of them, he leaves a rod (not the traditional lump of coal) by way of admonition, for he is a highly moral saint, though kind and forgiving. If the parents are too poor to buy gifts, the children say ruefully that the saint's horse has glass legs and has fallen down and broken his foot. The horse or ass of St. Nicholas is not forgotten; the children leave a wisp of hay for him, and in the morning it is gone.

As with us, the older people have their own festivities, suppers, exchange of gifts, surprises. But also as with our Christmas; the feast of Nicholas is primarily a day for Children.

Where did Santa Claus get his reindeer? And how did the grave saint become that gnome-like fat fellow so vividly described in this now famous poem, "*Twas the night before Christmas*?" The answers to these questions are only provisional, matters of conjecture. Your guess is as good as mine, but here goes my best effort I can describe from my research.

Notice that in the poem, the formal title Santa Claus does not appear. The title of the poem is *A visit from St. Nicholas*, and in the verses the visitor is St. Nicholas and 'Saint Nick'. The verses were written in the first half of the 18th century. In these verses the author is writing as a jolly human being, the father of a family taking a day off. This verses must represent the idea of Santa Claus that prevailed in this time, and long before the author's time in America and far outside this country for they spread all over and are still reprinted every year.

Who Really Wrote "Twas the Night Before Christmas"?

This poem has been giving credit to Clement Clarke Moore for many years. The problem was that for at least fifteen years before the poem saw the light of a Troy New York day, by 1808 at the latest, a group of children had been listening to Major Henry Beekman Livingston Jr. read them the poem. And all four of them - Charles, the oldest, and his next-door-neighbor bride Eliza, second son Sidney, and third son Edwin - all remembered the event and their pleasure in the poem.

The original handwritten version was destroyed in a Wisconsin fire at the home of one of his grand children. Though all the children remember it well and have told everyone they know about it, it is not very well documented.

A literary detective who could trace the origin of writing styles, Mr. Don Foster, discovered that around 1806 or 1807, Major Henry Beekman Livingston Jr. was reading this poem to his children. One account goes back to 1805 when this tradition first started.

Reading the styles of both men, I find it obvious that this poem is more than likely written by the Major than by Moore. The Major was fun loving, outgoing and always writing to give humor to everyone and especially children. On the other hand, Moore's writing was very sarcastic, and gloomy. Talking about bawdy women needing a strong man to control them and that children do not need to play but need books so they can be educated.

Reading about the views of both men was amazing. I recommend that anyone who wants to know the truth behind the poem read some of the history and background on both men. Then read both works. Major Henry Beekman Livingston Jr. passed away in 1826 leaving the way for Clement Clarke Moore to accept the role of the author of this poem. It appears that a nanny who knew the Major and privileged to his writings and readings went to work for the Moore's and brought the poem with her to the new household.

Did you know that the names for the reindeer came from Major Livingston's stable? Yep, he named the reindeer after his horses. Now how is that for an 1805 coincidence?

Now in this delightful jingling poem there is not a touch of religion. The 'jolly old elf' has not the slightest resemblance to a reverend saint. And there is no suggestion, except in the word Christmas, of any connection in thought or spirit with what is, excepting possibly Easter, the most sacred day in the whole Christian year. And similarly we may observe in our time many a Christmas party runs its course without any participants giving a thought to a birth in a manager from which our year is dated. So Santa Claus is strangely different from his pious namesake and also in some places and among some people estranged from the very religious occasion to which he is attached. This is another reason that I claim that Santa Claus has no religion. Religion belongs to the holiday and not the legend. This is also the reason I feel that Clement Moore (a minister in the church) did not write this poem.

But in some parts in America where the people are of Dutch or German descent there is a charming alliance between Santa Claus and the Christ Child. It came about in this way. Some parts of Germany after the feast of St. Nicholas had been moved forward and identified with Christmas it was felt that the real patron of the day, the true giver of gifts, should be Christ himself. This feeling probably arose from the Protestant objection to the worship of saints. So St. Nicholas was deposed from power; gradually, not by any sudden revolution, he disappeared in some places, from the customs long associated with him. But the customs remained and would not go away. On Christmas Eve there were gifts of sweets and toys for good children. Or they put bowls in the window, and behold, in the morning they found that the window pane has been taken out during the night and gifts laid in the bowls.

The bringer of these gifts was not St. Nicholas but the Christ Child, in popular German, Kris Kringle. But among the German people in America, the legend of Santa Claus still survived, and so Kris Kringle is a combination of Santa Claus and the Christ Child.

This combination gives us an inkling of what happened in the whole story of Christmas from earliest times, Santa Claus, the merry elf, is not Christian at all, but Pagan, coming down from times earlier than the Christian era or at least earlier than the times when the Teutonic people were Christianized. He belongs to the popular fairyland, the land of elves, gnomes, spirits, hobgoblins and such. In countless fairy tales there are good spirits and evil spirits. The evil spirits haunt the woods and molest innocent people. The good spirits aid the poor, bring gifts in the night, rescue princess' in distress and so on.

The modern image of Santa Claus is an amalgamation of several traditions. The figure of the Christmastime gift-giver is found in many cultures, showing up in the person of the "Christkindlein" (from which we get the name "Kris Kringle"), which was superseded by "Pere Noel" in France and "Pelsnickle" elsewhere in Europe. But the introduction of Santa Claus into American mythology stems from Saint Nicholas himself.

Now where did Santa Claus get his reindeer? There are no reindeer in Germany and probably never were, certainly not the kind that are broken to harness like horses. And oddly enough the reindeer does not appear in any of the surviving Christmas legends and customs in old Germany. The reindeer first paws the roof of American houses. But of course, he cannot be an American animal.

There are reindeer in northern Scandinavia where they have been domesticated from time immemorial. Scandinavian and German legends and mythology are closely related. The old German gods come from the north and many German folk-tales are of Scandinavian origin. The reindeer of our Santa Claus certainly came from Lapland, and Santa is an arctic explorer, exploring the other way: Major Livingston, with true poetic imagination, describes him as "dressed all in fur, from his head to his foot" not in the red flannel with which we are accustomed to seeing him clothed. Among the Germans or Dutch who came to this country there must have been a legend of a Scandinavian Santa and in German the reindeer inexplicably got lost. Perhaps their bones will be found in a German forest by one of the literary archaeologists who dig into such matters. But no, the bones will never be found, for the reindeer are still alive and fly over the house-tops.

The career of Santa Claus through the ages is as mysterious as his annual flight. One might suppose that he would have gone directly from Germany or Holland to their near neighbor England, as the Christmas tree was transplanted to England after the shortest possible journey. But it is very likely that Santa Claus, having become a good American colonist, re-crossed the Atlantic in an English Ship – or perhaps as the first transatlantic flyer. He has long been a well established figure in the Christmas customs and not only of the mother country but in all parts of the British Empire. The allegiance of English Children, however, is divided. Some believe that Santa Claus brings them their presents. Others believe in Father Christmas, a more recent creation, whom English artists represent as an old gentleman in what seems to be a sort of eighteenth century costume with gartered legs, a tail coat, and a squarest beaver hat.

It is rather strange that English Christmas customs are not more closely imitated by Americans. We know nothing of the Yule log, even in houses that have open fireplaces. Perhaps the reason that we borrowed little from the English Christmas is that the English who came to America, especially in New England, were not the merry-making kind; they would have abhorred the idea of making Christmas an occasion for mirth and happiness. They would have groaned at one petty custom, which is inherited directly from England. The singing of carols in the streets on Christmas Eve was unheard of and would have been frowned upon. In all New England literature of the classical period there is scarcely a reference in prose or verse to Christmas, and that was the time when Dickens and Thackeray and other English writers, eagerly read in America, were giving the holiday new spirit and brightness in England.

Customs differ in different countries. A Russian coming from the country of which Nicholas is the chief saint would not at first sight understand our Santa Claus. He would see no relation between his saint before whose icon he bows and the figure in a red suit with a long white beard standing in front of a department store and doing his bit to keep a spirit of good cheer in the enormous American institution – Christmas trade. An American tourist brought up as Protestant finding himself in an Italian city would look up in his guide-book an ornate Italian painting of St. Nicholas miraculously answering a prayer for help, and that tourist unless he had historical imagination might not realize the connection between the beautiful painting and the angel on his last Christmas tree at home and the letter that he wrote as a boy asking Santa Claus to bring him a new sled.

Yet these connections do exist, and they are very important, for they are bonds that hold the world together and help to give its disparate parts and antagonistic faiths a human unification. No other saint and few other men embrace such a wide variety of benevolent ideas as St. Nicholas, with such duration in time and such extent throughout the Christian world. And he is probably the only serious figure in religious history in any way association with humor, with the spirit of fun, for he is the patron of giving. And it is fun to give.

If you want to learn more about the traditions and how they began, try searching and looking up the different aspects we have today. Like why do we have turkey and ham at Christmas? When did we start giving gifts? Where did the first Christmas tree, wreaths, holly, mistletoe, and other traditions begin? If you dig deep enough, you will be totally surprised at what you find. I found it quite interesting to read about the Yule log. I also found it quite interesting to find out about mistletoe.

How did the lights we put on the trees come about? Was Thomas Edison also the inventor of the electric Christmas lights? What about the ornaments? Were Santa's boots and belts always black? What are the other colors that Santa wore and why? You will also find several questions that aren't answered and you will just have to be satisfied with the responses and explanations of others or make up your own version. For example, a friend of mine mixes some glitter and places them in a small baggie. He then attaches a short explanation that this is magic dust and needs to be spread around outside or around the tree so Santa will know where to stop and leave toys for all the good girls and boys.

What about the elf on the shelf? Where did that come from and how can you use it to your benefit? What is the story behind it? What is the truth and what is fictional? The more you search for answers to your questions, the more questions you will create. Discovery is the most fascinating part of this adventure. I truly loved my adventure into discovering the person who really wrote *T'was the Night before Christmas*. Reading all the background and the different works from several sources was fun and exciting.

Interesting Thoughts about the Different Parts of the Poem

Although a staple Christmas story for nearly two centuries, the full significance of Major Henry Livingston's poem is often forgotten. Major Livingston was considered very learned and was called a walking encyclopedia.

Published first in 1822, *T'was the Night Before* Christmas crystallized for many what would become the widely understood depiction of Santa Claus. This particular incarnation would later become intertwined with the European Father Christmas, creating the international figure we know today.

In fact, the author remained anonymous until Moore first claimed writing it. He worried that the secular nature of the poem could cause controversy for his position as a Baptist Minister. Once the popularity of the poem was assured though, Moore's name became known and he forever became famous as the man who designed a central part of our modern day Christmas.

In writing this poem for his grandchildren, we assume that Livingston drew upon his knowledge of anthropology and his fascination for ancient traditions at this time of the year. In weaving some of these traditions into his tale, many took on a new significance. This is just my opinion of how he may have thought, but since there is no record, we will not know the truth of what was going through Major Livingston's mind as he wrote down this poem.

There are so many Christmas traditions and concepts that find their beginning in this poem that it seems appropriate, particularly on this Christmas Eve, to pick through the verses and illustrate just how much our modern day Christmas owes to these 56 lines.

T'was the night before Christmas, when all through the house
Not a creature was stirring, not even a mouse;

The stockings were hung by the chimney with care,
In hopes that St. Nicholas soon would be there;

(Actually, the hanging of stockings had been around for some time by this point and is linked to the original tales of Saint Nicholas.) Not surprisingly, Saint Nicholas was a very popular historical figure for his tendency for generosity to the disadvantaged. One such story tells of how he was passing through a poor village when he overheard the troubles of one family. A father had three daughters, but unable to afford a dowry to secure a suitable husband for each of them, it was becoming increasingly likely that they would be forced into prostitution. Therefore, as each girl reached the appropriate age, Saint Nicholas passed by and dropped a bag of gold through their bedroom window. Each time, the family was able to use the gold as a dowry and the girl was able to marry. I found that this same story is also attributed to Saint Valentine!

One variation on the tale has it that Saint Nicholas tossed the bags of gold through the window and they landed in the girl's stocking, which had been hung out to dry. It is from this that we developed the tradition of hanging a stocking for Saint Nicholas to demonstrate his generosity.

Another variation comes from Knickerbocker's stories about the history of New York where he changed the tradition of placing wooden shoes out to collect the goodies, to those of stockings hung by the fireplace. This was further embellished by Nast with his artistry.

The children were nestled all snug in their beds,
While visions of sugar-plums danced in their heads;

Sugarplums was the treat of the day. As children of today dream of candy canes, sugarplums was the treat of the earlier days.

And mamma in her 'kerchief, and I in my cap,
Had just settled down for a long winter's nap,

Night caps and kerchiefs were worn to bed along with long night shirts; unlike the pajamas of today.

When out on the lawn there arose such a clatter,
I sprang from the bed to see what was the matter.

Away to the window I flew like a flash,
Tore open the shutters and threw up the sash.

When the days turned cold, the shutters were brought closed. This helped to keep the wind and cold out. One could still look out of the shutters to see the outside but only through small openings with limited visibility. If you wanted to look outside, most of the time you had to muscle the shutters open.

The moon on the breast of the new-fallen snow
Gave the luster of mid-day to objects below,

It was stated by a granddaughter of several generations after the Major as she stood on the staircase gazing out the front door at the snow on the ground. This must have been exactly where Grandfather Henry got his inspiration for the poem. It is beautiful outside and the new fallen snow is bright with the full moon tonight.

I would love to stand on those steps and look at the door at such a wonderful winter scene. My mind is already picturing this beautiful sight.

When, what to my wondering eyes should appear,
But a miniature sleigh, and eight tiny reindeer,

With a little old driver, so lively and quick,
I knew in a moment it must be St. Nick.

This is the first ever mention of St Nick using reindeer as a mode of transport, but it was not a random choice. Firstly, Livingston was familiar with the Northern European Christmas celebrations and their Christmas gift-givers such as Father Christmas and Old Man Winter. He probably drew many of his inspirations from Lapland, as a suitably wintery climate, and therefore included the traditional use of a sleigh with reindeer to reflect how a mythical figure from that part of the world would travel.

Also Knickerbocker wrote in his chronicles of New York that St. Nick was a Dutch creation. He was small and elf-like. The Major just may have borrowed this idea.

More rapid than eagles his coursers they came,
And he whistled, and shouted, and called them by name;

"Now, Dasher! now, Dancer! now, Prancer and Vixen!
On, Comet! on Cupid! on, Dunder and Blixem!

To the top of the porch! to the top of the wall!
Now dash away! dash away! dash away all!"

Some people may be surprised to see Rudolph is not included amongst Santa's roll-call of reindeer. In fact, Rudolph was a commercial creation that came about approximately a century later as part of an advertising campaign for a department store. Once the song, sung by Gene Autry, became popular, Rudolph cemented himself as the most famous of Santa's reindeer, despite never appearing in the 'official' line-up.

The choice of eight reindeer is also significant. Actually, eight reindeer would be incredibly impractical in pulling a sleigh, but Livingston was slipping in an obscure reference to another Northern European Christmas tradition. That was Odin or Woden's horse which he road had eight legs. He also had eight horses in his stable that he used (but not at the same time.) Their names happen to match the reindeer's names.

Before Christ, the Norse winter festival of Yule took place at the winter Solstice and is responsible for providing many of our modern traditions. One of them, and a precursor to the idea of the Christmas Eve visitor, is that the God Odin or Woden would ride around the world at night on the festival, deciding who deserves good or bad luck for their crops for the year ahead. Bestowing prosperity or hardship on the people he visits, the Odin or Woden tradition can be seen as a possible origin for the idea of Santa drawing up a list of who has been naughty or nice. The Major was able to slip in a reference to one of the original Christmas gift-givers.

As dry leaves that before the wild hurricane fly,
When they meet with an obstacle, mount to the sky,

So up to the house-top the coursers they flew,
With the sleigh full of toys, and St. Nicholas too.

**And then, in a twinkling, I heard on the roof
The prancing and pawing of each little hoof.**

So why the roof? Is there any significance to this? If we return to Lapland again and Northern climates, many traditional dwellings were built into the ground, with a covering of skins and other materials to keep out the elements. This meant that the roof rose out of the ground and it was therefore possible for a visiting sleigh to arrive on your roof, although what damage that would do, I am unsure…

**As I drew in my head, and was turning around,
Down the chimney St. Nicholas came with a bound.**

The chimney is one of the more bizarre aspects of the Santa Claus myth. Why would anyone choose this method to gain entry? Again, Livingston was showing his knowledge of Lapland housing. With Lapland dwellings built low into the ground, there was only one opening in the middle of the roof that served as entry and exit, as well as the chimney for the fire. So by entering a Lapland house, you were actually bounding down the chimney. A clue to this is contained in the poem as St. Nicholas doesn't climb down the chimney, but enters with one bound.

**He was dressed all in fur, from his head to his foot,
And his clothes were all tarnished with ashes and soot;**

At this period in history, there was no single image of how Santa Claus looked. He was just as likely to be depicted as a wine-soaked partier on a sled pulled by turkeys than he was a bearded old man in a cloak, and hundreds of other variations besides. Since Major Henry Livingston Jr. so loved children, he made the likeness after what he thought the children might enjoy.

Continuing his theme of borrowing from the Lapland tradition, Saint Nicholas is dressed as you would expect someone from that part of the world. Notably, the Major does not describe the colors of Santa's outfit, and the images inspired from this poem were free to use any colors they felt appropriate. It wasn't until Coca-Cola adopted Santa Claus for their annual Christmas advertising campaigns in the 1930s that he became commonly associated with the red and white outfit we know today, selected to reflect the Coca-Cola brand. This is yet another example of commercial advertising shaping Christmas.

A bundle of toys he had flung on his back,
And he looked like a peddler just opening his pack.

His eyes -- how they twinkled, his dimples how merry!
His cheeks were like roses, his nose like a cherry!

His droll little mouth was drawn up like a bow,
And the beard of his chin was as white as the snow;

The stump of a pipe he held tight in his teeth,
And the smoke it encircled his head like a wreath;

Commonly, Father Christmas or Santa was depicted actually wearing a wreath about his head, made of holly or other Christmas greenery. He had a white beard and the Dutch depicted him with a long clay pipe. This could explain the smoke that encircled his head like a wreath.

He had a broad face and a little round belly,
That shook, when he laughed like a bowlful of jelly.

He was chubby and plump, a right jolly old elf,
And I laughed when I saw him, in spite of myself;

Although Livingston describes Saint Nicholas as a 'right jolly old elf', this has been taken to mean that Santa is actually a magical elf. This is most likely the origination of the idea of elves assisting Santa at Christmas Eve as well as the other-worldly nature of the big man himself, but this is definitely an extreme extrapolation from this poem. It is quite clear that the Major is not necessarily defining Santa as an elf but is likening him to one due to his jolly nature. Also, this poem does not provide any other background for its creation – no North Pole refuge for example. All of these magical elements were later added by modern commercial depictions and Hollywood.

A wink of his eye and a twist of his head,
Soon gave me to know I had nothing to dread;

He spoke not a word, but went straight to his work,
And filled all the stockings; then turned with a jerk,

And laying his finger aside of his nose,
And giving a nod, up the chimney he rose;

Santa's exit up the chimney is also more interesting when put into the context of the Lapland dwelling. Although the poem implies magic has taken place in Santa rising back up the chimney, in Lapland, rising up the chimney means no more than leaving through the front door, as they are one and the same.

He sprang to his sleigh, to his team gave a whistle,
And away they all flew like the down of a thistle.

But I heard him exclaim, ere he drove out of sight,
"Happy Christmas to all, and to all a good-night."

And with that, Major Henry Livingston shaped our Christmas Eve celebrations forever. Don't forget to pull down a copy of the poem to read to your children in bed tonight and when you do, reflect on how different Christmas would be if the Major hadn't decided to favor his children on this occasion with his fascination for ancient traditions and true Christmas spirit.

A Visit from Saint Nicholas

by Major Henry B. Livingston

Twas the night before Christmas, when all through the house
not a creature was stirring, not even a mouse.
The stockings were hung by the chimney with care,
in hopes that St. Nicholas soon would be there.

The children were nestled all snug in their beds,
while visions of sugar plums danced in their heads.
And Mama in her kerchief, and I in my cap,
had just settled our brains for a long winter's nap.

When out on the roof there arose such a clatter,
I sprang from my bed to see what was the matter.
Away to the window I flew like a flash,
tore open the shutter, and threw up the sash.

The moon on the breast of the new-fallen snow
gave the luster of midday to objects below,
when, what to my wondering eyes should appear,
but a miniature sleigh and eight tiny reindeer.

With a little old driver, so lively and quick,
I knew in a moment it must be St. Nick.
More rapid than eagles, his courses they came,
and he whistled and shouted and called them by name:

"Now Dasher! Now Dancer!
Now, Prancer and Vixen!
On, Comet! On, Cupid!
On, Dunder and Blixem!

To the top of the porch!
To the top of the wall!
Now dash away! Dash away!
Dash away all!"
As dry leaves that before the wild hurricane fly,
when they meet with an obstacle, mount to the sky
so up to the house-top the courses they flew,
with the sleigh full of toys, and St. Nicholas too.

And then, in a twinkling, I heard on the roof
the prancing and pawing of each little hoof.
As I drew in my head and was turning around,
down the chimney St. Nicholas came with a bound.

He was dressed all in fur, from his head to his foot,
and his clothes were all tarnished with ashes and soot.
A bundle of toys he had flung on his back,
and he looked like a peddler just opening his pack.

His eyes--how they twinkled! His dimples, how merry!
His cheeks were like roses, his nose like a cherry!
His droll little mouth was drawn up like a bow,
and the beard of his chin was as white as the snow.

The stump of a pipe he held tight in his teeth,
and the smoke it encircled his head like a wreath.
He had a broad face and a little round belly,
that shook when he laughed, like a bowl full of jelly.

He was chubby and plump, a right jolly old elf,
and I laughed when I saw him, in spite of myself.
A wink of his eye and a twist of his head
soon gave me to know I had nothings to dread.

He spoke not a word, but went straight to his work,
and filled all the stockings, then turned with a jerk.
And laying his finger aside of his nose,
and giving a node, up the chimney he rose.

He sprang to his sleigh, to his team gave a whistle,
And away they all fly like the down of a thistle.
But I heard him exclaim, ere he drove out of sight,
Happy Christmas to all, and to all a good night!!

Chapter 2

So You Want To Be Santa

Who Is Santa? OK. You have already read about the history. Does that make you want to know more? Being Santa is not just putting on The Red Suit, a long white beard and running around yelling Ho! Ho! Ho! Being Santa is also an attitude and a famous character we portray to the delight of children of all ages. Not too many folks dislike Santa. Santa is as much a part of American tradition as Independence Day and any other day that we celebrate with a character.

Below is a poem to get you started on the season. I don't know who wrote it, but it sort of makes a valid point. What is said about the crabby old man can also be said about us as we portray Santa. I'll bet everyone of us can rewrite this poem and insert Santa for the old man.

Crabby Old Man

What do you see nurses?
What do you see?
What are you thinking ?
When you're looking at me?

A crabby old man,
Not very wise.
Uncertain of habit.
With faraway eyes!

Who dribbles his food,
And makes no reply.
When you say in a loud voice,
'I do wish you'd try!'

Who seems not to notice,
The things that you do.
And forever is losing, A sock or shoe!
Who, resisting or not,
Lets you do as you will.
With bathing and feeding.
The long day to fill!

Is that what you're thinking?
Is that what you see?
Then open your eyes, nurse,
You're not looking at me.

I'll tell you who I am,
As I sit here so still,
As I do at your bidding,
As I eat at your will.

I'm a small child of Ten,
With a father and mother.
Brothers and sisters,
Who love one another.

A young boy of Sixteen,
With wings on his feet.
Dreaming that soon now,
A lover he'll meet.

A groom soon at Twenty,
My heart gives a leap.
Remembering, the vows,
That I promised to keep.

At Twenty-Five, now,
I have young of my own.
Who need me to guide,
And a secure happy home.

A man of Thirty,
My young now grown fast.
Bound to each other,
With ties that should last.

At Forty, my young sons ,
Have grown and are gone.
But my woman's beside me,
To see I don't mourn.

At Fifty, once more,
babies play 'round my knee.
Again, we know children,
My loved one and me.

Dark days are upon me,
My wife is now dead.
I look at the future,
Shudder with dread.

For my young are all rearing,
Young of their own.
And I think of the years,
And the love that I've known.

I'm now an old man,
And nature is cruel.
Tis jest to make old age,
Look like a fool.

The body, it crumbles,
Grace and vigor, depart.
There is now a stone,
Where I once had a heart.

But inside this old carcass,
A young guy still dwells,
And now and again,
My battered heart swells.

I remember the joys,
I remember the pain.
And I'm loving and living,
Life over again.

I think of the years, all too few,
Gone too fast.
And accept the stark fact,
That nothing can last.

So open your eyes, people,
Open and see.
Not a crabby old man,
Look closer . . . See ME!!

Have you thought about what it takes to be a credible Santa? Have you thought about ethical issues with the job? What about some basic rules to follow? Do you think Santas need to follow some rules? And of course, the wardrobe! Along with that you need to figure out what type of Santa you want to be and are EXPECTED to be when you show up someplace as Santa.

I can see it now. You are asking yourself what does he mean by "What Type Of Santa You Want To Be?" So you thought there was only one type of Santa did you. Well, read on. There are some descriptions included here that can help you decided. You can also go back and reread a couple of sections of the traditions from different countries. Just look at the different drawings of Santa for the past 200 or so years and see how different he is in each.

To start, ask yourself what kind of Santa do I want to be? Make sure you write down everything you say. Ask what do you want to look like, how you want to act, what you will do, and as many different things you can think of. Now think about all the Santas you have known in the past. They could be mall, store, street, party, movie, play, book, any type of Santa you can recall. Now write down the features from each that you would like to incorporate in yourself as Santa.

Can you see where I am going with all this? Being Santa is difficult yet it is so rewarding when performed correctly, effectively and comfortably as you want him to be.

Don't forget to write down all the bad things you have seen in Santas too. This will help you eliminate any potential problems or bad habits before they begin. It will also make you wanted by many and asked for by all. You can become the number one Santa if you set your mind to it. Don't worry about the look too much until you can master the portrayal part. Once you can act and sound like Santa, then start working on your looks.

Have I Ever Seen a Bad Santa?

Have I ever seen a bad Santa? As a matter of fact, I didn't get to see this one, but I heard all about him.

I was working in a store for a couple of weeks when the store owner changed the hours I was supposed to be available. Since my calendar gets booked early, I couldn't accommodate the change and had my agent find a temporary replacement Santa.

Here is what I heard about him when I returned to work. He showed up and found the young lady responsible for ensuring that the Santa pictures came off flawlessly. She was terrific with that task. Well, this replacement Santa went straight to her and said he needed help. She walked with him out to his vehicle (with sleigh being towed on a trailer) and proceeded to tell her she would remember this moment for the rest of her life.

Well, she told me she would remember that moment, not because this Santa was nice, he really wasn't. Not because of the unique sleigh he brought with him that lights up and played Christmas music, but because of the poor attitude this man had. Once he had finished explaining his sleigh to her, he proceeded to pull his wardrobe out of the vehicle and handed it to her. He expected her to carry it all inside while he just walked behind and watched.

After struggling with the heavy wardrobe and managing to get it to the employee lounge, she left him and indicated she would be at the chair when he was ready to join them.

Upon entering the store, it was obvious that there were a number of folks ready to see Santa. The line already had about 100 folks standing there waiting patiently. Well, this Santa took his time and showed up almost 15 minutes later than the advertised start time. He complained about not having enough room to spread out so he could properly dress.

Once he got to his chair and the gates to Santa were finally opened, his cell phone rang. He held up his hand indicating that the children coming towards him should wait. He proceeded to conduct his personal business on the phone and then addressed the children. He wouldn't let anyone sit on his lap and his smile was so rough the young lady stated she was surprised that the kids wanted to see him.

He demanded the staff bring him water and find a table to put the candy canes on so he didn't have to reach for them. He also wanted cold water every time he had a thirst. He told the staff to shut down the line so he could leave to eat and to take brakes (which he took several in the middle of seeing all the children).

There was never a kind word from him, only demands. When he left, the employees talked to the manager about him and from what I understand, his name was put on the same list as the drunken Santa they had once before. This was the "Never to Hire Again" list.

I told my agent about what I heard and she told me that the store manager already called her to complain about him. I am assuming that he will not get another job from this agent.

There are several stories out there like that and I am sad to hear them. Thank goodness I strive to be the best I can be and to make the employees as happy to have me around as the children who bring their precious smiles to me.

A few weeks before I started this particular Santa gig, I was privilege to have the opportunity to sit down with several Santas from the area. They all seemed extremely nice. This same Santa couldn't help talking about himself and all the important folks he played Santa for. I had an immediate dislike towards him because of that self important image he was portraying.

After I heard this report from the employees, I decided to try and take away business from this guy. I hired another local agent and aggressively started marketing myself to all the business in the area. I don't know how well it worked since I don't keep in touch with any of these Santas. They just didn't seem friendly and as if they were only in the business for the money. I really didn't want to tell them how much I made because they might get upset. On the other hand, maybe I should have and watched them lose the last of their clients by overcharging them.

I really don't want to be vicious, but when I meet someone who is more interested in themselves than the children or adults around, than I don't like them as a Santa. I honestly feel that Santa needs to be kind and giving all the time. They need to not think of themselves and to think about others.

Teaching others how to be Santa brings great joy. Most of my lectures and courses include the ethics of being Santa. Here I try to explain that always one must try to think of Santa and try their best to live up to that image. Make a list of everything you can think of that makes Santa…. well you know, Santa. Now that you have a list of what makes up Santa, do you fit with everything you said? If not, you need to seriously rethink your role as Santa. Maybe you will want to try something else. Don't take your bad attitude and negative attitude around others and ruin Christmas for those of us who enjoy the season.

Just looking like Santa is not enough. You will need to act like Santa and to properly portray the jolly old gent. Reading my book, *Santas Book of Knowledge*, you will learn lots of thing to do to make you a better Santa and also bring in more money if that is what interest you.

You would not believe how something as simple as a laugh can get you remembered. When I started to laugh with a lower rumble in my chest and folks heard me chuckle, they just thought I was happy all the time. I was always smiling and laughing whenever I could and my laugh was from my gut and not my throat. As the years went by, folks enjoyed being around me because I always smiled and I had pleasant things to say. Even my laugh was infectious.

Now when I laugh, everyone says "he evens sounds like Santa." I love it when folks relate me to the real guy. Besides the long white beard and glint in my eye, I sound like the old guy too. What a complement! Now you must try things. Smiling all the time helps put that magical gleam in your eyes. They soon begin to sparkle and people will remark about your eyes. Keep smiling; you look more like Santa when you are smiling.

Start practicing all the good things you want to portray as Santa. It never hurts to start and practice. The more you practice, the more it will become second nature and the more natural you will be throughout your performance. Practice year-round so that when the season comes, you are well practiced and polished. Then go out and have some fun.

What It Takes To Be a Creditable Santa.

This is one of my favorite subjects. Look on the internet. Look at pictures everywhere and see the different likenesses of Santa. Are there any that make you say, "I would like to look like that"? Or are there ones that scream to you, "This is exactly what you don't want to look like?" Do your research and then try to achieve what you think is best. Don't be satisfied with second best, look to be the best.

Remember back to your childhood. What were your expectations? Ask kids today what is their idea of Santa. Do some research! There are so many types of Santas these days, which one would best suit you. Which one would you feel comfortable portraying and talking about?

If you are in the city, dressing like St Nicholas (a Bishop) would not be appropriate unless you were at a religious event or at a Dutch party. Dressing with a head dress of candles again would not be appropriate unless at a religions event or some event with a German or Scandinavian theme. Same with a wreath of holly as your crown.

What about wearing all white or all green outfits? That probably wouldn't fit unless you were someplace that expected to see that in Santa. Now which red outfit is best? Have you looked at Sundblom's Coca Cola looking Santa? What about Nast's Harper's Weekly magazine Santa? Those are two different looks. There's more. You just have to look for them.

Here is a picture of a work shop look. See how I am checking my Naughty & Nice list. This consist of a shirt by Adel's of Hollywood, knickers by Darlene Bush who makes Civil War costumes, suspenders from Wal-Mart, socks from the soccer sports store and shoes with a homemade buckle with Santa on it.

Here is a Continental look that I call my formal affair. It has a vest and I have a long coat to wear over it that makes it look traditional too. I like the shirt and jambeaux (the tie or neck scarf). Both are from Darlene Bush. The belt is by Peter Kilmer. It has a beautiful design of the reindeer pulling Santas sleigh on the back and holly on the front.

Check out all the costume shops you can and see what they have to offer. They may have various ideas and styles of Santa Suits. This might help you to decide what to wear.

If you are visiting a school, you might see if you can wear a workshop look. That might be more comfortable and give you the look of a toymaker that would impress the children. There you go, I have already given you five different ideas and looks. Do your research and see what you are comfortable with.

Don't forget the traditional and Coca Cola looks. They need to be a staple in your wardrobe. These are both from Adel's of Hollywood. Again the belt is from Peter Kilmer and the boots are custom made from Capri Shoes.

Coca Cola

Traditional

You may notice in the pictures that I have bells on my white cuffs over my boots. I do this for several reasons. First, when I walk, everyone knows I am coming so I don't startle the small children. Second, I wear them to create the sounds of Christmas. Nothing is more exciting than to hear the sleigh bells of my reindeer before you see me. After I appear, most folks forget about the bells and just enjoy the presence of Santa Claus.

Is Santa Claus Real?

To this question I must give you the answer I gave my daughter. When she was in first grade, I had taken an old Santa outfit I was using and made a little elf outfit for her. It consisted of a vest and skirt. I bought her a white shirt, Santa hat and white stockings to wear.

She went with me everywhere that year and helped me pass out gifts to everyone. The adults thought she was cute and the kids thought she was the luckiest girl on earth even though I tried to convince them she was a 300 year old elf. They could believe in me as Santa Claus but not my daughter as an elf.

Now as we were headed to a house where she knew the children, she asked me what to say when they ask her about helping out. I simply started to explain that as she knows, I help Santa during the Christmas season leaving Santa to do all the work Christmas Eve. She can tell her friends the same thing. She has been asked to help Santa on occasion and since this was the season of giving, she decided to help out by passing out some presents. But she decided to let them know that she would not be with Santa on Christmas Eve.

She also pondered if there really was a Santa since she knows all my secrets and heard all my talks with the different children. My answer to her was simple, "This is the season for giving." She nodded in agreement. I continued, "Santa is the biggest giver of all with all the toys and stuff he hands out each Christmas." Again she nodded in agreement. "So", I took a big breath and started, "if we give out gifts, than we must be considered to be like Santa. If we are like Santa, it never hurts to let others think that we are the Jolly Old Elf too! So, that means that Santa is alive and well in all of us."

I could see a light come on in her head. "Does that mean I'm Santa too?" she asked.

"Yep" I explained.

She continued helping me be Santa for a couple more years and then started spending more time with her friends during the season. I believe she just didn't think about Santa any more until many years later when she left her friends behind to go to college.

My daughter is now married and has three children of her own. She enjoys my visit with them after Christmas each year and has them looking forward to seeing Santa after he is through delivering all the toys to the children of the world. She took me aside one year after her twins were born and told me she still believes in Santa. I smiled and told her to remember to pass that on to her children when they are ready to know. She knew exactly what I meant as she nodded in agreement.

So is there really a Santa. I will most definitely say yes to that question. Anyone who gives a gift with love and kindness during the Christmas season is most definitely a Santa Claus. They perpetuate the positive image of good and kindness in the world. Those that say no there is no Santa Claus are the image of what I see is wrong in this world today. Not enough kindness and unconditional giving.

If everything has to be in black and white, then explain to me God, Mohammad, Buda and all the other deities of this world. Can you see them? How do you know they exist? If you believe . . . . . they exist!

One person wrote an article about some distinguished scientist who discussed matter and what gives matter its mass. They contend that matter has no mass until the God element is initiated. He likened it to an invisible soccer ball. You don't see it, but if kicked into the net, you know it is there by the bulge it makes in the net when it hits the back.

I just prefer to think of Santa as the Jolly Old Elf who enjoys giving gifts to children of all ages. Just look at me, I give out gifts year round to all the good boys and girls. Just last week a mom brought her teenage daughter to work. When they saw me, the mom stated, "See, there is a Santa Claus." The daughter stated, "But you told me there was no Santa Claus."

After a few minutes, I went to my sleigh (my truck throughout the year) and pulled a stuffed Teddy Bear out. When I saw them again, I told them that being nice throughout the year always produces a gift from Santa. With that I handed them a Teddy Bear and disappeared.

A few days later the mom found me and told me that her daughter is still talking about Santa and showed the Teddy Bear to all her friends. That one act of kindness has sure gotten some miles. Both mom and daughter are affected and now her friends. I'll bet mom has told this story to her friends too.

There is even more to this story. The lady keeps bringing by new hires to let them see Santa. They all want to see my smile and hear my laughter. I even had one request to see my truck and all the toys I keep in the back.

There is another story in my book about a boy learning there was no Santa from his sister and then asking his grandmother about it. I love that story. Grandma didn't explain about Santa but showed the young boy that Santa was alive and well no matter what anyone says.

Yes, I too believe there is a Santa Claus and **Bah Humbug** on all who think otherwise.

The Mrs. Claus and other Helpers

The most important part of being a Mrs. Claus or other elf helper is that you must remember you are in a supporting role. Santa is the draw and everything must be done to either enhance Santa or to make him look good. Saying this does not mean you have nothing to do. Mrs. Claus should assist with handing out the gifts, convince the shy ones to come and either talks to her or Santa and be ready to discuss important holiday recipes and craft activities.

Mrs. Claus plays a very important part with Santa. I prefer that my Mrs. Claus be responsible for collecting any fees due. This keeps Santa focused on the children. She also needs to work with the children. This includes placing children on your lap for pictures and talking with everyone. Make sure Santa's lap is full and only take children if Santa suggests it. Never try to put yourself out in front of Santa by asking for children or anyone else to sit on your lap.

For example; if you are sitting with Santa and receiving children, you must let Santa have all the children and only accept the overflow or the ones that don't want to get near Santa. Never try to entice a child to sit with you first. You must be the gentle talker and the one who convinces the child that Santa is a good guy.

Never ask a child what they want for Christmas. That is Santa's job.

Do not make comments about the children looking handsome or pretty unless you do that to all the children and it is after Santa greets them. Some children prefer to sit with Mrs. Claus and that is terrific. It will keep them calm and they will be able to talk to Santa from the comfort of Mrs. Claus. Also, never make a comment about your desires when folks are approaching you. This includes flirting with the guys.

Another good thing you can do is to greet the children first and bring them to Santa when he is ready. Be the kindly grandmother type and don't try to get attention focused on you. Remember, Mrs. Claus bakes the cookies and helps take care of the elves. She is the organizer and the one that ensures Santa looks his best all the time. Mrs. Claus comforts the crying children and entertains with stories and such with all. She gets them comfortable with singing and other entertaining activities.

The best of Mrs. Claus is ready to share recipes of cookies, cakes, ginger bread, hot coca, and many more. She is also ready to either read or tell a story to the children. Mrs. Claus could sing, make crafts, and just be around to make everyone comfortable. You will not find too many asking for just Mrs. Claus, but after a good one leaves, she will be asked to accompany Santa time and time again. If you pass out reindeer antlers and Rudolph noses, Mrs. Santa can do this.

How should Mrs. Santa look? Well she should complement Santa and never out do the jolly old gent. She should have white hair (see survey results within this book) and she should always be smiling and supporting the Christmas spirit. Be the grandmotherly person even though you may think yourself too young for that role.

It can't be said enough that Mrs. Claus needs to be the supporting person. This is the person Santa depends on the most. Mrs. Claus can control the visits, watches the time and ensures Santa sees every child. She is also the one that talks to the parents and explains to them the best way for them to get pictures and offers suggestions on how to get the picture with their crying child.

She tells the parents things like, "If you turn your child toward the camera and don't let them see Santa, you could probably get away with a drop and dash move where the photographer can get a good shot before the child realizes they are on Santa's lap." You could also do the same move only tell the parents to sit on Santa's lap holding the child facing the camera. This way the child is comfortable sitting on the parent's lap for the picture with Santa.

Mrs. Claus can also suggest other picture taking opportunities that Santa can do with the child. Some are mentioned in other places in this book. She can either sit slightly behind Santa at his side or stand behind Santa. Never should Mrs. Claus try to be Santa's equal or even to upstage him.

Remember to be supportive and do whatever it takes to make Santa look good. The supporting role is important and most appreciate how Mrs. Claus makes this operation a smooth one. I can guarantee that a supporting Mrs. Claus will be asked back again and again. She will not get the booking without Santa, but she will be a necessary part of his visit each year in the future.

The Basics of Being Santa

If you don't look the part, you will never be able to make everyone believe you are Santa no matter how hard you, "Ho! Ho! Ho!" and how many toys you give away. Something else you might do is to learn a Christmas phrase or two in other languages. That helped me over in England when I visited an orphanage. I knew enough French to totally surprise a young lad and enough Welsh to stop another in his tracks. If you don't know how to speak Christmas in American Sign Language, you might want to learn. That always impresses folks. They may not be deaf, but when they see you talking in sign to a deaf child, your tips go up and so does your credibility.

All mentioned above is not necessary to impress your children or the neighbor's children. But if you can find out something that they believe in that makes Santa special to them, then you are on the right track to being a creditable Santa. One trick is to contact the parents and make yourself a naughty and nice list you can read about each child. What a surprise when you bring out that list and begin to read. ***BIG NOTE***. MAKE SURE YOU END WITH THE NICE LIST AND SAY SOMETHING NICE TO THE CHILD.

When you have the wardrobe on, be sure you stay in character. You will never know who is watching or listening. Santa doesn't smoke, drink, chase women, gamble, or anything that might spoil the reputation or image in a child's eyes.

Always have something for the children. It is terrible to arrive someplace and not have enough to give out to everyone. I always carry extra stuffed animals in my bag just in case. Just so happens that one year this came in very handy as a young girl with a young family just signed up with a country club I was visiting, came to visit me at the club. Of course, being new, they didn't have a gift to give her, so I carefully reached into my bag and produced a stuffed teddy bear. That went over terrific with the child, the parents, and the club. It made me feel good too seeing the happiness all around.

Don't try to hide faults. Don't exaggerate them either. If you make a mistake, move on and don't do it again. I called a young child Mickey instead of Mikee. Next time around I got the name right.

Believe in yourself. If you think you are Santa and truly enjoy giving gifts to everyone and making everyone happy, you will be accepted as Santa. Even the adults will forget who you are and begin believing you are Santa.

Read the current Christmas stories and be ready to explain them; especially *Polar Express.* Included in the back of this book are several other stories you may use. The ringing bell and the non-ringing bell from the Polar Express story are particularly important. Know who the reindeer are and be able to name them. Be able to explain where they are right now and why the children can't see them.

Here again are the names of the reindeer as you will find them listed in the original poem. Later versions changed Dunder and Blixem to make a better rhythm and rhyme.

Dasher and Dancer
Prancer and Vixen
Comet and Cupid
Dunder and Blixem (Donner and Blixen)
And of course Rudolph.

Dunder and Blixem are the original names in the poem and were changed to Donner and Blixen to make the poem read smoother. Use which ever you choose but be consistent. I prefer the original names, but that is just my preference.

Just a little background information; Both male and female reindeer grow antlers each year. When they are growing, the antlers are soft, rubbery, and the living mass of blood and marrow is covered with a furry skin. The antlers grow rapidly and during this period the reindeer are said to be "in velvet". The antlers are finished growing in August, harden, and the "velvet" is vigorously rubbed off. The bulls then begin to rut. They become aggressive (remember, they are animals, keep safety in mind). Their necks swell. They become protective of the females in the herd, and the breeding season of several months begins. The older bulls generally lose or "drop" their antlers first, usually late December or early January, with the remaining bulls following this process until as late as March. The females generally keep their antlers until calving time, 7 months from when they were bred. Then the antler growing process is repeated all over again.

Talk to some reindeer breeders and found out some more interesting facts. Contact ROBA (Reindeer Owners and Breeders Association). They are willing to give you information and answer your questions. Look up reindeer ROBA on the internet or write to them. P.O. Box 883, Lake Crystal, MN 56055 U.S.A. phone - (507) 726-6996 email: **info@reindeer.ws.** Find the facts. Do you know what reindeer really eat? How about the weather they need to be in. How often do they shed their coats?

Do some research and be prepared. Enjoy finding out some facts.

Santa's Movements

This is going to be interesting. I am going to attempt to show you with words, how Santa should move. I know that Santa is supposed to be rotund, but let's not over play that part. Santa is also supposed to be fit and able to carry the toys and see all the boys and girls.

Let's start with very basic movements. When you first see Santa, does he waddle into your view or does he bound and bounce with every step. I have found that if I am smiling a lot, I walk a little taller and have a little more energy in my movements. Now there's a good term, ENERGY. If you have energy in every movement you do, you will look the part and the kids will really love you.

I prefer to get away from the grandfather look and actions. I don't want to look or act like I am old. I want to look and act like I was a teenager again, of course without the problems of a teenager.

If you laugh a lot, try putting your hands on your belt and making it move with your laugh. I just cracked up laughing one day when I saw a Santa laughing and he grabbed his belt and wiggled it up and down. It wasn't in time with his laugh and it really looked ridiculous. I tried to explain the movement but couldn't get it through to him. If you are going to grab your belt, make it move with your laugh. If you laugh properly, it should be easy to follow the movement of your belly as it wiggles and jiggles like a bowl full of jelly.

Other gestures you can add should be big and elaborate. For example; if you are explaining about some faraway place or a large patch of snow or some other large area, use your hands to show how it is spread out or far away. If you are talking about your reindeer, why not make the antler jester on your head. The kids will love it and copy it. Place your thumbs on the sides of your head and spread your fingers out. We used to draw that type of hand when making a turkey for Thanksgiving during the school year.

You can wiggle the antlers but don't wiggle them too much. It will make you look like you are trying to make a funny face to someone. Also if you are talking about Rudolph, why not touch your nose. That is his famous feature. Use it!

Something to always remember is that Santa NEVER reaches or grabs for a child. Let the child come to you and then put your hand out to them. Santa doesn't play with his hair or beard. Let it be. Let the children play with it.

Most kids see Santa and think of Santa as the cartoons they watch depict him. In those cartoons, he is playing games and such. Be ready for that type of movement. Don't be the cripple who can barely get around; be the person that has no problems getting around. I take a lot of Aleve during the season. It helps to combat the aches and pains I have from the movement. I never want to let a child down. I want to fulfill their greatest expectations of Santa.

Character Development

Speaking of a child's greatest expectations, what type of Santa are you? Does that sound like a strange question? If you were in a traditional English setting, you would want to be Father Christmas, very stately and very prim and proper. By the way if you are looking for a Father Christmas character to portray, he is an English gentleman and dresses accordingly. That is he wears a waist coat and britches (or knickers with stockings).

Now if you were in a Dutch community, you would want to have a robe and be more saintly. You would carry yourself around in a very distinguished manner and conduct yourself appropriately. You would also have a scepter with a sphere and a cross atop of it. This robe would be more like a long dress and is usually a royal red or burgundy.

What would you do in a Native American community? Well, one of the ways I dress is like a mountain man. I look like Santa but am very outspoken and outgoing. I am very loud and look like I have been living in the mountains for several years. Why that way do you ask? Well, it is simple, during the winter Pow Wow's the mountain men would come down and bring their customs with them. Someone playing Santa would look like he lived in the mountains because he did. It would be an animal hide jacket with buckskin pants and an animal fur hat. (I prefer the Davy Crockett type of coonskin hat.)

Now that I have you thinking about what you would look like, what type of character will you portray? Will you be the lively old elf full of energy and excitement or will you be more like the Bishop and saintly? Will you hand out switches or will every child get a toy? Are you the classic old guy that likes to give gifts or are you the studious guy that Nash drew in the Saturday Evening Post and other magazines? Maybe you are the Coca Cola Santa Tate Sundblom drew for the advertising campaigns and would rather be relaxing.

With this character in mind, you need to create a skit to perform when you are at a location. Being in character, you will need to perform to entertain your client. Yes, you are an actor and actors perform for a living. If all you want to do is sit in a chair and listen to what children want for Christmas and hand out presents, you have missed a lot of what Santa is. You need to interact with the children and do so in character.

Think of it like the folks who love the medieval reenactments. They are not only dressed in character, but they speak in character also. They speak as they are dressed, both prim and proper as a Lord or Lady or you might hear some gutter snipe talking as a serving wench or street entertainer. You will hear yet another and very different dialect from those in armor and carrying weapons.

If you were active, how would you act? If you were kicked back and relaxing, what would you say? Think of several things you as Santa in your wardrobe might say and do. Write them down. Create a script. Make yourself a little play so that you can perform for the folks around you. Watch the excitement of the children as you perform. It will make you want to do more and more for them.

Nothing is more pleasing than to see smiles on the faces of children. It makes your heart ring out with joy and happiness.

The Ethics of Being Santa

Ok, here are some issues. These shouldn't need to be brought up, but in light of some very poor people who haven't a clue of what it is to children to know their Santa is not really Santa is saddening. Never smoke, chew or sniff tobacco products when you are getting ready to portray the jolly old elf. Santa doesn't smoke, chew or spit. The smell of that on you will put children off.

Also, never drink while wearing the wardrobe. Go change if you must drink. Never drink before you portray Santa either. You don't need it on your breath and the adults won't think twice about not allowing their kids near you. Along with that, don't use drugs when you are going to be performing as Santa. You want to be in your right mind. So far these things have been just common sense. I write about them because there have been some Santas in the past that didn't heed this common sense stuff and really started giving us a bad name.

Be very careful of what you say. Don't be telling off color jokes or participating in groups that are telling off color jokes. Remember the kids are around and see you doing this. No matter how pretty the lady is, never tell her to come sit on your north pole or ask if she wants some candy. Nothing could ever repair the damage you cause by talking to someone (even to someone you know) and having a child over hear the conversation.

No matter how much fun it may be to get with the wife while wearing the wardrobe, wait until you are behind closed doors before attempting any intimacies. Never let a child or their parent ever see you doing anything that could remotely be misconstrued as inappropriate. More and more states are filling up with people who would rather sue you for their easy life. Don't give them any type of opportunity. Even best friends and family will sue so be careful all the time.

Other ethical issues include the placement of your hands. Never take a picture with anyone where BOTH hands are not visible. This may sound stupid and there may be an innocent reason, but don't do it. This is another way to get sued with proof. Always wear your gloves in pictures. This will help identify where your hands actually are, besides the side effects of keeping the germs of a sick child away from you.

No matter what your sexual preference may be, keep it to yourself. Sex has no business in being Santa. Santa is a child's friend and gift giver. Always remember that you are there to entertain the children and adults. Keep that in mind when you are working. The children come first always.

The movie *Bad Santa* did us a great disservice. Please don't think it is funny to do any of those things you saw in that movie. Think of what others might say before you say or do something. Something may seem funny to you at the time, but will it still be funny as you are standing in front of a judge pleading not to go to jail? Ethics is a fine line to follow. There just isn't enough space in the world to talk about all the ethical issues.

Think of yourself as being on display. You have to be perfect all the time you are in the wardrobe. If not, someone will say something to you. Remember that you are in a glass showcase whenever you have the suit on. Never think it is funny to portray the *Bad Santa*. It is not funny and can get you into a lot of trouble, especially if you are being compensated. If you are doing this for a friend, you could lose a friend. I know how I am around my children. If someone does something inappropriate around them, I will not only say something, but I may even act on it.

For goodness sake, turn off your cell phone. If you must really have it with you while you are performing and you really must answer the calls coming in, give it to an elf who can go away from the children and answer it for you. Nothing is worse than to hold up talking with children while you are on the cell phone. Santa does not need to disrupt the children like that. If you think that you are so important that you can't turn off your cell phone while performing, than I suggest that you hang up the red suit and let others who really care about the children take your place.

Here is something to ponder. Should you or should you not hand out candy canes? I personally do not because of an incident of a child having an allergic reaction or diabetic reaction right there in front of me. Also, I don't like it when the parents immediately grab the candy from them and tell them either they can have it later or they can't have it at all. To prevent that from happening, I started handing out little fleeced bears and stickers that say "I have met Santa". I am always looking for little trinkets I can give out. One year I was able to give out plastic coins that say Naughty on one side and Nice on the other. I even developed a magic trick with them.

You need to consciously make that decision before you go anywhere. If I am someplace and the person paying for me wants to provide candy to hand out, I don't mind, the onus is now on them if there is a problem. I prefer to remain on the safe side and keep the children safe and not have a parent take away a gift I have given a child. I think it is rude to ask a parent if you can give a candy cane to a child also. The child is there and can hear you. Don't make the child feel bad. Give them something they can have and the parents won't take away and won't cause them harm.

Handing out candy for one place I worked, I started asking the children if they like candy canes. This gave me an insight into what the children want. I would estimate that about one-tenth of the children did not want the candy cane. In that case I would always remind them that this is the season for giving and ask if they would take my gift and pass it on to someone else in the spirit of giving to others and wish them a Merry Christmas at the same time. That way they will be passing the spirit of Christmas along to others.

I have become more aware of sweets since I have been diagnosed as diabetic. Kids are becoming diabetic sooner. Their eating pattern and lack of exercise is doing them great harm and their parents don't even know it. Don't be a part of the problem. Help the kids of today (our future leaders) remain healthy.

Basic Rules to Follow

We have already gone over some rules that concern smoking, drinking, and ethical issues. Some others you might think of include; don't pick your nose. You are easy to spot and believe me, when in costume; you will be seen picking your nose, scratching your ass, giving that glare look or even the middle finger salute to someone who just upset you. Don't do it when dressed as Santa. You will be seen flipping someone off every time and with the cell phone cameras, you might even be caught and your picture placed on the internet.

You need to be concerned with your body odor too. Make sure you are freshly showered. Don't use a lot of cologne. Some cologne may cause an allergic reaction in sensitive folks. It may also make others choke. Make sure your costume is clean and not smelly or dirty. Make sure your teeth are clean and your breath is fresh. I don't recommend sucking on peppermint candy to smell like candy canes. I did that for years until I started losing my teeth. Use the mouthwash strips or just use mouthwash.

Instead of listing all the does and don'ts, I would like to just say, if it is something that you should not say or do in mixed company (men, women, children, old folks) than don't do it and don't say it. Also to assist with the hands in photographs, always wear gloves. This makes it easier to spot your hands. When wearing gloves, make sure the skin on your arms do not show from where your costume ends to the gloves. There are several tricks out that that will solve that problem. You can wear a special sleeve that goes under your suit, you can sew a ribbon loop at the end of a long sleeved T-shirt and hook it around a finger under your gloves (I picked up this trick from NASA) or you can purchase long gloves. I prefer to wear the long sleeved T-Shirt with the ribbon loop. This helps me to remain cooler and carries any perspiration I may have away from my body.

Though you may find a few children that are above your ability to lift because of their weight, never make a comment about it. The same goes for that darling little girl who is dressed to the nines and looks so cute. Don't mention anything about how pretty she looks unless you say that to everyone. Keep all your comments about the children to yourself.

One good rule of thumb is to not ask "non-Christmas" related questions. Most of the time you may get a funny story to tell others later, but there will be those times when it will either tear your heart out or the parents will become upset that you are trying to find out sensitive or private information. You cannot give advice or counsel to anyone unless you are a licensed psychiatrist or social worker. Even teachers have to be careful what they say. If you have any doubts about child abuse or domestic violence, you must contact a police officer and tell them what you know. Don't search for information. You could find yourself in jail or even at the wrong end of a lawsuit.

One of my beginning years before I learned about not pursuing non-Christmas related questions, I had a family visit me. There was a mother, father, a young girl about three years old and a young boy about five or six years old. They all came close and the young man jumped on my lap first. When I asked what he would like for Christmas, he boldly stated, "I want a new sister!" I looked at Mom who was horrified and indicated that she was not pregnant. Dad looked at Mom with an inquisitive look. So not knowing any better I asked "Why do you want a new sister?" To which I received the matter-of-fact statement, "because I don't like the one I have!" We all had a good laugh. I could see the relief come over Dad's face and Mom was at peace with that answer too.

This year what most kids ask for is a job for either mom or dad and sometimes both. The last couple years it was for a safe return of a parent or older sibling from the wars, but this year it is all about the job. Instead of telling them that Santa can't help with that, let them know that I am thinking about the person they are wanting the job for and will be looking everywhere for something they can do. Then I quickly change the subject to what they want for Christmas.

Being Santa is easy as long as you remember that you are in the public eye and should act accordingly. You are there to bring joy and happiness to those around you. You can't fix the problems of the world and shouldn't even try. Just smile and make those around you smile and feel better about the moment. Remember your job as Santa. You are to bring joy and happiness to everyone around the world.

This year I am prepared for the "I need a job" request. With the hard times being here these past few years, I know and understand that feeling of hopelessness. One thing I do say is that they need to remember I deal in toys. If they want a car, how does a Matchbox car sound? Or, if they want money, Monopoly money is the best I can do.

Several folks have sat on my lap in past years and asked for money or jobs. For those older ones who do so, I always say that the recession has to end soon and if they continue to hang in there, things will be getting better. I do promise them that I will be thinking about them throughout the season and wish them all the joy and happiness that surrounds this wonderful season.

Here is a rule that lots don't think about. No matter what the draw or what your motivation is, if you look like Santa, don't go anywhere near where another Santa is set up. A few years ago, I ruined a Santa's image because he brought his grand children to visit with the store Santa (me). I don't know if he secretly felt he could improve his image with the kids or what, but it must have backfired on him. His grandkids brought friends with them to see me when I was in a store setting. I overheard the kids talking and one told the rest that I was the real Santa and not the grandpa. They even told the grandpa that. What a shame to make the kids have to choose and decide between more than one Santa at Christmas time.

It is fun at gatherings of Santas to ask the kids to see if they can find the real Santa, but not during the Christmas season. Be kind; don't put yourself or another Santa in that position. Keep away from the kids while shopping or doing things during the Christmas season. It is not too much to ask for. Just be aware of your surroundings and don't get into that type of situation. It really isn't funny to make the kids have to make such a decision.

Santa's Survival Bag

Here is a utility device you will want to make up for yourself. I will tell you a few things and you decide if you want to carry them or add to the list. The most important thing about this survival bag is that it must be small enough to be inconspicuous and you can carry it with you everywhere.

The first thing I should mention is that this is a bag. I have a small, soft sided, ice chest (just big enough to fit a six-pack in.) In it I place 4 small freezer ice blocks. These are those chemical containers that you place in the freezer and use instead of ice. I prefer these because they don't sweat or get anything else I put in there wet. It just keeps things cold. Next I put in a bottle of water for every hour I plan to be active; (minimum of 4 bottles). If I am going someplace for an hour or less, I leave this in my truck.

Now we have water to hold us over and we don't need to ask the host or hostess for some ice water. Most of the time the kids and parents want to give you hot chocolate. This may be terrific on a cold winter day, but as you are sitting next to the roaring fire and are sweating like a stuck pig in July; that is last thing on your mind. If you are lucky, you may get offered a cold glass of milk.

Another important item I place in my bag is a wash cloth. Actually I have two. One I wet-down the night before and roll it up and set it in the freezer. This allows for me to place a cold, wet cloth on the back of my neck when I get too hot. The other is just a dry wash cloth to wipe away the sweat. I use a wash cloth instead of a towel for space. I use to have a golf/bowling towel, but someone decided they needed it more than I did. I haven't gotten around to replacing it yet because the wash cloth works just fine.

Having a snack helps me too. I usually have a pop tart or something like that so I can munch on the way to my next visit. This will stave off the hunger and allow me to keep my stomach from growling at the most inappropriate times. Another thing I carry is some Halls cough drops for those times when I feel I just need to cough and a package of those strips of mouthwash to keep my breath fresh.

I also add in an extra of several things I like to have, for example: a spare set of gloves, a spare D'Lite magic finger, a spare giggle box (I carry this box that has the sound of a child laughing when you squeeze it), a small pen light flashlight, Aleve, a hand sanitizer, and the last thing I put in there is something to clean my boots with and make them shiny again.

When I will be someplace for a long time, I carry this kit in with me. I try to keep it hidden and ask the host/hostess if they will bring it to where I will be after a while. I let them know it is my survival kit and I would like to have it handy. Having a small bag is non-intrusive and doesn't take away from any settings that may be established for pictures. Also, a small bag can be hidden.

Now in my truck I carry additional things. I always carry a complete costume change. You never know when an accident will happen. One year, I changed my pants on three different occasions the very same day. In the past three years, I haven't needed it but it sure felt good to have it. I also have a large staff I can use to help support me if I have a lot of stairs to climb. I leave the staff outside so not to have it get in the way inside people's houses as I try to maneuver about.

I also have a GPS and a huge map of the area. I prefer the books that get right down to the street level. It usually assists better with directions given by the client. I also carry my appointment book with all the information I need for that and other visits that night and a computer generated packet of directions to the location. The last thing I carry is enough money to hit a drive through to grab something to eat or something to snack on in the car. Something healthy instead of a greasy fast food burger is preferred, but when one is hungry, anything goes. I don't get into the messy stuff either; have to look neat for the next performance. This means Burger King and Taco Bell are out. I also don't do Sonic for the same reason.

You might want to look for a lint roller and a brush to clean your wardrobe between visits. Anything you can do to look neat is terrific.

Your Wardrobe

This is a costume. Make sure you take care of it. If you don't think you are an actor wearing a costume, you may need to seek help professional help for yourself. Remember you are an actor and need to look the part you are portraying. Take care of yourself and the clothes you wear to assist in portraying your character.

Let's talk about the costume you are going to wear. If you look on the internet, you will see the same picture with several different descriptions. Be very careful of what you purchase. A one-time purchase for a one-time use it really doesn't matter too much. But any type of pull over costume is easily torn and hard to keep clean. Find a reputable costume maker and have one made for you if you plan on portraying Santa for more than one year. If you need a costume idea, check out the section after this chapter that shows additional Santa attire and Mrs. Claus wardrobes. The cost is a tax write off and will be a better quality than most what you can get over the internet.

What do you wear the rest of the year. If you have a real beard, it really depends on your activity. If you are like me and portray different characters throughout the year, then you will want to dress accordingly. Always give a professional appearance no matter what you wear.

Now if you are a year-round Santa, I recommend a nice red three-piece suit. You can get some made fairly inexpensively in lots of places.

Just need to look in the Yellow Pages. Otherwise, if you are just going to be kicking it around, try some red overalls or red pants with a Hawaiian shirt. There are a lot around with Santa designs on them.

Always remember that you will be recognized as Santa so make your appearance match the man. Don't look like some homeless person looking for a handout. Be professional at all times. Look professional at all times. Wearing the red suspenders helps too!

Don't forget to include your T-shirts and those heavy socks that make your feet comfortable in those boots you wear.

Wide Selection of Costumes

Here are some places you might start in locating a costume. Note that the major department stores are not mentioned. I do recommend going to a costume shop and trying on different Santa costumes. Find the one you like and see if you can have one made like that. Do not, and I repeat DO NOT go out and spend $500 to $700 on a deluxe costume from Sears or any other similar type of store. Have one made that fits you. It will cost about the same. These are some sources for pre-made Santa Suits:

www.SantaSuitExpress.com
www.santasuitsandmore.com
www.santasuitsusa.com
www.planetsanta.com
www.Ebay.com
www.clowncostumes.com/index.html

Custom Made Santa Suits

These are not the only custom places to purchase. This list includes the ones I currently use. Look for a Theatrical Taylor or costume maker. They will do an excellent job too. If you use any of these, let them know I recommended them to you please. Robbie will also make you a Hawaiian shirt with Santa on it if you ask. Deborah makes clothes for several theatre groups and Adel does it for the movie industry. The more you look and seek these types of tailors, the more of them you will find.

www.santasuitorder.com
Adel of Hollywood – (323) 663-2231

If you would like to see Adel's work, log on to the Santa4hire website.

Robbie Hite rlrmhite@yahoo.com
Deborah Morrison yntvsxy@yahoo.com

For some sketches of what Deborah can do, check out the end of this section in the book. These are of both Mrs. Santa and Santa himself. The work is quality. I can vouch for that because I wear them and have several Mrs. Clauses who wear them now.

Santa Belts

I prefer the custom belts. These belts are better made and last longer. Plus you can get them with some very elaborate designs on them. Durability is necessary for a multiple use Santa. The plastic or pleather belts tend to wear out and crack. They don't hold up as well and also begin to curl after a while. Look neat and have a good belt. A good belt also helps support the back.

www.santabelts.com
www.santaclausbelts.com
www.santasuitsdirect.com
www.dellsleatherworks.com/santabelt.htm
www.RealSantas.com
heressanta@gmail.com - Santa Peter Kilmer, makes custom buckles and boots also

Santa Gloves

These are very important. I prefer the gloves with little rubber dimples on the fingers and palms. This allows me to turn the pages of a book without wetting the glove or taking them off. You will find that they also stimulate the imagination of the children. When one asks me about my gloves, I usually tell them that I can hold the reins to the reindeer better with them.

www.marchingworld.com
www.mccormicksnet.com
www.luckyclownsupply.com
www.anytimecostumes.com
www.gloves-online.com

Santa Boots

I recommend you find yourself some very nice boots that fit. It is worth the money to spend on your feet. If you are going to be wearing them for a while, cheaper boots will soon look old and tarnished with all the kids stepping on them. No matter how many inserts you put in them, they still are not comfortable. I have been wearing custom fit boots from Capri for over 5 years now and will never get anything else.

http://www1.shopping.com/xGS-Santa_Boots~NS-1~linkin_id-3056030
www.santaboots.net/
www.santaboots.com/
www.spearshoes.com
www.scaboots.com
www.santasuitsdirect.com/santaboots
www.Romans.com
www.threatrehouse.com
http://www.allthingsrenaissance.com/shoes/

www.caprishoes.com
heressanta@gmail.com - Santa Peter Kilmer, makes custom belts and buckles also.

Santa Stockings/Socks

If you are going to try different looks such as shorts, knickers, or other calf length or shorter pants, you will want some socks that will complement your outfit. Here are a few places to look.

www.sportsunlimitedinc.co/soccersocks
www.sportsauthority.com
www.dickssportinggoods.com
www.awesomesports.com
www.absolutesocks.com
www.clownantics.com/socks

Santa Shirts

The reason I list Darlene here is that she makes Civil War era costumes. She is very good, and the shirts are comfortable and easy to clean. Darlene also makes the knickers if you are interested in that type of look. I also have special shirts made through Adel of Hollywood. These shirts work well with the workshop look. The collar and cuffs have gold trim that matches the trim down the front of the shirt.

Darlene Bush sylvester98@earthlink.net
Adel of Hollywood – (323) 663-2231

Holiday Pins

The reason for the pins is that many Santas, on occasion myself included, like to wear a special pin on their hat. It adds to the pictures taken and makes you look more like Santa. I don't use anything flashy, but I do like a holly pin with red/white berry leaves or a reindeer head with antlers.

www.flashingblinkylights.com
www.pinmart.com.holidaypins.cfm
www.pinstocker.com
http://www.stockpins.com/christmas-lapel-pins.html

Stickers

In many places I talk about the year-round Santa carrying something to give children that recognize him. Well, if you are going to a performance or visit, you may be seen by children other than those you are visiting. Having some stickers that say something like "I Met Santa" are terrific to hand out. These are great to hand out to keep the kids interested. Look at all the different options available and choose one that you are comfortable giving out.

www.indianaclowns.com
www.clownsupplies.com

Suspenders

I cannot recommend these enough. Once you start wearing them with your costume (to prevent embarrassing moments) you just may find yourself wearing them for other occasions. I not only wear them to hold up my pants, but I also wear them for the aesthetic value. The look is terrific.

www.luckysclownsupplies.com
www.duluthtrading.com
www.store.suspenderfactory.com/suspenders-button-on-holidays.html
Wal-Mart has Red Suspenders at a great price.

Sleigh Bells

As you start performing more and more, you will find that you will need some type of noise maker to let everyone know you are coming. Nothing is worse than to enter a room, scaring the nearest child into crying because you startled them. Some Santas wear bells on their boots, others on their waist. Some Santa's have placed them on a walking stick or staff. Most have bells that they jingle as they move towards their performance location. I have found that if you are doing a daycare or elementary school, it is best to be noisy, even if it disrupts others. It is more fun that way.

Choose your bells wisely. No cheap bells. Make sure they are of good quality. You might even try looking up Native American Bell Dancer costumes.

www.classicbells.com
www.gbmcgee.com/bells
www.acmecarriage.com/sleighbells
www.nocbay.com/store/bells
Various sizes of bells and moderately priced:
Michael's Craft store, JoAnn's Fabrics and Hancock Fabrics.

Santa Schools

The last two schools are the most famous. The first two are traveling schools. I am sure there are many more, but these are the top rated schools around. I can also be contacted to travel and teach. My prices are reasonable and very cheap if you provide all the space required. I wrote the different courses for the Santa Claus Academy owned by Gary Casey. Check out my website or write me (snail mail or email) and I will ensure you get my information. I also include a copy of this book for all the students for a small fee.

Schools by the Noerr and Cherry Hill photography groups are mainly to teach Santas how to perform for them and what is expected of them. They don't really go into the mode of teaching one how to become a great Santa.

www.santaclausacademy.com – Direct Decedent's of Santa Claus School – Gary Casey
http://www.realsantas.com/iusc.htm - International School 4 Santas - Tim Connaghan's school
http://www.funwithsantaclaus.webs.net – My website
http://www.amerevents.com/school.htm - American Events Santa School
http://www.santaclausschool.com/ – Charles W. Howard's School
http://www.santaschool.com – Victor Nevada's School

Miscelanous Stuff

This section is here because as you get into being Santa, you will start looking for lots of "STUFF". Well here is a starting point for all your stuff. I like going to the dollar and discount stores. They usually have reindeer antlers I buy by the hundreds and flashing red noses that I also buy by the hundreds. Check out your local discount stores and see if they get them in. Usually you will find them at a terrific price.

www.bronners.com
www.1000bulbs.com/LED-Christmas-Lights-B
www.christmaslightsetc.com/led-christmas-lights.htm
www.backdropoutlet.com
www.dennymfg.com/store/index.php
www.samsclubus.pnimedia.com
www.brazos-walking-sticks.com/size_stick.html
www.santas.net/aroundtheworld.htm
www.coinsforanything.com
www.signsbyyou.com/gifts/cat_13.htm
www.centsibleholidaylighting.com/index.htm
www.santaexpress.net
www.amerevents.com

www.hotcards.com
www.jinglegram.com
www.atlanta.kijiji.com/f--W0QQCatIdZ0
www.atlanta.craigslist.org
www.clubflyers.com/index.php?cPath=25

The internet is a wonderful resource for Santa costumes and related accessories. Here I have given you a start but you should build your own library of resources for the items you are interested in.

This is just a start. I recommend that you travel to different costume shops and see what they have to offer. You might be able to purchase a used Santa suit that is in need of repair but of good quality and would be fairly inexpensive for your first one.

Yep, I did say your first one. After all, once bitten with the Santa bug, it is hard to stop. It is so much fun you will want to keep doing it all the time.

I am sure that most folks who have been portraying the jolly old elf himself for a couple of years have several costumes. I have 6 different looks and can modify some of them to give me an additional 12 different looks. I am currently looking into having two more different styles created for me. I love it. I hope that you too will also grow to love this as I do. I play Santa for charities usually in June, July, and August. Sometimes I get a request to do charity work in November and December but unless they are really important or I can get a lot of mileage out of it, I don't do those. I save November and December for my paying jobs.

Some folks like walking sticks, canes, shepherd crooks and other such devices to assist in walking. Don't over-decorate these. Some are so gaudy that they detract rather than add to the costume. Take a good hard look at what you do and ask others to give their opinion. Don't sway them one way or the other with how you ask the question. Let them make up their mind and keep track of the results.

For example: while teaching a Santa class, we had a discussion about what color Mrs. Claus' hair should be. Some ladies in the class swore up and down that red head, brunette, and Goth black were all acceptable.

My personal opinion is it should match Santa's hair and beard. So I set out to find out what most folks thought. I phrased the question as follows: In your opinion, what color should Mrs. Claus' hair be?"

Overwhelmingly, the Santa's stated that it should be as white as their hair and beard by a whopping 99 %. The other 1% had wives that assisted them and did not color their hair.

Conversely, the ladies who portrayed Mrs. Claus stated it could be any color by only a 65% margin. I guess they just were too vain about their looks and didn't want to look old yet so they wanted to keep their "younger look" with the darker hair color.

I asked others who did not portray either Santa or Mrs. Claus and they stated fairly matter-of-factly, that the hair should be white as snow. 86%.

Then I asked the kids. They all stated white for the Mrs. Claus hair 100%.

My conclusion, those Mrs. Claus who do not wish to have white hair, buy a wig. All others, the hair should be white as Santa's beard and hair. Sorry about those young ladies and those who wish to preserve their youth longer. I have a young Mrs. Claus who helps me occasionally. She wears a wig all the time. The wig is pure white. She won't have any other color. Even when she bleaches her hair white, she still wears the wig so she doesn't need to have a perm or other stuff done to her hair to make it look like Mrs. Claus.

Sketches of Wardrobes

T'is The Season

By Al Horton
T'is the season of Christmas
And all through the land,
If there really is a Santa
Than where is this man.

I see a white beard
In all the big shops,
And I know that my presents
Come from my Pops.

Each Christmas Eve
As I lay tucked in my bed,
Visions of Santa
Dance through my head.

Wonder I must
Fake beards or real,
Does somebody come here
Giving presents and not steal.

I dream of the reindeer
And wonder how they fly,
I dream of Santa's workshop
And how he gets by.

The noise down stairs
Sounds like they are assembling my bike,
I will have that surprised look
If it's something I like.

Christmas wrappings all over the floor
With bows for the gifts stuck on the door,
And the scribbled tags
From Santa on bags.

Is there really a Santa
Or does Mom and Dad do the work,
To make me so happy
Knowing my brother is a lying jerk.

He says there is no Santa
And I really want to know,
How does he get here
I thought he needed snow.

But again in the morning
I awaken to delight,
To see all the presents
Left in the night.

As I turn to my brother
And leer with a smile,
I got more than him this year
Much more by a mile.

He sneered and he jeered
He still loudly proclaimed,
There is no Santa Claus
Cause Daddy is his name.

Than Mom in her nightgown
And Dad in his robe,
Took us aside
This is what they told.

Santa is the spirit
The spirit of the year,
It's the giving of presents
And bringing joy and good cheer.

Everyone feels better
When they can give a gift,
For the love that is included
Gives everyone a big lift.

Now if giving is not good
Or if it bothers you both,
It will stop right here
I give you my oath.

But if giving is good
And you wish to partake,
Select an old toy
To the orphanage we'll take.

Away we all flew
To the home across town,
And gave of our gifts
To those children around.

As we sat down to breakfast
Later that morn,
I felt so much better
But I was still torn.

So if there is no Santa
Than who brings all the toys,
To all of the good
Girls and good boys.

My dad looked at me
And he winked and then smiled,
You do he said
Your name is now on file.

Welcome to the roster
Of Santa's everywhere,
Welcome to the club
My son so fair.

So now I do know
There is a Santa Claus,
He is in all of us
I say that without pause.

Santa is you,
And you, and he is me,
Santa is everywhere
And we are all he.

Chapter 3

Santa's Voice

A friend of mine, and another Santa, Lou Knezevich gave me lots of information for this section. He is not a voice instructor, but has accumulated a considerable amount of background information in this field. He also recommends you find yourself a voice coach.

One of the most important features of Santa is his voice. This voice projects soft spoken warmth, friendliness and security. It gives the listener comfort and makes them feel they are in the presence of a grandfatherly type of person. Santa is not to be feared.

If Santa's voice is used improperly it can make children cry, grown-ups wince and ruin your credibility. Most of us are not endowed with the rich baritone sound which commands respect and speaks of authority, so we must practice developing a Santa voice. Now I can't guarantee you will have the perfect voice, but you can work on modulating and controlling your voice.

Exercise Your Voice

One of the most discomfiting occurrences when you're speaking in public is to have your voice tighten up and come out as a high-pitched squeak or just give up and go away. It's so annoying and discouraging that it makes a person want to jettison the entire business of speaking in public. Perhaps the thought of being a mime becomes very attractive indeed.

Carole McMichaels answers this question best.

What can I do to prepare myself so that when I'm nervous I can still breathe?

First it's helpful to be aware of how you breathe normally. To ascertain this, sit on a straight chair. Put one hand on your upper chest and the other hand on your belly. Take a normal breath, and make these observations: Which hand moved? Did your belly go out or in?

You're doing well if both hands moved OUT, or if your belly moved OUT. What you want to avoid is having your belly suck in and your chest move out. That's probably the most common style of breathing, and it is something you definitely want to change, for the sake of your body's health as well as the strength of your voice.

Although breathing is a natural body function, breathing for proper singing or speaking requires training and strengthening the muscles of your diaphragm, back, and belly. The following exercise should be done daily:

1. Sit on a straight chair. Feet flat on the floor. Spine absolutely straight as possible, but not tense. (Feel as though you have a cord running straight up from your tailbone to the top of your head, gently and effortlessly keeping you in that straight position.)
2. Put your hands on your belly, fingers spread and just touching in the center slightly below your navel.
3. Take a great big breath right into your belly.
4. Let your lower jaw drop a bit and say a quiet "HA" as you pull in

your belly with your hands, slowly as you can remaining comfortable all the while.

Do this several times, always being aware of any tension that might occur. (Allow your tongue to lie inert on the bottom of your mouth, tip barely touching the teeth.)

<u>Now repeat the first three steps of the exercise, but substitute 4Aand later 4B below, for #4.</u>

4A. With your hands, pull your belly in pretty fast, and let out the air with a loud "sssss" sound. Then do the same thing, but with only one hand, and with your thumb on one side and your fingers on the other side of your throat, feel to be sure there's no tension during the "sssss".

As your control develops you'll be able to sustain your breath for longer and longer periods. Now try this next one.

4B. When you feel ready, release the breath with a soft hum. Any note in the middle of your register. Avoid the lowest notes.

Simple as they are, these little exercises can make your entire life easier. They feed your physical and mental body with health-giving oxygen. You'll find you're more relaxed and positive in your everyday activities.

Before we try any vocal renderings let us practice by warming up the vocal cords. We want to protect our vocal cords and exercise the diaphragm. Before the voice exercises, let's do like with any exercise program and stretch. We want to stretch the diaphragm. Reach one arm to the ceiling then the other, alternating inhaling and exhaling. Do you feel how open and connected your body starts to feel? Take a big breath in and then blow it all out. (Be careful if your uppers are a bit loose we don't want any flying missiles.). Sit on the edge of your chair, round your lower back by bringing your tailbone closer to the chair. Gradually arch your lower back, releasing your lower belly as you come up. Notice you get taller and shorter.

Bring the sounds from deep inside and let them rumble and reverberate up and out. You don't have to try and deepen your voice; it is automatically deepened, the lower you start the air. Practice relaxing before talking. Relax your vocal cords and use the air in your belly.

Using that air from deep below, make siren sounds. Make them glide up and down with a lip trill (raspberry) or tongue trill (rolled "r"). Notice how you are be able to go higher and lower in your range with this exercise. Start off in the lowest range you can. Now practice rolling your r's and keeping this going for as long as you can.

I do recommend that you find a voice instructor. The instructor will teach you information you did not know and will then coach you in making vocal improvements. You don't need to take singing lessons, but voice lessons would be a fabulous help. They will help you bring that deep air with the lower tones to the surface. Practice being a TV announcer. Listen to the announcer the next time you are watching a game show. See if you can imitate that person's voice.

Now get that Buzz going. Put your lips together, teeth slightly apart and do a descending "hum". Experiment with the sound until you feel vibrations. Try to keep that vibrating sensation in your face. Now try it saying "v-v-v-v". Continue practicing this exercise. Use whichever one creates the most vibration.

Go from low to high with the "hum" or "v-v-v-v". Now go from high to low. Don't go so high that your throat gets tight. Keep the low side of this exercise relaxed and stress free. Do not force the sounds or pitch to the point of strain.

Using the "buzz" sound you got in the earlier exercise, do a descending glide and then ascending glide with each of these syllables: "Ma", "May", "Me", "Moe", "Moo". Breathe before each glide.

Keeping the sound smooth and connected as possible as you move your voice high and low, say the following words and phrases.

Remember to take a low abdominal breath before uttering each phrase (abdomen moves out as you breath and in as you breath out). Keep the air moving to the end of each word and phrase.

Repeat: no-no-no-no-no-no-no-no-no. Now not now. Nearly noon. Never at night.

Bub bub bub bub bub bub bub bub bub, Bobby bought boats. Buy burgundy bottles.

Va-va-va-va-va-va-va-va-va-va. Very vain. Vote for vinny. Varni vamped very vivaciously.

Wuu" Kazoo sound. Hold onto the "w" sound and pulsate it. Feel the buzz? Try these sentences:

What's the weather like?

What did you do this weekend?

Where are you going?

What's for dinner?

Keep the air moving to the end of the word or phrase. Don't let the sound become raspy at the last word.

All right, is everybody warmed up?

Everyone is familiar with Santa's signature saying which denotes his pleasure and is used in all types of situations fitting to the character of Santa Claus. I'm referring to the loud, "Ho, Ho Ho," which comes from the bottom of your belly and thunders from every wall of the room. Somehow we Santas have come to believe that loud is good and the louder we are the more believable we will be.

Here are some tips from Jane Oakshott BA, MA, LAMDA (Gold) MBE, a voice and performance coach working with professional voice users in business, the professions and the arts; e.g. public speakers, lawyers, actors. Jane is Trustee of the Voice Care Network UK and an accredited trainer for the Law Society of England and Wales.

Nerves: Where we need to start is 'what do you need out of this?' Everyone has a key thing that if they get that right then everything else will fall into place. So, to make sure we cover the right stuff in this session, it would be useful to know what your particular problems are, and you'll probably find that a lot of your friends will say 'Oh yes! I do that too!' When you get nervous, what goes wrong in your performance? What do you want to combat? Do you get nervous and tend to run your words into each other. Maybe you tend to mumble. Does your voice get cluttered back in your throat? Do you speak much too quickly? How about stammering? Just can't seem to get the words really out? Is that just in presentations or otherwise...? Do have a very tight jaw and your lower lip is quite tense which means that the sound of your voice can't get out beyond your teeth? Something we need to work on.

Relaxation and Balance: The first set of exercises that we're going to do are for the whole body, to open out the area for your lungs to give you more breath space and to make you feel more centered, taller, wider, as if you're taking up the space you deserve. And the effect of that will be to make you feel less nervous and generally more assured because you know you look good, and once you know you look good you'll feel better about your audience.

Shoulder circle: Make your shoulders rounded, really work them up to your ears and a little bit further back so that your hands are quite loose and they're down around about the seam of your trousers, and then let your shoulders go aaahh, allowing the shoulders' weight slide down toward your buttocks. What you've done is taken them in a big circle, and then down your back. Instead of carrying your arms, which weigh something like 60 pounds, on these muscles and on the muscles on the back of your neck, you have the weight of your arms and shoulders sliding down your back and becoming counterbalanced by your feet. So instead of carrying around 60 pounds weight, you're actually just standing there carrying absolutely nothing.

Elastic rope: Right after the shoulder exercise the elastic rope, is a really good exercise to make you feel you own the world. It's a mind game. Imagine that you have a piece of elastic rope coming out of your spine, through the crown of your head and it's attaching you to the ceiling. Now that piece of elastic is just a fraction too short, alright. So it's pulling you slightly off the ground, not forwards, not backwards, your head's not going anywhere, but it is just pulling your spine up a little bit. Can you just feel that so that you're fractionally coming off the ground, in other words your weight is going slightly forward over your toes rather than back on your heels? So it's just a mind thing, you're not actually coming off the ground. Start like that but then gradually see if you can get the feeling without your heels leaving the ground; once you've got the feeling of the elastic rope coming up through your spine, move on to the next exercise.

Breath Capacity and Control: Having made space for the lungs to work, we need help for the muscles that do the breathing. That is the rib muscles and, very importantly, the diaphragm. Have you noticed when you're nervous, it's the diaphragm which seizes up? That's what makes the butterflies happen. If you can work your diaphragm at your own will, then nerves won't have an effect on you.

Whoosh: This is an exercise to help you relax. To do it, breathe out and then let air back in comfortably. With that air just say 'Whooshhhh...' Whooshhhh... Good, there's a lot of pressure there. Now when you said the 'shhhh' part, could you feel the tightening? That's where your diaphragm is. Do that again, in other words breathe out, get rid of stale air, allow fresh air back in and then again say 'Whooshhhhh...' and really feel that diaphragm muscle working to the very end of your breath.

Mosquito zapping: This another exercise which really gives force to that Whooosh sound, and also, as a side effect, gives you focus when you're talking to your audience. I'd like you to imagine that your mouth has a laser in it and that laser is the air coming out. Imagine you can see mosquitoes around the room, just above your eye level, and I'd like you to zap one at a time with that laser gun, and the sound is like when you make a sneeze. You know that sound 'ch'. Now imagine that 'ch' is actually a deadly dart coming at a mosquito, you have to aim at it with your eyes, and then 'ch'. So like any other breathing exercise breathe out, get rid of stale air, take in a comfortable breath, and then 'ch'. Ch. Now on the next breath we're going to breathe out, breath in comfortably do 3 mosquitoes, see each of them. Ch, ch, ch.

Clear speech obviously comes from talking to people. The place to begin is your need to have the other person hear what you're saying. Not at a loud volume either, you can talk REALLY LOUDLY and still be unclear. What's important is clarity of speech. This is much more important than being loud. So what do you do to make your voice clearer? Where the words are shaped is actually in your mouth, with the lips and the tongue. They chop up the sound as it comes through and turn into words.

Onion: This a really good exercise for relaxing your mouth muscles and making them more flexible. Shut your lips and say 'onion' four times over. [With lips shut] Onion. Onion. Onion. Onion. Now say it without shutting your lips. Onion. Enjoy the feeling of being able to open your mouth. So three times through, onion, with your mouth closed and then the fourth time, open your mouth! With lips shut. Onion. Onion. Onion. Now open. Onion.

Taffy: This helps with clarity. This is another exercise to help your words come out more clearly by working the muscles of your mouth. Place your tongue on the back of your teeth. Find the hard ridge to press against. In that ridge there's an arch right in the middle. Put the tip of your tongue on that arch and keep it there while you recite the days of the week very clearly. As in: Monday, Tuesday, Wednesday, Thursday, etc. The more you move your jaws and your lips, the better the words will come out. This is very important for working your mouth muscles and producing clear words.

Intonation and tone are important. Of course, the end product we will hope for in our own voice is attractiveness. People will want to listen to it. And a lot of that comes from the way the tune of the voice goes and the pitch variation. To a certain extent, if you do the exercises for clarity, in other words those which make the lips and tongue work harder, so all the lip and tongue sounds come out firmer, then your voice will gain interest. Your voice will gain energy and tune. Here's one to practice in varying your pitch. It is a favorite singer's exercise called 'Sirening' and to do that you find an 'ng'. This is the sound in the middle of 'ringing', 'ng.' The tongue goes up at the back and it all comes down your nose, 'ng'. Imagine you're going along a road and you're coming to a set of traffic bumps so instead of going 'ng' (in a monotone voice) you're going 'ng' [voice goes up and down] and the bumps are getting bigger so it's 'ng' [voice goes up and down but rising more]. Don't forget to breathe. You'd be surprised at how many more notes you've got there from the ones you will use in everyday life. Do you know most people only use about three notes out of at least three octaves available in their voice in everyday life?

As always, practice makes perfect

When and How You Use It

The loud, "Ho, Ho Ho!" should not be used when making an entrance except when needed to get the attention of a noisy crowd. Just imagine what a booming, "Ho Ho Ho" entrance will do to babies and small children. It's going to scare them and set off some hysterical crying which in turn diverts the audience's attention from you and your entrance. Now the time to consider the loud, "Ho! Ho! Ho!" is when you exit the event. If you've done your job well, there will be some happy faces wishing you goodbyes and a group well familiar with Santa. As you are about to leave the sight of the crowd is the time to utter those famous words; "Merry Christmas and to all a good night! HO! HO! HO!"

Let's practice a loud, "Ho! Ho! Ho!" remembering to bring that voice up from the depths of your stomach. When you're comfortable with it precede it with a departing, "Merry Christmas and to all a good night!"

There is another "Ho! Ho! Ho!" which is actually a chuckle. You probably should use a version of this when you enter a room so you do not frighten children. As we mentioned before the worst thing you can do is make an entrance and scare a child or toddler. This immediately distracts from you and misdirects your audience's attention. The chuckle is done in a modulated voice said as a soft yet deep rumbling, Ho! Ho! Ho!" Along with the chuckle at appropriate times your belly should shake with each, Ho! Ho! Ho!" or place each hand on your belly and give a shake with each chuckle.

Practice this as a normal laugh. Soon you will have this chuckle down so well that you don't have to think about laughing that way. It also gives incredible credibility to you. Folks will start commenting that you even sound like Santa. That low rumbling, Ho! Ho! Ho!" chuckle did the trick.

Practice the soft and gentle chuckle and build it into a bellowing and hardy laugh. It is more realistic and less apt to frighten the small children who may be timid around you anyway.

When talking with children it is best to speak very quietly and secretively. Remember you are being told a secret desire of a child who is placing their confidence in a red-suited character who fulfills wishes of good children. Talk to the child as you would an adult, don't baby talk or change the pitch of your voice.

You may wish to chuckle as you ask a child what they desire or sometime during their time on your knee. Animate the visit by facial expressions such as looks of surprise, pondering thought, and smiling. That way you can keep that twinkle in your eyes. Laugh often and loud if it calls for it.

Now in your best Santa voices, let us try the "Santa chuckle."

OK, we are all warmed up; now let's laugh until we can't laugh any more.

Just a little hint about your voice training, like any other part of your body that you want to train, repetition is the key. I love to practice while driving my truck. I keep the windows up, but the practice laughs keep me smiling and when someone pulls up to me at a traffic light or some other stop, I don't mind them thinking I am a bit touched. Because, when I turn to look at them I am smiling and a little wave usually gets them to smile back. What a wonderful world we live in when everyone smiles at each other.

So now we all know that we must practice. Remember, practice makes perfect.

Although we don't give much thought to our voices, his voice is one of Santa's most important assets. I'll illustrate my point.

I was hired for a photo shoot at a very exclusive country club which started early as over 70 families were scheduled for photos with Santa. The room we were using was narrow and long so from the entrance door to my Santa chair was a fair walk. The doors were kept closed until it was the next family's turn. It was very enlightening to see the reaction of children and adults when they saw me sitting beside the Christmas tree waiting for them. For many it was a happy laugh and some children ran the length of the room to jump upon my lap. Oh yes, there were one or two who took one look at me sitting in the chair and did an abrupt about face or tugged at the parents to leave.

A beautiful little girl of about three or four, dressed in her best Christmas dress started to enter the room with her parents and grandparents. Upon seeing me she stiffened and it appeared she was about to head back out the door. Her parents got her close to my Santa chair but things didn't look promising. One of the grandparents told me she was very frightened because of an experience with a mall Santa. I heard them say her name which was Julie, but none of my coaching was going to move her until I noticed a big band aid on her finger. When I inquired about it the parents quickly chimed in that she had caught her finger in a door. I stood up from the chair and slowly advanced towards the child. In a normal voice, I asked her if it hurt and how her finger got caught in the door.

As she answered me I slowly took small steps to the Santa Chair. I told her I could barely hear her as I lowered my voice speaking to her. I kept asking her to come closer so I could hear. Soon we were face to face and I told her very quietly about a time I caught my finger in a door and how much I knew it hurt her. She proudly displayed the bandaged finger and I quietly gained her confidence. In hushed tones I told her there wasn't enough light to really see her finger except by the chair. I sat down and after a few more words about her finger I asked her to sit on my knee so I could really see her bandage. She sat upon my knee to the amazement of the entire family and photo staff. Julie placed her hand in mine and with little encouragement gave the photographer the biggest smile she could. I could hear the sighs of delight from the family and photographers.

After the pictures were taken, Julie gave me the biggest hug and then happily exited with her mother and grandparents. Her father came over to me with a tear in his eye and thanked me over and over again for taking the pictures plus alleviating Julie's fears of Santa Claus. He told me I had a gift from God that no one had been able to do what I did and he asked what I had said to her. All I could tell him is we talked about her hurt finger and became the best of friends. If I had any intuitive feelings they were to speak very softly and to be genuinely concerned about Julie's injury. Had I spoken in a normal voice or not projected sincerity I would have never gained Julie's confidence. We Santas need to use our voices wisely, develop patience and speak to children with respect.

Do I Have Santa's Voice?

When you put on the red suit it transforms you into the Santa character and many things change within you. I'm from Texas and my normal speaking voice has a very recognizable accent. I lived in the South for many years yet most folks would comment "You must be from the North because of your accent," so I'm recognized and identified by my voice.

Of course this worried me until I realized I also have a Santa voice and yes, Santa lives in the north, the way north. I believe we all have a Santa voice which comes out when we wear the red suit and assume the role of Santa. This voice mimics the robust, Ho! Ho! Ho!" and carries within it the warmth of Santa. If you think about the voice you have when you are Santa you will soon realize your voice sounds different. It may sound deeper than normal or maybe you pronounce words with a different inflection then your normal speaking voice.

I have a theory that we have heard Santa's voice in a movie or a spoken story and this sound is what our minds are trying to emulate in our voices. If you have a "Santa" voice I encourage you to cultivate it and use it to make your portrayal of Santa Claus more believable.

My best advice is to find a voice coach and get some real practice in. Short of that, keep with the exercises mentioned above and keep practicing your Santa voice and laugh. Let everyone know you are Santa with your chuckle.

A friend once confided in me that he never though he had a Santa's voice until one day he decided to get the kids singing. So, he started out the song himself. His wife came around the corner to see who was singing and told him later that he had a wonderful voice. He had always thought he didn't have a Santa voice and certainly didn't think he could sing.

This leads to one comment. You would be surprised what you can do when you are Santa. Try everything. If it doesn't work out, don't try again. When it does, add it to your performance.

Chapter 4

Grooming

Basic Concepts

Grooming covers a wide area, all factors of which influence personal acceptance by others. Have you ever been around someone in a social setting and couldn't help notice their body order or even their bad breath? Wow! Those two factors alone could set you back quite a bit. Well, this chapter deals with your grooming habits, what are the standards, and what everyone sees, hears, and smells when they are around you.

Let's start with the easiest to control. Prior to each visit, make sure you are freshly bathed. Splashing on additional cologne only turns the children off. Cologne is usually too strong for a young child's nose. Definitely use a deodorant. Preferably one that is unscented. The elimination of Cologne and deodorant will assist you in finding out if a child has an allergenic reaction to us, or should I say our scent.

Cleanliness is not only bathing, it includes brushing your teeth prior to a visit. Brushing prior to your visit also removes things that may stick in your teeth and helps cut down on the bad breath. Don't forget to scrub that tongue while you are in there. Use mouthwash. A good strong mouthwash will assist in killing the germs that cause bad breath.

You might want to think about sprinkling a small amount of baby powder in your beard for a really fresh scent. Babies will smell and identify you as a friendly person. I only use this trick for private settings when I know or at least suspect to find babies there. Also, I don't put too much on because the white powder will get all over the place and on your costume. Then it just doesn't look right.

Along with this, you need to watch what you eat for at least 24 hours prior to your appearance. Certain spices and foods will leach through your skin and that may be offensive to some sensitive noses. I love garlic. That is definitely a no no during the season.

Mind your breath, make sure you don't eat anything that would cause you to belch or that may retain its odor in your mouth. Gassy foods include beans, broccoli, soda, beer, etc. Breath mints only cover up odors for a few minutes. Keep your breath fresh always. Hint: Parsley is great to chew after a meal. It clears the pallet and removes offensive orders. Mints are made of sugar, if you want bad teeth; use something with sugar in it to clear your breath. I also recommend using the breath strips. They are mouthwash in dissolving strips.

At many events food is plentiful which encourages people to ask you to eat and drink. Santas should make it a practice not to eat or drink in front of an audience for the basic reasons of dropping food on your beard, clothes' or accidentally spilling something. Water of course is acceptable and you should use a straw to keep the beard dry. Liquor is never acceptable before, during or on the premises after the event. When asked to eat Santa should reply: "No thank you I really can't eat anything while I'm here making sure the guests are happy." Or "I can't eat anything right now but I would enjoy a plate to go to have when I relax!" I know sometimes after you have had a long Santa day it's hard to turn down something to eat but we must remember to maintain the image even when an innocent temptation seems like the thing to do. Those cookies and milk are inviting, but don't do it.

Keep your wardrobe clean. Nothing is worse than arriving at a visit with yesterday's stains and smells on your clothes. Hint: smoking will stay with your clothes for more than 2 or 3 hours. Kids have sensitive noses and can smell it on you. Don't smoke before a visit and especially don't smoke on any break you take during a visit.

If your shoes are dirty, the children will know it. Always polish them so they are clean for each visit. Hint: a damp rag may do the trick, but always be prepared with polish. Most drug and food store carry the quick wax shine kits that fit in the palm of your hand which do a nice job on your boots.

Your Hair and Beard Are Very Important.

For the real beards, this means shampooing, (dandruff shampoo if necessary), use a conditioner. Your beard is perhaps your most important asset. Shampoo your beard and hair daily. Use a GOOD quality shampoo and plenty of a QUALITY conditioner. The shampoo can actually be a cheap brand, but you should never scrimp on the conditioner. Always use the best you can. You may find yourself in need of a good dandruff shampoo every couple of washings. Find one that is right for you. Shampoo and conditioners used for show horses' manes and tails produce spectacular results!

Your beard is a lot coarser than your hair and will require more conditioning to keep it soft. Avoid spraying your hair with hair spray, this defeats the effect achieved by the conditioner.

The softer your hair and beard feels to the touch, the better for the kids. Don't leave any greasy stuff in your hair for the children will touch it. (It is usually the adults and babies that pull it.) Always brush your hair and be ready for anything. If you curl your hair, be prepared to do it every hour. Hairspray is a terrific invention, but it makes the beard hard and brittle, it could feel uncomfortable to the child.

White hair is the standard. That is snow white! Any other color is not acceptable. Some folks acquire it naturally while others must bleach to achieve the desired results. If you bleach, enlist the aid of a professional. Losing your hair on your head or beard is devastating. Damage and or loss of your hair and beard can result from the incorrect use of bleaching products. I really can't mention this enough.

I have tried the spray on color and found it is only good for adult parties where I can remain at a great distance. Some swear by it, but I prefer to be able to touch my hair without the color coming off. You should strive to keep your beard and hair as white as possible. This may require the occasional use of a "Bluing" shampoo. The Blue or Purple shampoo will assist in removing any yellow in your hair.

For the designer or glue on beards and wigs, (Yes I did say glue on), make sure that you groom and clean your wigs before putting them up for the night. This will give them the chance to set in the proper form and will keep them lasting longer. The glue to use is what is used in make-up and movie industry, it is called spirit gum. To remove, just apply some spirit oil. All can be found at any good costume shop.

Even though you can remove your hair and beard, you should follow the instructions for proper care and take all the precautions to maintain them in their best condition. I actually wore a designer beard and wig for several years. Keeping them hung and clean allowed me to pass it on to another would-be-Santa when I grew my own. Always remember that the same principle for cleanliness in your personal hair also applies for designer beards & wigs.

There will be more information and recommend products at the end of this chapter. I won't vouch for how they will work for you so I suggest that any product you try for the first time, use in the off season when it won't matter too much what happens. ALWAYS FOLLOW THE DIRECTION PRECICELY.

The Art of Applying Makeup

Applying Make-Up is an art form in itself. Most department stores have a make-up counter and makeup artists who are ready to give advice. Don't be bashful, explain to one of the stylist you are a Santa and you need make-up advice. I think you'll find they will love helping Santa and you'll be getting useful advice to correctly apply make-up. Let the experts help you at first. Remember the best advice I can give you is less is best, none is worse.

Select a base color closest to your facial color. Apply in a light circular motion over facial scars, age spots or any facial imperfections. You are camouflaging and blending into the skin. This may be applied with either your finger tip or a cotton swab.

The white is used to lighten the skin beneath the beard areas any where your beard is not completely filled in. It is also used to lighten your skin beneath the eyebrows. Apply very lightly. This can be applied with either you fingertip or cotton swab.

It only takes a very small amount of the red to give your cheeks and nose tip that wind-burned look. Apply with your finger tip rubbing lightly in a circular motion. If you get too much red, you can tone it down by putting a little of the base over the red.

Sprinkle a small amount of powder on the powder puff, spread out evenly then pat your makeup with the powder puff. Always pat, never rub! Give the powder a couple of minutes to absorb any excess makeup, removing any shine, then brush off excess powder, spray with cold water to set the makeup and brighten colors.

This is theatrical grease paint and will not run if you perspire. You will need baby oil, baby magic, or a makeup remover to remove completely and easily. Wipe the areas with a soft towel moistened with the remover. Wash your face with warm water and soap or shampoo. Apply a skin moisturizer after use.

That is grooming in a nutshell. Below you will find many products that several Santas use. Remember, READ and HEED the instructions on the packages. Use a professional for first time help.

Just Some Products To Look At

Here are some products. I do not recommend any of them over the others. The notes are taken from product advertising. These are just some of the products our Santas use on their own. It is always recommended that everyone seek professional help so as not to lose their hair or cause other damage to it.

Time Renewal Conditioner

Multi-pro-vitamin system repairs up to 2 years of damage in 1 month** by restoring hair's sheen and silky feel.

Time Renewal – Undo up to 2 years of damage in one month

Time Renewal Shampoo

Multi-pro-vitamin shampoo helps target the hair's problem zones, restoring its beauty from root to tip.

Time Renewal Replenishing Mask

Dramatically quenches parched strands, leaving hair supple and restored

Breakage Defense – Get up to 90% less breakage in 1 month.

Breakage Defense Shampoo

Multi-pro-vitamin system strengthens weak hair to provide up to 90% less breakage in 1 month.

Breakage Defense Conditioner

Fortifies exhausted hair to provide up to 90% less breakage in 1 month.

Breakage Defense Strengthening Spray

Helps target, repair, and fortify weak hair, building strength against damage.

Breakage Defense Strengthening Lotion

Helps repair smoothness so weak hair can build strength against damage and breakage.

Breakage Defense Detangling Leave-In Crème

Conditioning formula helps detangle and protect rebellious hair from breakage.

Frizz Control – Get all day frizz control

Frizz Control Shampoo

Multi-pro-vitamin system repairs rebellious damage that causes frizz for all-day frizz control.

Frizz Control Conditioner

Locks in hair's natural moisture and helps seal out humidity for all-day frizz control.

Frizz Control Extra Strength Serum

Transforms prickly hair and helps seal out humidity for ultimate frizz control.

Frizz Control Ultra Smoothing Balm

Tames unruly frizz instantly—for brilliantly smooth hair all day.

Frizz Control Anti-Humidity Hairspray

Long-lasting flexible hold that locks your look through high humidity. Formulated with a touch of cucumber and green tea fragrance, the balanced formula of new Coo Moisture Conditioner leaves hair soft and feeling fresh. For all hair types.

COWBOY MAGIC® Shine In Yellowout™

SHINE IN YELLOWOUT™ Neutralizes Yellow Stains and Brightens Hair of All Colors

Black, White, Chestnut, Bay Brown, Roan, Palomino, Paint

Benefits:

There are benefits for both horse and human. SHINE IN YELLOWOUT™ takes yellow stains out of hair and gives dull hair of every color a more brilliant sheen. It leaves hair silky, shiny and smelling good.

COWBOY MAGIC® Rosewater Shampoo

COWBOY MAGIC® Concentrated Rosewater Shampoo with Silk Conditioners is easy to use and is formulated to:

1. Gently dissolve dirt and clean hair.
2. Condition the hair and skin.
3. It is easy to rinse.
4. To be used full strength or diluted up to 20 to 1.
    - **It works instantly:**
      The fast working ingredients break down dirt and unwanted matter quickly without damaging hair.
    - **It is a deep conditioner:**
      Panthenol and silk protein penetrate the hair and deep condition the skin, preventing dryness.

- **It creates a shine:**
  The silk molecules reflect prism light giving the hair a rich, natural shine as it restores vibrant beauty.
- **It takes a small amount:**
  The formula has a double action that allows gentle full strength use without damage.
- **It is easy to rinse:**
  Quick release sudsing surfactants cost us more, but give the user a fast and easy **rinse** action without buildup. You get more suds and less work because it is easier to rinse.
- **It works on people too:**
  Our double rich formula can be compared with some of the most popular and expensive "salon-only" shampoos on the market.

COWBOY MAGIC® Rosewater Conditioner

COWBOY MAGIC® Concentrated Rosewater Conditioner is a new innovation in the equine market. Hair neutralization and clarification has been a human hair salon service for a long time. It's use results in healthy looking hair.

- **It is concentrated:**
  To be used straight or dilute 20 to 1.
- **It works instantly:**
  As it is massaged in, the formula will dissolve mineral and chemical buildup deposited by water. After rinsing, the hair will be left in an ultra clean, almost virgin state.
- **It deep conditions:**
  Silk and panthenol penetrate hair and skin, moisturizing and adding body to hair.
- **It is long lasting:**
  Neutralizing the hair by demineralizing, it can last for more than a week depending on the water you use and what other treatments are put on the hair after neutralization. Whatever additional process you use, hair will look and feel better. It neutralizes static electricity, tangles are reduced and kept to a

minimum as static electricity is controlled by reducing the trace mineral in the hair.

- **It only takes a small amount:**
  The formula is very concentrated and a small amount goes a long way.
- **It works on people too:**
  Human hair care salons have been offering this special service for a long time. You can use COWBOY MAGIC® as a conditioner and body builder after shampooing. Hair will instantly look and feel soft and clean with full body and be more manageable.

<u>VitaTress Biotin Shampoo</u>
Conditioning cleanser especially formulated for the problems related to fine, fragile, and thinning hair.
<u>VitaTress Biotin Scalp Creme</u>
A metabolic scalp treatment fortified with Biotin to stimulate hair growth.
<u>Simply Silver Colour Toning Shampoo</u>
Make your grey hair sparkle!
<u>VitaTress Cystine Treatment</u>
A body-building, strengthening treatment.
<u>VitaTress NutriVolumizer</u>
Formulated with featherweight holding ingredients for control, body, and fullness
<u>Phyto Organics Nectaress Nourishing Conditioner</u>
This sheer, lightweight conditioner instantly detangles, restores, and smoothes to leave hair shiny, healthy looking, and full of body

Fanci-Full Rinse: *White Minx*

- Brightens gray and tones brassiness
- Rinse in, Shampoo Out
- No ammonia or peroxide

Wella WELLITE Creme Lightener - box
2 complete applications
Achieves highest degree of lightness

Fast lightening action reduces processing time
Will not run, remains moist during processing
Quick, easy and accurate mixing
Rinses out easily
Ideal for use with Color Charms Extra Mild Toners
Wella Color Charm 20 Volume Clear Developer 32 oz.
SKU: B53028
Clear Developer 20 Volume is a stabilized developer formulated for use with all permanent hair colors when covering gray/white hair

All of these products are good and affordable. The highest priced product on this list in the Cowboy Magic Detangler, but it doesn't take much so it last longer than the cheaper products. With this considered it isn't really that expensive in the long run because it lasts a long time.

Use these products and then determine which ones works best for you. No two beards are alike and what might work well on one does not necessarily mean it will work as well for others.

I highly recommend consulting a beautician. This will ensure you don't lose all your hair and beard the first time you try to bleach it. Ask questions. They will talk with you and pass on some of their secrets such as what to do to get the remaining yellow out of your hair once you have completed the bleaching process. Do not **over bleach** your hair. Follow the directions precisely.

The only product to use a lot of is a high quality conditioner. This is where you need to spend the most of your money. Any inexpensive purple shampoo will do, but a high quality conditioner will aid in the restoration of your hair will leave it soft and manageable. The kids and adults alike will remark about your hair and beard if you do so.

Do not put products in your hair that will leave it stiff and brittle. For example, hairspray is not necessary if you take care and manage your hair and beard. My beautician uses a moderate amount of hairspray before she begins curling my hair. There is no stiffness, she just wets the hair with the hairspray and then uses a curling iron to make a few curls to enhance my look. Works wonders every time.

I have spent a lot of time on the real bearded hair care. This is because when you purchase a quality wig and beard for your designer beard Santa look, you will also get instructions on how to care for them. Read and heed these instructions. If you purchased your wig and beard from a place that makes them or deals only in wigs and hair pieces, you can always ask them for any additional information they would be willing to part with. You see, they not only want to see their products remain in terrific condition; they also want you as a repeat customer.

These custom shops also want you to tell other potential Santas about their shop so that they can get more business. Designer wigs and beards need just as much attention as the real hair and beard. The care of these pieces is a little different, but just as necessary and just as important. Don't get caught up in just throwing your wig and beard aside when you are through. They are very important and should last longer than most of your wardrobe.

Again, my best suggestion is to get professional advice. Go see the folks in person and take your wig and beard with you.

Chapter 5

Fitness

We have all read *The Night Before Christmas*, which talks about and describes Santa. Now what I want to know is what part of "Lively and Quick" doesn't anyone understand? This chapter is designed to get you thinking about some ways that you can get started exercising and eating a balanced diet.

I can hear the groans now. There are lots of Santas out there that think fitness is for the young and those who want to look thin and sexy. Well, that is not so. Fitness is for everyone to remain healthy. I've seen Santas that can't go from their dressing rooms to their chairs without stopping for a break. Children see that and think what's wrong with Santa? Or ask if he really is Santa. Fitness includes being able to walk without being out of breath, doing an activity without gasping for oxygen, and talking with folks for a long period of time without needing to catch your breath. You should be able to get on the floor with a child and then get back up without too much difficulty.

Yes, Santa's belly shakes like a bowl full of jelly when he laughs, but he is **Not Fat** (we don't use the F Word any more) and lazy. He is more, let's say portly or maybe, "Jolly". Sitting in a chair 4 – 6 or 8 hours a day or more can and will wear on you. If you are a Mall Santa, that sitting time could reach 12 to 15 hours a day.

So what do we do to get into better shape? Especially if we aren't eating right or doing some sort of exercise at the gym. How do we keep in shape when we sit in a chair for 12- 15 hours a day, 7 days a week from the beginning of November through the 25th of December? Read on my friends and find out.

Regular Exercise

We all get heavier as we get older, because there's a lot more information in our heads. That's my story and I'm sticking to it.

We need to get the Yin and Yang back together. We need to align our chi. A great start is to learn Tai Chi. We need to keep the body in a harmonious balance. Practice keeping your balance through the following exercises and, you too can gain control over your body.

Every time I hear the dirty word 'exercise', I wash my mouth out with chocolate.

Walking is one of the most popular forms of exercise, and for a good reason. You don't need any special equipment. It is easy on your bones and joints. And, it fits into even the busiest schedules. Incorporate a hobby (Nature Walk) or learn something new (Audio Tapes) into your fitness schedule. This will make it more enjoyable, plus it will exercise your mind as well. Staying healthy is one way to keep being Santa for a long time.

I like long walks, especially when they are taken by people who annoy me.

A friend introduced me to some elastic bands that he uses to stretch his arms and legs. He does these exercises while sitting in a chair when no one is around. It is like having weight training without the weights. You pull against your own body mass and muscles so you can't really over do it.

This chapter will be talking about some ways that you can get started exercising.

Regular physical activity is good for almost everyone. It protects against heart disease and stroke and aide in weight management. If that isn't enough, exercise can also strengthen bones and tone muscles.

It increase energy and relieve stress. The best benefit is improving how you look and feel.

Regular physical activity can protect your heart, lungs, and blood vessels in several ways. It helps keep blood flowing freely through your arteries by reducing "bad" (LDL) blood cholesterol and increasing "good" (HDL) blood cholesterol. Regular exercise can also help lower blood pressure and reduce your risk of heart attack and stroke.

Exercise helps your body burn calories, making it easier to manage your weight. Diet alone does not help your body get stronger and lose weight. Regular exercise can help you burn body fat and build muscle. This can make your body stronger and increase your energy level. Exercise can also lower your risk of thinning bones (osteoporosis) by building bone mass, which makes bones stronger. Your appearance can improve as you build, tighten, and tone your muscles. Your body can become more flexible, and you may be less likely to injure yourself while exercising or doing other physical activity.

Exercise can help you feel better about your body and increase your sense of well-being. Now that you know about all these benefits, you may be wondering how to plan an exercise program and what type of exercise is best for you.

I know I sound like I am harping on this exercise thing, but high blood pressure can lead to other problems. We aren't those young chickens anymore. We also have to worry about diabetes and other ailments that come with age.

Get a checkup first! Before you begin an exercise program, see your healthcare provider for a physical examination. The checkup will help ensure that your exercise program will not lead to other complications.

First off, we need to start looking at exercise in a different way. Seek exercises complementary with our advancing years. Did you know that many experts now say that moderate exercise can benefit you as much as intense exercise. So, kick back and enjoy some moderate exercises.

You also don't need to do it all at once. You can split your workout into short sessions throughout the day. Exercising bit by bit throughout the day is very beneficial. Don't overdo anything!

A friend of mine once told me that he works out with potato sacks as much as four times a week. He started with 2 one-pound sacks. He would hold them in each hand and do curls, circular arm motions, hold them on his shoulders and do squats and bend toe touches. He told me that he had moved up in weight, 10-pound sack, 25-pound sack, and is now using a 50-pound sack every week. Next week he is moving up again. He told me he's now going to place 1 potato in each sack. Yes, I know it is just a funny story, but what I would like to express here is that doing things in moderation and slowly build up. You didn't get out of shape over night and you won't get back in shape over night.

What types of exercise are best? Moderate physical activity, such as brisk walking, is best. Walking is easy and you can do it almost anywhere. The only equipment needed is comfortable clothing and shoes and socks that fit well. Jogging, bicycling, swimming, and dancing are also great ways to get some exercise. Certain team sports, such as soccer or basket ball are good choices.

Find an activity you like. Choose an activity that you enjoy and that is convenient for you. You'll be more likely to stay with your exercise program if you like the activity and it is not too difficult to do. You may want to vary your routine to keep exercise interesting. For instance, you could take a brisk walk 3 times a week and do yoga or swim twice a week.

Walking can add minutes to your life. This enables you at 85 years old to spend an additional 5 months in a nursing home at $7000 per month.

The only reason I would take up walking is so that I could hear heavy breathing again.

I have to walk early in the morning, before my brain figures out what I'm doing.

If you are going to try cross-country skiing, start with a small country.

I know I got a lot of exercise the last few years,...... just getting over the hill is work.

Every time I start thinking too much about how I look, I just find a Happy Hour and by the time I leave, I look pretty damn good.

Senior Fitness

Try this website to learn about some senior fitness programs: www.vqactioncare.com/seniors.php.

For an all around harmony of your body and soul, try T'ai Chi. This website has some good information for you:

www.gaiam.com/product/id/1010390.do?SID=WG092SPRTAPEMACS&gcid=S18376x028&keyword=exercise%20for%20seniors.

Wall push-ups.

A. Place hands flat against the wall.
B. Slowly lower body to the wall. Push body away from wall to return to starting position.

Chair squats.

Begin by sitting in the chair. Lean slightly forward and stand up from the chair. Try not to favor one side or use your hands to help you. Something as simple as standing up and sitting down, while keeping your balance is great exercise. Doesn't take much.

Biceps curl.

Hold a weight in each hand with your arms at your sides. Bending your arms at the elbows, lift the weights to your shoulders and then lower them to your sides. Use anything that has some heft to it as weights. You don't need to go out and buy some expensive weights. I sometimes use cans from the pantry.

Shoulder shrugs.

Hold a weight in each hand with your arms at your side. Shrug your shoulders up toward your ears and then lower them back down.

I usually use heavier weights for this exercise. Try using two bleach or laundry detergent bottles for this exercise. The little bit of weight is definitely enough.

The advantage of exercising every day is so when you die, they'll say, "Well, she looks good doesn't she."

Seated Exercises

Here are some chair exercises you can do.
Many of these exercises were adapted from these sources:

National Institute on Aging, Exercise: A Guide from the National Institute on Aging, 2001, http://www.nia.nih.gov/HealthInformation/Publications/ExerciseGuide/.

Tufts University and Centers for Disease Control and Prevention, Growing Stronger: Strength Training for Older Adults, 2002, http://www.cdc.gov/nccdphp/dnpa/physical/growing_stronger/growing_stronger.pdf.

Prepared at The University of Georgia by:
Mindy Bell, BS, Primary Group Exercise Certified (AAFA, Aerobics and Fitness Association of America), Tiffany Sellers, MS, and Kathryn N. Porter, BS (Personal Trainer and Master Fitness Specialist from the Cooper Fitness Center; NASM Group Exercise Leader, Certified through ASCM and Cooper Fitness Center).

Illustrated by:
Krysia Haag, Computer Graphics Artist, The University of Georgia.

Reviewed by:
Bree Marsh, BS, Certified Personal Trainer (AFAA),
The University of Georgia.

For more information, contact:
Mary Ann Johnson, PhD
Professor of Foods and Nutrition
Faculty of Gerontology
Department of Foods and Nutrition
The University of Georgia
Athens, GA 30602

mjohnson@fcs.uga.edu
706-542-2292

Sunshine Arm Circles

Seated in a chair with good posture, hold a ball of any kind in both hands with arms extended above your head and/or in front of you, keeping elbows slightly bent. I have even just pretended that I had a ball in my hand but using a ball is much better. Visualizing the face of a clock out in front of you, begin by holding arms up overhead at 12 o'clock. Circle the ball around to go all the way around the clock in a controlled, fluid motion. When you've reached 12 o'clock again, reverse directions and circle the opposite way. Keep alternating circle directions for several repetitions. Rest. Do another set of repetitions.

Modification: A ball is not required for this exercise. Imagine that you are holding a ball while performing the motion. If it is difficult to bring your arms overhead, extend them out in front of you and move arms as if drawing a circle on the wall with or without the ball.

Tummy Twists

Seated in a chair with good posture, hold both hands close to the body, with elbows bent and pulled in close to the ribcage. Slowly rotate your torso to the right as far as you comfortably can, being sure to keep the rest of your body still and stable. Rotate back to the center and repeat in the opposite direction. Do this several times, with two twists counting as a full set. Rest. Do another sets (two twists each).

Modification: Try using a ball for this exercise or hold a small object such as a can of soup or water bottle to add resistance.

Neck Stretch

Seated in a chair with good posture, slowly tilt your head toward your right shoulder. Hold the head in this position, and extend your left arm out to the side and slightly downward so that your hand is at waist level. Release and repeat on the left side. Do this several times for each side.

Modification: For a deeper stretch, gently pull the extended arm behind your back.

Front Arm Raises

In a seated position with good posture, hold both hands with palms facing each other like you are praying. Extend the arms out in front of your body, keeping your elbows slightly bent. Starting at the knees, slowly raise your arms up to shoulder level (no higher), then lower them back to the starting position, taking about two to three seconds to lift and lower. Repeat several times. Rest. Do another series of sets.

Modification: A ball is not required for this exercise. Imagine you are holding a ball as you perform the motion, or hold a small object, such as a can of soup or water bottle for added resistance.

Knee Extensions

Sitting toward the edge of a chair with good posture and bent knees, hold on to the sides of the chair with your hands. Extend the right knee out so that the toes come up toward the ceiling, being sure to keep the knee slightly bent without locking it through the entire movement. Lower the leg back to a bent position and repeat this movement numerous times, using about 2 seconds each to lift and lower the leg. Switch to the opposite leg and perform several more repetitions. Rest briefly. Do another set of repetitions for each leg.

Modification: If you are more advanced, sitting in the same position as above, extend one leg out in front of you with toes pointed to the ceiling. Lift and lower the entire leg only as high as you comfortably can, keeping the knee slightly bent. The longer lever adds difficulty to the exercise.

Chest and Upper Back Stretch

In a seated position with good posture and shoulders back and down away from the ears, extend your arms out in front of you at shoulder height. Interlace the fingers or grasp one hand with the other, and press out as you round the upper back and shoulders forward, feeling the upper back fan out. Hold for 10 seconds and release. For the shoulders, pull extended arms back behind you and interlace the fingers or grasp one hand with the other, keeping your hands down toward the buttocks. Feel the chest and shoulders open up as you pull your shoulders back. Hold for 10 seconds and release. Repeat the upper back and chest stretches.

Chair Stands

In a seated position with good posture and feet flat on the floor, cross your arms over your chest or hold a ball with both hands at chest level. Keeping your weight on your heels, stand up, using your hands as little as possible or not at all. As you bend slightly forward to stand up, keep your back and shoulders straight. Take at least three seconds to sit back down. Repeat numerous times or as many as you can comfortably do with good form. Rest. Do more repetitions.

Modification: If you are more advanced, try doing squats. Beginning in a standing position with back facing the seat of a chair, slowly bend the knees to lower down toward the seat of the chair. Stick out the buttocks so that your knees do not extend beyond your toes. Just before your buttocks get to the seat of the chair, stand back up to the starting position in a fluid motion, squeezing your buttocks and putting all the weight in your heels as you push back up.

Overhead Arm Extensions

Seated with good posture in a chair, hold your arms straight out and raise them up over your head, without locking the elbows. Keeping the elbows pulled in toward the head, slowly bend the elbows to lower your hands down along the back of the neck, using about two seconds to go down, then two seconds to raise them up over your head. Repeat several times. Rest. Do another set of repetitions.

Modification: Try seated triceps extensions. Bending slightly forward with elbows tucked into your sides, slowly extend the elbows so that your forearms go back behind you, keeping the elbows pulled up and in for the entire movement. Return to the starting position and repeat. Hold soup cans or small weights for added resistance.

Elbow to Knee

Seated toward the edge of a chair with good posture and knees bent, start with your right arm extended up overhead. Slowly lift the left knee up as you lower your right elbow down toward your left knee, taking about two seconds to lower down. Try not to bend over at the waist. Release and go back to the starting position. Repeat. Switch sides and do several more repetitions, pulling one elbow to the opposite knee. Rest. Do another more repetitions on each side.

Modification: Try this (with a chair nearby for balance) exercise in a standing position for an increased range of motion.

Heel Raises

Seated toward the edge of a chair with good posture and knees bent, place feet flat on the floor. Raise heels up off the floor, coming up onto the balls of the feet. Hold for one second, then release. Do multiple sets of repetitions each, resting briefly between sets.

Modification: If you are more advanced, stand behind a chair and hold on lightly for balance. Come up to the balls of your feet to lift the heels up off the floor. Release and repeat as described above.

Overhead Reach with Side Bends

Seated in a chair with good posture, reach your arms up overhead. Hold for 10 seconds. Allow your right arm to relax down by your side (can rest hand on chair seat) while your left arm stays up overhead. Slowly lean to the right and reach your left arm over your head to the right. Hold for several seconds. Come back up to the center position, pulling both arms overhead again. Repeat by bending to the opposite side, relaxing the left arm to the side this time. Do another set.

Pliés

Holding the back of a chair, stand with legs a little wider than shoulder width apart, and toes pointed outward slightly toward the corners of the room. Bend your knees to lower yourself straight down, using several seconds to do this. Make sure that your legs are wide enough apart that your knees do not protrude beyond the toes when you go down. Return to the starting position by pushing through your heels as you come back up. Perform the pliés multiple. Rest. Do as many as you can comfortably do while maintaining good form.

Modification: For an added challenge, do not hold onto a chair. Try holding a ball, water bottle or can from the pantry in your hands instead. Or, change the count of the exercise by lowering down and holding for several seconds or doing short, pulsing pliés.

Rear Leg Extensions

Begin by standing behind a chair with the right leg slightly in front of the left, holding on to the back of the chair for balance. Keeping your back straight and leaning slightly forward, lift the left foot a few inches off the floor or as high as you comfortably can, squeezing the buttocks as you do this. Do not arch your back. Lower the leg back down and repeat the movement several times. Switch sides to work the other leg. Rest briefly. Do multiple repetitions for each leg.

Modification: For an extra challenge, change the count of the movement. Lift the leg and hold for 5 seconds, or do short, quick pulse lifts for 5 seconds.

Side Leg Lifts

Begin by holding onto the back of a chair as needed, standing with feet slightly apart. Take 2 to 3 seconds to lift your right leg 6 to 12 inches out to the side, keeping the knee and toes pointed forward. Hold the position for one second. Take two to three seconds to lower your leg back to the starting position. Perform several lifts. Switch to the opposite leg. Do more repetitions for each leg.

Modification: For a less advanced version, tap the toe out to the side and pull back in, rather than lifting and lowering the leg. For a more advanced version, change the count of the movement by lifting the leg and holding for 5 seconds or lifting and pulsing the leg and releasing back down.

Sit and Reach

Seated toward the edge of a chair, extend your legs out in front of you, keeping the knees slightly bent. With heels on the floor and toes pointed up toward the ceiling, extend your arms out in front of you and try to reach down to touch your toes. Bend at the waist to do this and do not bounce. Hold the stretch for about 10 seconds. Come back up to the starting position. Repeat the stretch several times.

Modification: Depending on your flexibility, you may only be able to go to your knees or shins. If you are very flexible, you may be able to reach your fingers out past your toes.

There Are Three Parts to an Exercise Program.

One is aerobic. This is any activity that raises your heart rate, and no, just looking at a pretty lady will not do. You must do some physical activity that is rhythmic in nature and uses large muscles. Aerobic activity, to be effective, must be conducted at least 20 minutes a day. If you want to lose weight, you will need to bump that up to 45 minutes to an hour a day.

Another is strength building. This works certain muscles or groups of muscles. This builds muscle mass so that you can retain more oxygen in your system. It also increases your strength. Strength building should be conducted 5-10 minutes a day.

The final one is stretching. This loosens muscles and joints while lengthening your muscles. This too should last 5-10 minutes a day. Do these at the beginning and at the end of each exercise period. Yes, you need to stretch to warm down after exercising.

All this will take less than 40 minutes a day. Now think about it. What is 40 minutes in your day?

Where to exercise appears to be a problem for some folks. Actually it is an excuse. You don't' need to hit the gym or have a gym built into your home. Here are some easy examples of where to exercise.

First there is your own home. It is probably one of the best places you could find. You don't have to travel to exercise. You can wear whatever you want, and I even like to watch television while I work out.

Believe it or not, you can exercise at work. You can either stop at a gym on your way to or coming from work. There are some Santa exercises you can do in your Santa Chair.

You can also do this on the road. Walking while on vacation or using the facilities at a hotel you are staying at is good for you. You don't have to spend hours, just a few minutes at a time.

Below are a few exercises that we (you and I) should practice to help get you on your way. Now we're not trying to make Santa look like Mr. Universe, just trying to get Santa to be more watchful of his own health. We do need Santa around for many more years to come.

Aerobic Exercises

These should be done for at least 20 minutes at a stretch.

Running the Vacuum Cleaner
Mowing the Lawn
Raking Leaves
Power Walking
Stair Climbing
Pushing your grandkids stroller around the block or mall.
March in Place *(Seated and Standing)*

Strength Building Exercises

These should be accomplished in at least 10 minute routines.

Toe Raises
Bicep Curls
Mini Squats

Stretching Exercises

These need to be accomplished to warm up the muscle groups you tend to work so as not to pull a muscle or injure yourself as you exercise.

Shoulder Stretch
Seated Hip Opener
Shoulder Rotations
Backward Bend

Head Tilt
Ankle Circles

Carbohydrate or "carb" counting is a tool many people use to make healthy food choices. Healthy eating, along with exercising regularly can help you achieve your goals.

This information came from the Veterans Administration.

Healthy Eating Goals

The basics for healthy eating are the same for people everywhere.

- Eat a wide variety of foods to get the energy, vitamins, and minerals you need.
- Eat more whole grains, vegetables, fruits, and fat-free and low-fat dairy products.
- Limit processed foods.
- Eat less cholesterol, saturated fat, and trans fat.

If you need to change your eating habits, it will take time. Start by trying to make one or two changes a week. Write down on a piece of paper the changes you would like to make this week. Then add new ideas to your list each week.

Here are a few foods and what they do for your health.

Apples	Protects your heart	prevents constipation	Blocks diarrhea	Improves lung capacity	Cushions joints
Apricots	Combats cancer	Controls blood pressure	Saves your eyesight	Shields against Alzheimer's	Slows aging process
Artichokes	Aids digestion	Lowers cholesterol	Protects your heart	Stabilizes blood sugar	Guards against liver disease
Avocados	Battles diabetes	Lowers cholesterol	Helps stops strokes	Controls blood pressure	Smoothes skin
Bananas	Protects your heart	Quiets a cough	Strengthens bones	Controls blood pressure	Blocks diarrhea
Beans	Prevents constipation	Helps hemorrhoids	Lowers cholesterol	Combats cancer	Stabilizes blood sugar
Beets	Controls blood pressure	Combats cancer	Strengthens bones	Protects your heart	Aids weight loss
Blueberries	Combats cancer	Protects your heart	Stabilizes blood sugar	Boosts memory	Prevents constipation
Broccoli	Strengthens bones	Saves eyesight	Combats cancer	Protects your heart	Controls blood pressure
Cabbage	Combats cancer	Prevents constipation	Promotes weight loss	Protects your heart	Helps hemorrhoids
Cantaloupe	Saves eyesight	Controls blood pressure	Lowers cholesterol	Combats cancer	Supports immune system
Carrots	Saves eyesight	Protects your heart	Prevents constipation	Combats cancer	Promotes weight loss
Cauliflower	Protects against Prostate Cancer	Combats Breast Cancer	Strengthens bones	Banishes bruises	Guards against heart disease

Cherries	**Protects your heart**	**Combats Cancer**	**Ends insomnia**	**Slows aging process**	**Shields against Alzheimer's**
Chestnuts	**Promotes weight loss**	**Protects your heart**	**Lowers cholesterol**	**Combats Cancer**	**Controls blood pressure**
Chili peppers	**Aids digestion**	**Soothes sore throat**	**Clears sinuses**	**Combats Cancer**	**Boosts immune system**
Figs	**Promotes weight loss**	**Helps stops strokes**	**Lowers cholesterol**	**Combats Cancer**	**Controls blood pressure**
Fish	**Protects your heart**	**Boosts memory**	**Protects your heart**	**Combats Cancer**	**Supports immune system**
Flax	**Aids digestion**	**Battles diabetes**	**Protects your heart**	**Improves mental health**	**Boosts immune system**
Garlic	**Lowers cholesterol**	**Controls blood pressure**	**Combats cancer**	**kills bacteria**	**Fights fungus**
Grapefruit	**Protects against heart attacks**	**Promotes Weight loss**	**Helps stops strokes**	**Combats Prostate Cancer**	**Lowers cholesterol**
Grapes	**saves eyesight**	**Conquers kidney stones**	**Combats cancer**	**Enhances blood flow**	**Protects your heart**
Green tea	**Combats cancer**	**Protects your heart**	**Helps stops strokes**	**Promotes Weight loss**	**Kills bacteria**
Honey	**Heals wounds**	**Aids digestion**	**Guards against ulcers**	**Increases energy**	**Fights allergies**
Lemons	**Combats cancer**	**Protects your heart**	**Controls blood pressure**	**Smoothes skin**	**Stops scurvy**

Limes	Combats cancer	Protects your heart	Controls blood pressure	Smoothes skin	Stops scurvy
Mangoes	Combats cancer	Boosts memory	Regulates thyroid	aids digestion	Shields against Alzheimer's
Mushrooms	Controls blood pressure	Lowers cholesterol	Kills bacteria	Combats cancer	Strengthens bones
Oats	Lowers cholesterol	Combats cancer	Battles diabetes	prevents constipation	Smoothes skin
Olive oil	Protects your heart	Promotes Weight loss	Combats cancer	Battles diabetes	Smoothes skin
Onions	Reduce risk of heart attack	Combats cancer	Kills bacteria	Lowers cholesterol	Fights fungus
Oranges	Supports immune systems	Combats cancer	Protects your heart	Straightens respiration	
Peaches	prevents constipation	Combats cancer	Helps stops strokes	aids digestion	Helps hemorrhoids
Peanuts	Protects against heart disease	Promotes Weight loss	Combats Prostate Cancer	Lowers cholesterol	Aggravates Diverticulitis
Pineapple	Strengthens bones	Relieves colds	Aids digestion	Dissolves warts	Blocks diarrhea
Prunes	Slows aging process	prevents constipation	boosts memory	Lowers cholesterol	Protects against heart disease
Rice	Protects your heart	Battles diabetes	Conquers kidney stones	Combats cancer	Helps stops strokes
Strawberries	Combats cancer	Protects your heart	boosts memory	Calms stress	
Sweet potatoes	Saves your eyesight	Lifts mood	Combats cancer	Strengthens bones	

Tomatoes	Protects prostate	Combats cancer	Lowers cholesterol	Protects your heart	
Walnuts	Lowers cholesterol	Combats cancer	boosts memory	Lifts mood	Protects against heart disease
Water	Promotes Weight loss	Combats cancer	Conquers kidney stones	Smoothes skin	
Watermelon	Protects prostate	Promotes Weight loss	Lowers cholesterol	Helps stops strokes	Controls blood pressure
Wheat germ	Combats Colon Cancer	prevents constipation	Lowers cholesterol	Helps stops strokes	improves digestion
Wheat bran	Combats Colon Cancer	prevents constipation	Lowers cholesterol	Helps stops strokes	improves digestion
Yogurt	Guards against ulcers	Strengthens bones	Lowers cholesterol	Supports immune systems	Aids digestion

Carb Counting

Carbohydrate is the nutrient in foods that raises blood glucose the most and the quickest after you eat. The other important nutrients – protein and fat – have much less effect on your blood glucose.

Carbohydrate counting can help you:

- Mange your blood glucose.
- Be flexible in your choice of foods.
- Eat more foods that you enjoy.
- Have more freedom in choosing your meal times.

To Carb count, you need to know which foods contain carbohydrate and then:

- Find the carb content of your favorite foods.
- Figure how much carbohydrate you need each day.
- Divide your carb allotment into meals and snacks.

Foods with carbohydrate are:

- Starches – bread, cereal, crackers, rice, and pasta.
- Starchy vegetables – potatoes, corn, peas, beans.
- Non-starchy vegetables – green beans, broccoli, lettuce.
- Fruit and fruit juice.
- Milk and yogurt (hard cheese contains very little carbohydrate).
- Sugary foods – candy, regular soda pop, jelly.
- Sweets – cakes, cookies, pies, ice cream.

The only food groups that don't contain carbs are:

- Meats and meat substitutes, such as eggs and cheese.
- Fats and oils.

Sweets are okay to include in your meal plan once in a while. But, be sure to read the nutrition label before you eat. Sweets often contain a lot of carbohydrate, calories, and fat.

Experts recommend that about half of the calories you eat come from carbohydrate. The number of calories you need each day depends on your height, weight, age, and activity level. You and your healthcare provider should decide how many calories you need each day.

FOOD	**Amount**	**Food Group**	**Grams of Carb**
BREAKFAST			
Bran flakes	1 ½ cup	Starch	30
Milk, fat-free	1cup	Milk	12
Banana	Small (4 oz)	Fruit	15
Meal Total			**57**
LUNCH			
Sandwich of:			
Roast beef, lean sliced	2 oz	Meat	0
Cheese, sliced (part skim)	1 oz	Meat	0
Whole wheat bread	2 slices	Starch	30
Mayonnaise, reduced fat	1 tbsp	Fat	0
Baby carrots and grape tomatoes	½ cup	Vegetable	5
With low fat dressing as dip	2 tbsp	Fat	0
Apple, large (8 oz)	1	Fruit	30
Meal Total			**65**
DINNER			
Winter Squash	1 cup	Starch	15
Whole wheat dinner roll with	1 small	Starch	15
Margarine, regular tub	2 tbsp	Fat	0

Broccoli, Steamed with lemon	½ cup	Vegetable	5
Salad greens, cucumber,	1 cup	Vegetable	5
Red pepper, and Italian dressing	1 tbsp	Fat	0
Broiled flounder with lemon	3 oz	Meat	0
Meal Total			**40**
EVENING SNACK			
Yogurt, plain, fat-free	2/3 cup (6 oz)	Milk	12
Meal Total			**12**
TOTAL			**174**

Portion Size Is Important

The best way to know your portion size is to use measuring cups or scales. Correct portions are important for healthy eating. If you are dining out, or unable to use measuring cups or scales, you can estimate serving sizes by using your hand.

- Your fist equals about 1 cup.
- Your palm equals about 3 ounces.
- Your thumb equals about 2 table spoons or 1 ounce.
- Your thumb tip equals about 1 teaspoon.
- A handful equals about 2 ounces (1/4 cup) of a snack food.

It is recommended that you get yourself an exchange list. An exchange list describes foods with similar carbohydrates and similar food groups. You can look this up on the internet for assistance. It is recommended you talk with your healthcare provided about this information.

The reason for this chapter is to help keep Santa healthy. The less exercise we get, the worse we eat, the more opportunity we have to get high blood pressure, diabetes, and many other complications that are no fun to have. We even are at a higher risk of a stroke or heart attack because of our size and age. Be careful and live longer.

Chapter 6

The Visit

You may be a mall Santa, just make visits to house parties or maybe you concentrate on charity events, whatever you do, that first impression you make with your audience will set the tone for your entire appearance. The rule of thumb is that what you do in the first **FIVE** seconds of your visit will dictate how you are perceived throughout your visit. So, make your entrance a fabulous one.

Now...... How do you make that entrance memorable? What you do and what happens in the first five seconds can make or break you. So, make if work for you. Figure out a small performance you can do to make life better for those watching. It doesn't have to be elaborate or extraordinary; it just has to be positively memorable.

Let's imagine you are standing on your client's front porch: You arrived on time and now hear the laughter of the guests. Sounds like a very happy party. A big plastic bag of gifts was left by the steps as you were told and now you have them stuffed them in your sack. When you telephoned this client a few minutes ago, they told you to come right in. OK, take a deep breath and ring the door chimes and its "Show Time."

Your Entrance

Hello everyone, it's so good to be here", is one type of comment you should make. Walk in extending your hand, primarily to adults, and to anyone who will shake it. Little children will be surprised so there may be some screams of excitement seeing Santa.

Chuckle a lot using that Santa Chuckle you learned back in the voice section, smile a lot, and be happy with a twinkle in your eye. While doing so look about the room, to see who is there. Do you see any elderly folks, what about young parents and of course notice all the children and where they are and what they are doing!

Where is Santa's chair? Locate where it is set up. Identify any obstacles that may hinder your progress towards that chair. Be attentive to what guests are wearing: you may compliment a Christmas vest, tie or Santa hat. Be attentive to prominent features of the guests. You may compliment Grandpa's white hair, "Just like Santa's" then saying in a hushed voice so everyone can hear. "Just don't make me take my hat off because I'm losing a bit of it." Here's a place for a controlled, "Ho! Ho! Ho"!

The host and guests are going to form an opinion of you in the first five seconds so you want to make a grand entrance. You're playing up to your audience as you enter and circulating around the room. Treat everyone with respect and gentle teasing to bring out a smile.

Now here is something to ponder. Who is your customer? You just can't say the kids because are they paying you? Who do you have to please? If you don't please the kids, will you be asked back? Know that the person who hired you is your customer and you need to please them. Know and understand what they expect from you and live up to and beyond those expectations.

Helpful Hints for a Positive Visit

Here are a few helpful hints to ensure you please your customer.

1. Find out ahead of time what to expect and what your customer's key objectives you are. Calling the client no less than seven days before the event serves several purposes. First it confirms the show time and second it gives you the opportunity to get any location descriptions for assistance in finding the address and parking space. You will also get last minute instructions during this time so be prepared to write things down.

2. Make sure you know if you are to locate a bag of toys to fill your Santa bag outside the building or are you supposed to get them inside?

3. What special requests does your customer have? Is there someone special you need to recognize? Do they have a Christmas elf that needs to appear? Is there a special song that needs to be sung?

4. Find out if you will be having helpers. Get a working contact cell phone number and a backup if possible. Always stay in contact with your client, calling them when you arrive at the address and see if there are any last minute changes. They may need you to enter by another door or wait a little for a straggler to arrive.

5. Think of any value added things you might be able to do to guarantee that return business. Always think of the future.

6. Have a little skit in character or some activity such as magic if it appears it will take some time to weave your way through the crowd.

7. Gather a helper or two along the way. - It is always a good idea to use at least one pre-teen or older to assist in reading the names on

the gifts. You really don't want Santa to pronounce a name wrong. Have something special to give them when you are through. You can use them to assist in diverting attention if the situation needs it. They can help with the rowdy kids, the overly helpful adults and the spoiled brat so you don't need to deal with them directly.

8. Sell yourself at all times. The more you can convince the children you are the direct descendent of Santa, the better your chances of getting another customer or a return visit booked.

Here are a few things you might do. Remember to practice and do them well.

9. Try reading a story. Pick a good one and be very expressive. Lead the group in a sing-a-long. Do you know any magic you can mystify them. What about balloon animals? That is fairly easy to learn.

Adding value to your visit with these additional actions will bring referrals and repeat business. I have found that some folks like to tip when they are pleased, even when the times are tough.

The object of this section is to get you started and let you know what you might expect. This will help you calm your nerves for the first few times of the season. Also included are some handy hints you might want to hand out ahead of time to make your visit smoother.

Now here is a question to ponder. What does everyone see when they look at you? Now don't answer this as to what you want them to see or what you see. Ask around to find out what others think. Don't influence them with your phrasing. Ask directly what folks see and think. Have them be very critical.

Do the same thing with your little skit or with your reading. Perform for some folks and see what they think? Ask them what was good and what was bad. Work to improve the bad parts and keep the goods parts the same. Practice, practice and practice some more. This will allow you to be more comfortable with what you are doing and to perfect the routine.

Difficult Situations

Ok, let's assume that you have made it to the party and things are going along terrifically. You are prepared and your portrayal of Santa is working out smoothly. Now you are faced with some very difficult situations. Work these situations out before you are confronted with them. Doing so will prevent you from needing to think on your feet and possibly getting the situation wrong or making it worse.

Some of the difficult situations you may encounter are; the scared child, the non-believers, the brat, and the pushy parent.

Think about all of these possible situations and think through what you may do. The scared child is the easiest to deal with. You need to tell the parent to not push the child to you. Have them hold the child and talk to the child. Find something you can talk to the child about. Keep your voice low and calm. Always have a smile on your face and be prepared to abandon all hope of having the child sit on your lap. Sometimes if you are lucky, you can coax the child to stand next to you but just be thankful if you can talk peacefully and quietly to the child.

Always reassure the child that receiving a gift from Santa is OK. Never force yourself on the child and never grab for the child. If the child does not want the present you have for them, see if the parent will take the gift and let the child sit down somewhere and open it. I have even given up my seat to let the child sit down. Then kneeling next to the chair, we get a good picture.

At one party, I had a scared child that wouldn't come near me. About an hour into the party, the child was sitting on my lap. What happened is that I saw the child was inching closer to me and watching what I was doing with the other children. Whenever there were no children on my lap or talking to me, I would smile at the child and say something to them. Most of time, I would speak just loud enough for the child to barely hear. That brought him in a little closer each time.

Not only was mom happy, but grandma was ecstatic to have a picture of her grandson with Santa. I even got the young boy to get his mom and grandma to come and have a family picture with me. Now that was really enjoyable, and the massive tip they gave me was appreciated too.

If the parent really wants the pictures and is trying to tell you a crying picture is better than none, than have the parent hold the child facing the camera and not looking at you. The parent can then sit on your lap and the child will be on their lap. This serves several purposes. First, the child is reassured while sitting on mom or dad's lap and second, if the child is screaming and wiggling around trying to get free, the parent has to deal with it and not you. You don't have to worry about holding a child against his will and you also don't have to worry about harming the child.

Pictures turn out much better if the parent is holding the child and sitting on your lap. If the parent stands next to you this reinforces the fear in the child. Make sure the parent that is holding the child is sitting on your lap. Don't let them try to sneak the child on your lap and run away. I prefer to let a crying child down and run to their parent than to try and hold on to the screaming kid.

How do you handle children with challenges? If they have a physical handicap, than you will have to get to them in their special chair unless the parents or the child's assistant picks them up and places them on your lap. That is the easy part. What about a mental handicap? Find something that makes the child smile and work with that. Keep the child happy for some terrific pictures. The parents will really appreciate that. Some special needs children need to be reassured that they are good. Do this a hundred times; even a thousand times in the short period you have them. Take some classes on autism and children with attention deficit. You will be surprised how easy it is to relate to these children and give them as much pleasure out of seeing you as any child will have.

Be prepared to give and receive lots of hugs. Physical contact is usually what a child needs and wants. This reassures them that they are loved and folks around them appreciate them. Have you seen the huggers at the end of events during the Special Olympics? That is to let them know that everyone is a winner when they try.

If a child tries to speak, let them. Don't try to put words into their mouth. Let them try to explain. Try to repeat what they are saying to show them that you understand. This holds true for the deaf. You don't need to know sign language while talking with a child who is deaf. Try to mimic a sign they are doing. They will love to correct you if you do it wrong and will be really happy to see that you understand their desires.

Again, take some classes. Learn to sign and learn all about other special needs children. There are some interesting facts out there that will amaze you once you learn about them. Volunteer to work at a special needs training center. That will surely open your eyes and give you a new understanding. It will also give you a new outlook on life.

How about those non-believers! What do you do with those that want to spoil the fun for all with their non-believing attitude? I sometimes bring out my Christmas bells. I have several miniature stockings that I carry with me. Half are filled with bells that ring and half are filled with bells that don't ring. I first ask the non-believer to pick a stocking. Of course their bell does not ring. Then I ask several others to select a stocking. And of course their bell rings. I will even let the non-believer select another stocking.

Here is a little story I like to relate to them so they better understand the purpose of Santa. It's called "I Believe in Santa". I wish I knew the author so I can give appropriate credit.

I Believe in Santa Claus

I remember my first Christmas adventure with Grandma. I was just a kid. I remember tearing across town on my bike to visit her. On the way, my big sister dropped the bomb: "There is no Santa Claus," she jeered. "Even dummies know that!"

My Grandma was not the gushy kind, never had been. I fled to her that day because I knew she would be straight with me. I knew Grandma always told the truth, and I knew that the truth always went down a whole lot easier when swallowed with one of her "world-famous" cinnamon buns. I knew they were world-famous, because Grandma said so. It had to be true.

Grandma was home, and the buns were still warm. Between bites, I told her everything. She was ready for me. "No Santa Claus?" she snorted .... "Ridiculous! Don't believe it! That rumor has been going around for years, and it makes me mad, plain mad!! Now, put on your coat, and let's go." "Go? Go where, Grandma?" I asked. I hadn't even finished my second world-famous cinnamon bun.

"Where" turned out to be People's General Store, the one store in town that had a little bit of just about everything. As we walked through its doors, Grandma handed me ten dollars. That was a bundle in those days. "Take this money," she said, "and buy something for someone who needs it. I'll wait for you in the car." Then she turned and walked out of People's.

I was only eight years old. I'd often gone shopping with my mother, but never had I shopped for anything all by myself. The store seemed big and crowded, full of people scrambling to finish their Christmas shopping. For a few moments I just stood there, confused, clutching that ten-dollar bill, wondering what to buy, and who on earth to buy it for. I thought of everybody I knew: my family, my friends, my neighbors, the kids at school, and the people who went to my church.

I was just about thought out, when I suddenly thought of Chris Geckker. He was a kid with bad breath and messy hair, and he sat right behind me in Mrs. Bradshaw's 2nd grade class. Chris Geckker didn't have a coat. I knew that because he never went out to play at recess during the winter. His mother always wrote a note telling the teacher that he had a cough, but all us kids knew that Chris Geckker didn't have a cough; he just didn't have a good coat. I fingered the ten-dollar bill with growing excitement. I would buy Chris Geckker a coat! I settled on a red corduroy one that had a hood to it. It looked real warm, and he would like that.

"Is this a Christmas present for someone?" the lady behind the counter asked kindly, as I laid my ten dollars down."Yes, ma'am," I replied shyly. "It's for Chris."

The nice lady smiled at me, as I told her about how Chris really needed a good winter coat. I didn't get any change, but she put the coat in a bag, smiled again, and wished me a Merry Christmas.

That evening, Grandma helped me wrap the coat (a little tag fell out of the coat, and Grandma tucked it in her Bible). We use the best Christmas paper and ribbons in the house and wrote, "To Chris, From Santa Claus" on it. Grandma said that Santa always insisted on secrecy. Then she drove me over to Chris Geckker's house, explaining as we went that I was now and forever officially, one of Santa's helpers.

Grandma parked down the street from Chris's house, and she and I crept noiselessly and hid in the bushes by his front walk. Then Grandma gave me a nudge. "All right, Santa Claus," she whispered, "get going." I took a deep breath, dashed for his front door, threw the present down on his step, pounded his door and flew back to the safety of the bushes and Grandma.

Together we waited breathlessly in the darkness for the front door to open. Finally it did, and there stood Chris.

Fifty years haven't dimmed the thrill of those moments spent shivering, beside my Grandma, in Chris Geckker's bushes. That night, I realized that those awful rumors about Santa Claus were just what Grandma said they were: ridiculous. Santa was alive and well, and we were on his team. I still have the Bible, with the coat tag tucked inside: $19.95.

P.S. Always remember: If you quit believing in Santa Claus, you get underwear for Christmas!!

Another Trick

Another trick I use is some magic. I perform some simple magic trick letting everyone know that the believers will make things work and the non-believers cannot make the trick work. This is wonderful, especially when I perform the lighting of Rudolph's nose. Once you purchase a D'lite finger tip, you will receive instructions on how to perform several tricks.

If all of this does not work, I try to get the non-believer close and ask them to not disrupt the fun for those who believe. Then I continue to have fun with all the other children making sure I exclude the non-believer until about half way through. Then I ask if they would like to participate and that makes them change their mind. Most of the time, you can get an adult to take the child aside and talk to them about spoiling the fun for the rest of the children.

Then you have the BRAT! Just look at the parents to see why they are that way. With the Brat, you let the crowd help you. If the Brat is pushy and demanding, you can always ask the crowd, who should be next and they usually will not choose the brat. I usually have something to say like it is time to share Santa with everyone else. Everyone gets their turn and their present. If you try your hardest to be patient and stay on my nice list, I will look for something special just for you.

If the brat brings his toy back and asks for another, I usually tell them they need to talk to their parents about that because that is what their parents told me you wanted. If you want something else, you will need to write me a letter so that my elves can assist in building, wrapping and putting in my sleigh for Christmas. The brat is the hardest to ignore.

If the brat is always asking questions, make sure you don't just answer the brat. Make sure you get everyone's attention and let them know what the brat is asking. Then see if someone else can answer it for you. This will get the focus off of the brat and on to other children. The more the attention is on other children, the less attention the brat has in their favor. Usually the brat just craves attention.

Along with the brat comes the pushy parent. I just love these types. These are the ones that want everything for themselves or their child right now. They want to be first. I usually address the parents and ask if they have been naughty or nice. Ask them what they did today to deserve to be on the nice list. This puts them on the spot. Pushy parents don't want to be in the spot light so when you do that to them, they usually back off. If you keep putting them in the spot light, soon they get the message and back off.

It is like the mom of a talented child. They want to push the child to perform in front of everyone. Ask the parent to perform or ask them to wait their turn and proper time. I usually try to get the pushy parent aside and let them know that their pushy style is making it very uncomfortable for others at the party. If they could just wait their turn, things would be much better. Most pushy parents don't realize they are pushy and feel that they deserve everything they are trying to get. They feel they should be first or their child should be first. They think that the world needs to revolve around them or their child. They have little to no consideration for others and could care less about those around them. These are the dangerous ones. These are usually the ones that cause you the most grief.

Pushy parents only think of themselves and no one else. This makes them dangerous and bears considerable watching. There are times when I either ignore them or ask someone in charge to take care of the situation if possible. Do not upset the pushy parent. That is a sure fire way of getting a lawsuit filed against you. Pushy parents usually think they are always right and everyone around with a different opinion is always wrong. Be careful around these types of folks and avoid confrontations when possible.

Know Your Audience

Now for the easier side of the visit. Your audience! You must understand group dynamics. If you ever get an opportunity to take a class on group dynamics or group psychology, I highly recommend you do so. This will lend you some insight into dealing with different groups.

Family gatherings are fun. Here you will find several generations together and will need to take a moment to get with each generation. Make sure you get a picture with each and as many as possible. There is a different culture when dealing with families. Some have very specific traditions and others are just unique. In the south, there are two different types of family gatherings. One is a very religious gathering where old acquaintances with relatives are renewed and the other is a typical "Redneck" gathering where everyone sees each other often so this is just another excuse to get together and party.

The stories you hear are different and the specific functions you perform are also different. Make sure you know before you arrive what is expected of you. Also you will need to find out who is giving the party. If it is the matriarch, you will have one set of rules to follow, if it is the parents of small children, you will have another set of rules and priorities to follow. Be sure to find out who the family leader is and give them some of your attention.

Mixed groups such as birthday parties are interesting. You never know what background the families are from unless you can get a heads up early. You may come across someone who is Jewish and say they don't believe in Christmas. Talk to them about Hanukah. Know what Kwanza is and discuss Mormon beliefs, Islam, Buddhism, and any others you can learn about. Yes, you must be prepared to help every child enjoy the party.

Concentrate on the reason for the party and don't over accentuate the Christmas aspect of your visit. Here is a terrific time to say again, "SANTA IS NOT RELIGIOUS!" the season of Christmas is religious, but nowhere in our history is Santa religious. This will probably upset those in the Bible belt area and others that like to think they are good Christians, but think about it. Look at what modern day Santa has become and our evolution. St. Nicholas is the only worthy religious icon in our past and he is not the only part of our past. Reread the history section of this book if you have any doubt.

You will also notice that each year, more and more folks are celebrating Christmas and they are not Christians. I once did a party for a Jewish lady who had special gifts for her Christian friends and another special set of gifts for her Jewish relatives and family. That was fun.

Moving on to other organizations; schools, scouts and every other organization that throws a party have an underlying theme of the organization. The same goes for corporate parties. Know what the background is for each party. Do your research. Find out about that organization and see if you can find something you can relate Santa to within the organization. Talk to that aspect. The more you can be a part of the organization; the more you will be accepted.

Here's an example for you to ponder. You are going to perform at a Christmas party for a local Girl Scout Troop. You find out that they just finished being honored with some badges they earned and you want them to feel very proud. See if there is something special that they do at their meetings that you can lead or participate with. See if you can help them start on the path to earning another badge.

I like to have reindeer antlers and blinking red noses with me. In these types of groups, I will pass out a few to some of the children and then have them sing Rudolph the Red Nosed Reindeer. This gets them involved and active. Plus they have something else to take home with them. That would be memorable for both the children and the parents. The plus side of this is that those parents with cameras and video camcorders will have a record of this visit and may call you for next year or recommend you to someone else they know.

Here is a tough question. Most parties have mixed age groups. There are younger and older children present. How do you keep all of them entertained and wanting more? Lots of time, I have the older children assist me with the younger children. Not watching them because older siblings get that enough from their parents. I usually have them help me read the names and find the child to talk to. I have a special gift that I bring for those who assist me like that.

The older children are great sources of information also. They can tell you who has been naughty and who has been nice. They don't mind telling on the parents either. I get the funniest tales from the older children. They also are the ones that help me understand if a child has a hearing or vision problem. They give me the first indications if a child is autistic or in some form disabled. These children don't mind giving you most information you seek.

The last section on group dynamics is the difference between a large and a small group. The larger the group, the less control you will have on activities. Try to get a small group of children together to listen to a story or to show some magic to. Another small trick I like to use is my magic key. I can make it turn over in my hand all by itself, which always gets a giggle from some. Learn something special. Maybe you can get some of the children to start singing. I found one time that there was a particularly talented group of kids that sang really well together. They loved to sing and I was treated to a myriad of terrific Christmas songs.

So, we have gone over quite a bit under this section titled "The Visit". Now for a few finishing touches and you are on your way.

Talking with Children

When should you listen to the parent and when should you listen to the child? That is an everlasting quandary. I use some very simple rules. When I am with a child, I listen and pay close attention to the child. I give them my undivided attention while at the same time I listen to what is being said around me. This gives me clues to the child's name, what they want, and what their fears might be.

Having your ears open all the time is the biggest secret of how Santa knows all. Other children will say something to a child and you can take it from there. If the parent or an older child wants to talk for the child all the time, start talking to the child and don't ask too many questions. Like for a boy that is shy and the parents want to talk for them, I usually ask them if they know what they want for Christmas. That usually gets a physical response, either a smile, a glimmer in their eye or a nod of their head. Once I get that first response, I talk a little more than ask the big question, what do you want for Christmas? If I get no response, than I usually continue by stating something like, "Let me see, you want a baby doll that wets her pants!" Then looking at the young man I can see the horror in his eyes.

If you can get any type of response than keep it going. Talk about a pretty dress or some other girly things. The young man will eventually give you lots of responses. Then I smile and say, oh that's right, you want a wagon or a ball or a bike or something that I remember his parents telling him to tell me. That brings out a smile and sometimes the child even talks to me. I never stop talking to the child and I always gear the conversation to simple responses so that reactions like a smile will let me know we are communicating.

Sometimes you might want to try the converse of this style by asking a shy boy if they want a Barbie or a dolly or a princess dress. A little girl you might want to ask if they want a football or a fire truck or a GI Joe. When you get them to indicate no, you can now state that you know what they don't want. Now, what do you really want this year? This usually works unless the child is determined to not talk to you, or look at you, or even acknowledge that you exist. The best thing then is to say thank you and send them on their way letting the parents know they wouldn't talk to you.

Always let the child leave with the understanding that if they wish really hard then I can hear that wish and will work in trying to get them what they want. Don't promise any special gift, always indicate you will work on getting it if they continue being on my NICE list. Never push the child to tell you anything. Always push to make the child comfortable.

Since we are on the topic of listening, be an effective listener. Listen to the child and respond accordingly. Listen intently with all your heart. When responding back to the child, repeat what they told you in the same manner they told you. If a young girl wants a dolly for Christmas, then you might repeat back to her that number one on your list is a dolly. Now you will get those children who have been practicing their list. They have about a dozen or two items memorized and rattle it off whenever asked what they want.

For these children, listen intently to any item they may emphasize and repeat that item back to them. I usually pick out two or three items to repeat back and finish by saying. "and a lot more". I also ask if they have written it down and sent it off so that I don't have to remember everything. If not, make sure you tell them to write it down for you.

Listen to what the child talks about. Some children love to hear their own voices so they ramble. You can stop this by repeating what they are saying and asking if they have anything else they want to add that is different. When they start repeating, you can remind them that you already have that down and want something new and different. If they continue to ramble, you can always ask them to write down their list and bring it back.

Listening to what a child says and responding to what you hear is the best method for active listening. This will also earn you credibility with the child. You are not just another adult that doesn't want to listen to them. You actually listen and understand.

My funniest story along these lines occurred when I was given a young lady about 12 to 18 months old to have our picture taken together. She was smiling so I asked her what she wanted for Christmas. Well, this young lady started talking. I couldn't understand a thing she was saying, but she babbled on and looked at me like I should understand. I kept smiling and looking at her. Every once in a while I would say something like, "You don't say", or "and is there anything else"? I even laughed when she paused to take a breath. This went on for about 60 seconds (which seemed like an hour) and all the parents started gathering. Yep, we were the talk of the party for the rest of the night. Dad did manage to get it on camera.

This also goes well with special needs children. Just listen to what they say and answer them. Pay them some attention and you will get the biggest smiles ever. Try repeating back to them what they tell you. That way they will brighten up as they realize that you really do understand them.

One thing you must always remember, as Santa, you never get involved with the children's problems. If times are hard you may sympathize with the child, but then change the subject. Always let the child know that no matter what the situation, you will not skip them this year or any other year. I had a family come and talk to me about a week after they were told that their father was killed in Iraq. They wanted to talk about that. What I did was to let them know that their father would always be with them if they continue to remember him and talk about him. Never forget and always include him in their thoughts and dreams. They were pleased with that and we moved on to the toys they wanted.

Let the child know that you love them and that you will always stop by on Christmas to leave them a present. Let them know you will leave them something special or a surprise. Don't promise them anything except that you will be there looking over them on Christmas Eve.

Always let them know that you love them. This helps reassure the child that they are good and will enjoy the holiday season. Try to give them a hug if they allow it and send them off feeling good about themselves.

No matter how hard the times nor what the situation, we lost our home and live in our car now, daddy is in jail, mommy and daddy don't have a job so we don't have any money, etc. Sympathize with the child and try to steer the conversation to things that are a more happy situation. Always let the children know that they are special and will receive something from Santa.

Special Needs Children

If you are talking to a child who is part of the deaf community, please pay particular attention to what they are signing. Try to duplicate the sign back to them. That will reassure them that you understand what they want. Usually if you can't figure it out, there will be somebody there who could translate for you. Just don't depend on them or talk to the translator.

Here are a few websites to visit to assist you with your signing.

www.lifeprint.com - This is by the Dr. Bill, William G. Vicars, Ed.D., Director, Lifeprint Institute

www.masterstech-home.com/asldict.html - Couldn't find the name of the husband and wife team who put this together.

www.commtechlab.msu.edu/sites/aslweb/browser.htm - Michigan State University website.

www.handspeak.com - Hand Speak

www.aslpro.com/cgi-bin/aslpro/aslpro.cgi - ASL Pro is a very good site to use also.

For those who want to learn to finger spell, here are a few starters.

Merry Christmas

Abbreviated Merry Christmas

MC

Santa Claus

Abbreviated Santa Claus

Cookies & Milk

Look up everything you can think about that has to do with Christmas and memorize those signs. Here is a short list to start you on your way. Don't try to finger spell everything on this list. There are short versions or short signs that you can use that mean the same thing. Look those up using one of the websites listed above.

Christmas
Merry Christmas
Santa Claus
Doll
Ball
Truck
GameBoy
Presents
Naught
Nice
Good

Now try to look up phrases such as:

Hang your stockings,
I like Cookies and Milk
Be good
Enjoy the holidays
Do what your parents ask.
The reindeer are on the roof.

What about autistic children. This is a terrific website to begin your learning about autism. http://www.aslpro.com/cgi-bin/aslpro/aslpro.cgi There are many more places to visit with terrific information, but I recommend starting here.

The best recommendation I can possible give you is to look up on the internet anything you possibly can about the different types of inflictions that affect the children you will be visiting. Know what to say and do around them. Most will tell you to pay them a lot of attention and continually give encouragement. Never treat them like they have a disability.

They have their own little world and community. Try to become a part of that community and don't try to force your values on them. Tell them over and over again how good they are. Always encourage them and never discourage them.

Know the Toys

Now the key to being successful when talking with the children is to know what toys are popular at the moment. Toys R Us and a few other major toy store chains usually have a website that you can look at that will tell you the popular toys of the day.

I try to listen to or look at the different advertisements so that I know what is coming up. I also visit many stores to see what they seem to be selling out of or having requested be brought in. I research this starting about October. This gives me a head start in looking at the right places for this information and making the right contacts. I also look up consumer goods and try to find what the bad products are and know why they are bad so I can talk to the children and possibly the adults about them. The "Toys R Us" website. http://www.toysrus.com/viewall/index.jsp?categoryId=3137242&viewAll=topRated&pmc=1) has a list of the top toys for the season along with a prediction of the top toys for Christmas.

Whatever you do, do not enter into any moral issues, such as suggesting that a fat child not ask for a computer or video game but instead ask for a bike or some other outdoor activity. Never push religion on a family. Never push your ideals on anyone. Keep your opinions to yourself and just talk facts and actual truths that you can back up. Know the toys and be able to talk to them. For example, when the American Girl doll came on the market, you should have known what types there were and why a child might ask for a specific one.

Do your research and know what is out there. As you start getting to know the different stores, you can also get your name out there as a Santa and possibly get a job with them. Work all the angles you can. Let one aspect of the position lead to others and always keep an open mind. Look for opportunities to learn something new that will enhance your visit and make it memorable for all.

The Best Picture Around

You have all probably seen those really awful pictures of children with Santa; those of crying or screaming children in the clutches of an old man in red with a beard. There is even a website devoted to some of those terrible pictures. I personally don't see the humor in it, but here are some hints to help make the Christmas pictures with Santa memorable for all.

First you want to make sure of the background. Don't do it in front of a fireplace that is blazing with a fire. That sounds like a terrific place, but most folks don't own an expensive camera so the bright light from the fire will tend to wash out a lot of things. With this in mind, don't have the background be in front of a window or mirror. You will lose a lot in both of those pictures too.

Check for what is in the background. If there is a pole lamp, bush, or anything that sticks up in the air, make sure it is not directly behind you or else recommend that it be moved. It is not good to have a lamp sticking out of your head in a picture.

Find a background that is close to a single color as possible and with as little design as possible. The simpler the background, the better the picture will be. Make sure that there are no other folks in the background. Who wants a picture of other folks?

Now that the background is set, make sure there is enough light for those folks that do not have a flash on their camera. Make sure there are no deep shadows. Ensure the background has enough light. If outside, have the camera's back to the sun or the existing light. Use a flash whenever possible to fill in the shadow areas.

The child does not have to be on the lap for a good picture with Santa. The child can be standing besides Santa or actually seated in Santa's chair. Santa could be beside the chair or even behind the chair.

You don't even need to see Santa's face to know its Santa. Hold the child over the shoulder. Take a picture of Santa's back with the child facing out. Maybe you can get the child to sit at Santa's feet. A picture of the child with Santa's boots is magical. Can you get down on the floor with the child? Can you get nose to nose and play with the child? Can you get a high five from the child? Can you hold a toy or a treat so the child is reaching for it?

What about a Christmas ornament? Can you dangle one in front of a child like you would play with a cat? Do you have reindeer antlers a child can wear? What about a Santa hat? There are lots of things. I even had a child in a high chair with a bib that said "I LOVE SANTA", and I was feeding the child. What a wonderful picture that ended up to be.

When working with a professional photographer, have a signal so that they can be ready when you do something special. This will alert them to be ready and they will get all the shots necessary. Remember, try working as a team and the pictures will turn out much better. My favorite shot is of a child that doesn't walk yet, I have them kneeling in my chair with me besides the chair. I am kneeling and leaning towards the child with my hand out. It looks like the child is trying to reach my hand.

Always be smiling and ready for the picture. The photographer may take the picture when you are not thinking they would and it is spoiled because your eyes are closed or you are not smiling. Be ready all the time. Think like you are going to be photographed constantly and always be prepared to look your best.

The Business of Santa

Chapter 7

Plan for the Holidays

Now the first part of this section is not built for the year-round Santa because they should be doing these activities all along. This section is designed for the once a year Santa whether you sport a real beard or designer beard. This is a brief checklist to help make your holidays easier to handle. One thought is preparing to become Santa again and the other is to make the experience (and season) more enjoyable for you and your family. Remember how happy and carefree the holidays were when you were younger?

Early Santa Planning

JULY: Let's begin our planning in the middle of summer. The Santa season may be a long ways off, but it is never too early to start your planning.

This is another magical month. The spectacular holiday of Independence Day and all the hoopla that goes with it make for a terrific and fun time to be a part of. If you don't want to be Santa during the summer, try dressing up like Merlin the Wizard or maybe an old miner. These can be fun characters too. Those that know you as Santa will also appreciate seeing you in different guises.

Use this month to experiment with new outfits and new ideas for promoting yourself. This is the time to be creative and starting looking for your place in this universe. A friend of mine decided to start making wooden toys. He set up his jig saw and started cutting, sanding, and sometimes painting. Lots of things he makes. Another friend started making comical handmade items like an Appalachian weather rock. Hangs a rock on a string and then has a hilarious set of instructions to go with it. He also makes other mountain folk type of toys for comical relief. Still another friend makes leather belts and still another makes magic tricks.

If you haven't made yourself a Christmas stocking change bag, then now is the time to do it. It is a quite simple task. I also purchase additional long-sleeved white T shirts and sew ribbons on the sleeves. If you want to know why, either have me come out and lecture about the Santa wardrobe or read my book. Another friend makes the magic coloring book. Flip through it once and it shows blank pages. Flip through it again and you see black outlined pages that need coloring. Flip through it a third time and see all the pages colored in. This too is simple to make.

Over the previous year, I have collected business cards from lots of Santas, Mrs. Claus, and elves. I look at them this month and organize them. Those that I would like to stay in contact with I place in my planner and in a contact list. Those whose card I think has a unique look to it, I set aside and try to see if I can incorporate it into the next card I make.

I like having different cards each year. This allows me to judge what is working and what is not working. It also lets me see when someone contacts me what they used. It gets me noticed on multiple occasions by those who forgot they had my card.

Though the months are long and hot, this is the time where I usually work the hardest building the actions that I will be working on over the next few months.

Create your Master Calendar for the Holiday Season. Include all personal and family activities, school and religious events, business trips, family trips, concerts, socials, annual parties, etc. Have everyone you care about give their input. Consider all of the activities that you are planning and especially those you don't want to miss.

Use an actual calendar for this. I have found that using a monthly calendar for the year works best and using a weekly or daily calendar for November and a daily calendar for December works best for me. I have a 3-ring binder that I use to put this calendar in. Once I have written on a page, I go back into the computer and put it in my electronic calendar and reprint that page so I can update my book. This has proven helpful on numerous occasions. My book travels with me year round.

Make a list of all the tasks and projects you want to complete for the Holiday Season. If you are like me, I like to add to my Christmas displays every year. I enjoy watching it grow. Now is the time if you are the handy man to start building. If you are a scrounger, start looking, or if you just like the attention but not the work, look for others to do the work for you. Schedule it in your Master Calendar for the Holiday Season.

There are some awesome companies that put up lights and adds music to it. Check out their website at: www.holidaytechnologies.com/showcase/showcase.asp or www.christmasmoon.com.

Next, schedule all of your known activities, plus your list of tasks and projects by putting them on your Master Calendar. This includes contacting those Mall and Photo Companies you may want to work for and send them the requirements and specifics they request of you. I suggest you get a current background check and update any insurance you have at this time. FORBS (Fraternal Order of Real Bearded Santas) is a terrific place for a background check and insurance. Mark your calendar. July, update insurance and get current background check. Look for agents if you use them.

Pull out your old decorations and lights. Decide what to keep and what to get rid of. Have a yard sale, or donate to your favorite charity, the things you don't want. Don't go overboard, Remember, most pre-1950 toys and decorations are now valuable collectibles. This is a terrific time to start building that special yard design you've had tucked away for the past couple of years. If you decide to start that project, schedule it on your Master Calendar.

You will want to pull out your entire Santa Wardrobe. Make sure it is clean and in pristine condition. If not, seek to repair, replace, and/or clean it immediately. This is a terrific time to make contact with other Santas to see if they found any place new you could use to build or enhance your wardrobe. Sign up for some Santa classes to see what the trends are for the coming year or just to get into the right mindset for the upcoming season. Get them on your schedule.

Make a list of the decorations and wardrobe items you would like to add this year. Then when you are out and about, you will know what you need to purchase and what ideas you are looking for. If you keep a small notebook with you, you will be able to refer to it when you are out. You would not believe what yard sales have to offer the Santa. You may need to clean or repair whatever you find, but you will have it. Make sure you ask about Christmas stuff when you are visiting these folks. They may have forgotten about them and would be willing to give you a terrific deal to cart off boxes and boxes of special Christmas stuff.

If you aren't already booked for the season, have some new Santa photos made and get out there and hustle yourself. The key here is to have new Santa photo's made! If you aren't interested in being a paid Santa, than start working on the schedule for the family and friends to have Santa visit. Let them know you are willing, but it will be first come first serve for a visit. Start practicing your visit plan. Add new activities to your visit and get them down pat now, so you don't look silly trying something new during a visit.

If you are interested in making an income from the upcoming season, than keep reading this book and look into as many opportunities as you can. This is the time of year that budgets are discussed in big business. Their big Christmas promotions are being discussed and you could get in on the ground floor.

AUGUST: This time of month everyone is getting ready to send the kids back to school and the last minute vacations are being enjoyed. This is the time when it is fresh in my mind to think of the kids, grandkids, and all parts of my family.

Now is the time to take all of those lists you have been creating and start working on them. I like using this month because the year is half gone and the Christmas season is rapidly approaching. Usually most companies have already created their budget for this season and contacting them will remind them they need to start working to get their holiday activities together.

Setup a Holiday gift idea file. Use a separate page or folder for each person on your list. At the same time, keep a master list of current toys on the market and start watching for what new toys are coming out this year. The "Toys R Us" website (http://www.toysrus.com/viewall/index.jsp?categoryId=3137242&viewAll=topRated&pmc=1) has a list of the top toys for the season along with a prediction of the top toys for Christmas. Visit it often, it helps. Having this information will assist you in talking with the children. You now have a basic understand of what the children are talking about.

Start clipping catalog pages, pictures from magazines, and Sunday newspaper inserts. This will assist you in keeping visual clues in your mind for aid in shopping for gifts or just looking to see what is new. I like doing this for the family gifts because now I can start watching for the sales and pick the items up a little cheaper.

At the same time, find a place to store gifts you purchase. Make sure that you label who they are for and mark them off your gift list.

Update your holiday card mailing list. Decide what kind of and how many cards you'll want this year. This is the time of year I review the private visits I made last year. I can send them a reminder that it is never too early to book Santa for this year. If you raised your fees, you might want to give old customers a discount coupon for this coming Christmas season.

My books are officially opened this month and my agents know it. They will start sending me bookings and I must track them all. I respond to each individual request so they know I received them and I make sure I call everyone to confirm. I have a daily log that I created to show where I will be performing, for whom, what is expected of me and the outfit I will be wearing. If money is due, I will not that also. These are than plotted on a map so that I will know my traveling distance and time. Keeping on top of these things ensures that when the time comes, I have no problems. Or at least I don't create any problems by waiting until the last minute.

Remind folks that for them to get what they want, they will need to plan early and to book early. This will also give you time to improve your talent if you have something special you like to do. I am not very good at singing, so I practice that a little. I love magic, so I start looking for other small tricks I can incorporate into my performance. I don't look to put on a complete show so I don't advertise that I do these things. I just do them to add a little sparkle to my visits.

My greatest inspirations come in this month. That is because as I begin to work on all the lists I have made, I come up with new ideas of better variations of the ideas. This makes me work even harder because this is fun to me. It is not common for me to stay up several hours past my normal bedtime and to get up earlier just to work on these items.

SEPTEMBER: This is a great time of year. The holiday seasons begin and the food is tremendous. If you are in need of some healthy life-styling, now is the time. Don't wait until next year and make that stupid comment about vowing to lose weight, start right now. Get into a regime now and enjoy the holiday foods.

Don't forget to continually update your Master Calendar.

Scheduled a day or two in November and December to bake cookies, make fudge, wrap presents take the Christmas picture and deliver gifts. Schedule some "me" time just for yourself. Also make a point to be with family and friends. Relax and enjoy life.

Make out a list of new things you would like to do this Holiday Season, i.e., attend a holiday concert; see a live performance of the 'Nutcracker,' visit a theme park or Holiday Village. See it they can be added to your Master Calendar.

If you want to add more visits to your Santa schedule, start contacting those places. Let them get to know you now. Visit other Santas and let them know you would be interested in filling in for them in case of emergencies or if they just need a break.

If you are planning to travel, you should be searching now for travel bargains on airfare, hotels, etc. The longer you wait, the higher the prices will be as the holidays approach. If you are driving to an unknown location or place that is new to you, check the internet or the auto club for maps and directions. If you perform a lot of visits either through your own bookings or those from an agent, it might be advisable to purchase a GPS unit to locate all the different address. (Garmin and Magellan are just two of the many.) I even pay for an annual subscription for road construction, accidents, and weather for the areas I travel in the most for my GPS unit. This has proven helpful on numerous occasions.

If you haven't already started ordering gifts, now is the time. Especially ones that require special touches or that may be going overseas.

If you like crafts or making your own decorations now is the time to start shopping for new holiday decorations. A few shops, such as Michaels and Jo-Anne's, will have pre-season displays and possibly sales on decorations, candles, lights, etc. I usually pick up mine in January or February, but the pre-holiday season sales are also good.

Order your holiday cards if you have them professionally printed. Get your holiday picture taken if you include a family photo with your cards. (Note: Many local photo studios have special packages for holiday family portraits. Some even have photos with Santa!) These would be another business opportunity.

OCTOBER: I love this time of year. This is when I really gear up. I visit local farms and zoos to see if I can have my picture taken with the animals. (This is another business opportunity; have your picture taken with family pets.) Making the rounds during this time of year is great, not only do I get to meet lots of folks, but I sometimes have great inspirations. Have you thought about seeing if the farmer wants to run a Christmas operation you can visit? Or maybe the Zoo is interested in hosting some children as a Christmas fundraiser you can assist with? These trips are valuable to get you seen. Dress appropriately.

Either make your holiday labels now or start addressing envelopes. If you do a small batch each week, starting now, you'll be done before you know it. Start checking local Department Stores for holiday decorations and other Christmas related items. The best selections are always available sometime in October, while everyone else is thinking of Halloween.

Review your calendar again, for changes or revisions. Now is a good time to schedule a few breaks, in November and December, especially if your calendar is getting full. Re-check school, church or other calendars for events that may have changed. Make all of your November and December appointments for haircuts, beauty salon, etc., now before all the good times are booked! Don't forget your pet's grooming too! Add a few appointments in December with yourself. These are buffer times when you can relax, get a massage, go to the movies, and reduce the stress. Plan for some quality family time, too!

Get out your recipes now and plan your holiday menus. Decide on your favorites. Do an inventory of the ingredients in your cupboards and then stock up when you catch a good sale. I love to grill so I always plan on one day in December to have friends over for a cook-out. Some may think I am crazy, but the cold weather brings lots of folks together. The Holidays are a tasty time, filled with all kinds of great food. Instead of trying to make it all, pre-order special baked goods, tamales and any special items that you prefer not to make. (Save yourself some time. If a local bakery can make a cake or cookies just as well, or better than you, why not order theirs? Your guests and family will applaud you.) Don't forget to continue on your exercise regime.

Get a Flu Shot. If you're a senior or someone who is very active, a flu shot can help you keep your immune system in shape. Be Healthy. Get one early so that any symptoms that you may get will disappear before the season.

Purchase Holiday stamps for the cards, labels for the computer, and holiday pocket cards for cash gifts. Be careful to not purchase too many. Remember the Post Office is a "For Profit" business and raise their rates periodically. You don't want to have a bunch of letters go out that have a multitude of additional stamps to make up for the slight raise in postal rates.

This is a great time of year to start writing your Christmas stories and poems. You actually have time this time of year to get yourself into the spirit of Christmas.

NOVEMBER: The weather outside is frightful, but the fire is so delightful...... I love the winter songs. It's what I sing all the time these days. I can't wait for the first snow of the season. I love a white Christmas. But there is still a lot to do.

Complete any catalog or online holiday ordering now before the November/December rush. This will also make your wallet feel better after the holidays. You would have bought and paid for things long before Christmas shows up. The after Christmas bill paying blues will not get you this year.

If you work year-round as Santa, you probably have several daycare centers, nursery schools, and other locations where you will have pictures made with the kids.

Remember the grooming standards and remember to always try to be the granddad. Find out from each photographer what you can do to make the picture time easier and more relaxed for the photographer and the children having their picture taken. Be prepared for anything.

Decide now, what gifts you would like to receive. Tired of getting something you really didn't want or need? Afraid you won't have an answer when someone asks you what you want. Why not be bold this year. Make a list you can give to those you exchanged gifts with. Have a variety of gifts in different price ranges to fit everyone's wallet. Then when someone asks that dreaded question, you can present them with your very special list.

This is the time to get your holiday decorations ready. Decide what you are going to use and where you will be putting these and the new items you bought these last couple of months. I usually have my decorations up year round but when I do need to add, I try to do it gradually so that no one notices, then all of a sudden, BAM!, it's there.

Review your calendar again, for changes or revisions. Always be prepared and continue to check everything twice. Remember, you are Santa.

Shop for any food staples or kitchen supplies you need before November 15th. Then all you need to do is your regular weekly shopping or shopping for fresh items.

Around this time of year I try not to be in desperate need for anything. I know that I will be stopped even if I am not in costume, sometimes the full Santa beard is enough and that I will stop to talk with kids. A normal 15 minute trip sometimes takes longer than an hour.

Address the rest of holiday cards before Thanksgiving. Getting them in the mail before the first of December usually relieves any stresses I have. If I can't get it on the calendar to go to the post office sometime the first week of December, I just aim to get them in the mail anytime after Thanksgiving.

Order any special gift certificates you want to give. Send all of your overseas gifts before Thanksgiving. I prefer to do this at the very beginning of the month. Lots of mail gets shipped from the middle of November on.

DECEMBER: Whoopee, the season has come!

Mail your U.S. cards, letters and gifts on December 1st.

Bake, wrap and deliver gifts and greetings to friends and those who cannot visit you. Check your lists twice, don't leave a friend unvisited. You want to make sure they don't feel like they are on the naughty list. Make them feel like they are on the nice list and you will have a friend for life.

Double check your gift lists and wrap all presents. Check your delivery schedule. Make sure you haven't left anyone out. Leaving someone out is very stressful. First the friend you left out will wonder why they weren't included this year and second your stress level with jump as you try to make amends.

Double check your calendar for parties and events. Missing a visit by Santa will definitely put you on the naughty list and reduce your schedule for next year. The rule of thumb is that when you book your visits; let the customer know that you will call them approximately a week away from the scheduled visit. If you haven't called, they should call you to double check on everything.

If all goes as planned, you can now do something special to de-stress. Enjoy your pre-scheduled Holiday massage or day at the Salon. You will find that those schedule "me" days are just what you need, very relaxing and very enjoyable. These days usually make me start planning for after Christmas holiday relaxing events.

And finally.... pat yourself on the back for actually getting ahead this year! Now you can relax and fully enjoy all of your Holiday events and time with your friends and family.

The Year Round Santa Plan

Let's change gears for a moment. Say you want to be a year round Santa. You have grown the beard and hair, and they are now as white as snow. What do you do next?

Usually I take my vacation in ***January*** and start looking for schools to attend to get more ideas for the next season. I relax in January and start working in February.

Though I take my vacation this month, this is not the month to totally goof off. This is the month to figure out the money you earned during the season and get your taxes together. You are in the habit of working hard, now continue with that theme and do the cleanup of your work.

Start with sending all your outfits to the dry cleaners and look to repair all the little things that went wrong during the season. Go out and purchase those things you saw during the season and thought you would like to have.

Make plans for a vacation next month and spending time with the relatives. January is the time to finish up with your season and put things away. I like making a list of what I want to purchase before next season and set that money aside or at least start saving. Figure out what you want to use to enhance your appearance both during the off season and during the season. Look for the best place to acquire those items.

Don't forget to take care of your vehicle. It has been through a lot these last two months. Get the oil changed and give it a good checkup. Look at the house too. You have probably been neglecting it but get back to maintaining it in tip top shape. The better shape you keep things in, the longer they will last. They will also be ready for any last minute activities you may want to do with them.

February has arrived and I am all relaxed. Where do I go from here? I use this month to look into college courses that would help me improve. I could find business courses so that I could be in better shape for running my Santa business or I could find other courses to assist in my visits such as psychology, group and organizational behavior courses, or even a class on how to make a musical instrument or magic.

This is the month to figure out the money you earned during the season and get your taxes together. You are in the habit of working hard, now continue with that theme and do the cleanup of your work.

Start with sending all your outfits to the dry cleaners and look to repair all the little things that went wrong during the season. Go out and purchase those things you saw during the season and thought you would like to have.

Make plans for a vacation next month and spending time with the relatives. January is the time to finish up with your season and put things away. I like making a list of what I want to purchase before next season and set that money aside or at least start saving. Figure out what you want to use to enhance your appearance both during the off season and during the season. Look for the best place to acquire those items.

Don't forget to take care of your vehicle. It has been through a lot these last two months. Get the oil changed and give it a good checkup. Look at the house too. You have probably been neglecting it but get back to maintaining it in tip top shape. The better shape you keep things in, the longer they will last. They will also be ready for any last minute activities you may want to do with them.

February leads into ***March*** and with the classes going, I am learning lots of terrific information. I have found a voice instructor who will make me into the perfect announcer type of guy. I even have taken some radio announcer courses so that I might get better with my interviewing and talking skills. I have joined Toastmasters and regularly attend their meetings. The local college that has film and other media courses know me quite well because I have volunteered to be part of their training. I even let the local High School Photo club know I am available for them.

Yes, March is just as busy as Christmas is every year. Not only do I get to include on my resume all the activities I have worked with, but I get the exposure I need and the practice I need. Any local improv group will be more than happy to have you. I never expect to be a comedian, nor do I ever expect to be funny. But, the standing up in front of folks gets easier each time I do it.

I usually find a good tax man this month and make a visit early. This way when they find something new that I don't track, I can go back and see if I have anything for that area. Finding a good tax man who will work with you and explain lots of things is terrific. These days of tight budgets and high prices, we need to watch every penny we have. It took me almost 5 years of asking the right questions and going to the tax man early to get all the information on what I could do to save money on my taxes. I keep getting little tips each year and am able to tweak my spreadsheets and tracking to make life easier.

I have several lists started this month. One is for places I would like to work next season. I have written to several train companies in the past and have been offered positions. Most I turned down because I wanted more reimbursement than they were willing to offer. I have written to several television stations and to several companies who make commercials for television. I have even tried movie theatres, car dealerships, high schools, colleges, community musical groups and lots of local clubs and organizations. Most don't pay much but that is all right since it is usually a one-time thing that doesn't last too long.

I look for agents if I need to replace one and try to contact some magazines and newspapers to see if they need a Santa for any reason. This year I approached my hairdresser and suggested they get the media out for my next bleaching and fix me up. They could provide the media and maybe they could get some mileage out of doing my hair and beard.

There is a local lady that travels the U.S. creating the wardrobe for several theatrical productions. I have her creating sketches of several different types of Santa and Mrs. Claus wardrobes for others to view on my website or in my book. She does a wonderful job and some of the outfits are really spectacular. This is the month that I start working with a talent promoter to see if we can get some Dickens singers together. I would love to be a complete package of entertainment.

April is what I call a fun month. This is the month that I contact all the corporations, photographers, actor organizations, theaters, and any place else I can think of to start looking to get more exposure and get my name out. No, they don't get tired of me doing this each year, and no I don't get work all the time, but there is that occasion when work does come and it is wonderful. Through many of these connections, I get other connections and sometimes referrals.

Believe it or not, I spend about 40 hours a week for the first two weeks of April researching and making a list of those I want to contact. The last two weeks I usually spend about two hours a day creating the cover letter I want to send them introducing me and figuring what type of promotional package I want to send them.

The end of April, I send them all out. One year it took a week of printing to get all the packages ready for mailing and another week to get all the e-mailed packages out. I didn't really mind the cost. It was fun building the promotional packages and introducing myself to new folks. That year, I did get quite a few visits booked.

I had a new idea this year and decided to try to become a Wizard at a local place that did the Medieval Times routine. That is a different story, but I just wanted something different. My long white beard made me a terrific Merlin. The outfit is wonderful and the fun interacting with the guests was an experience to remember.

Spring is here and it is time to do some spring cleaning. This time of year should be the time that you need to start getting rid of all your old stuff or at least packing it away in storage someplace. I like to recycle my old Santa suits. If I don't have someone I can give them too, then I try to make a little elf outfit, or part of a Mrs. Claus outfit, or even try to make a new look for me to wear in the future. Most of the outfits I throw away because they are getting to old and worn to be used.

I also like to take all my tax stuff and review to see what kind of tracking I need to do this year. Once I have that information down (or at least noted someplace) I tend to file those taxes away to keep for the obligatory 7 years. All my worksheets are also saved. I even clean out my computer of old files and put them on a CD for storage.

This is the time of year that I start to fill out my journal again. I write down all the things that happened over the Christmas season and review the past couple of years writing. Keeping this journal is what inspired me to write my book. I even write several articles a month from it to publish in different periodicals. If you want to publish something or don't know how to write effectively, get a copy of the writer's guidelines that each publication has. They want you to be published as much as you want to be published. Their hints are a good starting place.

Are you creative? Do you have artistic talents? Put them to use. Create or develop something that is uniquely you. Look at creating a new business card. The driver's license has been around for a while but is still a favorite. Try a different size card. Maybe you can try a post card size or something in between the standard business card and a post card. Either way, trying something new may be just the ticket for you. Update your Santa resume. For those of you that don't have one, think about creating one. You would be surprised how much that helps your bookings.

Don't get caught up in the petty squabbles of some folks. No matter what your opinion is on a specific person's actions or a specific organization's action, the best path to follow is to make no comment. Let other's ruin their image by mudslinging. I for one have no respect for someone who can't keep their mouth closed and voices a negative opinion of someone else. Now if you are defending against some mud being slung at you. Just state the facts and leave the opinions to others. This is the month that a lot of this starts. Don't be a part of it. If you don't like what an organization is doing or representing, don't belong to them. Find an organization that you like and can live with. I have left several organizations because of just this kind of activity.

Speaking of organizations, you really should belong to several. That way you can support the part of each organization you agree with.

Start your own organization if there isn't one in your area. Just have a gathering once a month over lunch to talk about being Santa and the different things you do. I recommend you do this in a public location for the visibility. Get a couple of folks together and enjoy. You can share ideas and feed off of each other.

If you haven't already completed your taxes, get to the tax man and have them ready to mail before the 15th. After all, your hard earned money should remain yours and not used to pay some late fees.

May is the get ready month. I have looked at my business cards and have decided what I want to change. I have researched the type of cards I want and the cost. I have also ordered these cards and hope to be preparing to hand them out in June. May is the time of year to hit the school districts. Find out who is in charge of the different booster clubs, the bands, and any other organizations that have Christmas events or fundraisers.

Use this month to start planning for the summer. If you do a lot of parades, this is the time to get signed up for them. The next three months are usually filled with festivals and parades. If you have a portable business, you can get that going too. Right now I sell stuffed animals but am seriously thinking about going into the popcorn business. No one can resist the smell of fresh cooked popcorn. Just thinking of that aroma in the air is making me want to get out and find some.

Jerky is growing in popularity right now. Maybe writing to a couple of placed that make the stuff will be enough to have them willing to tell me how to get into the retail end of their business. There are a lot of pre-packaged items that could be sold. Going through my mind brings up a lot to ponder. There really isn't a need to spend thousands of dollars in getting a business started. It is just as easy to spend a couple hundred dollars and start building from there. Who knows, you might be able to get some stuff on consignment. Look into eBay to sell your wares.

You might meet the newly elected to be Senior Class President and student body at your local high school. Let them know that you would be willing to help them with fundraising this summer. If they would put on a Christmas in July sale or event, you would love to be a part of it. I particularly like the local High School bands. I like listening to music and to work with them is a treat. I also look to work with the local symphony or orchestra. Unlike in Europe where every town has a brass band that plays, America does not have many bands or orchestras that give free concerts.

May is also the time to start creating your mailing list. Create two lists; one should be filled with email addresses and the other with postal addresses. These lists should be ideas of whom to contact for potential Santa visits. One year I sent out pictures, Santa resumes, and a letter that describes what I am looking for. Another year I sent out Christmas cards with my picture on it (received from one of the photographers I posed for) with a reminder that I am available and to start looking to book me in August if they want to ensure I make their date.

Yep, August is when I open my books. This is the month to create your calendar and your working sheets. I update my contract during this month so it is ready. I tell the folks who try to book me in January that they needed to contact me just before August or else I get their information and call them back. Once I get my calendar going, I call them and allow for early scheduling.

During May and into ***June***, start looking for bands that perform in the local area. See if they need any pictures with Santa or might be interested in some other sort of activity that may need your assistance. Also look for business that might want to have a Christmas in July sale or event. The local city council, usually the Chamber of Commerce or civics club, will put on some type of activity during the summer. Get involved. Plan to make a visit to a local hospital. Contact your local TV or radio stations to see if you can get involved.

I like this month. It starts the carnival and parade season and it is not too hot yet. I do parade around with my Santa workshop look on as I try to drum up more business for the summer. Make sure there are plenty of business cards to hand out.

This month is the time to start looking for more handouts to ensure Santa never runs out during the summer. Have a bag of trinkets as backup for what you prefer to hand out. Santa stickers are the easiest to carry around and you can carry a large quantity without it being bulky or getting in your way. I have a small red bag of fleeced bears that I carry with me. It looks like a miniature Santa bag. It is only carried when I run out of stickers or when it looks like I will be running out of stickers.

A Santa friend of mine has a shoulder bag you can purchase at Walgreens. It is a red bag that he carries all his important Santa stuff in. When he sees children, he can pull out stickers to give out. If he sees adults that are interested in him, he can pull out a business card. He also carries other things in there but they are all part of his Santa secret stash. Another Santa wears a fanny pack with all his stuff in it. Look around, you can make up a small bag of Santa necessities to carry everything. I personally like the miniature Santa bag. It can be tucked under the belt and gives a magical look when you pull it out to open up in front of the children. What's your trick?

The more publicity you can get, the more you get your name out to the public and the more business you will get. Now this leads us back to ***July***. In July, besides what is accomplished earlier in this section, you will want to start doing a lot of charity work. Donate lots of your time to visit those in need. Help with worthy causes. There are a lot out there and there are a lot of organizations that would appreciate your assistance. Get out there and get noticed.

Be a part of lots of parades. I enjoy the different fairs and events in the local and surrounding towns. Visit as many as you can. Make sure you have plenty of business cards. Always carry something to hand out to the children and some information about you for contacts. Continue this practice into August and September. Be sure you keep up with your master calendar.

Looks for ways to improve how you look, how you act, your business practices or anything else you can. Did you know that belonging to several Santa groups/organizations can help? Also attend different Santa events and classes. Most of the Santa schools out there you only want to attend once unless you think you need a refresher. They teach the same thing over and over again. I recommend that you attend all the schools at least once then start branching out on your own to find that specific class you need to get over the hump and improve your business or abilities.

Use this month to experiment with new outfits and new ideas for promoting yourself. This is the time to be creative and starting looking for your place in this universe. A friend of mine decided to start making wooden toys. He set up his jig saw and started cutting, sanding, and sometimes painting. Lots of things he makes. Another friend started making comical handmade items like an Appalachian weather rock. Hangs a rock on a string and then has a hilarious set of instructions to go with it. He also makes other mountain folk type of toys for comical relief. Still another friend makes leather belts and still another makes magic tricks.

If you haven't made yourself a Christmas stocking change bag, then now is the time to do it. It is a quite simple task. I also purchase additional long-sleeved white T shirts and sew ribbons on the sleeves. If you want to know why, either have me come out and lecture about the Santa wardrobe or read my book. Another friend makes the magic coloring book. Flip through it once and it shows blank pages. Flip through it again and you see black outlined pages that need coloring. Flip through it a third time and see all the pages colored in. This too is simple to make.

Over the previous year, I have collected business cards from lots of Santas, Mrs. Claus, and elves. I look at them this month and organize them. Those that I would like to stay in contact with I place in my planner and in a contact list. Those whose card I think has a unique look to it, I set aside and try to see if I can incorporate it into the next card I make.

I like having different cards each year. This allows me to judge what is working and what is not working. It also lets me see when someone contacts me what they used. It gets me noticed on multiple occasions by those who forgot they had my card.

Though the months are long and hot, this is the time where I usually work the hardest building the actions that I will be working on over the next few months.

My best advice for the year round Santa is to network. Get to know as many folks as you can and keep in contact. This way you will have someone to bounce off your new ideas and to hear the new ideas of others. You may hear that a particular Santa does something and you would like to know more. Talk to others about it and see what they know. Believe it or not, you will become an expert on the subject just by this little bit of research. Look for ways to change or improve yourself. Never be satisfied with status quo. Be the leader and the one that other Santas come to for advice. Know what you are doing.

Now is the time if you want to be a mall Santa to contact the companies that specialize in that. This way you will have your resume and photo out there and may get to pick which location you will be working in.

Christmas In July

By Santa Al Horton

There was no Christmas in July this year. With temperatures reaching above 100 degrees in a lot of places, most folks though it was too hot to think about this winter type of fun. I on the other hand think it is the perfect time to think about winter.

To break away from thinking about the heat and the beads of sweat rolling down your face, just think about Christmas. Not about the tree, nor the gifts spread all around. Not even about the lights that make the season so jolly. Think about the snow outside and the cool breeze that hits you in the face when you open the front door. Stomp the cold off your boots and sit down in front of the fireplace to get warm. Bundle up in a blanket and think about having a nice cup of hot chocolate. Maybe add some marshmallows.

Look out the window at all the folks having fun making snowmen and sledding down anything that resembles a hill. Watch the snowball fights get under way and the neighbor sweating up a storm shoveling their walkways. Everyone is bundled up like an Eskimo.

Now isn't that a cool thought? Don't you feel better? I surely do. I love listening to Christmas music year round and thinking about the snow in the mountains surrounding me. Seeing all the different kinds of animals that are foraging for food also brings a smile to my face. Yes, anything that will make me feel cool and smile at the same time can't be all bad.

Now back to this Christmas in July activity. Next year I think I will begin around February and start talking to businesses about starting this activity again. I need to sit down and plan out all the things that could be accomplished and prepare a proposal on how it should be created. I will gladly turn the reins over to someone else if they would like to plan it, but I need to make sure that it gets moving.

Now what can we have? First, I would love to bring all the children of the town into this idea. We could have a coloring contest for the younger children and an artistic creation competition for the older ones. Give them a theme and let them use their imagination to create something for the town to see. We could have a musical competition. Have any group of three or more get together to sing or play musical instruments in a talent show type of atmosphere. Keep the theme Christmas. Have a tree decorating contest with businesses donating the trees and different groups decorating them. To help raise money, have the community vote on the trees. Every quarter is a vote. Whichever group earns the most is the winner. Let the groups go out and bring folks by to vote.

Maybe we could have a craft section where there are several different categories to enter so that folks of all ages can show their skills. Make a sewing, baking, wood, paper, or flower arrangement competition. Also have many more categories to attract all kinds of things. See what businesses are willing to donate so that we can hand out prizes to lots and lots of folks.

Next bring in the Christmas theme. Make sure everything is related to Christmas in one way or another. Help with ideas about Christmas. Have folks write stories, poems and thoughts about Christmas. I am sure there are a lot of amazingly talented folks out there.

Get the town fired up about Christmas and try as they can to celebrate this fun in the middle of the summer.

Chapter 8

Working with a Mall or Photo Company

Basic Understanding

Besides talking about the basics of following the policy of the Company or the photographer, you want to ensure a good picture of you and the child is taken. Work here is a "team effort" so always strive to make the team work cohesively. Never try to give the impression you are in charge and never give the impression that you are a star and everyone needs to do your bidding. Wake up Santa! Do not expect the photo workers to be your servants. You need the artistic help of those poor young under-paid workers.

I recommend to never accept a crying child. Talk to the child and see if they will stand next to you. Try to see if they will sit in the big chair and let you kneel down next to them. Maybe you can get behind the chair so they don't see you. I like having the parent sit on my lap holding the child facing the camera. That way the child is comfortable and the parent will get a terrific picture of their child with Santa.

Work out a signal between you and the photographer. One that will let them know when you are ready and they can snap away at the appropriate time. Never let the photographer countdown to their shot or signal when they plan on snapping the picture. It never fails but the child or someone will always look away. Let them snap when they think they have a terrific picture framed in their camera.

Talk to the child and try different approaches. You can always get into the picture at the last moment and get the terrific shot. I have been known to allow a child to crawl around my feet and get a shot of them and my boots only. I can have a child looking over my shoulder and the shot is the child with Santa's back.

I have even been behind a chair and peeked out at the last minute to get the photo. I have also been on the floor with a child so that we are at the same height. I play with toys and totally enjoy myself with that child. The more you interact with the child, the better it makes for great pictures. The traditional picture of a child on Santa's lap is so passé. Just try to make the child enjoy themselves and things will get better. The better shots are when everyone is relaxed.

Never promise anything to the child to get them to take a picture. Also never promise to take something away if they don't take the picture. Remember, you don't need a picture with Santa to get your gifts this year. Don't allow that to be a threat. Santa never threatens a child. Now the European Santa traditionally carries switches for the bad children, but those are given to the parents. Santa never uses them so don't let your parent come out. Remain the grandparent and spoil the child.

Don't hold on to the child. When the child is ready to get down, let them down. When you are through with the shot, set the child down. Do not try to continue talking with the child. If you are in a situation with a line waiting to see you, holding on to a child longer than necessary will add time to those waiting. Think about it. Add 10 seconds on for every child and when you have 6 children in line that is an entire minute longer the last child has to wait. The longer the line, the longer the last child must wait.

Make sure you are the model Santa. Do the right thing all the time and you will never have to worry. Start doing stupid little things, and you won't be asked back or worse, you may get a law suit. Don't be a

Bad Santa. Always do the right thing. Let the child come to you and never grab them, never say anything mean to the child, and never let anyone know your opinion. You are not a social butterfly so just do your job. It is not only safer for you, but it is also appreciated more by those who hire you.

A Few Photo Companies That Hire Santas

Some of the larger mall photo companies who hire Santas are listed below:

Cherry Hill Photo Enterprises, Inc.
4 E. Stow Road Marlton, NJ 08053 / U.S.A.
PHONE: (800) 969-2440 / FAX: (856) 663-0880
www.cherryhillphoto.com

Noerr Programs
www.noerrprograms.com

One place to start looking for an agent that also does malls is with:

Nationwide Santa's
23441 Golden Springs Drive #211
Diamond Bar, Ca 91765
909-396-7363 phone
888-449-7464 toll free
909-860-6141 fax
baconbitz@roadrunner.com
www.nationwidesantas.com

Now some words of advice. Read the section on grooming and dealing with children. When working in a mall, you are there to sell photographs and that is how the company makes the money to pay you. If you can't do that, then don't work as a mall Santa. Also, another point, never grab at a child! Let them come to you or not. Grabbing at a child will only scare them more.

Be polite, listen to the child and remember you are there to make photographs which in turn make money for the company and money for you. As Santa, you are there for the children. As an actor, you are there for the photo company. Work as a team and both will be satisfied in the end.

A lot of the elves and photographers working these places are kids themselves. Treat them with respect. They are probably in their first job and could use some great assistance. Be a leader through coaching and guiding, not through demanding or bullying. Don't try to be their boss nor should you try to be in charge. Let them do what they were trained to do and only help if they need it.

If you are a *pre-Madonna*, don't work for a photo company or any other place. No one needs to work with someone who thinks they are the best and deserve star treatment. If you want star treatment, don't act like you deserve it nor should you demand it. I had a Santa replace me at a business for a day one year and when I returned, the workers told me all the horror stories such as him telling them they will remember his time for the rest of their lives. Well they do and not the way he intended it. He was put in the Bad Santa list with the Drunks they had in previous years. They will never hire him again for any reason.

He had them carry his suit to the dressing area, run get him water (which he demanded) had them jumping through hoops to find something to prop the candy canes he was to give out so he didn't have to move to reach them and was on his cell phone making the children wait for him to finish. He was totally unprofessional from start to finish. He will never be asked to take any of my performances ever again.

That gentleman was a very nice guy in a casual setting, but was a lousy Santa. Remember, you are not in charge nor are you the boss so don't act like one. You are there for the children so be there for the children. This guy even demanded a break in the middle of his 3-hour job. Hope he loves himself because if he treats all his clients like that he won't be doing many Santa jobs in the future. He brags about his past jobs. I believe that he doesn't have any repeat customers.

As a worker with the photo company you are there to make money for the company. The way you do that is to make the kids and their parents/guardians love you. They only way to do that is to be the true friendly and kid conscious Santa. Work the crowd. At least act like you love children. Sometimes you will need to bite your tongue as parents and children act up around you. Keep smiling all the time and be overly friendly. You get more with honey than you do with vinegar.

I never expect tips, but love it when they come. You know you must be a good Santa if you can get a tip in these hard times. One time a client opened his wallet and started to pull out 2 twenty's. He said Oops and put them back in his wallet. I did not see what he actually gave me until I was away from the area. When I looked, he had folded two one hundred dollar bills and stuffed them into my hand. I really liked that tip, but I must admit, that was out of the ordinary. Most tips were ten or twenty dollars which I also appreciated.

You can also have loads of props. I use my Santa bag and fill it overflowing with toys. I also have an oversized pocket watch that has a train running around the interior once you pop the lid. That musical watch has kept many youngsters amused.

On my boots I have jingle bells that I shake on occasion to get the child's attention. The sometimes like to get on the floor and play with them. That in itself is a cute picture. How about bringing one of your Night Before Christmas books or maybe the Polar Express. Any Christmas book will do that has a very distinctive cover.

If you think about it, I am sure you can come up with several more props. Use some of the magic you know. The D'lite finger tips or even balloon animals. Use whatever you can think of to produce a terrific picture. I never recommend using candy as a bribe. I spoke about candy in earlier chapters.

Chapter 9

Entertaining

Adding More to Your Visit

Are Are you an entertainer? If you answer that question no, then you need to get out of the business. Santa and those who portray him are actors. Actors are entertainers! Now that we have that straight, the next most important question to ask is, "What do you do to entertain the folks that hire you"?

If you just say "Be Santa" and "hand out the gifts", you are doing the folks that hired you a great disservice and you are killing your chances of a return visit to those folks next year.

Storytelling - Reading

The simplest thing you can add to your repertoire is..... That's right..... Storytelling. If you can read a story well or tell a made up story well, you will be a hit. Practice reading out loud. Practice is the key. There are also some other things to learn such as delivery elements and presentation elements.

Here is a version of "*T'was the Night Before Christmas*". It is meant to bring a tear to your eye and pride to your heart. See if you can read this and make those sentiments come across with your voice and actions.

Merry Christmas My Friend

First penned by Lance Corporal James M. Schmidt cir 1986.

This piece, which sees wide circulation every Christmas time, is generally credited to "a Marine stationed in Okinawa, Japan". Corporal Schmidt was serving as a Battalion Counter Sniper at the Marine Barracks in Washington, DC when he wrote this poem to hang on the door of the Gym in the BEQ (Bachelor Enlisted Quarters). The poem was placed that day in the Marine Corps Gazette, distributed worldwide and later submitted to Leatherneck Magazine.

Twas the night before Christmas, he lived all alone,
In a one bedroom house made of plaster & stone.

I had come down the chimney, with presents to give
And to see just who in this home did live.

As I looked all about, a strange sight I did see,
No tinsel, no presents, not even a tree.
No stocking by the fire, just boots filled with sand,
On the wall hung pictures of far distant land.

With medals and badges, awards of all kind,
A sobering thought soon came to my mind,
For this house was different, unlike any I'd seen,
This was a home of a US Marine.

I'd heard stories about them, I had to see more,
So I walked down the hall and pushed open the door.

And there he lay sleeping, silent, alone,
Curled up on the floor in his one-bedroom home.

He seems so gentle, his face so serene,
Not how I pictured a U.S. Marine.
Was this the hero, of whom I'd just read?
Curled up on his poncho, a floor for a bed.

His head was clean-shaven, his weathered face tan.
I soon understood, this was more than a man.
For I realized the families that I saw that night,
Owed their lives to these men, who were willing to fight.

Soon around the Nation, the children would play,
And grownups would celebrate on a bright Christmas day.
They all enjoyed freedom, each month and all year,
Because of Marines like this one lying here.

I couldn't help wonder how many lay alone,
On a cold Christmas Eve, in a land far from home.
Just the very though brought a tear to my eye,
I dropped to my knees and I started to cry,

He must have awoken, for I heard a rough voice,
"Santa, don't cry, this life is my choice,
I fight for freedom, I don't ask for more,
My life is my God, my country, my corps.

With that he rolled over, drifted off into sleep,
I couldn't control it, I continued to weep.

I watched him for hours, so silent and still.
I noticed he shivered from the cold night's chill.
So I took off my jacket, the one made of red,
And covered this Marine from his toes to his head.

Then I put on his T-shirt of scarlet and gold,
With an eagle, globe and anchor emblazoned so bold.
And although it barely fit me, I began to swell with pride,
And for one shining moment, I was Marine Corps deep inside.

I didn't want to leave him so quiet in the night,
This guardian of honor so willing to fight.
But half asleep he rolled over, and in a voice clean and pure,
Said "Carry on, Santa, its Christmas Day, all secure."
One look at my watch and I knew he was right,
Merry Christmas my friend, Semper Fi and good night.

Reading – How well do you read a story? Can you make a story sound scary, funny, exciting, or cause anticipation in others? How you read a story is just as important as the story itself. You don't give the audience what they are expecting, you will fail, no matter how great the story.

Voice inflection – Try telling a story soft. Tell the same story very loud. What does everyone think? Here is a phrase you can try. Softly and slowly say, "This is reindeer season, tonight we shall get Rudolph." Now say it loud and quickly. Can you see the difference? One sounds like you need to find Rudolph, the other sounds devious like your intention may be the destruction of Rudolph. You can ask a question with your voice. You can also make a profound statement, a comment, show agreement and disapproval. How you use your voice can attract attention, demand attention, and put you to sleep. Varying your pitch, volume, rhythm, and dynamics can make a great story even better.

Let's begin with the delivery elements. What is meant by this is how you tell the story. Do you have excitement in your voice at the exciting parts? Do you portray a sense of mystery at the write moments? What about laughter? Can your voice give the audience the sense of when they are supposed to laugh?

Delivery elements are essential. They include fluctuation in your voice pitch. Give your voice some high sounds when talking and low sounds when talking. Send the pitch higher as you build the suspense or lower as you want everyone to be on the edge of their seat. Pace is another element of delivery. If you talk at one steady speed, you will put everyone to sleep and folks (especially children) will lose interest in listening quickly. Vary your pace when speaking. Try reading aloud as fast as you can. Then try reading aloud very slowly. Both will show you how the story changes with the change in pace.

Don't get caught up with a monotone voice at a single pace. BORING! Some things just sound better when you say them fast. Think about these sentences. The boys ran as fast as they could and jumped on their sleds. Whoosh, down the hill they flew, laughing all the way. Now if you say them rapidly, it gives a sense of excitement and the joy everyone is having. If you say them slowly, there is no excitement and it is just another part of the story that is BORING!

Now try this slow section. "It was dark in the room when they opened the door. As the children crept further into the room, the door started to close with an eerie squeak". If you say this slowly, you can give everyone the sense of anticipation of what might happen next. If you say it rapidly, you lose all hopes at any suspense.

Vary your pace at which you speak and vary your pitch. Keep the highs and lows of your voice as you read a story. What about volume? Yep, volume is also important. If you want everyone on the edge of their seats anticipating the next part, just speak a little softer. If you want everyone to jump back a little, sharply increase the volume of your voice.

Try this phrase. "Whoa There!" If you say it softly and slowly, you give the impression that you are sneaking up on someone or something. If you say it quickly and loudly, it sounds like you want everyone to stop immediately.

Now try reading "Twas the night before Christmas". Don't forget to vary your speed, faster when you get to the part "and I heard on the roof such a clatter, I sprang from my bed to see what was the matter………" in the beginning when you are talking about "not a creature was stirring, not even a mouse….." you want to be talking softly.

After you have the pace down, try reading it again only this time change your pitch. Have a higher pitch when you talk about "the stockings were hung by the fire with care" and a lower pitch with "while visions of sugar plums danced in their heads".

As you read the poem, try different things. Go fast where you went slow. Read slowly where you were reading fast. Have a lower pitch in different places and higher pitch in others. Experiment! Once you have found what sounds nice to you. Practice it that way and read it to others to see what they think.

Don't forget to practice speaking softly and loudly in different places. Practice these few things and you will be well on your way to being a terrific storyteller. I like to envision myself as a TV or radio announcer. People can't see me so I must convey everything with my voice.

Now it was mentioned earlier about Presentation Delivery. This is what folks see when you are reading to them. If you were a ventriloquist, you would be trying hard to not move your lips when the dummy is talking. When telling a story, you want to be very animated. Speak with your eyes, your smile, your head, arms, hands and whole body movement. If you talk about shaking like a bowl full of jelly, than shake like a bowl full of jelly. It's very simple.

Animation – Are you stiff as a board? Do you make robotic movements? Do you know what is natural? How many times have you watched someone doing some activity and were mesmerized by them? How many times have you watched someone and wanted to go to sleep? Do you know why? Have you ever seen a painting that just seems to jump out at you? It's called natural animation. If you can move naturally, you can express lots of emotions. If you over emphasize a gesture, you bring it to the attention of the audience. Shrugging your shoulders is a gesture. But, if you put your arms out to your side with your palms up and shrug, the audience can see it clearly and understand what you are trying to convey. An easy example; if you are trying to be funny, how would you gesture greeting someone? If you are trying to be serious, how would you gesture greeting someone?

Animation should also be evident in how you turn the pages and how you may show pictures from the book you are reading. If you tell the story vividly, everyone will have visions in their minds of exactly what you are talking about.

Reindeer games – Ok, let's sing Rudolph the Red Nosed Reindeer. Now how do we spruce that up to entertain? How about adding antlers and a red nose. To make it more exciting, let's get the audience involved. Get them to wear the antlers and noses. You can do the same thing with the Polar Express. Have an engineer hat and train whistle; have some bells to ring.

The final item to cover with storytelling is probably the most important. Enunciate well. This not only means saying each word properly, but also saying it with the appropriate punctuation. Many comedians get paid to mispronounce their words. You are not one Rodney Dangerfield so speak correctly. Enunciate correctly, and ensure you follow the punctuation. Believe it or not, the writers of these poems, pros, and stories, write and get paid for having the words and punctuation correct.

Storytelling – Extemporaneous

Invent a story off the top of your head. Pick a subject then talk about it or maybe you might want to talk about an absurd variant on the truth. For example, if you have a theme of "Thunder", what would you talk about? I just might talk about my elves bowling during a break from their work of creating toys. Since the clouds are so low, they echo the noise. Sometimes the elves are right over top of you. Listen closely after the big boom (crashing of the bowling ball into the pins) and you can hear them laughing.

Now you try it. What kind of story can you come up with using the following words? Silver Bells, Super Stretch, Gold Coin, Key, Road, and Storm. Can you make up a joke or a funny story? Try it. It is not as easy as you may think. What makes up a funny story and who is it funny to?

Effective Storytelling

What is effective storytelling? Effective storytelling keeps the audience's attention. It keeps them on the edge of their seat with anticipation of what is to come. Your humor keeps them laughing so hard they are having trouble breathing? Audiences want more. Most of all, the audience retains a fond memory of the occasion and retains a principle or lesson learned. Applause is not a measure of success. We have been taught to applaud someone's effort. Not because it was good, but because of the effort.

- **Finding Stories**

Where do you find stories? That question is funny in itself. You can make a story out of anything. It can be a situation, a person, a place, a thing, an event, almost anything. Think about it. What happened today could make a terrific story if you know how to tell it. If you want to include yourself, start off your story with ...... So There I Was........ and build from there. Do you want it to be funny or heart wrenching? Figure out what you want and work towards that goal.

Like with everything else in this book, I am just giving you a start. Take classes. Talk to someone who tells a good story. Do your own research and discover what works best for you.

Here's something funny yet sad. Have you read the Warning Label on a tube of toothpaste? Yep, it says contact a Poison Control Center if more than a normal amount is swallowed. Poison Control Center and they recommend we put this stuff in our mouth? Wow!

Look everywhere and look closely. You can find lots of things to talk about.

- **Preparation**

Are you prepared to tell the story? Have you practiced it numerous times to the point that you probably have it memorized? Can you tell the story forward and backwards you know it so well? Do you know where to pause and where to change your voice?

The more you practice and the better prepared you are, the better the story will sound each time you tell it. I highly recommend you join a group such as Toastmasters to get used to being in front of people telling stories. You can practice on them and they will give you the honest feedback you need to improve how you tell it.

- **Concluding Your Story**

This is one thing that new story tellers have a problem with. Lots want to continue explaining the story and the twist and turns of the plot long after the story should be over. When the story is over, IT IS OVER! Stop and move on. If there are questions in the air, than use that opportunity to explain details, motivations and add color. You left your audience wanting more, a good thing. If they ask more questions than you want to answer, conclude by telling them, "Well, that's another story altogether!"

If you have to explain a part of a story, work on getting the description of that section better when you initially tell it. Make everyone more aware of what you want them to know. Don't tell them everything. Let them figure it out some of the puzzle for themselves.

Magic

Lighted Finger – simple "in-glove" actions. I prefer to use D'Lite soft finger tips. They appear to be more versatile and you have less trouble keeping them clean and hidden. I tried the glove that has a lighted finger but it just wasn't the same as a D'Lite.

With the D'lite, I can wear it under glove or on just a bare hand since it is flesh colored. I haven't had to worry about changing a battery. About every 4 years, I purchase a new one and the batteries are still going on the old one. I keep them around for spares.

My act with this is that I tell the children that I am going to create Rudolph's famous glowing nose. I rub a little red from my hat, I grab some magic from the snowball on the end of my hat, I cup my hands together and shake if vigorously so that it is mixed up well, then I let them peek in a small opening between my thumb and hand so they see the red light glowing inside. As they try to get into my hand to see the light better, I open my hands to show there is nothing there.

Magic Key – One method that works once a year. This is a terrific trick. I keep my magic key in its own little Christmas stocking and pull it out when children start asking about how I get into the houses. I place it in my hand and sprinkle some imaginary fairy dust on it and tell it to roll over. When it does, the children are delighted. I even let them play with it for a while. They can never duplicate how I make it roll over slowly and only on command.

Magic Coin – Now you see it, now you don't. Where is the coin? I like using the plastic coins that have Naughty on one side and Nice on the other. My trick here starts with showing that it tells if someone is good or bad. I place it in my hand with the Naughty side up, after showing both sides. I then ask a person to let me borrow their hand and quickly turn my hand over onto theirs so the coin is trapped in between.

Then I ask them what the coin should read. Are you Naughty or Nice? I remind them that the Naughty side was showing in my hand and that the Nice side was not showing. When they guess, I remove my hand to reveal that the Naughty side is up again in their hand.

After doing that for several children, I make the coin disappear and find a child who might like the coin and make it reappear from them. They then get to keep the coin.

Change Bag – Great with the Polar Express story. "Hear" the bell, "don't hear" the bell.

I do recommend visiting a magic shop in your area. Let them know that you are a Santa and want to perform some simple tricks that don't need a lot of setup and have a Christmas theme. Explain to them that a change bag in the shape of a Christmas stocking is an example of what you are looking for. Let them show you lots of things and see if you might be able to adapt it to your Santa act. Try new things.

Balloon Sculpture

There are several websites that deal with balloon sculpturing. I suggest you look them up and learn from them. Below are just a few simple things you can do. I don't like making the sword because the first thing a child does with it is to hit and stab folks with it. I prefer to do something they will cherish or show to others.

Something else to ponder for this section. Some folks have trouble inflating the balloons. In this day and age we don't call it blowing up the balloons. There are several methods to make this task easier. I used to stretch the balloons but they were still hard to inflate. Now I use a small hand pump to inflate the balloons. They are easy to use and can be carried in a pocket. Don't need a large one even though there are several styles to choose from. Select a simple one until you need to grow into a larger one.

Simple Dog
Simple Hat
For Laughs make a Worm
Pretzel
Horse

Singing

Have you tried singing? Here is a song that is humorous and easy to follow at the same time. Try singing this a couple of times. Who knows, maybe you will want to throw in part of this song in your performance.

Big Red

Sung to Night Riders in the Sky

He came from out of nowhere on that cold and wintry night.
His burglin' days were over and he vowed he'd put things right.
His sleigh was full of plunder as he hurtled through the black
They'd offered him a pardon if he'd put the whole lot

Yippie I oh Ho Ho, Yippie I A
That sleigh rider in the sky

The burgling fraternity all laughed as he passed by
They said he'd never make it so he knew he had to try
The Guinness Book of Records even scoffed at what he'd planned
In just one night he'd enter, every house throughout the land

Then at the stroke of midnight, Big Red began his famous run
Big Red was in his element, Big Red was having fun
His Laughter it rolled through the air, for every house he knew
Like a shooting star across the sky, or a comet down the slew

Yippie I Oh Ho Ho, Yippie I A
That Sleight Rider in the sky

At every house he took a nip to fight the winter cold
Big Red was getting tipsy, Big Red was getting bold
The poor folk and the gentry soundly slept and no one stirred
In every dream a smiling face, Big Red had kept his word

Yippie I Oh Ho Ho, Yippie I A
That sleigh rider in the sky

Big Red he got his pardon, he proved it could be done
Now every year you'll hear the shout – Big Red is on the run!
The laughter and the bells ring out and folks they cheer and say
We'll douse the fire and then retire, Big Red is on his way

Yippie I O Ho Ho, Yippie I A
That sleigh rider in the sky

He came from out of nowhere on that cold and wintry night
His burglin' days were over and he vowed he'd put things right
His sleigh was full of plunder as he hurtled through the black
They'd offered him a pardon, so he'd put the whole lot back

Yippie I Oh Ho Ho, Yippie I A
That sleigh rider in the sky

I am not a singer, but I do like to start my recitation of "Twas the night before Christmas" by singing it. When I get to the part about "I sprang from my bed to see what was the matter", I change to the storytelling mode and become very expressive.

I do manage to sing Rudolph the Red Nosed Reindeer with the kids. Here I usually bring out some antlers and a red nose for some of the children to wear. We start all over again and use the children as actors when we get to the different parts of the song. They love it and play along.

A Letter From Santa

My friend Santa Lou provided me with this information. I know a few other Santas that write letters from Santa, Frosty, Rudolph and a few elves. These letters are especially cute. I started writing them and they are a huge hit.

What child wouldn't be excited to receive a personal letter from Santa, especially if it's in reply to the one they sent Santa. Santa letters are one of the best ways to convey the magic we portray as Santa Claus and bring a lasting happiness to children. Santa letters are also an inexpensive way to promote yourself by offering them on your website, business cards or as hand outs.

There really isn't a need to worry about your grammar or writing style, as there are a number help aids built into your computer and online. In high school one of the classes I hated the most was English. Not only were adjectives, prepositions and i before e except after c, a mystery, but my teachers, were the most feared instructors in 3 counties. They were tough!

Over the years I've become a bit more comfortable writing but adjectives, prepositions and all the other rules of writing is still quite tough. Even as I worked as a technical writer, I had to look back into my different grammar books to make sure I did things right. I used the computer help a lot too. Thankfully, I have lots of help built into my computer to look over my shoulder and make me look much better than I really am.

Maybe you have had the same experiences and trying to write a letter from Santa brings back those memories. It will be hard to escape it but some time in your Santa Claus career you will be asked to write a Santa letter to some child either for a special reason or possibly you may want to offer it as a part of your Santa Service.

Let's explore writing a Santa Letter which I guarantee you is not going to be distasteful as those writing assignments in high school English class, and it's going to be a lot more fun. Don't worry about your grammar or what to say. By utilizing some of the resources already at your finger tips, you can become a pro.

Getting started is relatively cheap as you'll be utilizing things you already have or use.

What do you need to get started?

Basically you will need the following:

a. Computer
b. Printer and color print cartridge
c. Letter size Paper, White or maybe colored.
d. # 10 or suitable mailing Envelope
e. Postage Stamps
f. Foil Seal or a wax seal (gives an official look)
g. Lots of Imagination.

Where do I Find Santa Stationary?

There are numerous websites which offer free downloads of stationery with Santa-themed borders to use in your letter. You can find these by entering "Santa stationery free" or "Santa letters" into your browser and doing a search. You can also use Avery or even the Microsoft available borders and letter styles within the Microsoft Word documents.

You will probably find numerous sites listed as you search, but with a little bit of exploring you should find some themed stationery to your liking. There are literally hundreds to choose from. You can also build your own. I once bought some paper that was preprinted with the Santa theme around the borders. But that drives up the cost of the individual letters.

I have also found software that uses Microsoft Office Word as its word processor. Some have a small charge while others are free. These software programs assist you in writing letters to Santa and also in creating a letter from Santa. Some have certificates for Naughty and Nice with them while others have envelope dress up features along with post marks from the North Pole. Still others have a wide variety of graphics and fonts you can play with. Check them out. They are fun to play with.

What will I Say?

One of the easiest methods to write a Letter from Santa is to create a series of questions which you could use in your letter. Then build a couple of templates that sound good to you. These templates can be used over and over again or just as a sample as you write a personal letter to each child.

Below you will find some general questions which you might find useful. Place each on a separate index card to review them. Once you have selected the questions that you are comfortable with and will provide you the responses you would like, then make a letter template and develop a letter with instructions for completing and answering by the parents, grandparents or someone who has information about the child receiving the letter.

These questions are basic information, include the name and address to whom you're writing. Is it a boy or girl? Some information that only Santa will know such as a recent achievement, favorite sport, special present received last Christmas, etc. Also the names of brothers or sisters, ages and any special information should be included. Does the child desire a certain gift for this Christmas and are there any special requests or things that would really endear you to the child when you write them?

When you are composing your template letter to the child, keep a few things in mind; Write the letter in a conversational tone and avoid using words that are not usually in a child's vocabulary. Keep things simple and don't overdo descriptions or explanations. Be complimentary and respectful. Remember don't tell all about Santa. A little mystery is expected.

Include something from Rudolph and maybe find a hoof-print stamp to use. Maybe Frosty the Snowman could also write a letter or even one of your elves.

Let's Write the Letter

Practice composing a letter placing some of these idea's within. Begin with something similar as the following example.

You asked Emma's parents to fill out the questionnaire and here is the information you have. Emma, age 6, was in a dance recital, loved the Jasmine princess doll left last Christmas, her brother's name is Davis and they sing and dance together. Emma helps her Mom out a lot. She has an "Elf on the Shelf" named "Jingles." She wants a Snow White doll for this Christmas.

Dear Emma,

Greetings from the North Pole where it is now snowing. The snow is making everything a beautiful and sparkling white. We are all busy at work making toys for the coming holiday season. The elves had a short vacation after Christmas last year and when they returned to the toy factories there was a big mountain of orders waiting for them. It seems like they are always working so hard, including your elf "Jingles," to make sure there are enough toys to fill all the orders and special requests.

The elves in the Ballerina Doll Factory were all talking about you, Emma, and how well you danced at the Cumming School of Dance Recital. They thought you were one of the prettiest girls on the dance floor. I told them you were 6 years old and I wasn't surprised how well you danced since you are doing so well in school. I also told them that sometimes you and her brother sing and dance together. I told the elves I enjoyed it so much! I just can't stop saying "Ho Ho Ho!" with the biggest smile on my face from one ear to the other.

My elves have told me you want me to bring you a doll for Christmas. I know you want a special doll and her name is "Snow White." I'll try my best as I know your name is on the "Nice List."

Mrs. Claus just came in with some fresh baked cookies and a cup of hot chocolate so I'd better finish this letter. Oh yes, Mrs. Claus sends her love and requests that you keep up the good work you are doing. She's so proud of the way you help mom."

Your special friend,
Santa Claus

How to make it look good

I incorporated the information returned by Emma's parents into the body of the letter, trying to mention as many of the important items as possible. I checked the letter over, and being satisfied with the content, I'm ready to choose some stationery. You can easily find Letters from Santa with illustrated borders and/ or use clip art to make your own design.

I print what I have written as a word document while I download and print the colorful letter head I have chosen to send. Now some of you are adept at computers so you can skip over how I line up the letterhead.

I hold the word document up to the light to see if it fits within all borders and then adjust the word documents to fit accordingly. Not scientific but it works for me. The final step is to put the letterhead in the paper tray so when I download the word documents it will print within the borders. I normally don't preprint my Santa signature so I can do it free hand to personalize the letter.

Some Extra's

I mentioned in the "Things you'll need" foil stickers or sealing wax. Most office supply stores carry in their stationery area pressure sensitive foil stars and circles that look very official. You may wish to stick one at the bottom of your letter or across the envelope flap.

Mrs. Claus bought me a wax embossing kit which you can find online or at a Hallmark Store. The kit consists of Red Sealing Wax and the letter "S" in fancy script for embossing on a handle. I like to drip the melted wax over the envelope flap and then emboss the letter "S" into the hot wax. This leaves an official imprint from Santa and I can just imagine the excitement over the official letter from Claus.

You might think about adding a small plastic pouch of special Santa Magic Dust. This is approximately a pinch or two of different colored glitter. Include in the letter that they need to sprinkle this outside their door or near the road in the front yard to help guide me to their home to bring them that special present.

The Envelope is Important

The envelope is very important because it will be the first thing a child sees so you want to create some visual excitement right from the start. Many times when you download The envelope is very important because it will be the first thing a child sees so you want to create some visual excitement right from the start. Many times when you download letterhead there is a companion envelope with the same theme to make them as a matching set. Whenever possible try to use the companion envelope. It makes it look more professional.

If you use colored paper for your letterhead, buy the set with the envelopes the same color. Many online printing companies will print a return address label per your design. You can include a photograph of yourself in one corner and print something such as:

Santa Claus
Your Street Address
North Pole, Your State, and Your Zip Code.

This disguises your true location, however return or new mail will be delivered to your home.

One last thing is the postage stamp. You can have a postage stamp made with your likeness or maybe with Mrs. Claus. These may be purchased online and they are a terrific way to show everyone that the letter is coming from Santa Claus. Do try to order these as the season approaches and/or any postage price increases are not imminent. Otherwise you will have to paste on the additional postage stamp.

Writing Santa Letters is fun and can add much more to your

portrayal of Santa. Just be yourself, use your imagination and bring the joy to the little faces that wait to hear from you. After all, you are Santa! There are several software programs out there that will write the letter for you. You should try several before you decide to stick with one and sell it. You need to make sure you are satisfied with the program. If not, you can rest assure that your customers will not be satisfied with it. Find a good one. One that you can make moderate changes to.

Another similar trick I use is sending a PowerPoint slide show with animation and sounds. I do this to those parents who ask me to send their child something by email. This is a little different from the letter as it has pictures of some of my friends (animals, elves, reindeer, snowman and more), along with pictures of me wishing the children (by name) a Merry Christmas or whatever the greeting the parents would like.

This is quite simple to make if you know anything about PowerPoint. If you don't know anything about PowerPoint, a simple book or the tutorial within the product will guide you through this.

The thing you must be careful about is that this leaves your email address out there. I usually send it to the parents and ask them to remove my email address once they have downloaded the attached file.

I am sure you can think of lots of things to do. I have one friend who makes mini web movies where they talk to the child or children. This is too much fun but takes a little talent to create. Build your scrip so that you have less takes to get it the way you want it to look.

Have fun and be creative. Go off in numerous directions and experiment. I'll bet you can come up with at least a dozen more ideas. Some will work and others will just be learning experiences. Either way it will be fun to create and to add to your list of capabilities.

Chapter 10

Where Else Can You Perform

I have heard all the stories about needing your SAG (Screen Actors Guild) card to work in the movies or commercials. This is just not so. I used to have a card but quit the guild when I found out I could work without one and didn't have to pay the dues. Of course, membership does have its advantages and if you want to work ***full time,*** in the acting field, I highly recommend you look into acquiring your card and maintaining the dues.

Now don't let someone discourage you by them saying it cost several thousands of dollars to join and several thousands more each year to keep your membership. Look on their website and find out the facts. What it actually cost and the requirements you must meet to become a member. www.sag.org. Find out the facts for yourself.

With that said, let's move on to other things. These are things you can control and have fun talking to others about.

Performing at a Home Visit

First, you need to reread the visit information mentioned in chapter 6. You need to please the person who hired you and also pay a lot of attention to the children.

Have your skit ready and make sure you can perform it well. This will be your most critical audience. Make sure they enjoy your visit from the beginning to the end. I enjoy performing at homes. I can be with children who are more comfortable with their surroundings and find the most spectacular activities being performed there. I was allowed to play with some children for about half an hour at one party. It was so much fun.

At another home party, we made Christmas tree ornaments. Doing the craft thing was a blast. I even made a few suggestions for the following year. I was able to read not only one of my favorite stories, but I also was able to read one of their favorite Christmas stories. Wow was that fun. There are many books out there and some are really rare. Be prepared to enjoy a Christmas story you have never heard.

Special Events

These can be parades that the local communities have (Fourth of July, community celebrations, elections, etc) I have also found a car dealer organization that hired me to work their party. It was the most 2 hours worth of fun I had in a while, surprising people out of season! The perks with this event were terrific.

Other special events can include Special Olympics, fairs, carnivals, medieval fairs, and other things that take place in and around your city. Do you have a community that puts on plays or concerts? Try working with them. Christmas in July events work well too. I once assisted with sending special needs and cancer patients to a camp by seeing them off on their bus and giving each a gift to take with them. This took place in August.

I am sure that if you looked, you can find lots of different events you can participate in. These events don't have to be in November or December. They can be any time of year. Santa is always welcomed.

Parades

I like parades! You can either enter a parade by paying for an entry spot and being judged, or by a free spot. Most organizers will allow Santa a free spot if you don't advertise anything. Just this past September, I was Santa in a Fall Festival with a Professional Rodeo Competition rodeo and all. That was a load of fun. I did receive several bookings from that event.

I don't give anything out at parades. I don't want the children to be running up to me and I don't throw anything for fear that I might hit someone and do some harm. If I do have something to give out, I walk along side of the street and hand it out to the folks. This gets me closer to the children and on a personal basis.

Riding in a float is important too. Keep your eyes peeled for the anxious child and make sure you look at everyone and wave to everyone. Make them feel special that you saw them and wave.

Movie Theaters/Plays

This is a fun time for all here. Look to see if any Christmas types of movies or plays are being held in your area. Talk with the manager and see if they might be interested in having you there for opening night. You could be outside getting the crowd worked up to see the movie or play.

I also like going to a place where some Dickens Carolers might be performing. They are wonderful to listen to and a pleasure to work with. You might get some additional bookings through them.

Local Schools

Most folks think of only the preschool and elementary schools here. Look at the local high schools and colleges to. If they have a drama department or a film/photography department, see if they would like your services. You can either be a part of their performance or you can do like at the movie theatres and be outside or inside working the audience up to see what is coming.

What about the school bands. Do they put on a Christmas concert? Get with them for a quickie performance.

Check out the different clubs and organizations within those schools. Let them know that you are available if they are planning any Christmas time activities. You can be at their Christmas card/candy/calendar/etc kickoff sale. You can be a part of their publicity. What if they decide to sell Christmas trees this year? Be there one day and let them advertise that fact. It may also get you additional business.

Some schools have little carnivals and fairs. Get with them. Let someone make money by taking your picture with the kids.

Advertising Yourself

If you don't advertise yourself, who will? Get out there and push to be seen. Get to know the city council, chamber of commerce, city government, and all the civic organizations you can. Let them know you are available and willing to work.

You can put your resume together along with a current picture or group of pictures and pass them out to all the local photographers. You might want to hit the party shops and also any costume shops around. I went so far as to one year including all the TV, radio, newspaper, and magazines publishers in the local area. I even included all the advertising organizations.

Doing this you might get 10% back on your return with inquiries and 10% of those inquiries will turn into actual jobs. I placed over 300 of my resumes with photos in the area and received over 100 inquiries back. Out of those 100 inquiries, I had a job in September for publicity and 2 jobs in November for photo shoots. I even ended up with 1 job in December that led to 3 different other jobs in December. Now that is only 4 jobs out of 300, but at least I had work. If you live in an area, you don't need to do that every year. Have a postcard made up with your picture on the front and some contact information on the back. That will work for the next three or four years of contacts.

I have my truck slightly decorated so I can advertise year round. This also helps acquire jobs. Even a magnetic sign you can stick on the door of your car works. A friend of mine does that and claims he gets business that way.

I have gone a little overboard with my truck. I have since added antlers to both side and a large red nose on the front. My license plate reads RUDOLPH. Think anyone notices? You bet. As you approach from the rear, you get a different look.

I get folks zooming by me on the interstate and on the city streets. When they realize that I am driving, they usually slow way down to let me catch up so they can either wave or take a picture. Yes, I do have a Santa hat on the dash to wear on special occasions.

The website www.SantaClausAcademy.com relates back to when I worked for the Brotherhood of the Direct Descendents of Santa. I still teach, but I am out on my own and will come to almost any place and teach a class or two. Contact me if you are interested in having me talk to your organization or teach a class. My classes range from five full days to one hour lectures. I love to talk about being Santa and can expound on any subject in this book plus a lot more. Believe it or not, I have nine 8-hour days I can teach.

For example, one of the talents I have acquired is sign language. That is so much fun when you can communicate with someone who is deaf. I haven't mastered it yet, but it opened the doors to a whole new world out there.

Website

Now the one thing that I don't cover here is a website. Your best marketing tool this century is the internet. How can you best be seen by more folks and give out more information the public is asking for! Have a terrific website.

If you don't know how to build a website, try taking a class. Yes, I sound like a broken record. I highly recommend taking a website class. You will learn what it takes to operate a website and you will also learn how to work on the website.

When you create a website, make sure that the front page is eye catching and all the information is easy to figure out with easy to use links to all your information. I recommend you have your current background check on it (make sure you remove things like personal addresses, phone numbers, social security numbers and the like). Describe the type of Santa you are with lots of pictures and the areas and types of events you cover. Have a basic price list you are ok with and a method for folks to contact you to answer any questions you did not answer on the website.

If you start getting a lot of the same questions, that means it is time to put something on your website that approaches that subject and answers the questions before they are asked. Also let the folks know how you accept payment. Credit card transactions cost so be very aware of that. Know everything you need to accept credit cards before getting into that part of the business.

If you prefer to have someone help with your website, make sure you have all the codes from them for getting into the website and making changes. You never know when you will become dissatisfied with your current web-designer or find a better one. Look at all the websites out there and see what you like.

Remember, the longer it takes for a potential customer to load your website, the less you will have business from it. The rule of thumb with business types of websites, the faster it comes available to the public, the more money you make. With that said, make your website simple yet eye catching. If it is too plain, folks will not be interested in purchasing from you. If it so complex that it takes a while to load, than folks won't be bothered to look at your site.

As you look at other sites (not just Santa sites) see what you like about it and what you don't like about it. Make a list so that you do the things you like and don't do the things that irritate you.

Here are a few sample pages for you to look at. They were intended for the Santa Claus Academy website, but the owner opted to go more formally.

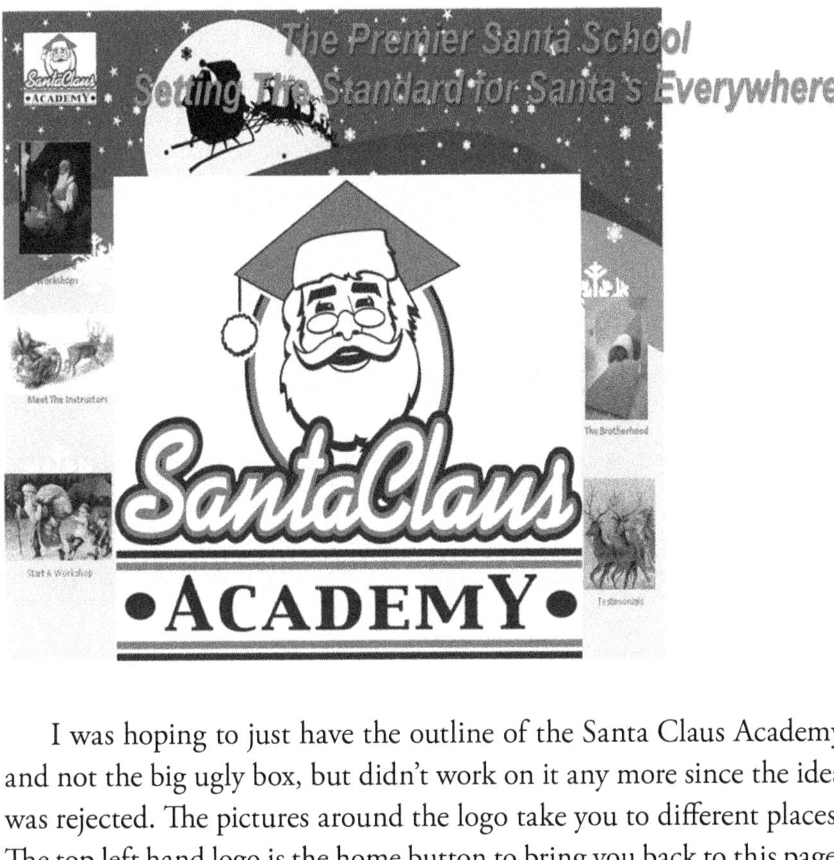

I was hoping to just have the outline of the Santa Claus Academy and not the big ugly box, but didn't work on it any more since the idea was rejected. The pictures around the logo take you to different places. The top left hand logo is the home button to bring you back to this page. The next one down is the Workshops where Santas, Mrs. Claus and elves/helpers can find what classes are available. The next one down is Meet the Instructors. Here we introduced the instructors for the session and the bottom one is where someone can create their own workshop and have the instructors travel to them to teach. On the right side of the page starting at the top, that is a direct connection/link to the Direct Descendents of Santa Claus website since they sponsored this webpage. The bottom is a link to testimonials from previous students exclaiming how great we are.

I didn't put music to it or snowfall since that would take longer to load. All the pictures are html compatible so they load quickly. Everything on the front page is simple and easy to understand. Anyone using it could easily find whatever they needed from the academy.

Make sure you include all the information from your information packet you developed earlier and more if possible. Try to hit every contingency you can. Include a copy or your Santa Resume. The more you have available, the fewer questions you will be asked and the better your booking will be.

Chapter 11

Build Your Santa Resume

What to include

– Photos or Cut Card.

Make sure you have at a minimum a head shot of yourself. I recommend that not only should you have a head shot, but also a full length shot of yourself. On a single 8 X 10 photo sheet, you should have the head shot cover the entire front or at least ¾ of the front. On either the side or across a small portion of the bottom of the front, have 5 or 6 other poses in other outfits if possible. Make sure one is seated and one is a full-length shot.

These photos will pay dividends when you include them with your Santa resume. Include all your contact information on the front. The reason I say this is that one place I returned to after giving my photo and resume too had my photo posted where their clients/customers can see it. With my information on the front, everyone knew how to contact me. Below is a sample of one of my cut cards.

- Your current background check

Why do you want a current background check? Well, you do if you are going to a private home or a business and they want to make sure you are safe to have. They don't want you robbing them or casing the joint for a later robbery. Also businesses want to make sure that you are safe for the kids. You know the routine, no sex offenders or pedophiles.

A current background check from your local Sheriff's Office should suffice. You could even get one from the different counties you will be working in. If you are big, pay for the big enchilada from the Federal Government (but start this one very early). The folks you are working for will appreciate this effort you made on their behalf.

Along with this, you might want to get a current physical. I use a trucker's CDL physical and carry the card with me. It shows that I am in good health. You can also carry a shot card with you that show your current inoculations. It will indicate your influenza vaccinations and your TB test. That too will give you a clean bill of health for visiting with children.

– The style of Santa you are

You really need to tell the folks this information. If they are expecting a Coca Cola Santa that will help build crafts and you are a traditional Santa that sings, you are not compatible and the event will not end on a positive note. Needless to say, you will not be asked back again.

If the only outfit you have is a workshop Santa, and the folks want formal pictures with the family, they too will not be happy or satisfied with your visit. Let everyone know up front what you do and can do.

– Where you have performed

Lots of folks ask me why they need to put this information down. My only comment is, if you are a mall Santa who has never performed at a private family party, you will probably not do so well on your first couple of visits. If you let folks know up front what capabilities are, you will get more business from more folks.

– References

References are very important. You do not need to put down addresses or phone numbers. Listing where you have been in the past is usually sufficient. This will give the potential customer an idea of your range of performance. If they want to talk to someone, they can look up the business number themselves.

I even go as far as putting down my references in this type of format so that the folks can see my background and capability.

- Private parties
- Family visits
- Major parties (commercial/corporate)
- Malls
- Hotels
- Charities
- Etc

References not only show your range, but they can show the level of performance you give. Some references will speak for themselves. For example, if you have a major store or corporation that you worked for, they will probably only hire someone who fits the part they expect. That is a plus for you.

How to write it

– Summarize VS Chronological

As with any resume, you can only answer this question once you have put your resume together. Gather all your information and put it down on paper.

I initially went with the summary method because I had very little to write. I would write that most of my profits were in the form of donations to the local orphanage or abused wives home. I even had money going to homeless shelters.

Then as I started performing more and more each year, and I changed my Santa appearance every few years, I started chronologically developing my resume. You will notice my resume (which I have attached in part) and see what I did.

A Sample Resume

Here is a summary portion: Note how it gives a brief description of my background in both private and Santa life.

RETIRED Air Force with thirty plus years of combined U.S. Air Force and private industry. Maintained a *Secret Clearance* within the government for the past 30 plus years and, delighted children all over the world as Kris Kringle. I have been portraying the Jolly Ole Elf for the children beginning with my own family and moving on to friends, orphanages and hospitals.

Now here is the Chronological part:

1970's

* Brought joy and happiness to children in the United Kingdom. Portrayed Santa to the Americans at several Royal Air Force stations and portrayed Father Christmas for five years at a British International disable orphanage. Had the local Chief of Police assist me as the Good Fairy. All Volunteered or raised money for charities.

* Wore a designer beard and wig.

1980's

* Provided happiness to young and old throughout the United States. Portrayed Santa Claus for both adult and children parties. Started performing at office parties and small business events. Charged donations to pass on to the local abused children's home.

* Wore special long-haired designer beard and wig.

1990's

* Began participating in parades.

* Had a few commercial shoots (still photography) for magazines. Never saw any results.

* Clientele increased to over 60 visits in the month of December.

* Portrayed Santa for government and private industry at the corporate level.

* Started charging as a business. My initial fee was $25 per visit.

* Began using theatrical glue and makeup to enhance the image and keep the beard in place.

2000's

* Grew a Real Beard.
* Went from a $25 a visit Santa to a $250 an hour performing Santa.
* Added singing, magic, balloon animals, story reading and storytelling.
* Clientele includes:

- *White Columns Country Club in Atlanta, GA*
- *AIM Marketing Solutions*
- *Cobb County Fire Department*
- *Four Seasons Hotel in Atlanta*
- *Numerous Photographers at Daycare Centers*
- *Boy Scouts*
- *Salvation Army*
- *Andretti's Speedway*
- *Numerous Hospitals*
- *Target*
- *Ogilvy Action Group*
- *Chateau Elan*
- *Several Pesticide Corporations*
- *Several Home Owner Groups*
- *Waffle House Corporation*
- *Alta Mill*
- *D & H Construction Company*
- *Twelve Resorts in Atlanta*
- *Sheraton Hotel Chain*
- *Lights of Life Festival in Atlanta, GA*
- *Television commercials*
- *Magazine Advertisements*
- *Bass Pro Shop*
- *And numerous families from the elite side of Atlanta and Las Vegas*

– How detailed?

This is an excellent question. You need to have your basic resume on one page. That is one side of one page. Your references should also be on that same side of the page if possible. Otherwise, they may be on the back of the page.

Make the resume as detailed as you feel necessary to get the potential client to hire you. You will notice that in my brief summary part I talked about my military background and my secret clearance. This will give most a sense of comfort around me knowing I am a veteran and that I was trusted enough to carry a security clearance. Also note, that I never described what I did in the military. I think it might shock them if I had something down like "sniper" or "Special Forces". They might be disappointed in me if I put down admin clerk or medic.

– Description of your services

This is important. You do not want to over-exaggerate your capabilities. I never claim that I could sing. I just happen to sing as part of my performance. If I could play a musical instrument, I would put that down. Always make sure that you make full arrangements with your client as to what you will do. If you have on your resume that you make balloon animals and you don't bring any balloons to the event, the client might be upset unless you coordinated ahead of time with the client that you would not be doing that.

Tell the client what you have to offer. I say I perform very moderate Christmas Magic. If you tell them you are a magician, they may expect a full magic show from you. Tell the type of Santa you are and what you can do for them.

– Schools and Training

If you want to talk about the different Santa schools you went to, by all means, let the client know. This will also put them at ease to know that you are a consummate professional trying to gain education as much as you can. They will be surprised with all the schooling you can receive and have taken just to bring joy and happiness to the family.

Here is what I included:

Master Degree of Santa Clausology, Santa Tim Connaghan 2006
Amalgamated Order of Real-Bearded Santas (AORBS)
Victor Nevada's School of Santa Claus 2005
Doctorate of Goodness 2006 – Santa Claus Academy – Brotherhood of the Direct Descendents of Santa Claus

– Publications I Write for

Sometimes I tell the client what publications I write for. This makes them seem to have a better connection with me since I do this more than just a little bit. They love going back and reading some of my work.

Here are a few Publications:

Red Suit Round Table Newsletter
AORBS Newsletter
Red Suit Gazette – BDDSC
Beatty, NV Journal

– Community Relations

Occasionally I include other community activities that I am involved with. Especially if this is for major clients I am courting. I want them to know I am a complete person and not just some homeless guy off the street trying to make a buck.

Here are some of the community activities I include:

Volunteered for the major events of the community, Desert Tortoise Days and the Regional Chili Cook-Off. Volunteered to assist the local boy scouts on several occasions and participated as a special guest in numerous other local events. Volunteered assistance to several city councils. Visited local homeless shelters, abused childrens' shelters, battered wives shelter, and many more as Kris Kringle. Brought cheer to an otherwise cheerless atmosphere.

The Audition/Interview

Here is where you will perform for the first time. Be in character all the time and answer truthfully. Give them the Santa answer to their questions and perform your best skit for them. Never slip out of character and never let them detract you from doing so. If they want to know about the real person behind Santa, have your real-life resume and background check available to hand them.

You are an actor. I can't say that enough. If you don't think you are an actor, than I suggest you see a psychiatrist immediately. They have a place for people who think they are someone they are not. Yes, play the part and play it well. Play it completely, but play the part. Study what you need to do and practice.

Some questions you might want to be prepared to answer during your interview could include:

1. Why do you want to work for us/me?
2. What makes you feel I/we should hire you?
3. What can you bring that will make you different and special?
4. What else can you do?
5. How much do you expect to be compensated?
6. We need a current background check.
7. We need a current drug test.
8. We would like a current DMV print out.
9. Can we give your name to others who might be interested?
10. Is there anything that would prevent you from completing your task if hired?

These are just a few interview questions. If you are auditioning, know who you are auditioning for and have your skit ready. Be prepared to improvise on the spot and answer some pretty strange questions. Each question asked will be designed to see how well you think on the go and how knowledgeable you really are.

Don't let the thought of an audition or interview bother you. Remember, they know nothing about you and are trying to learn as much as they can. Let them know everything you can without getting out of character. Enjoy this time as much as you would if you were working around children.

Talking to the Media

Here we also need to talk about working with the media. If you don't want to sound like a boob on the tube, then I suggest that you practice a little bit. The questions above are a good starting point, but make sure you are prepared to answer other questions like,

1. Why are you here this time of year?
2. What is Santa doing here?
3. What is it like being Santa year round?
4. Do you really like portraying Santa and having all the folks approach you?

There are a million questions the media will ask that seem sort of strange to you, but they are after a specific story. You need to figure out what that story is and make sure you stay in the Santa character and help them get to it. Have a purpose for everything you do. Make sure you get that across. Have a specific charity you like to work with and mention their name on the air. Promote yourself as available and willing to work year round for a good cause. Make sure you are always in character. I just can't say that enough.

Chapter 12

Setting Up Your Business

This section has some generally useful information and some really specific information. I suggest that if you want to set up a business, consultant a business accountant or business lawyer to assist with this endeavor. It will help immensely when trying to set up your corporation.

You will find some major differences from an expensive hobby to a full-fledged business. I suggest that you take lots of college courses and read all the free information on your State's Website. They provide lots of information to get you started. Their assistance also leads to others who will assist you for free. Take advantage of everything you can get.

I recommend that you use your search engine. Type in the name of your state and then business start up. That way you should get to your State's government web page with all the requirements. Just a hint, it is cheaper to start an limited liability corporation (LLC) in Nevada than it is in most other states. The most expensive states are New Jersey, California, and New York. There are several others that come close to these three, but they are the current leaders. State and local government websites will tell you how to develop your LLC, hot to create your business, and where you might go to find out more information about building your own business. Most of the information they give you is free. Take advantage of this. If you are looking to relocate to another state, look up that state's government webpage. I have even researched in other states where I knew I would be, or at least wanted to be, working. Each has a little bit different information, but they all have the same basic outline to follow in establishing your business.

Some states even list some pitfalls to watch out for so you don't close your business before you are ready. They also list how you should plan for closing your business. Me, I looked to see what information they would give me about selling my business so that I could carry on.

There is some information in this chapter talking about logs, that you will want to take note of. These are particularly helpful when it comes to tax time.

As always, I recommend education as the best answer for all questions and problems. If you want to learn how to start a business, go to your local college and enroll in a few courses. Business education is very specific. You will learn more about the rules in those classes than you will in this book. Find out for yourself. Take some accounting courses while you are at it. Unless you are independently wealthy and can hire an accountant, you will be doing all this yourself.

Setting Up Your Santa Business

Now what type of business do you want to set up? Do you want to just market yourself? Do you want to run a Santa Agency and market other Santas as well as yourself? Do you want to have a photo Santa business? How about a Christmas store or a Christmas book store? Do you have a special talent that other Santas could benefit from? You need to decide this before you get into anything else. Once you have decided what you want, then continue on with this chapter.

Now let's assume that you just want to market yourself and will possibly expand at a later date. That is a good idea unless you have the funds (and you will need no small amount!) to start your business.

Otherwise you will have to learn how to write a business plan, business prospectus and much more to ask for money. You will have to decide if you want to try for a grant or a business loan. If you are just going in this for marketing yourself, then read on. Otherwise, I suggest you find a lot of different business courses to take that will explain all the aspects of starting a full business.

First Things First

For those who didn't know, you do not have to carry on a regular full-time business activity to be self-employed. All that is necessary is that you make a profit in at least three out of the last five years. Otherwise it will be considered a hobby and you cannot deduct a lot of things you can with a business. Monitor this aspect of your taxes closely.

Create a Log of all your activities and track all your work. This log needs to have anything and everything you do as Santa. You must have records to show the source of income as well as to support the deductible expenses. I have several different logs for different purposes. One log tracks all my expenses throughout the year. A good place to look for the right questions is Schedule A on the IRS website. You can also acquire Publication 17 from the IRS and review their views on business activities and hobbies.

To be deductible, a business expense must be both ordinary and necessary. An ordinary expense is common and accepted in this business and a necessary expense is helpful and appropriate for this business. Generally, if more than one individual is an owner (you and your spouse), can elect to file two Schedule C's or Schedule C-EZ's. You must file an income tax return if the net earnings from self employment are $400 or more (as of 2010).

I deduct my gasoline expenses and all the things I purchase for my outfit, advertising, education, etc. Yes, I do include my prorated share of my internet bill when I use it a lot for emailing Santa related stuff. I also include paper and ink for my printer and anything special I purchased for the sole purpose of Santa Claus. Remember to estimate fair market value for all of your freebees and charitable activities. These are deductible. Keep a good record of where you did what and for whom.

Some other areas to think about deductions include:

- Cost of supplies that you give away throughout the year
- Clothes you purchase to enhance your Santa image, Including the summer outfit you wear to ensure you still look like Santa.
- Professional dues such as AORBS, FORBS, the Direct Descendents of Santa Claus and other organizations you pay a regular dues to.
- Subscription to different journals and magazines you use in your work.
- Special wardrobe components.
- Cost of cleaning these items.
- Safe deposit box used to hold your millions.
- Schools you attended to either help you with being Santa or assist you in running your business.
- Automobile depreciation (prorated)
- And many more. Just think about them and make yourself a list.

I create another log that documents my performances. It list the customer, their contact information, where I am to perform, what date and time I am to perform, any special requests I am to perform, payment information and the type of Santa I will be during this performance. This log is set up like a calendar. That way I can use it as the days pass and figure out what I have remaining to perform and what I have already performed. This keeps me from over-booking my day and also keeps me busy. I know where my available time is and can plan accordingly.

My last log is a spreadsheet. I list my dated Santa expenses and income event by event. I don't have as complete information as I do on my previous logs, but I do keep a running total of my money. Here I know exactly what I spend and how much I have made or am planning on making through the year. This is especially helpful when it comes to tax time.

Speaking of tax time, plan on itemizing your tax return. I still use a tax preparer/consultant each year. I find out different things doing this and the following year I tend to keep a little more of what I make. If you don't use a professional tax preparer/consultant, I honestly believe that you are cheating yourself. You probably won't find all the things you might and will probably be paying more taxes than you really need to. I have even taken some of the courses provided by the top 3 tax preparing companies, HR Block, Jackson-Hewett, and Liberty.

You don't need to incorporate but you will find becoming an LLC will help you a lot. I highly recommend doing so. This not only protects your personal accounts, but will also protect you. You don't need as much insurance. Clown insurance can get pretty expensive. FORBS has insurance at a fairly reasonable rate. Check out their website before you jump into purchasing insurance. Being an LLC will protect you personally from the eventual liability law suit. They can take from your business, but they can't take from you personally. Those that are not incorporated have the chance of losing everything to an injured party or an unscrupulous person equipped with a clever lawyer.

Make yourself a Santa Contract. Here is a funny one that some unknown author wrote. I have one that is more beneficial to me and covers all the necessary items of my visit including payment.

The New Santa Contract

Author Unknown

I regret to inform you that effective immediately, I will no longer be able to serve the Southern United States on Christmas Eve. Due to the overwhelming current population of the earth, my contract was renegotiated by North American Fairies and Elves Local 209. I now serve only the Northern United States and Europe. As part of the new and better contract I also get longer breaks for "fortified" milk and cookies. However, I'm certain that your children will be in good hands with your local replacement who happens to be my third cousin, Bubba

Claus. His side of the family is from the South Pole. He shares my goal of delivering toys to all the good boys and girls; however, there are a few differences between us.

1. There is no danger of a Grinch stealing your presents from Bubba Claus. He has a gun rack on his sleigh to prevent sleigh jackings, and a sign that reads: "These toys are insured by Smith and Wesson."

2. Instead of milk and cookies, Bubba Claus prefers that children leave an RC cola and pork rinds (or a moon pie) on the fireplace. Bubba doesn't smoke a pipe. He dips a little snuff, so please have an empty spit can handy.

3. Bubba Claus' sleigh is pulled by eight floppy-eared coon dogs instead of reindeer. I made the mistake of loaning him a couple of my reindeer one time, and Blitzen's head now adorns Bubba's fireplace.

4. You won't hear "On Comet, On Cupid, On Donder and Blizten ..." when Bubba Claus arrives. Instead, you'll hear, "On Earnhardt, on Wallace, on Martin and Labonte, on Rudd on Elliott and Petty."

5. "Ho, ho, ho!" has been replaced by "Yee Haw!" And you are also likely to hear Bubba's elves respond, "I hear'd dat!"

6. As required by Southern highway laws, Bubba Claus' sleigh does have a Yosemite Sam safety sticker on the back of the sleigh with the words, "Back Off!" and "Don't Mess with Santa!" The last I heard it also had other decorations on the back of the sleigh as well. One is a Ford or Chevy logo with lights that race through the letters and the other is a caricature of me (Santa Claus) going wee wee on the Easter Bunny.

7. The usual Christmas movie classics such as "Miracle on 34th Street" and "It's a Wonderful Life" will not be shown in your negotiated viewing area. Instead, you'll see "Boss Hogg Saves Christmas" and "Smokey and

the Bandit IV" featuring Burt Reynolds as Bubba Claus and dozens of state patrol cars crashing into each other.

8. Bubba Claus doesn't wear a belt. If I were you, I'd make sure you, the wife, and the kids turn the other way when he bends over to put presents under the tree.

Here's a more serious type of contract you can use with a client. Your contract with an agent needs to be more detailed about what you will receive.

Santa's Contract

Santa Your Name Here (Phone Number Here)

Client's Name:____
Print Clearly

Visit Date:____
Day Of Week   Day Month Year   From hour to hour

Location of Visit:______________________________________
Physical address   City State Zip

Contact Phone Number:_________________________________
Primary   Alternate

Special Directions:____________________________________
____
____

Payment: _____ Full Payment
_____ ½ Payment (remainder to be paid on the night)

Check _____ Ck #_____ _____ Cash

Special Instructions:___________________________________
____
____
____
____

________________________   ________________________
Clients Signature   Santa (Your Name Here) Signature

If there are any questions please call immediately. Santa (Your Name Here) will call approximately 1 week prior to the visit. If you don't hear from me, please call to confirm the visit. Also, Santa (Your Name Here) will call when he is 5 to 10 minutes away from your location to let you know he is almost there.

Santa Accounting

Tracking Expenses

Brainstorm types of expenses. I suggest that you write down everything you can possibly think of and then put the list aside. After several days, pick it up and try to add as much as you can. Get friends to help you think of ideas. No idea is too stupid of silly. It may lead to bigger and better ideas. All ideas need to be kept for constant review. You never know if something will spark that important piece of information you have been looking for.

Once you get this list together, write it in a spreadsheet. List every one of the ideas. If some are duplicates you can either combine them or eliminate one. As you figure out another expense, you might want to write that one down too.

Here are some ideas you might start with:

- Business Cards
- Advertising
- Schools you attend to learn more about being Santa
- Schools you attend to enhance your business knowledge
- Organizational Fees for Santa Organizations you belong to
- Background check fees
- Publications fees for pertinent information
- Track your miles traveled as Santa
- Gifts and giveaways you have to hand out

Save Receipts

This is sometimes hard to do, but I found if I carry a large envelope I am more likely to drop the receipts in there and save it. Of course this means I must go through the receipts at least weekly and find those I can put into my log. Even if you wait until the beginning of the new tax year to review them, at least you have them.

Track your Mileage

This part is so easy yet so hard. If you track your mileage for everything you do as Santa, you can use it as a tax deductible. I can remember one year that the allowable mileage rate changed in the middle of the year. I received a tax deduction at one rate for the beginning of the year and at a higher rate at the end of the year.

If you have advertisement on your vehicle all the time like mine, you can claim all the mileage you travel. I keep my mileage by the month just in case there is another increase in mileage. It isn't hard, just remember and put it on your need to do list for that month.

Identify Miscellaneous Santa Costs

This is a very important column. Once you have your spreadsheet working and you come across a once in a life time expense, put it in the miscellaneous column. If you notice that you have the expense more than once, make a new column with that expense in it. I have put my oil changes in the miscellaneous column unless I travel a lot and have more than two during the season.

Visit your Tax Preparer Early

If I could say this a million times, I would. This is very important. The reason for the early visit is so that when they ask if you have such and such information, you can go back home and look it up or create it in preparation for your next visit. This will also help you for your following year's visit. You will have an entire year's worth of information. Make sure you have all of your W-2's, 1099's and other forms that show income.

For example, I give out lots of stuffed animals. I claim them on my taxes. My tax preparer found out I did that when I gave her one for her child. That is when we started to claim them. That money adds up.

Charities

This is the best part. If you can, collect tax exempt receipts. Salvation Army, Goodwill, and all the major charities that accept donations will be able to do this for you. If you can't get a receipt, at least collect the name, address contact person, and all the contact information you can.

Track what you did and for how long. Estimate your normal cost and put that down.

If you just like to donate clothes and other stuff to some charity or church, you can estimate the fair market value. Think of it as a yard sale and price accordingly. The IRS will use this as a red flag so this is not a good practice to get into.

Tracking your charity work either visits or gifts is important. This will also lower the amount of taxes you will be required to pay. Also it gets you known about town and you will be sought out by many to assist more.

Know what deductions are and what refundable and non-refundable expenses are. Learn these from the IRS Publication 17 (which you can order free each year from the IRS website at www.irs.gov).

Another thing to keep in mind is that you can amend your taxes for up to 3 years past. If you have records for the previous years, go back and talk to a tax expert about this. You might be surprised at how much you can get back.

Record of Santa Visits

At a minimum, you will need the following information on any contract you design. It will be very useful in the future. I highly suggest you create a contract. This should be made in duplicate so that the individual has a copy and you have a copy.

Make sure your name, address and contact information is on the contract. This way the client will have that information in case they want to talk to you about something. Also having two copies giving the client a copy and you keep a copy for your records.

Keep in mind when you develop this contract, you need to know certain information to perform the visit. Make sure there is room to write all the information down. I also include if there is any special person that needs to be singled out and why. This way if I need to talk about the matriarch of the family, I will have something to say. Also if I am to talk about a child, I will need some ***Naughty*** and ***Nice*** information to talk about.

If a child is scared about something in particular, I need to know so we don't go there. I have had to give condolences to a child over a lost hamster. I also worked with a mom about a runaway dog of a child. Sometimes it is good to know.

I also let the client know during this contract that I have some handy hints that might assist them with making this a very memorable visit. I call it my handy hints for Santa. I have a check mark on the form to help remind me to give it to them. Use the examples below.

Handy Hints for a Santa Visit

If you are interested in selecting Santa your first name (Santa your full name) for your Holiday Event, here are a few handy insights for making Santa's visit a most enjoyable event. If there is something missing from this or your contract, please feel free to contact me.

1. **Have your camera/s ready**. Be sure to have all the film, videotape and batteries necessary to take the photos you want or need to get. Be sure to recharge your video and digital camera batteries.

2. **Reserve a <u>special</u> parking place for Santa.** It should be as close as possible to where he is appearing. And remember, Santa is a senior citizen. If he parks down the street or around the corner and has to walk all the way to your home, or office, he might be a bit winded or exhausted, when he gets there. And remember, he's wearing a heavy velvet suit that gets very hot, (even in December).

If the visit is at your home, leave an opening at the end of your driveway. Just put a temporary barrier in the space. Use a box, a chair or a sawhorse. Have some fun and put a sign out "Reserved for Santa!"

If your event is at a company facility, office building or hotel, try to make arrangements for Santa to park in valet parking or in a loading area. Again you can mark the area with a fun sign. This makes it easier for him to be fresh and ready to bring joy to your guests.

3. **Have your gifts ready.** Santa can carry in one bag of presents for

children or guests. They should be well labeled. We suggest a large black marking pen and writing directly on the gift because tags can easily fall off.

Have a "helper" available to read the names on the gifts. It is not proper for Santa to mispronounce a child's name. Having a helper to assist with calling the names and handing the gifts to Santa will be appreciated by everyone.

All packages should fit into one 55-gallon bag (Santa's current bag). Anymore and it may be too heavy or awkward for him to bring in. We all know of Santa's "Magic Bag." You know the bag that holds tons of toys and gifts and only weights ten pounds. Well that bag only works its magic on Christmas Eve!

If you have more than one bag, see if there is a way to have the gifts near his chair before he arrives or if there is a way for him to have "helpers" to bring the extra gifts in.

4. **Get everyone together, before Santa enters.** Timing is everything. Santa may only be there for a short amount of time. And, if everyone is scattered around the house or office, you lose valuable time. Santa and you can coordinate. He should call you when he is five minutes away from arriving. That's your cue to get everyone together, maybe to sing some Christmas carols, and to have someone go outside to meet Santa. If Santa is to bring in presents, the person meeting him can help fill Santa's bag. Then, at the right moment, Santa can pop in and join everyone in their singing. If you have a large group of children to see Santa, you should assign someone to be Santa's helper and coordinate the order of children as they each visit Santa

5. **Have a sturdy chair for Santa to sit in**. Folding chairs and low chairs (the one's you sink into) are not good. Santa usually likes a chair that is sturdy and stable. A good straight-back dining room chair works well. Santa likes to sit-up or on the edge of the chair. He should be able to sit comfortably and have a child on each knee.

6. **Place the Chair near your Christmas tree or in a holiday setting.**

In front of a fireplace with stockings hanging, the Christmas tree, or any festive type of backdrop is perfect. Your photos will have more impact when the background has a festive look. Place a wreath, a few Christmas cards or your children's drawings on the wall to make a wonderful difference. Leave a foot or two between the chair and the tree or wall. This will allow room for others to gather around and behind Santa's chair for group photos.

7. **Think about photos with everyone**. Yes, some teenagers will shy away or think it is too childish, to have a photo with Santa. Don't worry; Santa can stand up for a "buddy" photo. What about grandma and grandpa? Take a photo with Santa and Grandma Hugging. And, nothing is more fun than having Santa ask Grandpa if he's been a good boy!

8. **If there is a balance or payment due to Santa, place it inside a Christmas card or envelope**. It never looks appropriate when someone gives cash to Santa. So, as Santa is departing, hand him the envelope and say, "Thank you Santa and here is a Christmas card from all of us."

If you think about it, there is much more you can add. Never add things such as supplying water to Santa. Bring your own. Never mention about letters from Santa the child may give you or the cookies and milk you may be offered. Approach those subject is they arise. Keep thinking, I am sure you can add a few more to this list.

Chapter 13

Business Development

Overview

Business development is a combination of strategic analysis, marketing, and sales. Business development professionals can be involved in everything from the creation of marketing strategies, to the generation of sales leads, to negotiating and closing deals.

The job of the business development professional is typically to identify new business opportunities—whether that means new markets, new partnerships with other businesses, new ways to reach existing markets, or service offerings to better meet the needs of existing markets—and then to go out and exploit those opportunities to bring in more revenue.

Since the field is a cousin of marketing and sales, even when an organization doesn't have a stand-alone business development department or employees with the titles, you can bet that folks in sales and/or marketing are handling business development responsibilities.

You will be, no doubt, your own business developer and marketing specialist. Get to realize that right away and you are on your way to having a better business. Go to the local college and take some courses in business developing or marketing. You will be surprised at what you learn and how you can use it to improve your Santa business.

Identify New Business Opportunities

Your first job in marketing is typically to identify new business opportunities. Well, how do you do that? Don't just tell me you are going to be Santa. That won't fly. Tell me "how" things are important.

This means several things, in terms of what you'll do. First, you'll need to stay abreast of what's happening in your industry. Not only do you want to attend lots of Santa Schools and gatherings, but you will want to know what your competitors are up to in terms of products and service offerings, pricing, marketing strategies, and so on. Second, you'll need to make sure you understand what your strategy, how you compare to your competitors, and how you are perceived in the marketplace. Third, you'll need to understand the market. Who are the different kinds of people buying Santa's services and how are those people changing? Believe it or not, there are Jewish, Buddhist and other religions hiring Santa!

Next you'll need to think creatively about everything you know about the Santa business. This is the part of the job in which you identify possible ways to improve your sales, which can mean identifying anything from new market segments (or individual potential clients), to new sales channels to sell through, to other, related products or services in the marketplace with which your services can be combined into synergistic, "co-branded" offerings. What all this means is review the section on pricing and see some of the areas I market. That may get your creative juices flowing and get your potential markets identified.

The next part of the job is prioritizing the new business opportunities you've identified. To do this, you'll need to compare the potential returns of each new opportunity to the costs you would incur to exploit it. Which means spreadsheets—lots of spreadsheets.

Finally, you have to bring the new opportunities you've identified and prioritized to fruition. In other words, you'll be negotiating with those at other organizations who can help you take advantage of the opportunities you've identified. And, if you're good at what you do, you'll be closing deals with those other organizations to increase your bottom line. This means hitting the senior homes along with orphanages and other charitable type of communities too.

Business development might be better described as business-to-business sales. Cold-calling or prospecting for potential clients, members, or partners is often a task that most do not enjoy

If you think back to earlier segments in this book, you will already have some ideas on where to look for new business. I even talked about when I solicit and what I use in my solicitations.

The Marketing Concept

The term *marketing concept* pertains to the fundamental premise of modern marketing. This can be laid out as recognizing consumer needs/wants, and making your services that correlate with these consumer desires. This is why I recommend singing, magic and other Santa type of activities. Make sure you can read well at a minimum.

As an example, if you would employ market research to gauge consumer desires, use research and development to develop the revealed information, and then utilize promotion techniques to ensure the public knows the service exists. In Santa language, find out what the folks want from a Santa. Have folks survey their friends, talk to everyone you know and come in contact with then gear yourself to what you find out. If most only want a Santa to hand out gifts and tell a story, then set yourself up to be the best there is. Now let the public know that you offer that service.

In the early 1960s, Professor Neil Borden at Harvard Business School identified a number of performance actions that can influence the consumer decision to purchase goods or services. Borden suggested that all those actions of the company represented a "Marketing Mix". Professor E. Jerome McCarthy, at the Michigan State University in the early 1960s, suggested that the Marketing Mix contained 4 elements: product, price, place and promotion.

- *Product/Service*: The product/service aspects of marketing deal with the specifications of the actual goods or services, and how it relates to the end-user's needs and wants. The scope of a product/service generally includes supporting elements such as warranties, guarantees, and support. Think of this in terms of you being Santa. What marketing deals can you develop? What are you good at and what can you offer the public?

- *Pricing*: This refers to the process of setting a price for a product, including discounts. The price need not be monetary; it can simply be what is exchanged for the product or services, e.g. time, energy, or attention. Methods of setting prices optimally are in the domain of pricing science. Some of your pricing areas may include a phone call from Santa, a 15 minute visit, a 30 minute to an hour visit, picture sessions with day cares and photographers. I have also included a letter from Santa and a few more things. What can you offer?

- *Placement* (or distribution): refers to how the product gets to the customer; for example, point-of-sale placement or retailing. Often called *Place*, referring to the channel through which a product or service is sold (e.g., online vs. retail), which geographic region or industry, to which segment (young adults, families, business people), etc. also referring to how the environment in which the product is sold in can affect sales. This section is where your phone calls come into play.

- *Promotion*: This includes advertising, sales promotion, including promotional education, publicity, and personal selling. Branding refers to the various methods of promoting the product, brand, or company. There are so many ways to promote yourself, some have been covered in earlier chapters.

These four elements are often referred to as the marketing mix which you can use to craft a marketing plan.

Now that you have the basic idea, think of all the things you can do under each of the four sections above and make a list. Keep refining and improving the list. Spend a week or more doing so. This will give you an opportunity to let the brain relax and come up with more ideas.

I really like the marketing aspect. It gets my brain juices flowing as I try to figure out places that might employ me. Coming up with lots of ideas is fun. I make a game out of it and see if I can be very creative in what I can do. I have approached a lot of theatrical groups to see if they would like a Santa for any aspects of a performance. The local orchestra and even an opera group were in my sights. My next target is all the local bands. I want to see if they would be interested in having Santa at one of their performances. I even went to a couple of record producers to see if they needed any cover art with their clients and Santa. I am really pushing the limit on some of these ideas, but what the heck, the worst they can say is no. And, the best part is…. I can write off all of my efforts against my taxes.

I have also left the realm of Santa and opted for other work to include portraying Merlin the Wizard for medieval places and activities, an old miner for casinos and prospecting type of events and even a mountain man. I am looking into other characters I can portray.

Start-up Expenses Worksheet

Nearly everyone who has ever started a business has underestimated the costs, and then faced the danger of running with inadequate capital reserves. The key to avoiding this pitfall is to adopt a rigorous approach to your research and planning. A Startup Expenses Worksheet will lead you through the process.

Expenses

Begin by estimating expenses. What will it cost you to get your business up and running? The key to accuracy here is attention to detail.

For each category of expense, draw up a list of everything you will need to purchase. This will include both tangible assets (for example, equipment, inventory, etc.) and services (for example, remodeling, insurance). Then determine where you might purchase these goods or services. Research more than one vendor; i.e., comparison shop. Do not look at price alone; terms of payment, delivery, reliability, and service are also important.

Contingences

Add a reserve for contingencies. Be sure to explain in your narrative how you decided on the amount you are putting into this reserve.

Working Capital

You cannot open with an empty bank account. You need a cash cushion to meet expenses while the business gets going. This cash cushion should be enough to meet expenses for several months. You will need to pay the bills even though there is none to little money coming in at first. Make sure this cushion will take you through the hard times until you do start making money.

Eventually you should do a 12-month cash flow projection. This is where you will work out your estimate of working capital needs. For now, either leave this line blank or put in your best rough guess. After you have done your cash flow, you can come back and enter the carefully researched figure. Just a quick thought on cash flow. Figure out what you need in the way of expenses every month and what you anticipate bringing in every month. This is your cash flow. Enough must come in to meet the expenses.

Start with a Spreadsheet and enter your company's Name

Next add your name as the owner

How much are you going to invest? __________

Are you going to make any purchases? ___________

List everything you need.

This includes any Santa costumes or additions you will need in the near future. It also includes any advertising and a whole horde of things that you will need.

What is your working Capital Equipment? ___________

List everything.

Don't forget to list your vehicle. Insurance is part of the next section. I have a machine that assists me in stuffing animals. That too is a part of my capital.

What are your Locations and Administrative expenses? _________

Rentals
Utility Deposits
Legal and Accounting Fees
Prepaid Insurance
Office Supplies
Other

Do you have Opening Inventory?___________

List everything and its cost.

Advertising and Promotional Expenses___________

Paper/Ink
Internet time
Signs
Commercial Printing
Travel/Entertainment

Schools
Other Category

Other Expenses ____________
List them out.

Startup Expenses ____________
Buildings/real estate
Leasehold improvements
Capital Equipment
Location/Administration expenses
Opening Inventory
Advertising/Promotional expenses
Other Expenses

Information Kit

Build yourself an Information Kit. This is something that you can hand out to prospective clients so that they can review to see if they want to hire you. It doesn't have to be anything elaborate. You can just have your Santa Cover Letter, generic, your Santa Resume' and your photograph. Make sure you have lots of contact information included.

Other things you might want to include are:

- Your current background check
- Your current DMV printout
- Your current medical certificate (a food handler's card is also acceptable)
- A list of references (Client raves and contact information)
- Strong description of what type of Santa you are, what character you play and what activities/entertainment you provide.

I would include several different types of poses as Santa with several different activities shown. This will give the prospective client an opportunity to know you on their terms. If they like what they see and read, than you will get a call and potentially a job.

This information kit is great, especially for cold calls. That is for going places you haven't been before and trying to get a job without them even realizing that they need you.

Pricing

You also need to include prices. Now pricing is unique and different. I can make a recommendation of what to charge, but some would tell you that is too high while others will tell you that is too low. I recommend that you do some research for your area and determine what the going rate is. Set your prices to just below or just above depending on how comfortable you are at being Santa and how well you perform.

Here are a few types of services you need to consider when establishing prices;

1. Phone call from Santa
2. Letter from Santa
3. A quick 15 minute visit of saying Hi and giving out gifts to a single family
4. A 30 minute visit to visit more than a single family. Listen to the children and give out gifts.
5. An hour visit to be with up to 30 children, read a story, listen to their wishes and pass out gifts.
6. A photo session with a photographer that last less than an hour.
7. A photo session with a photographer that last an hour or more.
8. Price in any giveaways you may have.

Figure out not only what pay you want, but what you are willing to do for each of the above and write that down so that you have a record of actions. When you book yourself, you will not only know what you will be charging, you will also know what you will be doing. Keeping this record will have you being consistent in your business. That is very important. Someday compare expenses per job versus income per job to see where you are making your biggest profit or loss.

The Freebee or Charity Work

Never pass up the opportunity to do charity work. Giving freebies is also good for the business. Just don't make it a habit of doing everything for free.

Charities are a wonderful thing. Not only do you get to give back to those who have nothing, you have an opportunity to bring joy and happiness to children and adults alike. It is also good at tax time. I keep track of all the charity and freebee work I do and write them off at the end of the year. There are times when you cannot deduct the value of your labor, but if it is consistent with your normal charges, you can talk to the tax preparer about doing so.

Freebies are good because they attract more attention. I give away at least 100 if not 1,000 stuffed animals every year. I don't worry about the cost. That is a write off. The reason I give them away is that it brings in folks who don't normally think about Santa. I volunteer at different places, schools, community activities, etc., just to get myself out there and noticed. A freebie will provide other leads that will lead to more leads. Pretty soon, you are well known and are sought by many.

This doesn't happen overnight so plan on spending a few months just to start. It will take at least 3 months of getting out and doing freebies before you will start to get noticed. If you continue this through the next season, you will see an increase. The more you do this year after year, the more you will notice that the word of mouth has gotten around and the more business you will have. If you stop, you will have to start the process all over again.

I noticed that it took three years to establish myself as a credible and trustworthy Santa and another two years to be sought out to be the Santa of choice for different places. Don't lose that credibility or you will have to start over. That was five years spent on building my business.

There are a lot of charities out there. Look up the local community and county services. They have orphanages, abused and battered spouses/ childrens' homes and homeless shelters. Look up the local hospitals and see what they have. Maybe they have a ward they would like you to visit.

Try the different churches, civic organizations, (e.g. Moose, Elks, Legions, VFW's, etc.) and see what they come up with. It isn't hard to find a lot of charitable organization. All you have to do is get out there and look. You can get with several food banks and assist in delivering food to needy families.

Chapter 14

Agents – Good and Bad

This is a double-pronged chapter to begin. First off, let me tell you about a few agents. These are the ones that send you prospective Santa job information and it is up to you to be first one to call back and accept the call. These potential jobs may come from different organizations you are in or they may come from a company or individual that is in the business of finding jobs for actors.

Besides Tim and Gary, there are several organizations that do this service for a fee. AORBS has sent out letters, FORBES has sent out letters to its members, Peachtree Santas and the Palm Tree Santas also communicates with their members and there are so many more. The more organizations you belong to, the better the opportunity of someone within that group sending out a note to everyone stating that they cannot make a performance and the first one that calls will get the action. Look up and join a Santa organization near you. Another nationwide company which I use occasionally is: www.nationwidesantas.com. Gina is very helpful and is willing to work with you.

Now there are others that you can use and I have used in the past. Instead of naming names, I would just like to state that most organizations that have clowns and other characters for hire will also peddle you if you desire. These types of organizations are constantly looking for talent and are looking for talent in specific areas.

There are a number of other types of agencies out there and they fall into two basic categories; ***Employment Agencies*** and ***Talent Agencies***. Both of them will get you exposure – but they will expose you to different types of clients and groups of potential clients. An employment agent will get you exposed to malls, home/corporate parties, overseas jobs, media advertisements and the occasional commercial. A talent agent is more likely to expose you to the film industry and television. Depending on what you are looking for and wanting to do, getting the right agent is important. Some agents are very local and only work in a certain county or city while others have expanded out more and cover multiple counties and states. Still others have expanded internationally. Have your passport ready and enjoy the travel.

Let's talk about payment for the agent. An employment agent will place a bid on a job and give the employee (Santa) a fixed amount. This amount is usually agreed upon up front and you know what to expect by the contract you sign. A talent agent will place a bid on a job and give the actor (Santa) a fixed quote, and then subtract the agent's commission from the quote given. Your contract with this agent will identify the commission rate they will take. Again, you will know up front what you will be paid.

If you use one of these agencies, make sure they have good contact information. Usually you will need to provide them with terrific pictures to get hired out. Use a professional photographer and have high quality photos for your agent. After all, it will be these photos that will give the potential client their first impression of you. Make it a good one.

This will get your foot in the door. It is than the agent's responsibility to sell you. If they are good at their job, they will sell you a lot of the time.

Do not, and I repeat DO NOT give any agent money up front to work for you. A good agent will get their money when they hire you out. Paying up front is usually a scam and even the best places that claim they have a school to teach you their method are not good to pay. What can they teach you that you don't already know about Santa?

I'll even wager that you know more than they do about that aspect of the business. If you don't have your own suit, you may need to pay something up front for the use of their suit.

You may need voice training and I recommend that. You may need some acting lessons, and I also recommend that. But find these on your own and don't take any courses contingent on having an agent.

What might you expect to pay an agent? Some agents are pricey while others are quite reasonable. I try to find one that charges a reasonable amount for my services and then doesn't take too high of a commission. I am hoping we can come to an agreement that volume will make them their money and not high prices. I made one such agent fairly wealthy one year until I found out he was charging 50% of the fee for his service. That is a bit much by any standard. He made well over $120,000 that season from all his Santas.

My current agents and I have a negotiated price. I get X amount of money for a certain type of visit and anything over that the agent can get from the client is theirs. That is a fair deal. Of course when it comes to movies, television or advertisement, we re-negotiate what I get and what my fair share would be. That begins at $500 per day and goes up from there depending on what is needed from me.

So, finding an agent is not difficult. If you look for a theatrical agent, you will be disappointed. They are only look for acting and modeling types. If you look for one that handles, clowns, the Easter Bunny, look-a-likes and other such types, you have a better chance of getting some performances from their efforts. These folks usually have websites and advertise year round to keep the clients informed. They also have a regular client list they canvass periodically to see if there is a need for their services.

One other point about agents! If you have more than one, your chances of being employed more often through the season, is higher. Having only one agent really limits your exposure. I personally have three right now and I am looking for at least two more. Why? Well like I stated before, I have more exposure with more agents. One may look through advertisements while another looks at family parties, still another looks at corporate events and yet another looks at grand openings or annual parties and parades. I just acquired an agent that specializes in conventions and such.

The more folks I can get out looking for me, the better I feel and the more work I end up with during the season. I don't mind telling an agent that because they took so long in getting job information to me that I cannot accept the work they found. I would rather turn down work than to not have any at all.

I even have the agents looking for charity events they can book me into and I will pass out their business cards if they give them to me. That will bring in more business for them and possible for me. Make sure they don't charge you if they don't get any payment.

Chapter 15

Stories and Other Goodies

I have found the following collections in my travels and visits with other Santas. They were more than willing to share. Where I know the author, credit is given. I take no credit in the creation or writing of them. Some folks have talent and then there is me. HO! HO! HO!

Also, this is only a small selection of my collection. I continue to collect all year round and would love to collect some more. The parodies of "Twas the night before Christmas" are a particular favorite of mine. I would love to add more in this area. The story at the end of this section is particularly nice and was written by an Australian friend.

A Christmas Carol

English author Charles Dickens created the classic holiday tale, A Christmas Carol. The story's message—the importance of charity and good will towards all humankind—struck a powerful chord in the United States and England and showed members of Victorian society the benefits of celebrating the holiday.

The family was also becoming less disciplined and more sensitive to the emotional needs of children during the early 1800s. Christmas provided families with a day when they could lavish attention—and gifts—on their children without appearing to "spoil" them.

As Americans began to embrace Christmas as a perfect family holiday, old customs were unearthed. People looked toward recent immigrants and Catholic and Episcopalian churches to see how the day should be celebrated. In the next 100 years, Americans built a Christmas tradition all their own that included pieces of many other customs, including decorating trees, sending holiday cards, and gift-giving.

Although most families quickly bought into the idea that they were celebrating Christmas how it had been done for centuries, Americans had really re-invented a holiday to fill the cultural needs of a growing nation.

Fun Versions

Twas the night before Christmas in the USA

Michael Raff

Twas the night before Christmas, and all through the skies,
Air defenses were up, with electronic eyes.
Combat pilots were nestled in ready-room beds,
As enemy silhouettes danced in their heads.

Every jet on the apron, each SAM in its tube,
was triply redundant, linked to the Blue Cube.
ELINT and AWACS gave coverage so dense
that nothing that flew could slip through our defense.

When out of the klaxon arose such a clatter
I dashed to the screen to see what was the matter;
I increased the gain and then, quick as a flash,
Fine adjusted the filters to damp out the hash.

And there found the source of the warning we'd heeded
an incoming blip, by eight escorts preceded.
"Alert status red!" went the word down the wire,
As we gave every system the codes that meant "FIRE!"

On Aegis! Up Patriot, Phalanx and Hawk,
And scramble our fighters--let's send the whole flock.
Launch decoys and missiles, use chaff by the yard!
Get the kitchen sink up! Call the National Guard!

They turned toward the target, moved toward it, converged.
Till the tracks on the radar all finally merged,
And the sky was lit up with a demonic light,
As the foe met his fate in the high arctic night.

So we sent out some reconnaissance to look for debris,
Yet all that they found, both on land and on sea
Were some toys, a red hat, a charred left leather boot,
Broken sleigh bells, white hair, and a deer's parachute.

Now it isn't quite Christmas, with Saint Nick shot down.
There are unhappy kids in each village and town.
For the Spirit of Christmas can't hope to evade
All the web of defenses we've carefully made.

But a crash program's on: Working hard, night and day,
All the elves are constructing a radar-proof sleigh.
So let's wait for next Christmas, in cheer and in health,
For the future has hope: Santa's coming by stealth!

Politically Correct Version

Author Unknown

'Twas the night before Christmas and Santa's a wreck...
How to live in a world that's politically correct?
His workers no longer would answer to "Elves"
"Vertically Challenged" they were calling themselves

And labor conditions at the North Pole
Were alleged by the union to stifle the soul

Four reindeer had vanished, without much propriety
Released to the wilds by the Humane Society

And equal employment had made it quite clear
That Santa had better not use just reindeer
So Dancer and Donner, Comet and Cupid
Were replaced with 4 pigs, and you know that looked stupid!

The runners had been removed from his sleigh;
The ruts were termed dangerous by the E P A
And people had started to call for the cops
When they heard sled noises on their roof-tops

Second-hand smoke from his pipe had his workers quite frightened
His fur trimmed red suit was called "Unenlightened"

And to show you the strangeness of life's ebbs and flows
Rudolf was suing over unauthorized use of his nose

And had gone on Geraldo, in front of the nation
Demanding millions in over-due compensation

So, half of the reindeer were gone; and his wife
Who suddenly said she'd enough of this life
Joined a self-help group, packed, and left in a whiz
Demanding from now on her title was Ms

And as for the gifts, why, he'd ne'er had a notion
That making a choice could cause so much commotion
Nothing of leather, nothing of fur
Which meant nothing for him. And nothing for her

Nothing that might be construed to pollute
Nothing to aim. Nothing to shoot
Nothing that clamored or made lots of noise
Nothing for just girls. Or just for boys
Nothing that claimed to be gender specific
Nothing that's warlike or non-pacific

No candy or sweets ... they were bad for the tooth
Nothing that seemed to embellish the truth
And fairy tales, while not yet forbidden
Were like Ken and Barbie, better off hidden

For they raised the hackles of those psychological
Who claimed the only good gift was ecological

No baseball, no football ... someone could get hurt;
Besides; playing sports exposed kids to dirt

Dolls were said to be sexist, and should be passé;
And Nintendo would rot your entire brain away

So Santa just stood there, disheveled, perplexed;
He just could not figure out what to do next

He tried to be merry, tried to be gay
But you've got to be careful with that word today
His sack was quite empty, limp to the ground;
Nothing fully acceptable was to be found

Something special was needed, a gift that he might
Give to all without angering the left or the right
A gift that would satisfy, with no indecision
Each group of people, every religion;

Every ethnicity, every hue
Everyone, everywhere ... even you
So here is that gift, it's price beyond worth ...
"May you and your loved ones enjoy peace on earth"

The Technical Version!

Author Unknown

'Twas the nocturnal segment of the diurnal period preceding the annual Yuletide celebration, and throughout our place of residence, kinetic activity was not in evidence among the possessors of this potential, including that species of domestic rodent known as Mus musculus.

Hosiery was meticulously suspended from the forward edge of the wood burning caloric apparatus, pursuant to our anticipatory pleasure regarding an imminent visitation from an eccentric philanthropist among whose folkloric appellations is the honorific title of St. Nicholas.

The prepubescent siblings, comfortably ensconced in their respective accommodations of repose, were experiencing subconscious visual hallucinations of variegated fruit confections moving rhythmically through their cerebrums.

My conjugal partner and I, attired in our nocturnal head coverings, were about to take slumberous advantage of the hibernal darkness when upon the avenaceous exterior portion of the grounds there ascended such a cacophony of dissonance that I felt compelled to arise with alacrity from my place of repose for the purpose of ascertaining the precise source thereof.

Hastening to the casement, I forthwith opened the barriers sealing this fenestration, noting thereupon that the lunar brilliance without, reflected as it was on the surface of a recent crystalline precipitation, might be said to rival that of the solar meridian itself - thus permitting my incredulous optical sensory organs to behold a miniature airborne runnered conveyance drawn by eight diminutive specimens of the genus Rangier, piloted by a minuscule, aged chauffeur so ebullient and nimble that it became instantly apparent to me that he was indeed our anticipated caller.

With his ungulate motive power travelling at what may possibly have been more vertiginous velocity than patriotic alar predators, he vociferated loudly, expelled breath musically through contracted labia, and addressed each of the octet by his or her respective cognomen - "Now Dasher, now Dancer..." et al. - guiding them to the uppermost exterior level of our abode, through which structure I could readily distinguish the concatenations of each of the 32 cloven pedal extremities.

As I retracted my cranium from its erstwhile location, and was performing a 180-degree pivot, our distinguished visitant achieved - with utmost celerity and via a downward leap - entry by way of the smoke passage.

He was clad entirely in animal pelts soiled by the ebony residue from oxidations of carboniferous fuels which had accumulated on the walls thereof. His resemblance to a street vendor I attributed largely to the plethora of assorted playthings which he bore dorsally in a commodious cloth receptacle.

His orbs were scintillate with reflected luminosity, while his sub maxillary dermal indentations gave every evidence of engaging amiability. The capillaries of his malar regions and nasal appurtenance were engorged with blood which suffused the subcutaneous layers, the former approximating the coloration of Albion's floral emblem, the latter that of the Prunus avium, or sweet cherry.

His amusing sub- and supralabials resembled nothing so much as a common loop knot, and their ambient hirsute facial adornment appeared like small, tabular and columnar crystals of frozen water.

Clenched firmly between his incisors was a smoking piece whose grey fumes, forming a tenuous ellipse about his occipital, were suggestive of a decorative seasonal circlet of holly. His visage was wider than it was high, and when he waxed audibly mirthful, his corpulent abdominal region undulated in the manner of impectinated fruit syrup in a hemispherical container.

He was, in short, neither more nor less than an obese, jocund, multigenarian gnome, the optical perception of whom rendered me visibly frolicsome despite every effort to refrain from so being. By rapidly lowering and then elevating one eyelid and rotating his head slightly to one side, he indicated that trepidation on my part was groundless.

Without utterance and with dispatch, he commenced filling the aforementioned appended hosiery with various of the aforementioned articles of merchandise extracted from his aforementioned previously dorsally transported cloth receptacle. Upon completion of this task, he executed an abrupt about-face, placed a single manual digit in lateral juxtaposition to his olfactory organ, inclined his cranium forward in a gesture of leave-taking, and forthwith effected his egress by renegotiating (in reverse) the smoke passage.

He then propelled himself in a short vector onto his conveyance, directed a musical expulsion of air through his contracted oral sphincter to the antlered quadrupeds of burden, and proceeded to soar aloft in a movement hitherto observable chiefly among the seed-bearing portions of a common weed.

But I overheard his parting exclamation, audible immediately prior to his vehiculation beyond the limits of visibility: "Ecstatic Yuletide to the planetary constituency, and to that self same assemblage, my sincerest wishes for a salubriously beneficial and gratifyingly pleasurable period between sunset and dawn."

A Microsoft Christmas

Author Unknown

'Twas the night before Christmas, when all through the house
Not a creature was stirring, except Papa's mouse.
The computer was humming, the icons were hopping,
As Papa did last minute Internet shopping.

The stockings were hung by the modem with care
In hope that St. Nicholas would bring new software.
The children were nestled all snug in their beds,
While visions of computer games danced in their heads.

PageMaker for Billy, and Quicken for Dan,
And Carmen Sandiego for Pamela Ann.
The letters to Santa had been sent out by Mom,
To santaclaus@toyshop.northpole.com -

Which has now been re-routed to Washington State
Because Santa's workshop has been bought by Bill Gates.
All the elves and reindeer have had to skedaddle
To flashy new quarters in suburban Seattle.

After centuries of a life that was simple and spare,
St. Nicholas is suddenly a new billionaire,
With a shiny red Porsche in the place of his sleigh,
And a house on Lake Washington that's just down the way

From where Bill has his mansion. The old fellow preens
In black Gucci boots and red Calvin Klein jeans.
The elves have stock options and desks with a view,
Where they write computer code for Johnny and Sue.

No more dolls or toy soldiers or little toy drums (ahem - pardon me)
No more dolls or tin soldiers or little toy drums

Will be under the tree, only compact disk ROMS
With the Microsoft label. So spin up your drive,
From now on Christmas runs only on Win95.

More rapid than eagles the competitors came,
And Bill whistled, and shouted, and called them by name.
"Now, ADOBE! Now, CLARIS! Now, INTUIT! too,
Now, APPLE! and NETSCAPE! you are all of you through,

It is Microsoft's SANTA that the kids can't resist,
It's the ultimate software with a traditional twist -
Recommended by no less than the jolly old elf,
And on the package, a picture of Santa himself.

Get 'em young, keep 'em long, is Microsoft's scheme,
And a merger with Santa is a marketer's dream.
To the top of the NASDAQ! to the top of the Dow!
Now dash away! dash away! dash away - wow!"

And Mama in her 'kerchief and I in my cap,
Had just settled down for a long winter's nap,
When out on the lawn there arose such a clatter,
The whir and the hum of our satellite platter,

As it turned toward that new Christmas star in the sky,
The SANTALITE owned by the Microsoft guy.
As I sprang from my bed and was turning around,
My computer turned on with a Jingle-Bells sound.

And there on the screen was a smiling Bill Gates
Next to jolly old Santa, two arm-in-arm mates.
And I heard them exclaim in voice so bright,
Have a Microsoft Christmas, and to all a good night.

A Red Neck Christmas

Author Unknown

'Twas the night before Christmas and all through the trailer
Not a creature was stirrin' 'cept a redneck named Taylor.
His first name was Bubba, Joe was his middle,
And a-runnin' down his chin was a trickle of spittle.
His socks, they were hung by the chimney with care,
And therefore there was a foul stench in the air.

Than Bubba got scared and rousted the boys.
There was Rufus, 12 Jim Bob was 11
Dud goin' on 10 Otis was 7.
John, George and Chucky Were 5, 4, and 3:
The twins were both girls so they let them be.

They jumped in their overalls, no need for a shirt,
Threw a hat on each head, then turned with a jerk.
They ran to the gun rack that hung on the wall.
There were 17 shotguns they grabbed them all.

Bubba said to the young'uns, "now hesh up ya'll!
The last thing we wanna do is wake up yer Maw."
Maw was expecting and needed her sleep,
So they crept out the door without making a peep.

They all looked around, and then they all spit.
The young'uns asked Bubba, "Paw, what is it?"
Bubba just stared he could not say a word.
This was just like all of The stories he'd heard.

It was Santy Claus on the roof, darn tootin'
But the boys didn't know they was about to start shootin'!
They aimed their shotguns and nearly made a mistake

That would have resulted in venison steak.
Bubba hollered out, "don't shoot, boys!"
That's Santy Claus And he's brought us some toys.

The dogs were a-barkin' and a-raisin' cain,
And Bubba whistled, and shouted, and called them by name.
"Down, Spot! shut up Bullet! quiet, Roscoe and Enos!
Git, Turnip and Tater and Sam and Bosco!"

"Git down from that porch! git down off that wall!
Quit shakin the trailer, or you'll make Santy fall!"
The dogs kept a-barkin' and wouldn't shut up,
And they trampled poor Pete Who was only a pup.

Santy opened his bag, And threw out some toys.
Bubba got most, but left a few for the boys.
Since the guns had been dropped he just might not die.

He jumped in his sleigh, told his reindeer to hurry.
The trailer started to wobble Santa started to worry.
Just as the reindeer got into the air,
The trailer collapsed, but Bubba didn't care.

He was busy lookin' at all his new toys.
Then a thought hit him, and he said to the boys:
"Go check on yer Maw, make sure she's all right.
That roof fallin' on her could-a hurt just a might."

But Maw was OK, and the girls were too.
They fixed up the trailer it looked good as new.
And as for Bubba, he liked Old St. Nick,
But Santa thought Bubba was a pure-in-tee hick!

Bubba had a nice Christmas, and the boys did, too.
And the Taylors wish a Yee Haw Merry Christmas to you!!!

'Twas The Night Before Christmas for Moms!

Written by Karen Spiegler. Originally published in "Maniac Moms: A Humorous Newsletter for Crazed Mothers" in December/1993.

Twas the night before Christmas, when all thru the abode
Only one creature was stirring, & she was cleaning the commode.
The children were finally sleeping, all snug in their beds,
while visions of Nintendo 64 & Barbie, flipped through their heads.

The dad was snoring in front of the TV,
with a half-constructed bicycle propped on his knee.
So only the mom heard the reindeer hooves clatter,
which made her sigh, "Now what is the matter?"

With toilet bowl brush still clutched in her hand,
She descended the stairs, & saw the old man.
He was covered with ashes & soot, which fell with a shrug,
"Oh great," muttered the mom, "Now I have to clean the rug."

"Ho Ho Ho!" cried Santa, "I'm glad you're awake."
"your gift was especially difficult to make."
"Thanks, Santa, but all I want is time alone."
"Exactly!" he chuckled, "So, I've made you a clone."

"A clone?" she muttered, "What good is that?"
"Run along, Santa, I've no time for chit chat."
Then out walked the clone - The mother's twin,
Same hair, same eyes, same double chin.

"She'll cook, she'll dust, she'll mop every mess.
You'll relax, take it easy, watch The Young & The Restless."
"Fantastic!" the mom cheered. "My dream has come true!"
"I'll shop, I'll read, I'll sleep a night through!"

From the room above, the youngest did fret.
"Mommy?! Come quickly, I'm scared & I'm wet."
The clone replied, "I'm coming, sweetheart."
"Hey," the mom smiled, "She sure knows her part."

The clone changed the small one & hummed her tune,
as she bundled the child in a blanket cocoon.
"You're the best mommy ever. I really love you."
The clone smiled & sighed, "And I love you, too."

The mom frowned & said, "Sorry, Santa, no deal."
That's my child's LOVE she is trying to steal."
Smiling wisely Santa said, "To me it is clear,
Only one loving mother is needed here."

The mom kissed her child & tucked her in bed.
"Thank You, Santa, for clearing my head.
I sometimes forget, it won't be very long,
when they'll be too old for my cradle & song."

The clock on the mantle began to chime.
Santa whispered to the clone, "It works every time."
With the clone by his side Santa said "Goodnight.
Merry Christmas, dear Mom, You will be all right."

Twas The Night Before Christmas for Dads

Author Unknown

On the night before Christmas,
It's still in the house.
My whole family is sleeping,
So I'm quiet like a mouse.

I look at my watch
And midnight is near.
I think I'll sneak out
For a cold glass of beer.

Down at the corner,
The crowd is so merry,
I end up by drinking
About twelve Tom 'n' Jerry.

I get to bed late and,
Gee whiz, how I'm sleeping,
When onto my bed,
Those darn kids come leaping!

They sit on my face
And they jump on my belly,
And I'm shivering all over
Like a bowl full of jelly.

They scream, "Merry Christmas!"
My poor wife and me,
We stumble downstairs
And she lights up the tree.

My head is explOdin or Wodeng!
My mouth tastes like a pickle!
I step on a skate
And fall on a tricycle!

Just before Christmas dinner,
I relax to a point,
Then relatives start swarming
All over the joint..

On Christmas, I hug
And I kiss my wife's mother.
The rest of the year,
We don't speak to each other.

After dinner, my aunt
And my wife's uncle Louie
Get into an argument;
They're both awful screwy!

Then all my wife's family
Say Louie is right,
And my goofy relations,
They join in the fight.

Back in the corner,
The radio's playing,
And over the racket,
Gabriel Hader is saying,

"Peace on Earth, everybody.
And good will toward men."
And, just at that moment,
Someone slugs Uncle Ben.

They all go outside whooping
So the neighbors will hear.
Oh, I'm so glad Merry Christmas
Comes just once a year!

A Soldier's Christmas

Written by By Major Bruce W. Lovely
This poem was written by Lt Col Lovely for Christmas Eve 1993 while assigned to US Forces Korea (USFK), Yongsan Garrison, Seoul, Korea.

Twas the night before Christmas, he lived all alone
In a one bedroom house made of plaster & stone.
I had come down the chimney with presents to give
And to see just who in this home did live.

I looked all about a strange sight I did see,
No tinsel, no presents, not even a tree.
No stocking by the fire, just boots filled with sand,
On the wall hung pictures of far distant lands.

With medals and badges, awards of all kind
A sober thought came through my mind.
For this house was different, so dark and dreary,
I knew I had found the home of a soldier, once I could see clearly.

I heard stories about them, I had to see more
So I walked down the hall and pushed open the door.
And there he lay sleeping silent alone,
Curled up on the floor in his one bedroom home.

His face so gentle, his room in such disorder,
Not how I pictured a United States soldier.
Was this the hero of whom I'd just read?
Curled up in his poncho, a floor for his bed?

His head was clean shaven, his weathered face tan,
I soon understood this was more then a man.
For I realized the families that I saw that night
Owed their lives to these men who were willing to fight.

Soon 'round the world, the children would play,
And grownups would celebrate on a bright Christmas day.
They all enjoyed freedom each month of the day,
Because of soldiers like this one lying here.

I couldn't help wonder how many lay alone
On a cold Christmas Eve in a land far from home.
Just the very thought brought a tear to my eye,
I dropped to my knees and started to cry.

The solder awakened and I heard a rough voice,
"Santa don't cry, this life is my choice;
I fight for freedom, I don't ask for more,
My life is my God, my country, my Corps."

With that he rolled over and drifted off into sleep,
I couldn't control it, I continued to weep.
I watched him for hours, so silent and still,
I noticed he shivered from the cold night's chill.

So I took off my jacket, the one made of red,
And I covered this Soldier from his toes to his head.
And I put on his T-shirt of gray and black,
With an eagle and an Army patch embroidered on back.

And although it barely fit me, I began to swell with pride,
And for a shining moment, I was United States Army deep inside.
I didn't want to leave him on that cold dark night,
This guardian of honor so willing to fight.

Then the soldier rolled over, whispered with a voice so clean and pure,
"Carry on Santa, it's Christmas day, all is secure."
One look at my watch, and I knew he was right,
Merry Christmas my friend, and to all a good night!

A Sailor's Christmas

Author Unknown

T'was the night before Christmas, the ship was out steaming,
Sailors stood watch while others were dreaming.
They lived in a crowd with rack s tight and small,
In an 80-man berthing, cramped one and all.

I had come down the stack with presents to give,
and to see inside just who might perhaps live.
I looked all about, a strange sight did I see,
No tinsel, no presents, not even a tree.

No stocking were hung, shinned boots close at hand,
On the bulkhead hung pictures of far distance land.
They had medals and badges and awards of all kind,
And a sober thought came into my mind.

For this place was different, so dark and so dreary,
I had found the house of a sailor, once I saw clearly.
A Sailor lay sleeping, silent and alone,
Curled up in a rack and dreaming of home.

The face was so gentle, the room squared away,
This was the United States Sailor today.
This was the hero I saw on TV,
Defending our country so we could be free.

I realized the families that I would visit this night,
Owed their lives to these Sailors lay willing to fight.
Soon round the world, the children would play,
And grownups would celebrate on Christmas Day.

They all enjoyed freedom each day of the year,
Because of the Sailor, like the one lying here.
I couldn't help wonder how many lay alone,
On a cold Christmas Eve on a sea, far from home.

The very thought brought a tear to my eye,
I dropped to my knees and started to Cry.
The Sailor awakened and I heard a calm voice,
"Santa, don't cry, this life is my choice."

"Defending the seas all days of the year,
So others may live and be free with no fear."
I thought for a moment, what a difficult road,
To live a life guided by honor and code.

After all it's Christmas Eve and the ship's under way!
But freedom isn't free and it's sailors who pay.
The Sailor say's to our country "be free and sleep tight,
No harm will come, not on my watch and not on this night.

The Sailor rolled over and drifted to sleep,
I couldn't control, I continued to weep.
I kept watch for hours, so silent, so still,
I watchd as the Sailor shivered from the night's cold chill.

I didn't want to leave on that cold dark night,
This guardian of honor so willing to fight.
The Sailor rolled over and with a voice strong and sure,
Commanded, "Cary on Santa, It's Christmas and all is secure!"

A Fireman's Night Before Christmas

Author Unknown

Twas the night before Christmas and all through the town,
The fire siren echoed blaring its sound.
The firefighter's came running from far and from near,
And raced to the trucks quickly donning their gear.

And I in my bunkers my boots and my hat,
Jumped to the engine to see where the fire's at.
Down the corner of Fifth and of Oak,
The dispatcher informed us of a house filled with smoke.

Smoke poured from the sides, from up and from down,
Yet up on the roof there was none to be found.
So up to the rooftop we raised up a ladder,
And climbed to the top to see what was the matter.

I came to the chimney and what did I see.
But a fellow in red stuff past his knees.
Well we tugged and we pulled until he came out
Then he winked with his eye and side with a shout.

"These darn newfangled chimneys they make them too small,
For a fellow as I, not skinny at all."
With a twitch of his nose he dashed to his sleigh,
And called to his reindeer, "away now, away."

As we rolled up our hoses he flew out of sight, saying
"God bless our firefighters" and to all a good night.

Cops Night Before Christmas

Author Unknown

'Twas the night before Christmas,
Yet he slept all alone.
In a one-bedroom house,
Made of plaster and stone.

I had come down the chimney
With presents to give,
And to see just what man
In this small house did live.

I looked all about,
What a strange site to see.
No tinsel, no presents,
Not even a tree.

No stockings by the fire,
Just boots spit shined bright.
Then something else gleamed,
Reflecting the moonlight.

They were medals and badges,
Awards of all kinds.
And a sobering thought
Soon came to my mind.

For this house was different,
Unlike any I'd topped.
This was the home of an officer,
The home of a cop.

I'd heard stories about "them",
And I had to see more.
So I walked down the hall,
And pushed open the door.

And there he lay sleeping,
Silent and alone.
Curled up on his bed,
In this one-bedroom home.

He seemed so gentle,
His face weathered tan,
I soon understood
That this was more than a man.

For I realized the families
That I saw this night,
Owed their lives to these people
Who were willing to fight.

Soon round the nation
The children would play,
And grown-ups would celebrate
On a bright Christmas day.

They all enjoyed safety
Each month, and all year
Because of officers like him,
This man lying here.

I couldn't help wonder
How many were on patrol.
All alone on Christmas Eve
Out in the shivering cold.

I watched him for hours,
So silent and so still,
And I noticed that he shivered,
From the cold nights chill.

So I took off my jacket,
The one made of red.
And I covered this officer
From his toes to his head.

Then I put on His jacket
With the badge of silver and gold,
With the words "Police Officer"
Emblazoned so bold.

Though it barely fit me
I began to swell with pride,
And for one shining moment
I was an officer inside.

I didn't want to leave him
So quiet in the night,
This guardian of justice,
So willing to fight.

But half asleep he rolled over,
And in a voice clean and pure
Said, "Carry on Santa - it's Christmas,
All here is secure."

One look at my watch
And I knew he was right.
Merry Christmas my friend,
Code four and good night.

Twas The Computer Nerds Night Before Christmas

Author Unknown

T'was the night before Christmas, when all through the Net,
There were hacker's a surfing. Nerds? Yeah, you bet.
The e-mails were stacked by the modem with care,
In hopes that St. Nicholas soon would be there.

The newbies were nestled all snug by their screens,
While visions of Java danced in their dreams.
My wife on the sofa and me with a snack,
We just settled down at my Mac.

When out in the Web there arose such a clatter,
I jumped to the site to see what was the matter.
To a new page my Mac flew like a flash,
Then made a slight gurgle. It started to crash!!

I gasped at the thought and started to grouse,
Then turned my head sideways and clicked on my mouse.
When what to my wondering eyes should appear,
My Mac jumped to a page that wasn't quite clear.
When the image resolved, so bright and so quick,
I knew in a moment it must be St. Nick!

More rapid than mainframes, more graphics they came,
Then Nick glanced toward my screen, my Mac called them by name;
'Now Compaq! Now Acer!', my speaker did reel;
'On Apple! On Gateway!' Santa started to squeal!
'Jump onto the circuits! And into the chip!
Now speed it up! Speed it up! Make this thing hip!'

The screen gave a flicker, he was into my 'Ram',
Then into my room rose a full hologram!
He was dressed in all red, from his head to his shoes,
Which were black (the white socks he really should lose).

He pulled out some discs he had stored in his backpack.
Santa looked like a dude who was rarin' to hack!
His eyes, how they twinkled! His glasses, how techno!
This ain't the same Santa that I used to know!

With a wink of his eye and a nod of his head,
Santa soon let me know I had nothing to dread.
He spoke not a word, gave my Mac a quick poke,
And accessed my C drive with only a stroke.

He defragged my hard drive, and added a 'Dimm',
Then threw in some cool games, just on a whim!
He worked without noise, his fingers they flew!
He distorted some pictures with Kai's Power Goo!

He updated Office, Excel and Quicken,
Then added a screensaver with a red clucking chicken!
My eyes widened a bit, my mouth stood agape,
As he added the latest version of Netscape.
The drive gave a whirl, as if it were pleased,
St. Nick coyly smiled, the computer appeased.

Then placing his finger on the bridge of his nose,
Santa turned into nothing but ones and zeros!
He flew back into my screen and through my uplink,
Back into the net with barely a blink.
But I heard his sweet voice as he flew from my sight,
'Happy surfing to all, and to all a good byte!'

Twas the Night Before Finals

by Chad W. Sclove

Twas the night before finals,
And all through the college,
The students were praying
For last minute knowledge.

Most were quite sleepy,
But none touched their beds,
While visions of essays
Danced in their heads.

Out in the taverns,
A few were still drinking,
And hoping that liquor
Would loosen up their thinking.

In my own apartment,
I had been pacing,
And dreading exams
I soon would be facing.

My roommate was speechless,
His nose in his books,
And my comments to him
Drew unfriendly looks.

I drained all the coffee,
And brewed a new pot,
No longer caring
That my nerves were shot.

I stared at my notes,
But my thoughts were muddy,
My eyes went ablur,
I just couldn't study.

"Some pizza might help,"
I said with a shiver,
But each place I called
Refused to deliver.

I'd nearly concluded
That life was too cruel,
With futures depending
On grades had in school.

When all of a sudden,
Our door opened wide,
And Patron Saint Put It Off
Ambled inside.

His spirit was careless,
His manner was mellow,
He started to bellow:

"What kind of student
Would make such a fuss,
To toss back at teachers
What they tossed at us?"

"On Cliff Notes! On Crib Notes!
On last year's exams!
On Wingit and Slingit,
And last minute crams!"

His message delivered,
He vanished from sight,
But we heard him laughing
Outside in the night.

Twas the Night Before Christmas for Teachers

By Joyce Luke

‘Twas the week before Christmas and all through the school
Not a pupil was silent, no matter what rule.
The children were busy with paper and paste;
The mess that they made with it couldn’t be faced.

The teacher half frantic and almost in tears,
Had just settled down to work with her dears,
When out in the hall there arose such a clatter
up sprang the kids to see what was the matter!

Away to the door they all flew like a flash;
The one who was leading went down with a crash.
Then what to their wondering eyes did appear
But a green Christmas tree! (To decorate I fear!)

When the teacher saw this, she almost grew sick.
She knew in a moment it must be Old Nick!
She ran to the door (all her efforts were vain)
But she shouted, and stamped, and she called them by name;

“Now Tommy! Now Sandy, Now Judy and Harry!
Stop Billy! Stop Robert! Stop Donny and Sherry!
Now get to your places get away from the hall
Now get away! Get away! Get away all!

As leaves that before the wild hurricane fly
The pupils, pell mell, started scurrying by.
They ran to the blackboard and skipped down the aisle;
Their faces were shining and each had a smile.

First came a basket of popcorn to string
Then came the Christmas tree (menacing thing).
As the tree was brought in there arose a great shout;
The pupils were merrily romping about.

The state they were in could lead to a riot;
The teacher was sure, if allowed, they would try it.
Her nerves how they jangled! Her temples were throbbing!
The rush of her breath sounded almost like sobbing!

The lines of her face were as fixed as a mask;
It was plain that she didn't feel up to her task.
The look in her eye would have tamed a wild steer,
But the children ignored it; they did every year.

A tear from her eye and a shake of her head
Soon led me to think that she wished she were dead.
She spoke not a word but went straight to her work,
Strung all the popcorn which broke with a jerk.

But at last it was finished and placed on the tree;
Then came the bell and the children were free.
Their shrill little voices soon faded away
And peace was restored at the end of the day.

As she looked at the Christmas tree glistening and tall,
She smiled as she whispered,
"Merry Christmas to All"

'Twas the night before Christmas and all through the kitchen ...

Author Unknown

I was cooking and baking and moanin' and bitchin'.
I've been here for hours, I can't stop to rest.
This room's a disaster, just look at this mess!

Tomorrow I've got thirty people to feed.
They expect all the trimmings. Who cares what I need!

My feet are both blistered, I've got cramps in my legs.
The cat just knocked over a bowl full of eggs.

There's a knock at the door and the telephone's ringing.
Frosting drips on the counter as the microwave's dinging.

Two pies in the oven, dessert's almost done;
My cookbook is soiled with butter and crumbs.

I've had all I can stand, I can't take anymore;
Then in walks my husband, spilling drink on the floor.

He weaves and he wobbles, his balance unsteady;
then grins as he chuckles, "The egg nog is ready!"

He looks all around and with total regret, says,
"What's taking so long....aren't you through in here yet?!!!!"

As quick as a flash I reach for a knife;
He loses an earlobe; I wanted his life!

He flees from the room in terror and pain and screams,
"MY GOD WOMAN, YOU'RE GOING INSANE!!"

OK! Now what was I doing, and what is that smell?
Oh darn it's the pies! They're burned all to hell!

I hate to admit when I make a mistake,
but I put them on BROIL instead of on BAKE.

What else can go wrong? Is there still more ahead?
If this is good living, I'd rather be dead.

Lord, don't get me wrong, I love holidays;
It just leaves me exhausted, all shaky and dazed.

But I promise you one thing, If I live 'til next year,
You won't find me pulling my hair out, in here.

I'll hire a maid, a cook, and a waiter;
and if that doesn't work, I'LL HAVE IT ALL CATERED!

The Night Before Christmas for Dieters

Author Unknown

'Twas the night before Christmas and all round my hips
Were Fannie May candies that sneaked past my lips.
Fudge brownies were stored in the freezer with care
In hopes that my thighs would forget they were there.

While Mama in her girdle and I in chin straps
Had just settled down to sugar-borne naps.
When out in the pantry there arose such a clatter
I sprang from my bed to see what was the matter.

Away to the kitchen I flew like a flash,
Tore open the icebox then threw up the sash.
The marshmallow look of the new-fallen snow
Sent thoughts of a binge to my body below.

When what to my wandering eyes should appear
A marzipan Santa with eight chocolate reindeer!
That huge chunk of candy so luscious and slick
I knew in a second that I'd wind up sick.

The sweet-coated santa, those sugared reindeer
I closed my eyes tightly but still I could hear;
On Pritzker, on Stillman, on weak one, on TOPS
A Weight Watcher dropout from sugar detox.

From the top of the scales to the top of the hall
Now dash away pounds now dash away all.
Dressed up in Lane Bryant from my head to nightdress
My clothes were all bulging from too much excess.

My droll little mouth and my round little belly,
They shook when I laughed like a bowl full of jelly.

I spoke not a word but went straight to my work
Ate all of the candy then turned with a jerk.

And laying a finger beside my heartburn
Gave a quick nod toward the bedroom I turned.
I eased into bed, to the heavens I cry–
If temptation's removed I'll get thin by and by.

And I mumbled again as I turned for the night
In the morning I'll starve… 'til I take that first bite!

Twas the Night in the Casino

Bill Burton

'Twas the night before Christmas.
I hit the casino.
I went there to play,
More than just Keno.

The dealers were assigned to their tables with care.
Chatting with patrons who were gambling there.
I walked to the Slots and started to Play.
I had a feeling this would be my Day.

I put in my coins and gave the handle a yank.
As the coins started dropping I heard them go "Clank."
The wheels started spinning, they whirled and they glowed.
Alas! I saw three 7's, lined up in a row.

The lights started flashing, the bells all were ringing,
Out came the Jackpot with that old familiar jingling.
I reached down and scooped up all of my winnings.
I headed for the tables. I couldn't stop grinning.

A table was open so I sat for Blackjack,
Put down money for chips and purchased a stack.
The Dealer was smiling, I was having such fun.
Drew a Jack then an Ace, I had Twenty One!

Now off to Roulette but which numbers to choose?
The way things were going I just couldn't lose.
I watched the ball spinning, it clicked and it Popped.
Right into my number, that little ball dropped.

"Thirty five to One", the dealer pushed me my chips.
Then she said, "Thanks!" for the toke that I flipped.
Then out on the floor, I heard such a clatter.
I rushed to the Craps Table, to see what was the matter.

There was this Fat Guy so lively and quick,
I thought to myself, he looks like Saint Nick.
I watched the dice as they flew from his hand.
He made his point, ever time they'd land.

"Place the six and the eight and a dollar on YO!
"He blew on the dice before letting them go.
"To some these dice are more fun than toys.
I almost forgot, hard six for the boys!"

He handled the bones so smooth and so swift.
The timing was right, to ask for a gift.
"Oh Santa please share some of your lucky charm."
He whispered to me, as he took my arm. "If you want to keep winning when rolling the dice,
Just listen to Santa and heed my advice.
""I've learned from the Experts, Scoblete, Burton and Wong.
The secret of winning is PRACTICE hard and long."

"You MUST use your head and this is no fable.
If your Luck starts to turn, You must leave the table"
In the Blink of an eye he was headed for the door.
I pleaded with Santa, "Please, Tell me more!"

He called back to me
as he flew out of sight.
"Every day will be Christmas.
If you learn to play the game right"

'Twas The Night Before Christmas, Legal Version

Author Unknown

Whereas, on or about the night prior to Christmas, there did occur at a certain improved piece of real property (hereinafter "the House") a general lack of stirring by all creatures therein, including, but not limited to a mouse.

A variety of foot apparel, e.g. stocking, socks, etc., had been affixed by and around the chimney in said House in the hope and/or belief that St. Nick a/k/a/ St. Nicholas a/k/a/ Santa Claus (hereinafter "Claus") would arrive at sometime thereafter.

The minor residents, i.e. the children, of the aforementioned House, were located in their individual beds and were engaged in nocturnal hallucinations, i.e. dreams, wherein vision of confectionery treats, including, but not limited to, candies, nuts and/or sugar plums, did dance, cavort and otherwise appear in said dreams.

Whereupon the party of the first part (sometimes hereinafter referred to as "I"), being the joint-owner in fee simple of the House with the parts of the second part (hereinafter "Mamma"), and said Mamma had retired for a sustained period of sleep. (At such time, the parties were clad in various forms of headgear, e.g. kerchief and cap.)

Suddenly, and without prior notice or warning, there did occur upon the unimproved real property adjacent and appurtent to said House, i.e. the lawn, a certain disruption of unknown nature, cause and/or circumstance. The party of the first part did immediately rush to a window in the House to investigate the cause of such disturbance.

At that time, the party of the first part did observe, with some degree of wonder and/or disbelief, a miniature sleigh (hereinafter the "Vehicle") being pulled and/or drawn very rapidly through the air by approximately eight (8) reindeer. The driver of the Vehicle appeared to be and in fact was, the previously referenced Claus.

Said Claus was providing specific direction, instruction and guidance to the approximately eight (8) reindeer and specifically identified the animal co-conspirators by name: Dasher, Dancer, Prancer, Vixen,

Comet, Cupid, Donder and Blitzen (hereinafter the "Deer"). (Upon information and belief, it is further asserted that an additional co-conspirator named Rudolph may have been involved.)

The party of the first part witnessed Claus, the Vehicle and the Deer intentionally and willfully trespass upon the roofs of several residences located adjacent to and in the vicinity of the House, and noted that the Vehicle was heavily laden with packages, toys and other items of unknown origin or nature. Suddenly, without prior invitation or permission, either express or implied, the Vehicle arrived at the House, and Claus entered said House via the chimney.

Said Claus was clad in a red fur suit, which was partially covered with residue from the chimney, and he carried a large sack containing a portion of the aforementioned packages, toys, and other unknown items. He was smoking what appeared to be tobacco in a small pipe in blatant violation of local ordinances and health regulations.

Claus did not speak, but immediately began to fill the stocking of the minor children, which hung adjacent to the chimney, with toys and other small gifts. (Said items did not, however, constitute "gifts" to said minor pursuant to the applicable provisions of the U.S. Tax Code.) Upon completion of such task, Claus touched the side of his nose and flew, rose and/or ascended up the chimney of the House to the roof where the Vehicle and Deer waited and/or served as "lookouts." Claus immediately departed for an unknown destination.

However, prior to the departure of the Vehicle, Deer and Claus from said House, the party of the first part did hear Claus state and/or exclaim: "Merry Christmas to all and to all a good night!" Or words to that effect.

The Night Before Chanukah

Author Unknown

'Twas the night before Chanukah, boichiks and maidels
Not a sound could be heard, not even the dreidels
The menorah was set by the chimney alight
In the kitchen, the Bubbie was hopping a bite
Salami, Pastrami, a glaisele tay
And zoyere pickles mit bagels-- Oy vay!

Gezint and geschmock the kinderlach felt
While dreaming of taiglach and Chanukah gelt
The alarm clock was sitting, a kloppin' and tickin'
And Bubbie was carving a shtickele chicken
A tummel arose, like the wildest k'duchas
Santa had fallen right on his tuchas!

I put on my slippers, ains, tzvay, drei
While Bubbie was eating herring on rye
I grabbed for my bathrobe and buttoned my gottkes
And Bubbie was just devouring the latkes
To the window I ran, and to my surprise
A little red yarmulka greeted my eyes.

When he got to the door and saw the menorah
"Yiddishe kinder," he cried, "Kenahorah!"
I thought I was in a Goyishe hoise!
As long as I'm here, I'll leave a few toys."
"Come into the kitchen, I'll get you a dish
Mit a gupel, a leffel, and a shtickele fish."

With smacks of delight he started his fressen
Chopped liver, knaidlach, and kreplach gegessen
Along with his meal he had a few schnapps
When it came to eating, this boy sure was tops
He asked for some knishes with pepper and salt
But they were so hot he yelled out "Gevalt!"

He loosened his hoysen and ran from the tish
"Your koshereh meals are simply delish!"
As he went through the door he said "See y'all later
I'll be back next Pesach in time for the seder!"
So, hutzmir and zeitzmir and "Bleibtz mir gezint"
he called out cheerily into the wind.

More rapid than eagles, his prancers they came
As he whistled and shouted and called them by name
"Come, Izzie, now Moishe, now Yossel and Sammy!
On Oyving, and Maxie, and Hymie and Manny!"
He gave a geshrai, as he drove out of sight
"A gut yontiff to all, and to all a good night!"

`Twas Da Night Befo` Christmas

Author Unknown

Twas da night befo' Christmas and all in the hood
Not a homie was stirring cuz it was all good
The tube socks was hung on the window sill
and we all had smiles up on our grill

Mookie and BeBe was snug in the crib
in the back bedroom cuz that's how we live
and moms in her do-rag and me with my nine
had just gotten busy cuz girlfriend is fine

All of a sudden a lowrider rolled by
Bumpin phat beats cuz the system's fly
I bounced to the window at a quarter pas'
Bout ready to pop a cap in somebody's--
well anyway

I yelled to my lady, Yo peep this!
She said, Stop frontin just mind yo' bidness
I said, for real doe, come check dis out
We weren't even buggin, no worries, no doubt

Cuz bumpin an thumpin' from around da way
Was Santa, 8 reindeer and a sleigh
Da beats was kickin, da ride was phat
I said, Yo red Dawg, you all that!

He threw up a sign and yelled to his boyz,
"Ay yo, give it up, let's make some noise!
To the top of the projects and across the strip mall,
We gots ta go, I got a booty call!"

He pulled up his ride on the top a da roof
and sippin on a 40, he busted a move
I yelled up to Santa, "Yo ain't got no stack!"
he said, "Damn homie, deese projects is wack!

But don't worry black, cuz I gots da skillz
I learnt back when I hadda pay da billz."
Out from his bag he pulled 3 small tings
a credit card, a knife, and a bobby pin.

he slid down the fire escape smoove as a cat
and busted the window with a b-ball bat
I said, "Whassup, Santa? Whydya bust my place?"
he said,"You best get on up out my face!"

His threads was all leatha, his chains was all gold
His sneaks was Puma and they was 5 years old
He dropped down the duffle, Clippers logo on the side
Santa broke out da loot and my mouf popped open wide.

A wink of his eye and a shine off his god toof
He cabbage patched his way back onto the roof
He jumped in his hooptie with rims made of chrome
To tap that booty waitin at home

and all I heard as he cruised outta sight
was a loud and hearty.....
"WEEESST SIIIDE!!!!!!!"

Twas The Night Before Christmas and Santa Was Pissed

Author Unknown

T'was the night before Christmas – Old Santa was pissed
He cussed out the elves and threw down his list
Miserable little brats, ungrateful little jerks
I have good mind to scrap the whole works

I've busted my ass for damn near a year
Instead of "Thanks Santa" – what do I hear
The old lady bitches cause I work late at night
The elves want more money – The reindeer all fight

Rudolph got drunk and goosed all the maids
Donner is pregnant and Vixen has AIDS
And just when I thought that things would get better
Those a**holes from IRS sent me a letter

They say I owe taxes – if that ain't damn funny
Who the hell ever sent Santa Clause any money
And the kids these days – they all are the pits
They want the impossible …Those mean little sh*ts

I spent a whole year making wagons and sleds
Assembling dolls…Their arms, legs and heads
I made a ton of yo yo's – No request for them
They want computers and robots…they think I'm IBM!

If you think that's bad…just picture this
Try holding those brats…with their pants full of piss
They pull on my nose – they grab at my beard
And if I don't smile..the parents think I'm weird

Flying through the air…dodging the trees
Falling down chimneys and skinning my knees
I'm quitting this job…there's just no enjoyment
I'll sit on my fat ass and draw unemployment
There's no Christmas this year… now you know the reason
I found me a blonde… I'm going SOUTH for the season!!

'Twas The Day After Christmas

David Frank

'Twas the day after Christmas and all through the house
Children sat slack-jawed, bored on the couch.
Wrappings and toys littered the floor,
An incredible mess that I did abhor.

With Mom in her robe and I in my jeans,
We waded in to get the place clean.
When suddenly the doorbell: it started to clatter,
I sprang to the Security-View to check out the matter.

The new-fallen snow, now blackened with soot,
Was trampled and icy and treacherous to foot.
But suddenly in view, did I gasp and pant:
An unhappy bill collector and eight tiny accountants.

The door flew open and in they came,
Stern-looking men with bills in my name.
On Discover, on Visa, on American Express,
On Mastercard too, I sadly confess,

Right to my limits, then beyond my net worth,
Over the top I had charged, in a frenzy of mirth.
The black-suited men, so somber, so strict,
I wondered why me that they had first picked.

They stared at me with a look I couldn't miss,
That said "Buddy, when are you for paying for this?"
I shrugged my shoulders, but then I grew bolder,
Went to the cabinet and pulled out a folder.

"As you can see," I said with a smile,
"It's bankruptcy that I'll have to file!"
And with a swoop of my arm, my middle digit extended
I threw the bills in the fire: the matter had ended.

The scent of burnt ash came to my nose,
As up the chimney my credit-worthiness rose.
Without another word they turned and walked out,
Got into their limos, but one gave a shout:

"You may think that's the answer to all of your fears,
But it's nothing you'll charge for at least seven years!

T'was The Week After Christmas

Author Unknown

'Twas the week after Christmas, and all through the house
Nothing would fit me, not even a blouse.

The cookies I'd nibble, the eggnog I'd taste
All the holiday parties had gone to my waist.

When I got on the scales, there arose such a number!
When I walked to the store (less a walk than a lumber).

I'd remember the marvelous meals I'd prepared;
The gravies and sauces and beef nicely rared...

The wine and the rum balls, the bread and the cheese
And the way I'd never said, "No thank you, please."

As I dressed myself in my husband's old shirt
And prepared once again to battle the dirt...

I said to myself, as I only can
"You can't spend a winter dressed like a man!"

So...away with the last of the sour cream dip,
Get rid of the fruit cake, every cracker and chip.

Every last bit of food that I like must be banished
'Till all the additional ounces have vanished.

I won't have a cookie, not even a lick,
I'll want only to chew on a long celery stick.

I won't have hot biscuits, or cornbread, or pie,
I'll munch on a carrot and quietly cry.

I'm hungry, I'm lonesome, and life is a bore...
But isn't that what January is for?

Unable to giggle, no longer a riot
Happy New Years to All and to All a Good Diet

Christmas Comedy

Provided by some friends

How do you know Santa has to be a man?
No woman is going to wear the same outfit year after year.

What did the reindeer say before launching into his comedy routine?
This will sleigh you.

When is a boat like a pile of snow?
When it's adrift.

What do you call the fear of getting stuck in a chimney?
Santaclaustrophobia

How do snowmen get around?
On their icicles.

What does Santa call reindeer that don't work?
Dinner.

Why was Santa's little helper depressed?
Because he had low 'elf' esteem.

T'was the night before Christmas and all through the house, Not a creature was stirring, not even a mouse. The stockings were hung by the chimney with care. They'd been worn all week and needed the air.

Did you know that according to the song, "Rudolph the Red-Nosed Reindeer", Santa has eleven reindeer? Sure, in the introduction it goes "There's Dasher and Dancer and Prancer and Vixen, Comet and Cupid and Donner and Blitzen..." That makes eight reindeer. Then there's Rudolph, of course, so that makes nine. Then there's Olive. You know,

"Olive the other reindeer used to laugh..." That makes ten. The eleventh is Howe. You know, "Then Howe the reindeer loved him..." Eleven reindeer. The proof is in the song!

What do you call Frosty the Snowman in May?
A puddle!

Where do reindeer go to dance?
Christmas balls!

It's a romantic full moon, when Pedro said, "Hey, mamacita, let's do Weeweechu."
Oh no, not now, let's look at the moon!" said Rosita.
Oh, c'mon baby, let's you and I do Weeweechu. I love you and it's the perfect time," Pedro begged.
"But I wanna just hold your hand and watch the moon." replied Rosita.
Please, corazoncito, just once, do Weeweechu with me."
Rosita looked at Pedro and said, "OK, one time, we'll do Weeweechu."
Pedro grabbed his guitar and they both sang.....
"Weeweechu a Merry Christmas, Weeweechu a Merry Christmas, Weeweechu a Merry Christmas, and a Happy New Year."

Why does Santa always go down the chimney?
Because it soots him!

Where does Santa stay when he's on holidays?
At a Ho-ho-tel!

What does Mrs. Claus sing to Santy on his birthday?
"Freeze a jolly good fellow!"

What does Santa put on his toast?
"Jingle Jam"

What do you get if you cross Father Christmas with a duck?
A Christmas Quacker!

An honest politician, a kind lawyer and Santa Claus were walking down the street and saw a $20 bill. Which one picked it up??
Santa! The other two don't exist!

What do you do if Santa Claus gets stuck in your chimney?
Pour Santa flush on him!

What does Santa say to the toys on Christmas Eve?
Okay everyone, sack time!

Who delivers Christmas presents to pets?
Why, Santa Paws of course

Why does Santa like to work in his garden?
Because he likes to hoe, hoe, hoe!

What do you call a kitty on the beach on Christmas morning?
Sandy Claws!

Who delivers presents to dentist offices?
Santa Jaws!

Who delivers Christmas presents to elephants?
Elephanta Claus!

What do you get if Santa comes down the chimney while the fire is still burning?
Crispy Kringle!

Why does St. Nicholas have a white beard?
So he can hide at the North Pole!

What do you call Santa when he has no money?
Saint "Nickel"-less!

What smells most in a chimney?
Santa's nose!

What does Kris Kringle like to get when he goes to the donut shop?
A jolly roll!

What do you call someone who doesn't believe in Father Christmas?
A rebel without a Claus!

What is invisible but smells like milk and cookies?
Kris Kringle burps!

What did Santa get when he crossed a woodpecker with Kleenex?
Rapping paper!

What does Santa like to have for breakfast?
Mistle-"toast"!

Why does Santa take presents to children around the world?
Because the presents won't take themselves!

What does Santa use when he goes fishing?
His north pole!

How do we know Santa is such a good race car driver?
Because he's always in the pole position!

What is twenty feet tall, has sharp teeth and goes Ho Ho Ho?
Tyranno-Santa Rex!

What's red & white and red & white and red & white?
Santa rolling down a hill!

What did Santa say to Mrs. Claus when he looked out the window?
Looks like "rain", "Dear"!

What's red and green and flies?
An airsick Santa Claus!

How does Saint Nick take pictures?
With his North "Pole"-aroid!

Why does Santa's sleigh get such good mileage?
Because it has long-distance runners on each side!

What goes Ho, Ho, Swoosh! Ho, Ho, Swoosh?
Santa caught in a revolving door!

What kind of motorcycle does Santy ride?
A "Holly" Davidson!

Where does Father Christmas go to vote?
The North Poll!

What's red and white and falls down the chimney?
Santa Klutz!

What do you call Saint Nick after he has come down the chimney?
Cinder Claus!

What nationality is Santa Claus?
North Polish!

Why does Santa owe everything to the elves?
Because he is an elf-made man!

What goes oh, oh, oh?
Santa Claus walking backwards!

How many chimneys does Saint Nick go down?
Stacks!

What do you call Santa's Helpers?
Subordinate Clauses

What do you get when you cross a Snowman with a Vampire?
Frostbite

What does Santa get if he gets stuck in a chimney?
Claustrophobic!

What would you call Father Christmas if he became a detective?
Santa Clues!

Questions and Some Answers

Children are going to ask you the strangest questions. They are quite unafraid as a rule to ask the most embarrassing and at times the most heart wrenching questions.

Art Linkletter is a famous entertainment personality and he had a saying that "Kids say the darndest things." For years he had a Radio and then Television program interviewing children. He would ask a question and the children would respond in their own innocent way. He never knew what the answers would be except they would be spontaneous and often hilarious.

Today children are very intelligent and seek to solve the riddles of how Santa does things. You must prepare yourself for these questions with answers to establish yourself as the real Santa Claus.

Here are some of the most asked questions:

1. Typical questions from children
    a. **Where are your reindeer?**
        - Now that's a very good question. The reindeer are at a farm not too far from here and the farmers are feeding them special corn so they can be real strong to pull my sleigh.

    b. **How do you get down the chimney without getting burned?**
        - I knew you were going to ask me that so I am going to share a secret with you. One of my elves is a bit of a magician and he mixed up some magic dust. I sprinkle it down a chimney and the fire is out. When I am ready to leave, I put my finger aside my nose and up the chimney I go. I sprinkle some magic dust down the chimney and everything is as it was.

    c. **How many elves do you have?**
        - (Santa chuckle) I don't' know if we ever stopped to count how many elves at the North Pole. I do know we

are building more factories and houses so the elves can keep up with the demand for toys.

d. **How can you eat all those cookies and not be fat?**
   - I love to eat cookies but Mrs. Claus has asked me to watch my diet. I take a bite of a cookie here and there and some places I eat them all. I am trying to listen to Mrs. Claus but I sure love cookies and milk.

e. **Who is your favorite reindeer?**
   - Now that's a tough question. Lets see, there is Dasher, Dancer, Prancer, Vixen, Comet, Cupid, Donder, Blitzen, and Rudolph. I really like them all. But did you know that Dasher likes pickles?

f. **What do you feed your reindeer?**
   - Not too many people know this but one of my elves grows some magical corn. We feed the reindeer the corns so on Christmas Eve they can fly.

g. **What if there is not chimney?**
   - I either use some magic to make a chimney appear and then disappear when I am done, or I use a magic key. It unlocks all the locks of the worked on Christmas Eve.

h. **What if we move, or visiting someplace else on Christmas?**
   - Believe it or not, I can find all the children on Christmas. We always know where to go on Christmas Eve.

i. **What if there is no snow.**
   - A lot of placed do not have snow at Christmas time. It doesn't stop me from coming. Alan Jackson told one of my secrets in a song . In the South, Santa arrives in

a pick-up truck. I have other secret ways to traveling around too.

j. **Is there any food Santa doesn't eat?**
   - Venison (reindeer meat)

k. **How does Santa visit the whole world in one night.**
   - Time zones help, but so do the reindeer and some special magic.

l. **How does Santa get all the toys into the sleigh at one time?**
   - Actually my red toy sack is magical in that it is bottomless and continues to stay full until all the delivers to all the children around the world are completed.

m. **Does Santa have any children?**
   - Yes, I consider all the children in the world part of my family.

n. **Why does Santa not bring me what I want all the time.**
   - Sometimes I ask your parents what is best and they help me decide when you ask for so many things.

o. **Why does Santa wear red?**
   - So I won't get lost in the snow.

p. **Why do you live at the North Pole?**
   - It is miles from everywhere so I won't be disturbed while making my toys and checking my list.

q. **What kinds of treats do the reindeer like?**
   - They like to eat carrots and sugar cubes.

2. Typical questions from parents
    a. Most often parents want to "fill in" the question a reluctant child won't ask. Parent can be very insistent the child ask you. What are the names of you reindeer? Sometimes you may feel the parents have a certain joy in their voices hoping you will trip up.
    b. Most of the time parents are trying to help the child communicate with Santa and the questions they ask are much the same as asked by the young ones.
    c. Parents often give the clues for Santa. We Santa's have to listen carefully because the parent is setting a scene for us
        - The mom has the little one in tow and they are in front of you for the little one to tell you his wishes. He's very shy and doesn't want to speak. Mom isn't bashful at all and she prods the little one to ask a question they have discussed. The mother says, "Remember when we were baking Christmas cookies you had a question for Santa? Now's your chance to ask him."
        - Santa replies, This was so nice for you to help Mom bake cookies, I like all kinds of cookies but I do have some favorites. What kind of cookie is your favorite? They young one my answer or mom may pipe in with a favorite cookie, whatever cookie they name, you should respond by saying, Guess what? That is my favorite cookie. We both like the same cookie.
    d. Parents may become frustrated by their child's reluctant to talk to Santa or perform as they wish. Here's a scenario we often see during children's visit to Santa
        - You are sitting in the chair and a line of children awaits to see you. The chatty, smiling little one who stood between their parent and you is now before you. As you slowly raise your arms to greet them they cry hysterically and tries to break the grip of the parents The mother says if you don't tell Santa what you want he won't bring you anything for Christmas. Isn't that right Santa

- This is a situation I dread because the parents have now portrayed Santa as a person to fear. The child is upset and the parents threat only adds to the child's fears. Does have any suggestions?
    - One way to handle this is to tell the child, Don't worry Santa knows what you want for Christmas so be a good girl and look for some surprises. Santa loves you?
    - I tell the parents to bring the child back another time and Please don't' say I won't bring them anything for Christmas.

e. Some harder questions are
    - Asking you how much you charge while in front of children
    - Where else can we find you?
    - Can I hire your for Christmas Eve?

The Life Story of Santa Claus

 email...
bryangriffin@thelifestoryofsantaclaus.com

Chapter One
The Storm

Long, long ago, in a tiny village on the shores of a distance Sea, a fisherman and his wife lived in a simple stone cottage with their two children, Nicholas a boy of five and his baby sister Kathy. One afternoon, as Nicholas sat by the window carving a small piece of driftwood, he watched the fury of the storm clouds building. In the distance he could hear the roar of the waves breaking on the shore and his thoughts were for his father who must be being tossed about in his frail fishing boat. It was not long before Nicholas could no longer hear the waves above the rattle of wild hailstones hammering at the windowpanes.

It was growing dark as Nicholas asked in a concerned voice, "Mother, do you think father will be safe out there?" He received no answer. His mother was too busy looking after baby Kathy who was lying in her cot tossing feverishly.

Eventually she rose from beside the cot and with a worried look on her face confided in Nicholas. "Your sister's fever is becoming worse and I can't wait for your father any longer. Nicholas, I want you to stay by Kathy and wipe her forehead with this damp cloth. Oh, and make sure she stays covered. I'll be as quick as I can." she said patting Nicholas' head absentmindedly.

After putting on her long overcoat she hurried out into the cold, wild, black night, a flurry of snowflakes rushing in through the door as she left. Patiently, Nicholas watched Kathy for many hours until she stopped pushing the covers aside and her face became white and her hot little forehead grew cooler to his touch.

As the ashes in the fire turned from black to grey Nicholas' head nodded and he fell asleep on the floor beside the cot. That was the way the villagers found him next morning when they brought the sad news that his father had been drowned in the storm. To make things even worse they also had to tell him that his poor mother had been killed by a tree falling on her on the way to fetch the doctor. Now of the once happy family of four, there was only Nicholas. He was an orphan.

Chapter Two
The First Christmas Toys

Who would take care of little Nicholas now that he was all alone in the world? The fishermen and their wives had a meeting to discuss his plight. "We would take care of him of course," said one, "but it's not easy with five mouths to feed already, and he's a growing boy." "It's now the middle of winter and good fishing days are few and far between," said another. "With luck we'll just scrape through until spring."

Then kind, plump Mrs. Bavran spoke. "We have a reserve of food for this winter and there's an old bed in our store room, so we could take in the poor little mite. But mind you, a fisherman's life is never easy," she added. "Who knows what might happen between this year and next? I think that we should all share Nicholas. There are ten of us here now, so if we each agree to have him for one year that will take care of him until he's fifteen and without a doubt he'll run away to sea long before that."

Everyone agreed, and so Nicholas went to live with the Bavran family, moving in on Christmas Eve, the day before the Christmas feast. The children's excitement only made him feel more miserable and he curled himself up in a corner of the storeroom, and with heartbroken sobs for his lost mother, father and beloved Kathy, Nicholas tried to drown the sounds of merrymaking in the cottage. But the door opened slowly, and a little form was seen in the ray of light. "What do you want?" asked Nicholas almost roughly. "Go away. I want to be alone."

Standing in the doorway, the little boy's mouth quivered. "My boat's broken," he cried; "the new one given to me for the Christmas feast." Father's gone out fishing and mother can't fix it. What shall I do?" he asked holding up a broken toy fishing boat.

Nicholas dried his eyes on his sleeves and took the broken toy in his hands. "I'll fix it for you." he said as he turned back to his lonely corner. "Oh, come in here where there's more light," said the young Bavran. So Nicholas went in where there was more light, more children, and more laughter and for a while he forgot his sorrows.

As the months passed, Nicholas grew very fond of the Bavran children, Otto, Margaret and Gretchen. He loved playing with them, but he knew it couldn't last forever. When Christmas day was approaching again and the Bavran family talked of Nicholas leaving them, he became very confused and frightened, yet his main thoughts were of how he could repay them for their kindness.

Nicholas wished that he could give them all a gift, but the only things he owned in the world were the clothes that he wore, an extra coat and trousers, an old sea chest and the pocketknife that had belonged to his father. He just couldn't part with any of these.

Suddenly a wonderful idea came into his head. He would carve some toys for the children just as he had done for his dear little sister Kathy. So for the last two weeks of his stay with the Bavran family, Nicholas worked secretly in the dark storeroom, hiding his knife and wood whenever he heard anybody approaching. He struggled furiously during the last few days so all the gifts could be finished by Christmas morning, because, it was Christmas when the Bavrans had taken him in last winter and now the time had come that he must be passed onto another family.

The children wept quietly as Nicholas packed his meager belongings and Mr. Bavran, waited to take him to the home of Hans the rope maker. The little orphan drew from out of his bag the rough little toys he had made and on seeing the children's delight in their gifts he was so happy that he didn't feel like crying himself. A lovely glow spread over his heart when he saw their happy faces and heard their cries of thanks. "Next Christmas I shall be able to make you even better toys." said Nicholas, an air of determination in his voice. "Just you wait and see!"

With this promise, Nicholas now six years old, bravely left them, his small figure turned away from the happy scene to face the uncertainty of the year ahead with the new family. His face was sad, yet his bright blue eyes were warm with the thought of the happiness he had left behind. "Well," he thought to himself as they approached the rope maker's house "maybe the five children here will be just as nice to me as the Bavrans and I can make toys for them too. Christmas can be a happy time for me even if it's my moving day."

Chapter Three
The Sled Race

At the rope maker's cottage most of the winter evenings were spent by the children learning how to wind and untangle masses of twine, and to most of the simple net mending. Nicholas discovered that by loosening strands of flaxen colored hemp he could make the most realistic hair for the little wooden dolls he still found time to carve. When he left at the end of one year, the rope maker's five little children found five small toys waiting for them on the mantle of their fireplace. Nicholas did not forget his promise to the three Bavran children, but made a special trip to their house on that Christmas morning with their gifts.

As the years went by, Nicholas became more and more skilful with his father's pocketknife and all the children came to expect one of Nicholas' toys on Christmas day. No child was ever disappointed, for the young wood carver always knew exactly what each child would like.

Christmas was only a week away when Nicholas, now aged fourteen, arrived at the school playground to find all his friends in a group chattering excitedly. "What's happening?" he enquired. "There's going to be a sled race on Christmas morning," said Otto. "It will start from the Squire's gate at the top of the hill and finish at the big pine on the far side of his house.' "And the prize," interrupted Hans, "is a grand new sled with metal runners." "Nicholas, you'll enter won't you? That's not a bad sled you have, even though you..." "Hush Jan." whispered another. "It's not nice to remind Nicholas that he built his own sled, just because our fathers had ours made for us." But Nicholas was not listening to the conversation. He was thinking swiftly. Finally he turned to the others and asked, "What time does the race begin?" "Nine o'clock sharp on Christmas morning." was the reply. Nicholas shook his head doubtfully. "I don't know if I can make it," he said slowly. He was thinking of the chest full of toys which he had planned to deliver to all the children on Christmas morning, especially the one for Elsa the wood cutter's daughter, as she lived outside the village. "Perhaps if I get up very early and really hurried," Nicholas said to himself, then suddenly he realized that the race would pass right by Else's cottage. The doll could be dropped off in a few seconds, allowing him to continue without losing any time at all. "I'll be there! I'll be there! At nine o'clock sharp and you had better watch out for that prize!" he shouted gleefully.

Christmas morning was bright and sunny, with fresh crisp snow. Nicholas had been up long before the sun, and as usual had left toys in every doorway. As the children set off with their sleds for the race, the whole village followed behind to watch the excitement. But there was no sign of Nicholas.

Unfortunately one of his old sled's wooden runners had broken under the strain of carrying the heavy load of toys. As he desperately tried to lash it together with rope, he could hear the faint echo of the Squire's horn coming from the top of the hill. The race had started. Nicholas was deeply disappointed because he knew he had missed the chance to win the new sled, but as he had to go to the woodcutter's cottage anyway to deliver Elsa's present, he turned the battered sled upright and made a dash for the hilltop. As he reached the starting line, Nicholas saw his friends speeding off, looking like little black specks in the distance. "Come on Nicholas," called the villagers, "Let's give you a good push to get you started, one, two, three, off you go."

Nicholas flew down the hill, his face stinging in the wind, faster and faster he went, the wooden runners hardly touching the hard packed snow. The black specks were becoming larger and Nicholas knew he must have been catching up to the other children. Larger and larger they became until Nicholas nearly fell off his sled with amazement. They had stopped and were waiting for him just in front of the woodcutter's cottage. "Hurry up Nicholas." encouraged little Josef, "We would have waited for you at the top, but the Squire became impatient and made us start when the horn blew. You know we'd have waited for you if we could." "Yes," shouted Otto, "now go and leave that doll in Elsa's doorway, and let's go! From now on just see how long we'll wait for you! First come, first served for the new sled with metal runners."

With a noisy whoosh, twenty children were off and the race continued over the frozen creek, through patches where they had to carry their sleds, zigzagging between trees and then the long hard pull up the hill behind the Squire's house. Nicholas could only see one boy in front of him just as the big pine tree came into view. His mind was on how much he needed that new sled for his Christmas deliveries.

Nicholas flew along so fast that for a moment he thought he would sail right through the tree splitting it in two, but just in time he steered his sled to one side and jumped off. When he pulled off his woolly hat, he could hear the shouts and cheers from the villagers. He had won the race. It was like a dream come true. All the children pulled Nicholas home on his new sled and each mother and father that they passed, waved and smiled proudly, as happy as if it was their own child that had won the race.

Chapter Four
The Evening Before Christmas

After the crowd of villagers had dispersed on that merry Christmas day of the sled race, Nicholas was stopped at the door of the cottage where he had spent the last year by a lean, dark looking man who looked as though he had never smiled in his life. It was Bertram Marsden the wood carver of the village, who all the children called "Mad Marsden" because he lived alone, rarely spoke to anybody and chased the children away from his door with black looks and harsh words.

"You haven't forgotten have you Nicholas that you move to my house today?" Marsden asked gruffly. Nicholas looked up. Oh no, he hadn't forgotten, and he well knew why Marsden had offered to take him in for the last year of his life as a wandering orphan. The only reason he was willing, even eager, to feed and clothe Nicholas was because for almost five years now he had watched the work he had been doing with his old pocket knife, and realized that Nicholas would make a very good and cheap apprentice for him.

Once again Nicholas packed his few belongings onto his new sled, said a grateful farewell to the family he was leaving, and followed Mad Marsden home to his mean looking cottage on the outskirts of the village. On entering the cottage, Nicholas stepped immediately into the main workroom of the wood carver. Here was found his bench, work table, tools and an assortment of wood. Marsden pointed to a door in the corner and said, "You can store your belongings in there. Nicholas stood in the middle of the untidy room, looking around in dismay.

"There's a bed you can sleep on and you might as well put that pretty sled away for good. We have no time here to go romping in the snow. Come now Nicholas, don't stand there gawking. Put away your belongings; you have much to learn here. "I'm going to make a good wood carver of you. There'll be no time for silly little dolls and wooden toys. You'll have to earn your keep here. Oh, by the way you can keep that tribe of young children that always follow you about away from here, do you understand me boy?" Nicholas bowed his head and went silently to work putting away his small bundle of belongings.

So Nicholas started to work for the mad old wood carver and learned that his father's old pocketknife was a clumsy tool compared with the beautifully sharp knives and chisels that Marsden used. He learned to work for hours on end, bent over the bench beside his master, patiently going over a piece of wood until it was smooth as a piece of glass.

Sadly Nicholas could not learn to get used to the dreadful loneliness of the cottage, and longed for the days when he had been in friendlier ones surrounded by laughing children. Over the months, so as not to make it obvious to Marsden, Nicholas gradually cleaned and brightened the cottage to make his enforced home bearable.

One night as Marsden sat in front of the fire, silently smoking his long curved pipe, he noticed that Nicholas was still bent over the workbench engrossed in some task. “Here lad,” he said almost kindly, in his gruff voice. “I’m not such a hard master that I would have you work night as well as day. What’s that you’re doing? Why don’t you go to your bed? “It’s only a small piece of wood you threw away,” said Nicholas quickly, “I’m trying to make a copy of that chair you finished today, but this is a little one- a toy,” he ended fearfully, for he well knew that the word “toy” would mean children to old Marsden, and for some strange reason just to mention a child in his presence sent him into a terrible rage. Tonight however, he contented himself with merely a black look, and said, “Let me see it. Hmm, not bad, but you have the scroll on the back larger on one side than the other. Here, pass me that small knife.” Nicholas hastened to give him the small tool and watched admiringly as the old craftsman deftly corrected the mistake

“There,” Marsden said finally, holding the work away from him so that he could study it, “that’s the way it should be done.” Then, instead of handing the little chair to Nicholas, who was waiting expectantly, he continued holding it in his hands whilst a sad expression came into the fierce old eyes as he remembered the toys he had made for his own two sons many, many years ago. Slowly a smile grew on the tired old face, Nicholas blinked and looked again. Yes a real smile was tugging at the corners of that stern mouth which had been turned down for so many years.

Marsden lifted his head, and looked at the strong young face with the kind blue eyes. “You’re a good lad Nicholas, and,” he added almost shyly, for it wasn’t easy for a harsh man to change so quickly, “I think I’d like to help you with some of those little things you make. We’ll make them together these long winter evenings, eh, shall we Nicholas. You can deliver them on Christmas day in that fine sled of yours. Perhaps by then you might even like to stay and live with me next year,” the old man added in such a soft voice it sounded like a plea. He grasped Nicholas’ arm almost roughly, then a peaceful expression crept into the lonely old face as the boy answered simply, “Yes, of course master. I’ll stay here with you just as long as you want me to.”

So every winter evening saw two heads bent over the workbench. A grey head with thick, shaggy hair and the smooth yellow head of a boy. They worked feverishly during the weeks before Christmas and with the old man helping with the carving, Nicholas was able to add delicate little touches to the toys, which made them far more handsome than any he had made before. He painted the dolls' faces so that their eyes were blue and their cheeks and lips were as rosy as the little girls who would soon clasp them in their arms. The little chairs and tables were stained with the same soft colors that Marsden used on his own work; the little boys' sleds and boats were shiny with bright new paints, red, yellow, blue and green

Only two nights before Christmas, everything was finished. Although a toy for every child in the village was packed onto the sled with metal runners, Nicholas and the old man were still working at the bench. This time, they were desperately trying to finish a chest, which had been ordered by a wealthy woman in the next village twenty miles away. It was late on Christmas Eve when it was eventually finished.

"I'm sorry," said old Marsden reading Nicholas' thoughts. "You'll have to take it over tomorrow. I'd go myself, but I'm not as strong as I used to be. It's an all day trip, twenty miles over, and then you'll have to wait a few hours to rest the horses, and the twenty long miles back. "If only she didn't want the chest tomorrow," said Nicholas. "Well," answered his master, "We did promise it, and it has to be delivered on time. Now the toys weren't promised..." "No, but I have given them," interrupted Nicholas. "I was going to say lad that they weren't promised for Christmas day. Now you know that little children go to bed early. Why can't you..." "Why of course!" Nicholas jumped to his feet shouting, "Where's my list? Where's my sled? I'll have to hurry."

Outside, the village was asleep. No one saw the lone figure, wrapped up against the crisp icy air, dragging a sled from house to house, leaving a small pile of toys in each doorway until it was empty. It was three o'clock on Christmas morning when Nicholas turned away from the last doorway. His sled was now much lighter to pull, but his feet were tired from trudging through the heavy snow, but he was happy it was

Christmas and once again he had kept his unspoken promise to the children of the village.

Chapter Five
The First Christmas Stocking

Nicholas did not leave the wood carver on that Christmas day, or the next, or the next, but stayed on learning to be as good a wood carver as his old master. Marsden realized this and as he was now becoming too old to spend a full day carving, decided to retire and live with his sister in a nearby village. He was very proud of Nicholas and knew that he would be quite able to carry on by himself, and so it was that Nicholas became known as "Nicholas the Wood Carver."

The village had grown so large that Nicholas did not know every child in the village the way he used to, and the only way that he could tell if a house had children was by a bag hanging on the door on Christmas Eve. With this increase in children his small sled could no longer carry the enormous number of toys and Nicholas had to use Old Marsden's horse and sleigh for his now large rounds. It had become the custom of the children to leave a brightly decorated bag filled with oats on their doors and when the horse had eaten the oats, Nicholas would fill the bag with the toys he had made.

Nicholas' life was not all work. One day he looked up from his workbench and saw some children having a snowball fight in the fresh snow. They were having so much fun that he couldn't resist the temptation to join in. One of the children, whom Nicholas had never seen before, was standing watching shyly. "Here," said Nicholas, handing him a large hard snowball, "try this one for size. Justin looks like a good target over there." "Oh no! I have to gather some firewood and get home quickly," said the small boy as he moved away pulling his empty sled.

"Who's the new fellow?" Nicholas enquired from the children when the boy was out of earshot. "That's Frederick. He's just moved into the village. His father had an accident at sea which paralyzed him and now he has to stay in bed all day. The family is really poor so Frederick and his little brother Wilhelm don't have any time to play because they are always helping their mother.

Later, as Frederick was pulling his sled of firewood home, he had only one thing on his mind. He had heard so much about Nicholas and how he only left toys at the doors that had bags hanging on them. It was only a few days until Christmas and Frederick could imagine his little brother's face if he had a new toy on Christmas morning, but how could he arrange it so that Nicholas would know that there was a little boy in the house? He looked everywhere for a bag without success.

On Christmas Eve he tried to interest his mother in the problem. "Mother." he began slowly. "Mother, do you suppose we have a bag in the house?" "A bag! What sort of bag Frederick?" she inquired in astonishment. "Well, it should be embroidered really, but I suppose any sort of bag would do. We have to hang it outside the door on Christmas Eve, and when Wilhelm wakes up tomorrow there will be a beautiful toy in it for him. Nicholas the wood carver does it for all the children of the village and I thought if there was only some kind of bag around here..." His mother sighed, "Things like flour and potatoes come in bags and those we haven't seen for ages. Goodness knows, with all my other worries, I have no time to embroider a bag or even make one. Anyway I'm sure this Nicholas person wouldn't come to poor little children like you. Now go and get Wilhelm ready for bed. That might take your mind off your silly ideas."

So sadly Frederick was forced to abandon the idea of putting a bag outside the door for his little brother's Christmas gift, but he couldn't forget about Nicholas. He thought about how he looked such a kind, jolly man there out there by the forest. He felt sure Nicholas wouldn't pass a child's house just because they were poor. He thought and thought, and while sitting by the fireplace helping his little brother undress, he pulled of his warm, bright and woolly stocking. As Wilhelm held it up he said jokingly, "Now that would hold some kind of gift just a well as any embroidered bag. And why not?" he murmured to himself. "Why not indeed?" and with one leap he flung open the door and soon had the stocking tied to the door.

Once again this Christmas Eve, everything in the village was blanketed with white snow, sparkling under the bright winter moon. No lights were showing in the village and everyone was asleep... except Nicholas, of course, who was busy going from house to house leaving bulging bags filled with gifts. At Frederick's doorway he paused. In the bright moonlight he saw a funny object dangling on the door. A child's woolen stocking! Nicholas laughed silently to himself, a kind tender laugh, then reached down into his bag and filled the lonely little stocking up to the top, and then with a snap of his whip and the jingle of sleigh bells he was off to the next house on his rounds.

When Frederick opened the door on Christmas morning, he and his little brother found not one, nor two but three toys each. Right down in the toe of the stocking he found five large coins, enough to keep the whole family all through the winter. The boys shouted with joy, while their father almost sat up in his bed with the excitement. Their mother's eyes although always bright, were filled with happy tears as she watched Frederick and his brother hugging close to their hearts, the first Christmas stocking.

Chapter Six
The Red Suit

Squire Kenson, the richest man in the village, came driving up to Nicholas' cottage one day with an order for a new chest of drawers. Nicholas was attracted by the sound of silver bells and reindeer hooves on the snow. He looked out of his window and was impressed by the way the squire had arrived in his shiny red sleigh drawn by two beautiful reindeer. Donner and Blitzen were their names because they travelled so swiftly, like thunder and lightning.

Nicholas looked at the two beautiful animals and thought how much quicker they would pull him around the village on Christmas Eve than his old horse Lufka, who was now getting slower and slower as the years passed by.

All the time the squire was talking, the woodcarver was gazing admiringly at the fine suit of red deerskin he was wearing. The coat was rather long and belted at the waist, the trousers loose and tucked into shiny black leather leggings. Soft white ermine fur was around the coat at the collar, cuffs and the bottom, with the same beautiful fur around the close-fitting hat.

After the squire had left, Nicholas carried on with his work but his mind was on the beautiful red suit. "There's no reason why I can't have one too," he said to himself. "I've been going around dressed like an orphan instead of a wood carver for far too long." The very next day Nicholas paid a visit to Widow Arpen, the best dressmaker in the village. "I want a fine red suit, Mrs. Arpen." he started. "You know the one the squire wears?" The woman nodded. "Well unfortunately I can't afford such fine soft deerskin and of course I know I can't have mine trimmed with real ermine, so what do you suggest?"

The widow thought for a moment, then said, "We could get a bolt of strong homespun from the weaver which I could dye a rich red with rowan berries. As for the collar and cuffs, well pure white rabbit skin would look just perfect." "Done!" cried Nicholas, and he poured a handful of gold coins onto the table, "That should cover the materials and your work." "But that's far too much." exclaimed the widow, "Why half of this would keep my whole family right through the winter." "Keep it woman." smiled Nicholas. "You've had a hard time and I'll not be the man to die with a chest full of gold buried under the fire place.

"The widow stood at her door and watched Nicholas drive away through the snow. "Now there's a fine man." she murmured, the gold coins jingling through her fingers. "A fine big man." And so she bought the home spun which she died a beautiful bright red, but a strange thing happened. She had no pattern to go by as Nicholas was wearing the only tunic he owned, so the widow cut and sewed the suit with the image of a fine big man constantly in front of her. Nicholas was not a short man by any means but he was rather thin, and yet as Mrs. Arpen cut out and sewed the suit together, she knew she was sewing for a fine generous man and she made the suit to fit his heart instead of his body.

On the day the suit was finished and the last loving stitch placed in the soft rabbit trimming, Nicholas arrived to try it on. He went into the widow's little changing room and came out a few minutes later - and what a picture he made. "I can't see myself Mrs. Arpen," said Nicholas doubtfully, "because the little mirror in your room only shows part of me at a time, but it did seem to go on rather loosely," he finished tactfully, not wanting to hurt her feelings.

The widow gave one look at him and burst into tears. "Oh Nicholas, I've spoilt your suit. I've ruined it. I thought you were bigger. Oh, what shall I do?" "There, there, don't worry about it. Look at the length, that's all right. It's only that I'm not as fat as I should be. Why if I ate all the food the villagers sent me why, I guarantee in a few months time you wouldn't notice it. The trousers will be fine as soon as I buy a pair of boots to tuck them into, and what a nice cap this is! See how closely it fits and how warm looking the fur band is!" So Nicholas kept his oversized red suit and soon the villagers became used to the tall figure in the bright red trousers and tunic, the close fitting stocking cap trimmed with fur and the shiny black leather belt and boots. And what do you think happened after Nicholas ate more porridge, vegetables and milk, week after week? Yes his face became full, his chest filled out and he even began to acquire - whisper it - a belly!

Chapter Seven
The Reindeer

The next Christmas Eve Nicholas did not have such an easy time making his rounds of the village. To begin with, he was considerably amused and rather dismayed to discover that instead of one embroidered bag for each house, the children had followed little Frederick's example and had each put out a woolen stocking. So with some families having five or six children, there was often quite a row of stockings nailed to the door.

Of course Nicholas couldn't very well just put one toy in each stocking as it made the rest of it look so flat and empty. Since he hadn't stocked his sleigh with enough toys so that there would be several for each child, he found himself with an empty sleigh, and only half way through his list! "Luckily I have an extra supply of toys at home in the chest," he said to his horse Lufka as they returned to the cottage for more.

Nicholas quickly loaded up the sleigh and off they went again to finish the rounds. When there were only a few houses left to visit, the tired old horse began to falter. "Come on old boy," encouraged Nicholas, but Lufka was getting too old to spend all night struggling around the village, and this particular night he had made two trips.

As he plodded through a deep snow bank Lufka stumbled and the sleigh slid into a ditch. Crack! went one of the runners. Nicholas climbed down and after making sure that his horse was alright, shook his head at the sight of the disabled sleigh. Nicholas had to finish his rounds on foot that Christmas and the first pink streaks of dawn were brightening up the sky when he and Lufka finally returned to the cottage, Nicholas, fat and rosy, puffing heavily, while poor Lufka dragged his tired old bones straight to the stable door. For many days after that disastrous Christmas Eve, the villagers heard sounds of sawing and hammering coming from Nicholas' wood shed. They wondered what he was building, and whenever anyone asked him what it was he would jokingly say, "Just wait and see."

The villagers soon forgot their curiosity when an exciting piece of news spread through the village. "What's this I hear about the squire, Otto?" Nicholas asked his old friend. "Ah," said Otto, puffing away on his pipe. They say things have not gone too well for him over the last few years, so now he's going to sell some of his land and furniture to pay back the people he owes money to. The sale is tomorrow, so why don't you come up with us Nicholas?" "Now what would I be wanting to buy from the squire?" I don't need any more land and I can make furniture every bit as good as any he has in the house. As a matter of fact I made some of it." "What about his animals?" asked Otto? "He has two fine horses and a team of reindeer." "That's true," said Nicholas, finally interested enough to put down his work. "Lufka is too old to be of much help to me now. I think I will go up there with you tomorrow and see some of the excitement."

The next morning the squire's house and surrounds thronged with eager people. Some had come to buy while others just to watch or be nosy. Nicholas strode past the horses straight to the stables where the reindeer were kept. "He's after Donner and Blitzen," the men whispered to each other. "He's always admired the way they go so fast." The squire, now a bent old man with a worried look on his face, seemed somewhat bewildered by all the people talking about his house and possessions. When Nicholas showed his interest in the two reindeer he replied sternly, "Well you can't have Donner and Blitzen alone. The set of reindeer go together or not at all. Why Donner would go raving mad if she was separated from the rest of her family."

"Family!" exclaimed Nicholas. "But Squire I only need two reindeer. How many more...?" Eventually Nicholas weakened and became the proud owner of not two, but eight prancing reindeer, Donner and Blitzen, the mother and father with their six children, Dasher and Dancer, Comet and Cupid, Prancer and Vixen.

This year Nicholas was planning for a bigger and better Christmas Eve than ever before and worked day and night to finish the toys. Finally the great night arrived. Nicholas finished tying the eight reindeer to each other with a harness bright with jingling silver bells. He slowly backed them up to the wood shed door, which he proudly opened, disclosing a most beautiful sight. There stood a bright, shining red sleigh, trimmed with silver stripes, the runners curving up in the front to form a swan's head, the back roomy enough to hold toys for children of several villages.

Nicholas guided the reindeer into the shafts and climbed up onto the high seat, so beautifully padded with cushions made of soft doe skin. He took out of its holder, a long shiny black whip, cracked it in the cold air, and they were off.

That night the villagers were woken from their sleep by a merry jingling of silver bells, the stamp of reindeer's hooves on the hard snow and the sharp crack of a whip. They peeked out from behind their curtains and saw by the white light of the moon, a shinning red sleigh drawn by eight prancing reindeer whose flying hooves moved as fast as lightning. Perched high up in the seat, snapping a long whip with one hand and guiding the reindeer with the other was a large round man, dressed in a belted red tunic trimmed with white fur, baggy trousers stuffed into high black boots and a close fitting red stocking cap which flew in the wind. Of course they weren't close enough to see his face, but one and all, as they returned to their warm beds murmured kindly, "That's Nicholas on his way to the children. God bless him."

Chapter Eight
The First Christmas Chimney

When Nicholas was about fifty years old, and his hair and beard were becoming as white as the snow, a strange family came to live in the village. Not much of a family you may think, just one small old man, brown and wrinkled like a nut and a skinny little girl who drew back shyly from the crowd of villagers, who had gathered as they always did when someone new came to live.

"His name is Carl Dinsler." one woman whispered. "The old squire's housekeeper told me about him. She said that he was very rich. He must be rich to be able to buy the big old house up on the hill." "He may be rich but he doesn't look it." remarked another. "Did you notice that poor little child he had with him? She looks as though she needs a good square meal. Who is she anyway?" "She's his grand-daughter. Her parents died a little while ago and they say the old man bought the house on the hill so that they could be alone." "Do you know what he has done?" asked one little boy of the interested crowd. "He's nailed up all the gates and left only the front one open and that one he keeps locked with a bolt as large as this." He spread out his hands to show the size.

"And that's not all. I don't know how you would get into the house any way because he's put up boards over the windows and the front and side doors. There's not a sign of life anywhere in the old house now. You would think that it was disserted." "Why, the old man must be crazy."

they all said. "He must be afraid of somebody." "Afraid nothing." one man remarked, "The only thing he's afraid of is that someone will steal his money." "I'm sure Nicholas the wood carver will be interested in this news," said another. "One more child in the village, and such a lovely one too."

"Nicholas already knows about her." they heard a deep voice say and the villagers turned to see it was the wood carver himself who had joined the group unnoticed. "Her name is Kathy. I once knew a girl with that name." he went on with a sad faraway look in his usually merry blue eyes as he remembered his little sister. "I'd like to do something special for the poor little girl."

"How did you find out her name, Nicholas?" "She was wandering around in her yard just like a forlorn puppy who had been locked in," Nicholas answered. "I was passing that way and stopped at the gate so that I could talk to her. She says that she's not allowed outside the fence and can only play in the yard for one hour a day. She also told me that her grandfather doesn't want her to play with the other children from the village in case she talks about his gold and where he keeps it."

"As if we'd touch his money," the villagers said angrily. "He's a nasty old man. Why I'll bet he won't even let her put out a stocking on Christmas Eve." "That's a safe bet," laughed Nicholas, "he wouldn't open the front door even to let in something that was free!"

The crowd broke up and Nicholas went back to his work but over the following months he often thought of lonely little Kathy. He saw her several times and she told him she wouldn't be allowed to hang out her stocking at Christmas. The last time he visited her, old Dinsler shook his stick at him and told him to keep away from his house. After that, Kathy wasn't seen again but Nicholas still made a few toys for her and packed them away, just in case.

A few days before Christmas, Nicholas took a walk around the big boarded up house. He looked up at the covered doors and windows and his eyes brightened as he noticed the huge stone chimney on the roof. He chuckled to himself, "I'll try it! I might get stuck but it's worth the try."

Christmas Eve was dark and moonless with the wind whistling

through the streets and the light snow stung Nicholas's face and covered the sleigh and reindeer with a shining coat of ice. "Come on," he encouraged the reindeer, "Only the house on the hill left." He shivered in his red coat and must have looked like a giant snowman with the snow forming icicles on his white beard.

He tied the reindeer to the front gate, took his sack from the back of the sleigh and climbed from his high seat to the top bar of the fence and jumped into the yard. He stopped to listen but could only hear the banging of shutters in the wind. He crept over to the side of the house where a vine covered one door and this made an ideal ladder to the roof.

Being so fat and bulky and with the sack on his back it was hard work, but finally he puffed his way to the roof. This was the dangerous part as it was slippery with the snow and ice, and he had to hack away with his knife to make footholds. Finally a large shape loomed up above him. It was the chimney. Nicholas stopped and rested for a moment, then leaned over the edge and looked down the chimney into the inky blackness.

"Just as I thought," he murmured, "the old miser lets the fire go out at nights.... even on such a bitter cold one as tonight." He climbed over the edge and began his dangerous decent, feeling carefully with his feet for the jutting bricks, pressing his hands flat on the sides and bracing his back against the wall. Slowly he inched his way down until he felt solid earth beneath his feet. He stepped out of the fireplace into a room almost as dark as the chimney.

Gradually as his eyes became accustomed to the dark, he could make out a table and by groping in the darkness eventually found a stub of a candle, which he soon had lit. He drew out from the sack a bright blue woolen stocking, and filled it up to the brim with toys. Also he left nuts and lollies as he thought the hungry little girl wouldn't have had treats like this for some time.

Nicholas the hung the stocking on the mantelpiece, weighed it down with a heavy candlestick and stood back to admire the good job he had done. Just as he was about to blow out the candle Nicholas was startled by the sudden opening of a door and old Dinsler rushing into the room. "Sneaking into my house, are you? After my gold I suppose? I'll show you what I do with thieves, I'll show you!" The old man picked up a poker and swung it at Nicholas, who jumped to one side so that the table was between them.

"Don't be so foolish," he said quickly, realizing that Dinsler was in a rage and dangerous. "I haven't come after your gold. Look..." "Haven't you. Well then what brings you into my house in the middle of the night?"

"I'll tell you what! Look behind you at that stocking. The other children in the village leave their stockings outside their front doors, but you have so frightened your grandchild that she is afraid to ask you for anything. I only wanted to make her feel wanted like other children, and that she should get gifts the same as they do on Christmas morning."

"Gifts!" exclaimed the old man, bewildered and lowering the poker. "You mean you give things away?" He looked at Nicholas with a very strange look.

"Yes," replied Nicholas, relieved to see the poker being put away. "I'll even give you a Christmas gift, you mean old man." He reached inside his deep pocket and poured a stream of bright gold coins onto the table in front of Dinsler. "Here, if gold is all you care about, take this. and more... more to add to your hoard! And now," Nicholas said with an air of authority as he brushed some soot from one eye, "Will you please show me to your front door. If I have to climb back up the chimney I'll never get this suit clean again."

With that he marched from the room, in some ways a ridiculous stout figure covered in soot, yet he looked very impressive to old Dinsler, as he hurried ahead to open the door for Nicholas to return out into the cold black night.

The next week the village buzzed with excitement. Something was happening up on the hill. The old miser had ripped the boards off the windows and doors. He had bought a horse and cart and had been down to the village to buy huge quantities of food. He had also spoken to the school teacher and within a few days Kathy and her grandfather were seen on the road leading to the school, the little girl's face beaming up at the old man, her feet skipping along to keep up with him and her warm little hand tucked into his fist. All this because Nicholas had climbed down a chimney to fill ONE stocking!

Chapter Nine
The First Christmas Trees

Very close to Nicholas' cottage was a thick grove of pine trees, tall, beautiful dark trees that lifted their branches high up into the sky and formed a perfect shelter for the ground underneath. Scattered in among the larger trees were a cluster of firs, brave little trees, which kept their sturdy branches green all through the cold northern winter and came through each heavy snow storm with their shiny needles still pointed towards the sky. The children used to play in this grove, because no matter how stormy the weather was outside, here they could find a warmer, more sheltered spot away from the bitter winds. In the summer time it was a charming place, with the sharp keen scent of the pine trees and the soft murmuring of their branches in the breeze.

Nicholas loved this little grove, for in order to get there, the village children had to pass his cottage, and hardly a group went passed his door without one or more of them dashing in to say "Good day" to their old friend and to watch him at work at his fascinating toys. One day as Nicholas glanced out of his window, he noticed a group of children running from the grove. As they became closer he could see that they were frightened and as they ran into his cottage for cover, puffing and panting, Nicholas asked, "What's happened? You all look so frightened." "They've got long black hair," one boy cried out, "And the men wear rings in their ears," piped in another. "We couldn't understand a word they spoke." "Slow down, Slow down," said Nicholas, "Who are you talking about?" "Strange people with dark skin and hair." "Did they have horses and carts with them?" asked Nicholas with a knowing look. "Yes, and big covered wagons. " "They sound like gypsies to me," replied Nicholas, though they don't usually come so far north. They must have lost their way, and now they'll camp here until spring. There's no need to be afraid of them. They are people just like you and me."

Reassured, the children ran back into the grove to investigate these new people. They soon made friends with the gypsies and discovered that the children played the same games as them, as well as some interesting new ones. As Christmas drew near, they told the gypsy children about Nicholas, and how he drove up on Christmas Eve on a red sleigh pulled by eight shiny reindeer and filled their stockings with beautiful toys that he had made. "Once, when he couldn't get into Kathy's house because it was all boarded up, he climbed down the chimney!" "He can't visit us," joked one gypsy girl, "We don't have any doors, nor do we wear stockings. We certainly don't carry chimneys with us," she laughed.

Little Sonya, who wanted everybody to be happy, reported some of these things to Nicholas, and came away from his cottage with a contented mind, for she knew that the wise smile on his face meant that he had a plan in his kind old head.

On Christmas Eve, the reindeer were surprised to find that when their usual sound was over, Nicholas drove them right past his cottage and out towards the forest, stopping on the edge of the pine grove. A dark figure with a wide grin stepped forward. This was Grinka, the leader of the band of gypsies.

"Here you are Grinka," said Nicholas, giving him a bundle of small white candles. "You go ahead with these and I'll follow." Grinka stopped at every small fir tree in the grove and tied candles to their branches. Nicholas followed behind, covering the branches of each tree with nuts, shiny red apples and of course a sample of every one of his toys. It was almost dawn when the pair had finished, but there was a tree for each family with children.

"Now for the lights," said Nicholas and they went from tree to tree, touching a taper to each candle, until the whole dark grove was twinkling and glowing like the centre of a warm hearth fire. "I think that's the prettiest part of it all," said Nicholas, "and you must be sure to wake the children before the sun gets through the pine trees and spoils the effect."

"Alright," said Grinka, "I'll go and wake them now, before you go." "Oh No!" said Nicholas alarmed. "They mustn't see me. The children must NEVER see me. It would spoil it all. Now I must go!" Nicholas jumped onto his sleigh and was off, with the familiar jingling of silver bells and the crack of his long silver whip.

A few minutes after his departure, Grinka had aroused all the children in the camp. Nicholas should have stayed just to see the joy on the thin little faces as they scampered among the trees, each one discovering something new to shout about. "It's the lights on these lovely little trees that makes everything so beautiful," said one child. "No, it's the presents! Exclaimed another. "Just look at this pretty little doll I have!" "It's the fruit and nuts," added one hungry child stuffing his mouth with goodies. "I think everything is so beautiful because it's Christmas," decided one wise little boy. "Yes, yes, because it's Christmas!" they all shouted, dancing around. "And these are our Christmas trees!"

Chapter Ten
Holly

Holveg, who everyone called Holly, was a timid little girl who was sometimes frightened by the dark. Her skill at growing flowers in the harsh climate was remarkable and nothing gave Holly more pleasure than to repay Nicholas' generosity by sharing flowers with him.

One day as she was arranging the flowers for him she queried, "Are you afraid of goblins?" Nicholas put down the toy he was working on and turned a surprised face toward the little girl. "Goblins!" he exclaimed. "Now here am I, well past sixty years old and I've never heard of goblins. What are they Holly?" he asked in an interested tone.

Holly looked confused, then a doubtful tone crept into her voice, "Why I don't exactly know," she confessed, "but I've heard of them and when I'm lying in my bed at night I'm sure that's what I see creeping about my room."

"They must be shadows," said Nicholas, "I've never come across goblins, or for that matter ghosts either," he added.

Holly looked very impressed and said, "If I think I see a goblin in my room, I'll just say to him, Nicholas says you just aren't, you old goblin!" They both laughed and Nicholas hugged the little girl and told her it was time for her to run home for her supper.

The winter months passed by and when spring arrived and it was time again for planting the flowers, Holly fell very sick. All through the summer weeks she laid on her bed, weakened by a fever, recognizing no one, not even her beloved Nicholas. He brought flowers to her, hoping that they might bring back the wandering little mind, but she only pushed them away and went on with her delirious ravings of big black giants and horrible goblins. For with her illness, her almost forgotten fears had returned and with a heavy heart Nicholas realized that their friendly little talks had been completely wiped from her mind.

She gradually recovered but the fever left her the same pale, timid little girl she had been when she had first brought a bouquet to Nicholas. Holly was sadder than she had ever been during her entire life. Everything seemed black to her and her nights were filled with terror in spite of all that Nicholas had told her. But more than anything else, he worried because she had no flowers to take to him.

Holly pressed her thin little face against the window pane and looked with tear filled eyes out into her bleak front garden. As some boys passed her gate they paused to wave kindly to her. Holly waved back and wiped her eyes. She pushed open the window a little and called out, "What's that green bush you have in your sled Karl?"

The boys came over to the window and Karl held up an armful of branches with lovely little warm red berries scattered among shiny pointed green leaves. "Why it's so beautiful!" exclaimed Holly, clasping her hands. Her dull eyes began to sparkle a little as she asked, "What is it? Where did you get it Karl?" "We found it in the woods; way back in the part they call the dark forest. It grows like this even in the middle of winter but I don't know what it's called."

"Oh, it's so pretty," said Holly again, "but, but, did you say the dark forest?" "Yes," answered Karl, "and it's dark alright. The sun hardly ever gets through those trees and if you get lost in there I guess you'd stay lost forever." "Yes added another boy."I wouldn't go in there alone I can tell you," and off they went waving some of their prize and leaving Holly picturing the bright red berries and shiny green leaves in her mind.

How Nicholas would love some of that cheery little bush. But the dark forest! She shuddered. "There must be all kinds of terrible things in there," she thought. "Wild animals and strange noises and maybe, behind the trees - goblins!" Holly shook a little and then suddenly she had a mental picture of herself when she was in Nicholas' cottage saying, "I'll just look at him and say, Goblin, Nicholas says you just aren't." Holly buried her little face in her hands. "Oh, if only I dared to do it," she almost sobbed.

"Nicholas says to do anything when you are really afraid is braver than if you felt no fear at all. But that's a horrible place. Even the boys are afraid to go there alone. But I haven't any flowers for him and he's always so kind to us and spring is so far away!" So she sat there for a long time, her mind turning from one decision to another. "Maybe there would be some sun in the forest and if I hurried and found the berries quickly, perhaps I could be back again before dark. I'm going to do it!" She ran for her cloak before she had a chance to change her mind and before her mother returned from the village.

Nicholas looked up from his work and saw a little figure flying along the road, right past his cottage and into the forest. "That looked like Holly," he thought startled. "No, it can't be. She's not well yet. Besides," he shook his head sadly, "The poor little thing would be too terrified to go into the forest as it was dark enough for goblins," he said with a chuckle.

An hour later however, he was interrupted from his work by Holly's frantic mother. "Oh, I thought she was here," she cried. "When I came home and found her gone, I was sure I would find her with you. She's still so weak and look, it's beginning to snow!"

Nicholas was soon pulling on his bright red coat and fur trimmed cap. "I'll find her, don't you worry." He looked out at the grey afternoon sky filled with black clouds. Already the air was filled with millions of snowflakes, scurrying and tumbling in every direction. "I know where to look," said Nicholas. "I'll take the small sled with Vixen and we'll have Holly back here before the snow covers my path."

Holly meanwhile had found the red berries and her joy on seeing the cheerful little bush almost chased away the thoughts of what awful things might be lurking behind the huge tree trunks or hiding on the bough, waiting to spring down at her. She gathered a large armful of the berries and started back again, her heart beginning to pound as the light inside the forest grew dimmer and dimmer. As she started to run, the snow whirled in white mists around her. The wind whistled through the branches and moaned high up in the tree tops. It caught Holly's cloak and wrapped it around her head, making her think that some ghostly hand was plucking at her and trying to keep her in this terrible place.

She ran faster and faster, her arms clutching the bundle of berries, her head bent against the wind, and her feet tripping over rocks and stumps hidden in the snow. She breathed heavily and in spite of the biting wind she felt her head grow hotter and hotter. Her heart was pounding so hard she thought it would burst through her ribs. "I can't see anything," she sobbed, "It's getting darker and darker. I can't lift my feet and the trees are falling on me. "OH!" she shrieked aloud as her terrified eyes saw a huge form looming at her through the clouds of snow. She closed her eyes and fell in a faint, face down in front of Nicholas and Vixen.

When she next opened her eyes she was in the wood carver's cottage with her mother holding her in her arms and Nicholas' kind face looking anxiously down on her. "Where are my flowers?" was her first question. "I went into the dark forest alone to get them for you. Where are they?" Nicholas put the red berries and branches in her arms. "Here they are my dear. Did you bring them for me?" "Yes Nicholas and I was afraid, but I'll never be again, I know that now."

Nicholas wiped a tear from his eye. "You shouldn't have gone so soon after being sick, but I do love the little berries. What are they called?" "I don't know, but I liked them because they remind me of you, so round, red and shiny," said the little girl with a mischievous laugh.

"That's funny," answered Nicholas, "they remind me of you somewhat, so brave growing out there in the darkness and cold. Those little berries have the deep red of courage in them, so I think I'll christen them and from now on we'll call them 'Holly'."

Chapter Eleven
The Last Stocking

The years passed and Nicholas was now a very rich man even though he shared all he had with his friends in the village. Every Christmas morning the children would wake to find their stockings filled with toys and sweets. The poorer families would also find food... such things as chickens, vegetables and hams and often bundles of clothing would be left on their doorsteps.

But as you would expect, each year he would be a little feebler and the villagers who loved and respected him began to worry. Each Christmas morning as the children excitedly took the gifts from their stockings; the fearful thought in every parent's heart was "Maybe next Christmas he won't be with us."

A few days before one Christmas, a number of villagers called on Nicholas with a suggestion. "We thought Nicholas," said one man a little hesitantly, "we thought that you must get so cold filling the stockings outside the door, especially when there are five or six in the family, that it would be better if the children left their stockings inside by the fire." "Then you could come in and sit by the fire and take your time about it," added one woman kindly.

Old Nicholas looked up from the work he was doing and smiled. He placed his hand on the man's shoulder. "Ho, ho, ho. Fancy you coming here to tell me how to do my work." he joked. "Why I remember filling an embroidered bag for you when you were smaller than your own children are now. Then things changed when they started putting out stockings instead of bags and now you want me to change again and leave them inside. Well I suppose I must keep up with the times and if you all think it's better to have them inside, then inside I will go."

So from then on Nicholas would quietly creep into the houses on Christmas Eve and sit in front of the fire, slowly filling the stockings. Often the children would leave him a drink and a piece of cake, as they knew that he had a long night of exhausting work.

One Christmas Eve, old Nicholas found it harder than usual to leave each home. The warm fire made him feel drowsy and his old bones ached as he wearily pulled himself up to go. He made slow progress from one house to another until thankfully he arrived at his last stop, his back hurting from carrying his bulky sack, his head drooping with tiredness and his heart heavy as he realized how old he must be. The work he had done with such enthusiasm for so many years was now almost too much for him.

He dropped into a chair by the fire with a deep sigh of relief and it was a long time before he recovered enough to start filling the stockings. Even then he did it very slowly and it hurt as he reached down into the bottom of the sack, each time straightening himself with growing difficulty. He finished filling four of the five stockings but with the fifth one still empty in his hand he fell sound asleep.

About an hour later he woke with a start when he felt a hand shaking him. "Are you alright Nicholas?" asked a worried voice, "I got up to see if the fire had gone out and found you still here. Why it's nearly dawn." Nicholas shook himself then stood up wearily. "Yes, its Christmas morning and I haven't finished my work." "Never mind. I'll finish the last stocking for you," said the man. "Just leave the presents and go home to bed, but hurry before the children wake up and see you."

Nicholas, thinking of his warm comfortable bed, handed over the stocking and presents and wearily headed outside. A few minutes later a little boy in his pajamas stood in the doorway. "What are you doing daddy?" he asked in a disappointed tone. "I thought it was Nicholas who gave us the toys." The child looked ready to cry but his father reassured him, "Your Nicholas is getting old," he said, "and sometimes we fathers have to help him, but remember, it's Nicholas who leaves the toys for you."

"That's alright then," said the little fellow. "It isn't half as much fun if you think it's your mother or father who leaves the gifts." "I should say not," said the father very sternly, "and you must never doubt Nicholas. Why he would be so hurt at a little boy thinking he didn't fill the stockings that he might never come to his house again. Wouldn't that be terrible?' "Yes," whispered the boy in a frightened voice. "What would Christmas be without Nicholas?"

Chapter Twelve
Nicholas Sleeps

Holly was no longer little Holly, but a lovely slender young girl who led a happy life, her childish terrors long forgotten. She still continued the practice of bringing flowers to her old friend and every Christmas Eve she would go into the dark forest to gather holly to decorate his cottage on Christmas morning.

It was almost noon, and as she approached the cottage she noticed how silent and empty it looked without Nicholas bending over his work and no smoke coming from the chimney. She stole silently into the cold little cottage and quietly opened the door to his bedroom. "Why the darling was so tired he fell asleep with his clothes on," she murmured tenderly. For the fat round figure lay there, still dressed in the bright red suit with the white fur, the shiny black boots and the close fitting cap.

"Here's your holly," whispered the girl, bending over Nicholas. Then with a startled exclamation she dropped the red berries over the still figure and sprang back frightened. It was a few moments before Holly realized what must have happened and as she edged back close to him she sobbed, "Poor Nicholas. Why did you have to die? We all loved you so much."

She gently arranged the holly around his bed then ran out into the snow and with tears running down her face called loudly for the villagers. They gathered in little groups to listen to her story. The women murmured in broken tones between sobs, "He's dead!" and clasped their wondering little children closer, as if to comfort them for the loss of their dearest friend. The men looked everywhere except into each other's eyes, for no man wanted to see the tears that were there. "Yes he's dead," they all sighed deeply. "Who's dead mother? Is it Nicholas?" asked the children. "Won't he come to visit us any more on Christmas Eve?" And the parents had to turn away from the wide childish eyes because they didn't want to say that awful sentence, "Yes, Nicholas is dead."

The bells tolled and the village was in darkness that Christmas night. Vixen and his family whimpered in their stalls and holly glowed red over the still, loving heart in a red suit.

Chapter Thirteen
Santa Claus Is Born

The year that followed Nicholas' death on that Christmas morning was a very sad one for all the villagers. They had tenderly put Nicholas to rest in the pine grove near the spot where the children had played with him in the past. The eight reindeer were no longer in the stall behind the empty cottage, but had been taken by Kathy to the stables at the big house up on the hill.

In the months that passed, many a mother would pick up a little doll from the floor and gently wipe the dust from its face with a suddenly tear dimmed eye for the generous heart who had made the little toy with so much love. It gradually entered even the youngest mind that Nicholas was dead and would no longer fill their stockings at Christmas. They cried a little, but gradually the image of the fat, cheerful old man faded from their memories and so the year passed until it was again Christmas Eve.

"Mother, are we going to hang up our stockings?" "No child. Have you forgotten that Nicholas is no longer here and can't come to fill your stockings?" This question was asked and similarly answered in almost every house in the village on that Christmas Eve.

All over the village, children went sadly to bed without hanging up their stockings, except for one little boy, Stephen, who refused to believe that Nicholas wouldn't come. He astonished his parents when he calmly went about hanging up his stocking just the way he had done every Christmas Eve since he could remember. "But Stephen, he's dead," said his mother. "He can't come" "Of course he'll come," said a determined Stephen, "we must keep the fire burning for him."

So that night, all the doors were shut and the fires put out, apart from Stephen's house, where a lonely stocking hung beside a cheerful blaze. Just after midnight, Holly woke up. "I thought I heard sleigh bells and reindeer hooves," she said sleepily. "It must have been a dream" and she turned over and drifted back to sleep.

Christmas morning dawned bright and clear, the village silent under a blanket of snow. Suddenly the tranquility was shattered by a wild shout as the door of one cottage burst open. "He's been!" shrieked Stephen. "He's been. Look at my stocking! It's filled just the same as last Christmas and there's a big new sled by our fireplace. I knew it. Look everybody, Wake up, wake up! Nicholas has been."

Men, women, and children jumped from their beds to see what all the noise was about, and the children leaped right into the largest piles of toys they had ever seen. They were all around the fireplaces, on the tables and chairs, and even beside their beds. The entire village opened its doors and poured out into the streets, the children dragging handsome new sleds laden with the most beautiful toys the village had ever seen. "Did you see this? Look at my boat." "He must have come down the chimney when he found the door locked. There was some soot on the floor." "Isn't it wonderful? It's the happiest Christmas we've ever had!"

"Little Stephen found a fir tree in a tub, decorated with more gifts, fruit and candles, the same way the gypsy children found their gifts many years ago." "Yes, and Stephen says there's a big, shiny star at the very top." "That's because Stephen believes in him," they said ashamed of themselves, "But now we believe too." An old woman watching all the happy faces, said in her cracked voice, "He's a saint, that's what he is!" "Yes he's Saint Nicholas now!" They all took up the cry and the whole village joined in shouting, "Saint Nicholas! Saint Nicholas!"

A little boy's voice tried to add his stumbling speech to the general shouting. "Sant Clos! Sant Clos!" he lisped. "We believe now," the children and their parents all said to each other. "How could Saint Nicholas be forgotten by us. We believe he will always visit us on Christmas Eve as long as there is one child left in the village" "In the village," echoed little Stephen, "You mean in the whole wide world," he shouted triumphantly.

Reference List

"Santa's Elves in Alaskan Town Reply to Letters". AOL News. Dec. 9, 2006.

Barnard, Eunice Fuller. "Santa Claus Claimed as a Real New Yorker." New York Times. December, 19, 1926.

Baum, L. Frank. The Life and Adventures of Santa Claus. 1902; reprint, New York: Penguin, 1986.

Belk, Russel W. "A Child's Christmas in America: Santa Claus as Deity, Consumption as Religion." Journal of American Culture, 10, no. 1 (Spring 1987), pp. 87-100.

Bowler, Gerry, Santa Claus: A Biography McClelland & Stewart Ltd, Toronto, 2005

"R Cendella Gallery - Theme: Commentary," at http://www.rcenedellagallery.com

Christoph, Peter R., "Saint Nicholas," The Encyclopedia of New York State, Sample Entries

Clar, Mimi. "Attack on Santa Claus." Western Folklore, 18, no. 4 (October 1959), p. 337.

Clark, Cindy Dell. Flights of Fancy, Leaps of Faith: Children's Myths in Contemporary America. Chicago: University of Chicago Press, 1995.

"The Claus that Refreshes," at: http://www.snopes.com/cokelore/santa.htm

"Father Frost," at: http://www.bobandbabs.com/

Dini, Paul. Jingle Belle various issues

Felix Octavius Carr Darley Website

Flynn, Tom. The Trouble with Christmas. Buffalo, N.Y.: Prometheus Books, 1993.

"A Glimpse of an Old Dutch Town," Harper's New Monthly Magazine, Harper and Brothers, New York, Vol. 62, Number 370, March 1881.

Linda Sue Grimes, www.bellaonline.com/articles/art5431.asp

Hageman, Howard, Book review: Saint Nicholas of Myra, Bari, and Manhattan: Biography of a Legend by Charles W. Jones, Theology Today, October 1979

Horowitz, Joseph. Classical Music in America: A History of Its Rise and Fall. New York: W. W. Norton, 2005.

http://www.2think.org/hii/santa.shtml

http://www.baltimoremd.com/humor/santaengineer.html

"Is There a Santa Claus?" New York Sun. September 21, 1897.

Jones, Charles W., "Knickerbocker Santa Claus," The New-York Historical Society Quarterly, Volume XXXVIII Number 4, October 1954

Kenezevich, Lou. Numerous stories, ideas, and philosophies attributied throughout this entire book. 2009

King, Josiah. The Examination and Tryal of Old Father Christmas; Together with his Clearing by the Jury . . . London: Charles Brome, 1686.

Krythe, Maymie R., All About American Holidays, Harper and Row, 1962

Lalumia, Christine. "The restrained restoration of Christmas". In the Ten Ages of Christmas from the BBC website.

Ian Lancashire, University of Toronto (English Department) http://rpo.library.utoronto.ca/poem/1312.html

Moore, Clement Clarke. "A Visit from St. Nicholas." Troy (N.Y.) Sentinel. December 23, 1823.

Nissenbaum, Stephen. The Battle for Christmas. New York: Alfred A. Knopf, 1996. Otnes, Cele, Kyungseung Kim, and Young Chan Kim. "Yes, Virginia, There is a Gender Difference: Analyzing Children's Requests to Santa Claus." Journal of Popular Culture, 28, no. 1 (Summer 1994), pp. 17-29.

Ott, Jonathan. Pharmacotheon: Entheogenic Drugs, Their Plant Sources and History. Kennewick, Wash.: Natural Products Company, 1993.

Plath, David W. "The Japanese Popular Christmas: Coping with Modernity." American Journal of Folklore, 76, no. 302 (October-December 1963), pp. 309-317.

Quinn, Seabury. Roads. 1948; facsimile reprint, Mohegan Lake, N.Y.: Red Jacket Press, 2005.

"Rudolph," at: http://www.snopes.com/holidays/xmas/

"St. Nicholas of Myra" in the Catholic Encyclopedia at NewAdvent.org. "St. Nicholas of Myra," The Catholic Encyclopedia, at: http://www.newadvent.org/cathen/11063b.htm

"St. Nicholas of Bari (Fourth Century)," Catholic Information Network, at: http://www.cin.org/nichbari.html

"The Claus that Refreshes," at: http://www.snopes.com/cokelore/santa.htm

Seal, Jeremy, Nicholas: The epic journey from Saint to Santa Claus Bloomsbury, New York & London, 2005

Sedaris, David. The Santaland Diaries and Seasons Greetings: Two Plays. New York: Dramatists Play Service, 1998.

Shenkman, Richard. Legends, Lies, and Cherished Myths of American History. New York: HarperCollins, 1988.

Siefker, Phyllis. Santa Claus, Last of the Wild Men: The Origins and Evolution of Saint Nicholas, Spanning 50,000 Years. Jefferson, N.C.: McFarland, 1996.

Twitchell, James B. Twenty Ads that Shook the World. New York: Crown Publishers, 2000.

The Urban Legends Reference Pages (www.snopes.com/cokelore/santa.htm)

Mary S. Van Deusen, 2001, www.iment.com/maida/familytree/henry/writinghenryjr.htm

Barbara G. Walker, "The Woman's Encyclopedia of Myths and Secrets." Harper & Row, (1983) Pages 725 to 726.

Walsh, Joseph J., Were They Wise Men or Kings, Joseph J. Walsh, Westminster John Knox, 2001

"Why Track Him?" at NORADsanta.org.

Wikipedia, the free encyclopedia, Major Henry Livingston Jr. Biography, http://en.wikipedia.org/wiki/Henry_Beekman_Livingston

"Yes, Virginia, there is a Santa Claus," at: http://www.stormfax.com/virginia.htm

A special thanks to all those Santa's, Mrs. Claus and Elves that provided me with some insight into their world and allowed me to print some of their ideas and suggestions. There are hundreds out there that helped and I would love to mention them all if I could.

About the Author

Santa Al Horton (Santa to the World since 1980)

His journey in the world of Santa began in the United Kingdom while in the United States Air Force Stationed at RAF Alconbury. There he donned the suit to play for his children and then was asked to portray Santa again for the children of those in the organization where he worked. With this looking like a long term performance, he purchased a long wig and hairpiece that he used for the English Father Christmas look.

From this humble beginning, he was asked to play Father Christmas for a group of children in the local town and then asked to do it again for a national orphanage. For five years Santa Al was privileged to be asked to portray Father Christmas in central and southern England and for all types of activities. He learned a few Welsh terms and a few Scottish terms to help make the local children believe in him. His high school French came in handy at a local orphanage where he surprised a young French child. Pere Noel did thing write by this young man.

Upon returning to the States, Santa Al decided to continue his love affair with Santa and started performing at office parties, Christmas parties with various organizations and even began riding in a few parades around Christmas time. Soon he was asked to perform for the local community at several private parties and special occasions. His fondest memories of these early years include delivering a puppy to a young girl on Christmas Day.

As he performed more, Santa Al continued to enhance his wardrobe. Over the next 20 years that wardrobe expanded to 3 suits. When he finally retired from the Air Force, he grew a real beard. He has been a "Real-bearded" Santa ever since.

After working as a private contractor for the government, he decided enough was enough and began to travel. Santa Al found ***Santa Atlanta*** in Georgia where he joined ranks with Gary Casey and developed the courses for the newly formed school "The Santa Claus Academy," Not only was he considered the Dean of the school, but he taught for several years before moving back to the West where he now reside.

Santa Al has performed in several movies, been in several commercials and used for numerous commercial advertising ventures. Several folks have told him that they are modeling themselves after him because to them, Santa Al is what a Santa should look like. He has been told that he have a natural twinkle in his eyes that is no less than magical. He is also told that his constant smile is infectious and he is always trying to be happy. Santa Al firmly believes that the sparkle and smile he wears year round is what brings the joy and happiness to all he comes in contact with.

His next adventure is taking him into the medieval times as he tries to perfect the image of Merlin the Wizard. Joy and happiness surround him and he firmly believe that if you don't smile all the time you aren't really happy. Most folks can't help but be happy and smile when they talk to him. Santa Al continues to work on having his smile and happiness shine through in his voice. He believe that if you are truly happy and smiling, folks can tell it in your voice.

He does hope to be teaching and performing as Santa for many more years to come. Santa Al is honestly trying to get back into a good physical condition so that, as he puts it, he can live long and give something for his grandchildren to remember.

Loving what you do is half the battle of happiness. If you aren't happy, you shouldn't be Santa. Share the love and treat everyone as a child you plan to bring gifts to at Christmas time. Even the adults love that friendly and special feeling you give them.

Yes, Virginia, we have come to the end of this little book and hopefully it is just the beginning for most of you. Enjoy your new adventure and enjoy a life and life style that will bring terrific memories. Keep in touch and let me know how things are working out for you.

Santa Al

CPSIA information can be obtained
at www.ICGtesting.com
Printed in the USA
FFHW022357110419
51692629-57113FF

9 781463 4240